IDEALA

VALANCOURT CLASSICS

IDEALA

A Study from Life

BY

SARAH GRAND

"Dieu n'a voulu pour elle que les grands et âpres sentiers."
RENAN.

Edited with an introduction and notes by
Molly Youngkin

Kansas City:
VALANCOURT BOOKS
2008

Ideala by Sarah Grand
First published in 1888
First Valancourt Books edition 2008

Introduction and notes © 2008 by Molly Youngkin
This edition © 2008 by Valancourt Books

Library of Congress Cataloguing-in-Publication Data

Grand, Sarah.
Ideala : a study from life / by Sarah Grand ; edited with an
introduction and notes by Molly Youngkin. – 1st Valancourt Books ed.
p. cm. – (Valancourt classics)
Includes bibliographical references.
ISBN 1-934555-60-6 (alk. paper)
1. Feminists–England–Fiction. 2. Grand, Sarah. Ideala.
I. Youngkin, Molly, 1970- II. Title.
PR4728.G112134 2008
823'.8–dc22
2008035074

Composition by James D. Jenkins
Published by Valancourt Books
Kansas City, Missouri
http://www.valancourtbooks.com

CONTENTS

INTRODUCTION

IN 1888, shortly before Sarah Grand (Frances Bellenden Clarke McFall) left her husband and came to London to live as a writer, she published her first novel, *Ideala,* with her own money. The story of a woman who develops a feminist consciousness as the result of an unhappy marriage to a man with a roaming eye and the tendency toward violence, *Ideala* was the first of several important novels written by Grand in the 1880s and 1890s that explore the difficult issues surrounding gender relations in the nineteenth century. After publishing *Ideala,* Grand would go on to write her most famous novel, *The Heavenly Twins* (1893), which features three different women working to overcome gender biases, as well as the largely autobiographical *The Beth Book* (1897), which returns to a single heroine who is much like the central female character in *Ideala.* With the publication of *The Heavenly Twins,* Grand became a central figure in public debate over the role of women in society, sought after for her opinions on the issue but often ridiculed for her ideas by the periodical press. While *Ideala* is not as well-known as Grand's other novels, primarily because it remained out-of-print in the twentieth century, reading it provides insight into the development of Grand's influential ideas about gender, as well as her development as a writer who employed an innovative and proto-modernist narrative technique while still drawing on the realist tradition of the Victorian period.

* * *

While the "Woman Question" (as the debate over the role of women in society often was characterized) had begun before the late 1880s, it became even more vigorously debated during this period and into the 1890s. The 1890s New Woman novel, in particular, became a site for expressing multiple perspectives on the topic, and the New Woman, who refused to follow the Victorian tradition of middle-class marriage and motherhood, became the heroine in these novels. Thomas Hardy, author of *Tess of the d'Urbervilles* (1891) and *Jude the Obscure* (1895), called for franker discussion of "the relations of the sexes" in his 1890 article "Candour in English Fiction," and he caused serious controversy by highlighting these relations in his novels. Other male authors of the period followed suit: in *The Odd Women* (1893), George Gissing brought renewed attention to the "superfluous" woman (the woman who could not marry, even if she wanted, due to a shortage of marriageable men), and Grant Allen raised eyebrows when he published *The Woman Who Did* (1894), the story of a woman who proudly refuses to marry and lives "in sin" with her lover instead.

While the works of male authors who wrote about women were added to the literary canon in the twentieth century and, therefore, shaped much of the discussion of representations of women in literature, women writers of the late-Victorian period wrote as eagerly as male authors did about new roles for women in society. Only in recent decades have these women received attention from scholars and been brought into the literary canon; among them are Olive Schreiner, Mona Caird, Ménie Dowie, and Grand herself. Schreiner's *The Story of an African Farm*, published in 1883, set the stage for later works about the New Woman, since the heroine of the novel, Lyndall, seemed to embody the new ideal of women's independence. In works from the 1890s, New Woman characters possessed many of the qualities we associate with feminism of today: an awareness of the cultural conditions that create obstacles for women and the effort of women to speak out and act against these conditions in order to create a better world for themselves and other women. In Caird's *The Daughters of Danaus* (1894), readers are introduced to the independent young woman who uses the spoken word to articulate her need for a new way of living, and, in Dowie's *A Girl in the Karpathians* (1891), readers experience the more action-oriented variety of this type, who is not afraid to travel the world on her own.

Of these women writers, Grand remains the central figure, in part because she did much to popularize the term "New Woman" in an article titled "The New Aspect of the Woman Question," which ran in *The North American Review* in 1894. Of the New Woman, Grand writes that she has been quietly waiting for men, referred to as the "Bawling Brotherhood," to recognize her intellectual abilities, but she has been overlooked in favor of less intelligent women, whom Grand refers to as the "cow-woman" and the "scum-woman."

> Both the cow-woman and the scum-woman are well within range
> of the comprehension of the Bawling Brotherhood, but the new

woman is a little above him, and he never even thought of looking up to where she has been sitting apart in silent contemplation
all these years, thinking and thinking, until at last she solved the
problem and proclaimed for herself what was wrong with Home-
is-the-Woman's-Sphere, and prescribed the remedy.[1]

In making this statement, Grand not only declared that the New
Woman existed but she was a *thinking* woman, one who had been
reflective for some time but had finally turned her thinking into
action.

Grand's early life does not immediately suggest she would be an
important participant in the public debate over the roles for women
at the end of the century, yet she was active in the social issues that
would influence her fiction long before most women were. Born
in 1854 in Donaghadee, Ireland, Grand grew up in a family shaped
by military life. First, she lived as the daughter of a lieutenant in
the Royal Navy and then as the wife of a military surgeon, David
Chambers McFall. McFall was the youngest of 14 children; his father,
Thomas, had a coaching inn and owned commercial property in
Magherafelt, Derry, Northern Ireland. Grand married McFall, then
a widower with two sons, at age sixteen primarily to continue her
education: she was schooled at home until age fourteen and had only
two years of formal schooling, at the Royal Naval School in Middle-
sex and at a finishing school in London, when she married McFall.
Yet while attending the Royal Naval School, Grand learned about
Josephine Butler's campaign to repeal the Contagious Diseases Acts
of the 1860s, which punished women for the sexual vices of men,
and she organized a club at the school to back Butler's cause. At age
fifteen, then, she had already taken a stance on women's issues.[2]

Grand's marriage to McFall was, like the marriages of many
of her heroines, not ideal, though they did have one son, Archie,
together. The early years of the marriage were spent traveling

[1] Sarah Grand, "The New Aspect of the Woman Question," *North American
Review* 158 (1894): 271-276. Reprinted in Ann Heilmann and Stephanie Forward,
eds., *Sex, Social Purity, and Sarah Grand* (London: Routledge, 2000), 29-30.
[2] Stephanie Forward, "Introduction," in *Sex, Social Purity, and Sarah Grand: Volume 2, Selected Letters*, ed. Forward and Ann Heilmann (London: Routledge,
2000), 1-2. Information about McFall's family history provided by Sarah Greenhous, whose great-great-grandfather's brother was McFall.

through the Far East as McFall served in the military, but, in 1879, the family returned to England, living first in Norwich and then in Lancashire. In 1890, when Grand was thirty-six, she left McFall and their then-grown son to live in London. Once in London, Grand changed her name due to McFall's concern about being linked with her causes, and she became an important figure in the community of activists working for the advancement of women. She was a member of the Pioneer Club, which held regular debates on important social issues, the Women Writers' Suffrage League, and the Women Citizens' Association. She was vice-president of the Women's Suffrage Society and, later, after she moved out of London, president of the Tunbridge Wells chapters of the National Council of Women and the National Union of Women's Suffrage Societies.[1]

In addition to participating in these groups and writing novels with a feminist angle, she wrote a number of nonfiction essays focused on women's issues, including "The Modern Girl" (1894) and "On Clubs and the Question of Intelligence" (1900), in which she argued for the inherent intelligence of women and their ability to contribute to the betterment of the world. After the turn of the century, Grand wrote less and lectured more, traveling throughout England and also to the United States, though she did write two more novels, *Adnam's Orchard* (1912) and *The Winged Victory* (1916). After women won the vote in 1918, the nature of her activism changed somewhat. In 1920, she moved to Bath, where she became the mayoress of the town for nearly a decade, in order to help her widowed friend, Cedric Chivers, who was then mayor. In 1942, when Bath experienced the air raids of World War II, Grand moved to Calne, in Wiltshire, where she died in 1943.[2]

Grand's unique contribution, as an activist and writer, can be seen as early as *Ideala*, which clearly contains feminist themes. Still, Ideala's transformation is complicated by Grand's decision to portray this transformation through the eyes of a first-person male narrator, Lord Dawne. While Dawne (whose name is revealed only in *The Heavenly Twins*, where he and Ideala reappear as characters) certainly sympathizes with Ideala's struggle, his counsel of her is influenced by his own admiration of her and his impulse to protect her

---

[1] Ibid., 7-8.
[2] Ibid., 5, 8, 10, 15.

from other men. As Ideala considers the alternatives to her unhappy marriage, including an affair with a man named Lorrimer, Dawne encourages her to seek a different solution—in charity work with other women. Ideala travels to China, where she sees women fighting against the tradition of foot-binding, and this experience serves as the impetus for her own work to dismantle the constraints placed on English women by nineteenth-century society. Ultimately, Ideala is transformed from a woman who lacks consciousness about her own place in the world to someone who is committed to improving the lives of other women, yet she does not necessarily achieve the full level of freedom many New Women desired at the close of the nineteenth century.

Grand recognized the limitations placed on women as they struggled to become transformed in the preface to the novel, which indicates the story is about the development of Ideala's mind, especially the stages of this development under difficult conditions. Grand does not want readers to look for "perfection" in Ideala's mind but for how it goes through a "transitional" maturation process. Still, by paying attention to this transitional process, which reveals all the flaws of the mind as it develops, readers can learn from Ideala's experience and apply her experience to their own lives. Writes Grand, "[W]hy exhibit the details of the process? you may ask. To encourage others, of course. What help is there in the contemplation of perfection ready made? It only disheartens us . . . . The imperfections must be studied, because it is only from the details of the process that anything can be learned" (5). The preface, then, prepares readers for the fact that woman's consciousness will be central to this novel but is still in a developmental state.

Ideala's story of transformation is informed by a number of nineteenth-century historical and cultural contexts, including Victorian views of marriage and challenges to this institution via public debate. As documents from the period indicate, views about marriage were diverse. When the novelist Mona Caird published an article on the topic in the *Westminster Review* in August 1888, Caird's unorthodox view that marriage was a cultural construct and a complete failure for women prompted 27,000 people to send letters expressing their own perspectives about marriage to another paper, *The Daily Tel-*

egraph.[1] Along with the informal debate that occurred in the press, more formal debate about marriage took place in Parliament across the nineteenth century, via discussion of specific legislative acts designed to give women more power within their own marriages. In some ways, Ideala is the beneficiary of the improved legal status of women over the course of the century. The novel is set after the passage of the 1857 Marriage and Divorce Act, which allowed both men and women to file for divorce in the newly formed civil court rather than being forced to seek dissolution from the Church of England and/or Parliament. Still, Ideala is subject to a double standard regarding the conditions for divorce. While men only needed to prove adultery on the part of their wives, women had to prove adultery as well as other extreme circumstances, such as physical cruelty, bigamy, or incest. So, while Ideala can divorce her husband, who has cheated on Ideala and has been particularly cruel to her, she lacks the proof needed to do so. Although in 1870 women retained the right to their own property after marriage, which created more options for independence if they ended up in marriages similar to Ideala's, Ideala still suffers from lack of choice in terms of how to separate financially from her husband, though she benefits from the help of friends, particularly Lord Dawne and his sister, Claudia, who welcome Ideala into their home.[2]

As Ideala's awareness of her difficult circumstances grows, she exhibits many of the qualities of the yet-to-be-defined New Woman. Like other women of the late-Victorian period, Ideala searches to find alternative ways of living, and, as the separate-spheres model of the mid-Victorian period begins to dissolve, she is willing to take risks in order to explore these alternatives. Her greatest risk is pursuing a friendship with a man named Lorrimer, who works at a local mental hospital and provides Ideala with a place to read and think in the hospital library. Lorrimer is different from any other man in Ideala's life: he is able to see Ideala's intelligence in a way her hus-

---

[1] These letters, but not Caird's original article, are reprinted in Harry Quilter, *Is Marriage a Failure?* (London: Swan Sonnenschein and Co., 1888; repr. New York: Garland Publishing, 1984).

[2] For more on specific legislation related to marriage, see Lee Holcombe, *Wives and Property: Reform of the Married Women's Property Law in Nineteenth Century England* (Toronto: Toronto University Press, 1983).

band cannot, and he is willing to let Ideala take her time opening up to him rather than forcing her to talk about her unhappy marriage. Ideala and Lorrimer spend many afternoons working together, not necessarily talking much but simply sharing a quiet space together.

At first, Ideala's relationship with Lorrimer is one in which she is characterized as *losing* consciousness rather than gaining it, but this is Lord Dawne's view, not Ideala's. She sees the relationship differently, as one that gives her clarity of thought: "I was wandering in some such mental mist," she explains to Dawne once he realizes the relationship likely will become intimate and confronts her about it, "lost and despairing, when Lorrimer came into my life, and changed everything for me in a moment, like the sun. Would you have me believe that he was sent to me then only for an evil purpose?" (141). Clearly, Ideala's perspective is different from Dawne's, and her discussions with Dawne become the site for exploration of issues regarding individual liberty for women, which Grand valued but did not privilege over duty to the wider community of women. This tension between individual liberty and duty to a wider community is taken up by other women writers of the period, most notably Mona Caird, who addresses the issue in *Daughters of Danaus*. Caird upholds the right to individual liberty on all matters, including sexual liberty, and her heroine, Hadria Fuller, differs from Ideala, since she does have an affair after her marriage turns sour.

Caird and Grand often are distinguished from each other precisely on this issue.[1] In Grand's novel, Ideala at first is firm in her belief that she is a "free agent," with the right to decide how she will live her life and whether she wants to break from convention and run the risk of being perceived as an outcast. But Lord Dawne argues against an affair—or "arrangement," as he and Ideala refer to it—with Lorrimer, since Dawne believes Ideala has a responsibility to society rather than to herself only. Readers with early-twenty-first-century feminist sensibilities may perceive Lord Dawne as yet another man trying to stifle Ideala's individuality, especially since he

---

[1] Ann Heilmann, *New Woman Strategies: Sarah Grand, Olive Schreiner, Mona Caird* (Manchester: Manchester University Press, 2005), 158-161; Angelique Richardson, "'People Talk a Lot of Nonsense about Heredity': Mona Caird and Anti-Eugenic Feminism," in *The New Woman in Fiction and in Fact*, ed. Richardson and Chris Willis (London: Palgrave, 2001), 185-188.

talks to her about "self-sacrifice," and critics such as Teresa Mangum and Ann Heilmann have shown the ways in which Dawne
does impose certain limitations on Ideala as he counsels her about
her situation. Mangum's argument that Ideala must "wrestle free"
not only from Dawne but also from the two other "old-fashioned
men" in her life, her husband and Lorrimer, indicates both the overt
and more covert forms of pressure put on women in the period.
For Mangum, "Ideala's husband embodies the legal authority men
wield over women; her lover suggests the tempting but dangerous
attractions of romance; and, most significantly, the narrator repre-
sents the power of narrative authority, that ability to control women
by idealizing them."[1] And Heilmann's point that Dawne, who is a
painter and objectifies Ideala by thinking about her from an artistic
point of view, reveals at least one of the personal motivations for
Dawne's interest in Ideala's case. Citing the moment when Dawne
talks about the pictures he has of Ideala, in which he focuses on the
details of her dress and her beauty as she appears in this dress, Heilmann argues that "Lord Dawne's sexual desire transforms Ideala
into a sequence of erotic stills."[2] When Dawne realizes that Lorrimer may take his place as the primary male adviser in Ideala's life,
he is threatened by this reality.

Dawne's pressure on Ideala to resist Lorrimer and his emphasis
on self-sacrifice (a term used in the separate-spheres philosophy that
had oppressed women for much of the nineteenth century) as the
appropriate alternative for her, should make readers cautious about
his full commitment to Ideala's freedom. Nevertheless, as Barbara
Caine and Phillipa Levine have pointed out, it is also important to
recognize that there were multiple forms of feminism in the nineteenth century, and these different forms of feminism mapped out
different paths for women to attain freedom. Liberal feminism,
which drew on J. S. Mill's writing about individual liberty and put
emphasis on freedom and happiness for the individual, took a different approach than that of social purity feminism, which put emphasis on the double standard for men and women regarding sexual

---

[1] Teresa Mangum, *Married, Middlebrow, and Militant: Sarah Grand and the New
Woman Novel* (Ann Arbor: University of Michigan Press, 1998), 63.
[2] Ann Heilmann, *New Woman Strategies: Sarah Grand, Olive Schreiner, Mona
Caird* (Manchester: Manchester University Press, 2005), 56-57.

freedom and recommended that women resist sexual freedom and insist men become more chaste, in order to ensure all women would progress together.[1] In the earlier sections of *Ideala*, Grand puts these two forms of feminism in dialogue with each other via conversation between Ideala and Lord Dawne. Grand uses Ideala to articulate the liberal-feminist perspective, which maintains Ideala's right to make her own choices, including pursuing a relationship with Lorrimer. On the other hand, Grand uses Lord Dawne to advocate purity feminism; he discourages Ideala from actions based on achieving individual happiness and suggests she channel her energy into community-oriented action, which will help all women.

Through Ideala's discussions with Dawne about this topic, Ideala begins to develop a new awareness of herself as someone who does have a responsibility to others and not just to herself. She is open to this new form of feminism, yet she cannot make the transition until she separates herself from *both* Lorrimer and Dawne by traveling to China, where she observes the resistance of Chinese women to footbinding and realizes English women also are bound by the restrictions placed on them by their own society. Upon Ideala's return from China, it is clear her definition of consciousness has changed dramatically and is more distinctly community-oriented. When asked about her plans for the future, Ideala draws a parallel between the oppression of women in China and the oppression of women in England and commits herself to the women of England:

> Certainly the Chinese women of the day bind their feet. And yet they do a wonderful thing. When they are taught how wrong the practice is, how it cripples them, and weakens them, and renders them unfit for their work in the world, they take off their bandages. . . . When I learned that, and when I remembered that my country-women bind every organ in their bodies . . . [i]t seemed to me that there was work enough left yet to do at home. (177)

In responding to the question about the type of work she will do, Ideala makes it clear *increased consciousness* is key to changing the world and feminist action should be aimed at changing conditions for all women, not just for herself. Says Ideala, "Women have never

[1] Barbara Caine, *English Feminism, 1780-1980* (Oxford: Oxford University Press, 1997), 102-115; Philippa Levine, *Victorian Feminism, 1850-1900* (Tallahassee: The Florida State University Press, 1987), 130-133.

yet united to use their influence steadily and all together against that of which they disapprove. They work too much for themselves, each trying to make their own life happier. They have yet to learn to take a wider view of things, and to be shown that the only way to gain their end is by working for everybody else" (184). Only now does Ideala realize she has something to contribute to English society, and her decision, as Lord Dawne puts it, to "gather the useless units of society about her, and [make] them worthy women" (189) is the sign she has moved from liberal to purity feminism.

Ideala's transition to purity feminism is informed by two additional historical and cultural contexts: 1) women's involvement in charity movements across the nineteenth century and new variations on these movements at the end of the century, and 2) the rise of "thought-influence," the idea that people could influence others through good thoughts and, as a result, change the world. Just as debate over marriage brought out diverse perspectives, the notion of women providing charity to others evoked differing opinions. An anonymous article in *Fraser's Magazine* in 1859 argued that women should not do charity work, since it encouraged them to leave the domestic sphere and become less "womanly."[1] On the other hand, an article in the *Quarterly Review* in 1860 supported women in this role, arguing that women were doing the work no one else would do.[2] Regardless of these differing opinions, many middle- and upper-class women were involved in charity during this period, and leaders in the movement such as Angela Burdett-Coutts, in *Woman's Mission* (1893), reported on the real work women were doing to help others.[3] While the charity work done by women extended to a wide range of people, especially the poor and the sick, much of this work centered on women helping other women. Burdett-Coutts herself was actively involved in Dickens's project of rehabilitating "fallen" women, who came out of prisons and into his Urania Cottage. Their enterprise confirms the Victorian belief that upper- and middle-class women might be of help to working-class and poor women, and the goal in this class-structured charity was to rehabilitate women so they might someday lead a traditional, middle-class life.

---

[1] Anonymous, "A Fear for the Future, That Women Will Cease to Be Womanly," *Fraser's Magazine* 59 (Feb. 1859): 243-248.

[2] J. H. Howson, "Deaconesses," *Quarterly Review* 108 (Oct. 1860): 179-203.

[3] Angela Burdett-Coutts, *Woman's Mission* (New York: Scribner, 1893).

By the latter part of the century, women's involvement in charity work seems to have become widely accepted, and the rise of
feminism added a new twist to the type of charity work done by
women. Aware that the "superfluous" woman could not marry even
if she wished, due to a shortage of marriageable men, charity pro-
viders no longer had the goal of rehabilitating working-class and
poor women in order to become "angels in the house" but, instead,
began to focus on ways in which women could become productive
members of society, not by marrying but by acquiring new skills
and entering the workforce. While it is unclear what exactly Ideala is
doing with the "useless units" she turns into "worthy women" at the
end of the novel, she does not seem to be rehabilitating women for
marriage. Her actions seem to be more along the lines of educating
women about their status in society, and her approach anticipates
the type of charity work done by women such as Rhoda Nunn and
Mary Barfoot in Gissing's *The Odd Women*, who open a secretarial
school to train superfluous women for new professions. In the process, Rhoda and Mary also educate the women at the school about
their cultural status, through lectures on topics such as "Woman as
Invader," in which Mary calls for the women to become part of "an
armed movement, an invasion by women of the spheres which men
have always forbidden us to enter."[1] Ideala's decision to do something similar at the end of the novel, then, is a step forward for the
women's movement, and the fact that Grand published her novel five
years before Gissing published his (and completed her novel an additional five years earlier, in 1883) indicates that Grand was ahead of
her time. Though Gissing's novel has been more readily available to
late-twentieth- and early-twenty-first-century readers, Grand's novel
highlights the same important theme of women helping women.

Another important historical context for understanding Ideala's
transition from liberal feminism to purity feminism is the notion of
thought-influence, the idea that one can change the world through
good thoughts. As Sally Ledger and Roger Luckhurst's compila-
tion of documents about "psychical research" in *The Fin de Siècle: A
Reader in Cultural History c. 1800-1900* shows, the formation of groups
such as The Society for Psychical Research in the early 1880s signified

---

[1] George Gissing, *The Odd Women*, 1893, ed. Elaine Showalter (New York: Penguin, 1983), 153.

the interest in various forms of psychic power, including "thought-reading" (the passing of thoughts from one mind to another).[1] Influenced by the interest in psychical research, the emerging feminism of the late century emphasized the power of the mind, since it provided a supplement to the *actions* and *speech* used by women to advance their cause. In fact, late-nineteenth-century feminists advocated a three-step approach to resisting cultural norms that involved thought, speech, and action, with feminist thought as the impetus for the other two methods. Feminist newspapers such as Margaret Sibthorp's *Shafts*, which featured on its cover a woman shooting arrows of wisdom, truth, and justice into the atmosphere, especially focused on the power of thought. In "Shafts of Thought," an article in the inaugural issue of *Shafts*, Edith Ward discusses the advances of psychical research and the importance of it to social movements. Describing the process of how thoughts move through the atmosphere, Ward writes, "Every human soul is constantly engaged in creating and throwing off germs of thought, good or bad, exactly as germs are being created and thrown off by the physical system. . . . [I]f the receptive organism be affinitive, the germs find congenial soil for development, if, on the other hand, in the one case, the germs of physical disease fall upon a perfectly sound body they find no conditions suitable for their growth, or in the other, the thought germs are fructified or sterilised according[ly,] as their character, good or bad, meets with minds receptive to their influence."[2]

Then, discussing the significance of this process for people with the potential to change the world through their thoughts, Ward states, "Such a belief is full of terrible significance. . . . It means that each one of us who is living a life of apparent honour and respectability may be responsible to a greater or less degree for [sending] some erring brother or sister into the slough of actual crime. . . . [O]n the other hand, we have the glorious assurance that every pure unselfish aspiration streams forth no less potently to aid and strengthen the struggles of upstriving souls."[3] In other words, there are moral implications, bad and good, for the person who wants to impact the

[1] Sally Ledger and Roger Luckhurst, eds., *The Fin de Siècle: A Reader in Cultural History c. 1800-1900* (Oxford: Oxford University Press, 2000), 269-278.

[2] Edith Ward, "Shafts of Thought," *Shafts*, 3 November 1892, 2.

[3] Ibid.

world. Still, the opportunity for positive change should encourage those involved in social movements, and thought-influence even allows the person who cannot participate in the movement in traditional ways to become active. "To the invalid who reads SHAFTS upon a couch of suffering which incapacitates her for active philanthropic work," concludes Ward, "it may perchance bring weekly reassurance that from her own room she can send forth germs of helpful vigour to men and women engaged in active work."[1]

Grand's use of thought-influence in *Ideala* is evident toward the end of the novel, after Ideala has returned from China and says, "I thought for a long time that everything had been done that could be done to make the world better; but now I see that there is still one thing more to be tried. Women have never yet united to use their influence steadily and all together against that of which they disapprove. They work too much for themselves, each trying to make their own life happier. They have yet to learn to take a wider view of things, and to be shown that the only way to gain their end is by working for everybody else, with intent to make the whole world better, which means happier" (184). To do this, Ideala says, "they must be taught that they have only to *will* it—each in her own family and amongst her own friends; that, after having agreed with the rest about what they mean to put down, they have only to go home and use their influence to that end, quietly, consistently, and without wavering, and the thing will be done. Our influence is like those strong currents which run beneath the surface of the ocean without disturbing it, and yet with irresistible force, and at a rate that may be calculated. It is to help in the direction of that force that I am going to devote my life" (185). Here, Ideala incorporates the principles of psychical research into her philosophy about how change will come about, since to "will it" involves thoughts as well as speech and action.

★ ★ ★

While Grand's influence in debates about gender in the late-Victorian period is significant, her influence on literary style at the turn of the century is equally important. Not only does *Ideala* set the scene for *The Heavenly Twins* and *The Beth Book* through emphasis on simi-

---

[1] Ibid.

lar themes, but the novel also establishes a certain literary style for Grand's later work, which anticipates the modernist aesthetic made famous by writers such as James Joyce and Virginia Woolf. With their emphasis on subjective experience and shifting perspectives, Grand's novels include many of the techniques employed by modernist writers after 1900, yet Grand does not entirely abandon nineteenth-century realism, since she typically uses a third-person narrator who lays out the setting and characters in traditional realist fashion. *The Heavenly Twins* typifies Grand's approach, since the novel is told in third person but shifts from the story of one woman to another, in order to show their varying circumstances and differing perspectives on those circumstances. The novel is further complicated by the introduction of an "Interlude" in the middle, which critics often see as the most modernist aspect of the novel; John Kucich characterizes the interlude as a "stylized pastoral" that "strikingly breaks the novel's realist frame by creating a shadow world of artificial sexual being."[1] Finally, the novel ends with a section written in first person by the character Dr. Galbraith, who gives his impressions of one of the primary female characters from both a medical and a personal point of view, and the inclusion of his subjective perspective adds yet another layer to an already multilayered story.

Ideala differs from *The Heavenly Twins* in its narrative technique, but it too anticipates modernism, albeit in different ways. Grand's use of first-person narration, which I have already discussed in some detail, indicates readers are receiving a subjective experience throughout. One must filter through Lord Dawne's subjective narration in order to get at Ideala's experience, and we are well aware that Dawne's impressions of Ideala are shaped by his admiration of her. Still, even after readers negotiate Dawne's subjective account, we find that Ideala's experience is extremely complex; she is completely unaware of herself in relation to her surroundings, especially at the beginning of the novel, yet she also is an extremely *thoughtful* person, focusing on her own inner emotional experience more than the outside world. This focus on consciousness is a key element in modernist fiction.

Another key element in modernist fiction is a rejection of linear

---

[1] John Kucich, "Curious Dualities: *The Heavenly Twins* (1893) and Sarah Grand's Belated Modernist Aesthetics," in *The New Nineteenth Century: Feminist Readings of Underread Victorian Fiction*, ed. Barbara Harman and Susan Meyer (New York: Garland, 1996), 195-204.

modernist time, which often manifests itself in different approaches to plot. Sometimes the plot of the story moves more slowly, as in Woolf's *Mrs. Dalloway* and Joyce's *Ulysses*, both of which take place in a single day, and sometimes the plot is virtually non-existent, as in Joyce's *Finnegan's Wake*. The first half of Grand's novel, while not as extreme as any of the aforementioned works, is marked by very little plot. Instead, it seems to consist of a string of conversations Dawne has with Ideala, and it is only about twelve chapters into the novel that readers begin to learn the details of Ideala's marriage and see her take action to change her life. After that, the plot moves fairly quickly and in a linear fashion, yet there still are occasional lyrical disruptions to that narrative, where Grand uses stream-of-consciousness questions or quotation of poetry to focus on the psychological effects of the events of the story on certain characters. For example, when Ideala asks Dawne to travel to Lorrimer's hospital and give him the letter indicating that she will not come see him anymore, Grand fills Dawne's narration with questions that indicate a heightened psychological state as a reaction to this duty. "Was there no peace on earth for Ideala?", Dawne thinks, as he travels by train to see Lorrimer, "No one who could be all her own? I felt responsible for this last hard blow; had I done well? The rush and rattle of the train shaped itself into a sort of sub-chorus to my thoughts as we sped through the pleasant fields: *Was it right? Was it right? Was it right?*" (153). Dawne's thoughts turn to Ideala, whom he imagines

> with soft, sad eyes, pleading—mutely pleading—pleading always for some pleasure in life, some natural, womanly joy, while youth and the power to love lasted. By an effort of will I banished the question. I told myself that my action in the matter had been expedient from every point of view; but presently
>
> The rush of the grinding steel!
> The thundering crank, and the mighty wheel!
>
> took me to task again, and the chorus now became: *Expediency right! Expediency right! Expediency right!* which, when I banished it, resolved itself into: *Cold, proud Puritan! Cold, proud Puritan!* for the rest of the way. (153)

Here, Grand's use of repeated phrases, offset lines, and italicized

thoughts put readers thoroughly inside Dawne's mind, in the same
way a modernist novelist might. Then, a page later, Grand uses a
similar technique, interspersing lines from Tennyson's "Recollections of Arabian Nights" with realistic narration of Lorrimer's reaction, to show the effect on Lorrimer when he reads Ideala's letter.

> I heard him open the envelope; I heard the paper rustle as he
> turned the page; and then there was silence—

> Full of the city's stilly sound—

> a moment only, but filled with

> > Something which possess'd
> > The darkness of the world, delight,
> > Life, anguish, death, immortal love.
> > Ceasing not, mingled, unrepress'd,
> > Apart from space, witholding time—

> a moment's silence, and then a heavy fall. Lorrimer had fainted. (155)

Again, the disruption of the plot with more lyrical language to indicate the psychological states of characters anticipates the modernist
aesthetic.

Along with stream-of-consciousness questioning and intersper-
sion of poetry into the linear plot, Grand also uses more general
intertextuality to create a proto-modernist effect. Not only are there
direct quotations from over forty different texts, many of which are
poems by Tennyson, but in a number of places in the novel, these
quotations are couched in dialogue so that they are not obviously
quotations. For example, when Dawne comments on Ideala's struggle within her marriage, he incorporates a line from Tennyson's
"Locksley Hall" into his commentary: "She fought hard to preserve
her dignity, and was determined that 'as the husband is, the wife is,'
should not be true in her case" (41). And, when Ideala argues with
Claudia about the ways in which men limit the progress of women,
she incorporates a line from one of Prime Minister Benjamin Disraeli's speeches into her conversation: "We must stop when we cannot go any further, and all this old-womanish cackle on the subject,

the everlasting trying to prove what is already said to be proved—the looking for the square in space after laying it down as a law that only the circle exists—is a curious way of showing us how to control the 'exuberance of our own verbosity'" (182). The result of the strong intertextuality is that readers must continually negotiate the text, much in the way T. S. Eliot's *The Waste Land* forces modernist readers to take an active part in deciphering the various references in order to understand the broader message of the text.

Grand clearly made specific choices in terms of narrative strategies that push the boundaries of realism and anticipate modernism, yet she seems to have been aware of the ways in which critics and the general public were still invested in realism even at the end of the century, since the subtitle of the novel is "A Study from Life." As the materials included in the appendix of this edition show, Grand articulated her commitment to realism in an interview done with Sarah A. Tooley for the *Humanitarian* in 1896. "To be true to life should be the first aim of an author," she said, "and if one deals with social questions one must study them in the people who hold them, not invent a puppet to give forth one's views."[1] Further, in the Preface to *Our Manifold Nature: Stories from Life*, a collection that appeared in 1894, Grand states that her approach is one of realism, since the stories in the collection are "simply what they profess to be—studies from life."[2] Still, her realism may differ from that produced by other writers. "Fiction has always been held to be at its best when it was true to life,"[3] she states, but she also believes critics define realism too narrowly, arguing that "in order to be convincing, a study from life must be a garnished interpretation rather than a literal translation."[4] According to this definition, says Grand, "An actor has to paint his face to make it look natural in the glare of the footlights, and some analogous process must be resorted to by the writer who would produce the effect of life in his work."[5] Ultimately, she does not want to wear the mask most authors don, and that is why some critics will find her work "strange."[6]

---

[1] See Appendix to this edition, p. 211.

[2] Sarah Grand, "Preface," *Our Manifold Nature: Stories From Life*, 1894, Short Story Index Reprint Series (Freeport, NY: Books for Libraries Press, 1969) iii.

[3] Ibid, iv.

[4] Ibid, v.

[5] Ibid.

[6] Ibid.

Still, Grand's defense of her literary aesthetic should be understood in relation to the pressure put on women writers to conform to a marketplace shaped by male critics. As the appendix in this edition also indicates, reviews of *Ideala* were mixed, and one of the issues raised by the critics was the degree of realism in the novel. The reviewer for *The Saturday Review* thought the novel an example of naturalism and thus "the story of a nasty-minded woman,"[1] whereas the reviewer for *The Spectator* thought Grand had fulfilled the "unwritten contract which exists between a good author and his readers" by making Ideala "a real living character."[2] While Grand seems to have recognized that she needed to defend her aesthetic to some of the critics who reviewed *Ideala*, there were favorable reviews of the novel, including Margaret Oliphant's in *Blackwood's Edinburgh Magazine*. This review is particularly interesting, since Oliphant criticized other works about the New Woman, especially Allen's *The Woman Who Did*, Hardy's *Tess of the d'Urbervilles* and *Jude the Obscure*, and Dowie's *Gallia*. Contrasting *Ideala* with *Tess*, Oliphant writes that the former novel is "the expression of a great many thoughts of the moment, and a desire which is stronger than it ever has been before, cultivated by many recent agitations and incidents, for a new development of feminine life, for an emancipation."[3] Further, Ideala is "an example of the new sentiment which has been developed by, or which has been the cause of . . . the singular and scarcely recognised revolution which has taken place in the position and aspirations of women during the last generation."[4] Though Oliphant questions the realism of some of the actions portrayed in the book, such as Ideala's husband locking her out of the house one night, she credits Grand for preventing Ideala from taking the "fatal step" of having an affair with Lorrimer.[5] She also admires Dawne, whom she describes as "a man not carried away by the passion which forces Ideala; thinking, indeed, more of her than himself."[6]

Even more enthusiastic about the novel than Oliphant were

---

[1] Appendix, p. 190.

[2] Appendix, p. 193.

[3] Appendix, pp. 197-198.

[4] Appendix, p. 198.

[5] Appendix, p. 198.

[6] Appendix, p. 205.

the more thoroughly feminist critics, who were able to appreciate Grand's work fully. Mona Caird, mentioned earlier as the author of the 1888 controversial article about marriage, did not share all of Grand's beliefs, but she used *Ideala* in another article that ran in *The Westminster Review* in 1888, "Ideal Marriage," to indicate the ways in which the institution of marriage restricted women's liberty. She recounts the scene in *Ideala* in which Ideala discusses with the Bishop the hypothetical case of a woman signing a marriage contract, only to learn later she was kept "in ignorance of the most important clause in it."[1] Caird argues Ideala is right to be enraged that such a thing might occur: "Surely no one will seriously deny that Ideala's principle is perfectly right, and that to substitute a legal form for the sentiment that possesses the real binding force between two persons, is to found our kingdom upon sand, to base our social world upon a mockery and a sham."[2]

Particularly after *The Heavenly Twins* was published and Grand's reputation as a feminist writer was established, feminist reviewers drew attention to *Ideala*. *The Woman's Herald*, which ran frequent articles about Grand throughout the 1890s, reviewed *Ideala* in 1893. Acknowledging that the peculiarities of Ideala's character might seem odd to the reader, the reviewer nevertheless believes that as the novel progresses, "one forgets [the] peculiarities, and can find little but sympathy and admiration for the many noble qualities of a very complex character."[3] Further, the reviewer believes the novel anticipates the "fearless denunciation of social evils" that receive "eloquent utterance" in *The Heavenly Twins* and calls for a new edition of *Ideala*, which should be popular in the wake of the "tremendous success" of *The Heavenly Twins*.[4] Later, after *The Woman's Herald* became *The Woman's Signal*, it again reviewed the novel, describing it in 1895 as "the life story of a deeply sensitive, highly bred, delicately nurtured woman," whose "anguish and degradation" is "poignantly and powerfully suggested."[5] *The Woman's Signal* review also tells the story of Grand's attempt to publish *Ideala* as early as 1883 (only to be turned down because Ruskin did not like the book) and her deci-

---

[1] Mona Caird, "Ideal Marriage," *The Westminster Review*, November 1888, 620.
[2] Ibid., 621.
[3] Appendix, p. 208.
[4] Appendix, p. 208.
[5] Appendix, p. 209.

sion in 1888 to publish the novel with her own money.[1] By reviewing *Ideala* well into the 1890s, *The Woman's Herald* (later known as *The Woman's Signal*) affirmed Grand's continuing influence in the feminist community.

Although the mainstream reviewers seem not to have fully appreciated Grand's contribution to feminist content and modernist form, the feminist reviews indicate that Grand's novel was appreciated by at least a portion of the public in its own time. A century later, the overall reception of Grand remains favorable, yet criticism still is limited, in part because the novel previously has been out of print. However, interest in Grand's body of work continues to grow, and bringing *Ideala* into print once again will contribute significantly to our knowledge of a writer who was controversial yet immensely influential in her own time.

Molly Youngkin
Los Angeles

February 1, 2008

Molly Youngkin is Assistant Professor of English at Loyola Marymount University in Los Angeles, where she specializes in Romantic and Victorian literature, as well as gender studies and narrative theory. Her first book, *Feminist Realism at the Fin de Siècle: The Influence of the Late-Victorian Woman's Press on the Development of the Novel* (Ohio State University Press, 2007), examines the influence of feminist ideals in the debate over realism in the work of male and female authors writing in the 1890s, including Sarah Grand. She has also published articles on related topics in a collection of essays titled *Kindred Hands: Letters on Writing by Women Authors, 1860-1920* (University of Iowa Press, 2006) and in the journals *Victorian Periodicals Review*, *Studies in the Novel*, and *English Literature in Transition*. She currently is working on a new book, which focuses on the relationship between art and literature in nineteenth-century women's writing.

---

[1] See Appendix, p. 209.

Acknowledgments

I would like to thank the following individuals and institutions for their help on this project:

The Department of Special Collections, Charles E. Young Research Library, UCLA, which holds the first edition of the novel. Thanks to the staff members in Special Collections, especially Robert Montoya, who eagerly assisted me as I worked with the first edition.

Lisa deRubertis, who worked as my research assistant early in the project. Lisa provided suggestions about sections of the novel in need of annotations and gathered information for many of the annotations that appear in the final manuscript. Thanks to Graduate School at California State University, Dominguez Hills, which provided a one-semester stipend for Lisa to work on the project.

Michael Engh, Dean of the Bellarmine College of Liberal Arts at Loyola Marymount University, who provided financial support for the copyright issues involved with this project.

Sarah Greenhous, a relative of Grand's husband David Chambers McFall, who enthusiastically supported this project and provided information about McFall's family line.

Ann Heilmann, who provided significant leads regarding copyright issues. Ann's previous work on Grand was instrumental to my ability to complete the project, and her enthusiasm for the project pushed me to complete it more quickly than I otherwise would have.

James D. Jenkins, editor of Valancourt Books, who patiently oversaw the manuscript to print process and whose commitment to publishing the works of lesser-known authors is much appreciated.

David Killoran, Chair of the English Department at Loyola Marymount University, who provided financial support for travel to UCLA Special Collections.

Ayra Laciste and Erin Moore, who worked as my research assistants in the final stage of the project. Ayra typed and edited the documents included in the appendix, provided good suggestions for the Introduction and final annotations, and helped me check the final manuscript against the editions in UCLA Special Collections. Erin read proofs of the edition. Thanks to the Rains Research Assistant Program at Loyola Marymount University, which provided year-long stipends for Ayra and Erin to work on the project.

The many members of the VICTORIA listserv, who helped with the more difficult annotations and who generally encouraged the project with promises to use the edition in their courses. Also, thanks to Lois Feuer (CSU Dominguez Hills), Chris Foss (University of Mary Washington), Michael Galant (CSU Dominguez Hills), Don Lewis (CSU Dominguez Hills), Barry Milligan (Wright State University), Takako Naruse, J-Son Ong (Long Beach City College), Renée Pigeon (CSU San Bernardino), Stephen Shepherd (Loyola Marymount University), and Jacqueline Young (University of Glasgow), who offered their expertise with the more difficult annotations.

Every possible effort has been made to contact possible copyright holders of the novel. Thanks to employees at the Authors' Licensing and Collecting Society, the Book Trust, the Society of Authors, the Writers' Guild of Great Britain, the Public Lending Right, and the Bath Library, who provided useful information regarding copyright issues. All copyright holders are encouraged to contact the editor at Valancourt Books.

Bibliography

Anonymous. "A Fear for the Future, That Women Will Cease to Be Womanly." *Fraser's Magazine* 59 (Feb. 1859): 243-248.

Burdett-Coutts, Angela. *Woman's Mission.* New York: Scribner, 1893.

Caine, Barbara. *English Feminism, 1780-1980.* Oxford: Oxford University Press, 1997.

Caird, Mona. "Ideal Marriage." *The Westminster Review,* November 1888, 616-636.

Forward, Stephanie. "Introduction." In *Sex, Social Purity, and Sarah Grand: Volume 2, Selected Letters.* Edited by Stephanie Forward and Ann Heilmann. London: Routledge, 2000, 1-12

Gissing, George. *The Odd Women.* 1893. Introduction by Elaine Showalter. New York: Penguin, 1983.

Grand, Sarah. "The New Aspect of the Woman Question." *North American Review* 158 (1894): 271-276. Repr. in *Sex, Social Purity, and Sarah Grand.* Edited by Ann Heilmann and Stephanie Forward. London: Routledge, 2000, 29-35.

Heilmann, Ann. *New Woman Strategies: Sarah Grand, Olive Schreiner, Mona Caird.* Manchester: Manchester University Press, 2005.

Holcombe, Lee. *Wives and Property: Reform of the Married Women's Property Law in Nineteenth Century England.* Toronto: Toronto University Press, 1983.

Howson, J. H. "Deaconesses." *Quarterly Review* 108 (Oct. 1860): 179-203.

Kucich, John. "Curious Dualities: *The Heavenly Twins* (1893) and Sarah Grand's Belated Modernist Aesthetics." In *The New Nineteenth Century: Feminist Readings of Underread Victorian Fiction.* Edited by Barbara Harman and Susan Meyer. New York: Garland, 1996, 195-204.

Ledger, Sally, and Roger Luckhurst, eds., *The Fin de Siècle: A Reader in Cultural History c. 1800-1900.* Oxford: Oxford University Press, 2000.

Levine, Philippa. *Victorian Feminism, 1850-1900.* Tallahassee: Florida State University Press, 1987.

Mangum, Teresa. *Married, Middlebrow, and Militant: Sarah Grand and the New Woman Novel.* Ann Arbor: University of Michigan Press, 1998.

Quilter, Harry. *Is Marriage a Failure?* London: Swan Sonnenschein and Co. 1888. New York: Garland Publishing, 1984.

Richardson, Angelique. "'People Talk a Lot of Nonsense about Heredity': Mona Caird and Anti-Eugenic Feminism." In *The New Woman in Fiction and in Fact*. Edited by Angelique Richardson and Chris Willis. London: Palgrave, 2001, 183-211.

Ward, Edith. "Shafts of Thought." *Shafts*, 3 November 1892, 2.

Note on the Text

The Valancourt Books edition follows the first edition of 1888, published by E. W. Allen of London, though we have silently corrected errors in this edition that would have resulted in confusion for readers. The 1889 Bentley edition follows the 1888 edition, but at least one of the American editions, the undated Donohue, Henneberry & Co. edition published in Chicago, includes formatting changes, especially in terms of paragraphing and punctuation. The Donohue, Henneberry & Co. edition also contains several significant deletions of text, especially in the sections about Ideala's experience in China. Significant deletions have been indicated in the footnotes.

IDEALA

A STUDY FROM LIFE

"Dieu n'a voulu pour elle que les grands et âpres sentiers."
— Renan.[1]

LONDON :
E.W. ALLEN, 4, AVE MARIA LANE, E.C.
WARRINGTON: GUARDIAN OFFICE
1888.

---

[1] "God wished for her nothing but the lofty and rugged pathways." From Ernest Renan's *Henriette Renan* (1862). This quotation is not included in the Donohue, Henneberry & Co. edition.

"L'esprit ne nous garantit pas des sottises de notre humeur."
—Vauvenargues[1]

---

[1] "The mind does not protect us from the follies of our temperament." From Luc de Clapiers, marquis de Vauvenargues's *Réflexions et maximes* (1746). Vauvenargues was a French moralist, who lived from 1715-1747.

"It is that life of custom and accident in which many of us pass much of our time in this world; that life in which we do what we have not purposed, and speak what we do not mean, and assent to what we do not understand; that life which is overlaid by the weight of things external to it, and is moulded by them, instead of assimilating them; that which, instead of growing and blossoming under any wholesome dew, is crystallised over with it, as with hoar frost, and becomes to the true life what an arborescence is to a tree, a candied agglomeration of thoughts and habits foreign to it, brittle, obstinate, and icy, which can neither bend nor grow, but must be crushed and broken to bits if it stands in our way. All men are liable to be in some degree frost-bitten in this sort; all are partly encumbered and crusted over with idle matter; only, if they have real life in them, they are always breaking this bark away in noble rents, until it becomes, like the black strips upon the birch tree, only a witness of their own inward strength."—Ruskin.[1]

---

[1] From John Ruskin's *The Seven Lamps of Architecture* (1849). Ruskin (1819-1900) was the leading art critic in the Victorian period. This quotation is not included in the Donohue, Henneberry & Co. edition.

PREFACE.

You will ask me, perhaps, even you who are all charity, why parts of this book are what they are. I can only answer with another question: Why are we what we are? But I warn you that it would not be fair to take any of Ideala's opinions, here given, as final. Much of what she thought was the mere effervescence of a strong mind in a state of fermentation, a mind passing successively through the three stages of the process; the *vinous*, alcoholic, or excitable stage; the *acetous*, jaundiced, or embittered stage; and the *putrefactive*, or unwholesome stage; and also embodying, at different times, the characteristics of all three. But, even during its worst phase, it was an earnest mind, seeking the truth diligently, and not to be blamed for stumbling upon good and bad together by the way. It is, in fact, not a perfect, but a transitional state which I offer for your consideration, a state which has its repulsive features, but which, it may be hoped, would result in a beautiful deposit, when at last the inevitable effervescence had subsided.

But why exhibit the details of the process, you may ask. To encourage others, of course. What help is there in the contemplation of perfection ready made? It only disheartens us. We should lay down our arms, we should struggle no longer, we should be hopeless, despairing, reckless, if we never had a glimpse of growth, of those "stepping-stones of their dead selves"[1] upon which men mount to higher things. The imperfections must be studied, because it is only from the details of the process that anything can be learned. Putting aside the people who criticize, not with a view to mending matters, but because a

$$...... \text{low desire}$$
Not to seem lowest makes them level all;[2]

---

[1] Alfred, Lord Tennyson, *In Memoriam A.H.H.* (1850), section 1, lines 3-4.

[2] A slight misquotation of Tennyson's "Merlin and Vivien," *Idylls of the King* (1891), lines 825-826, which reads "low desire / Not to feel lowest makes them level all."

the people who judge, who condemn, who have no mercy on any faults and failings but their own, and who,

> . . . . . . if they find
> Some stain or blemish in a name of note,
> Not grieving that their greatest are so small,
> Inflate themselves with some insane delight,[1]

and would ostracize a neighbour for the first offence by ruling that one mistake must mar a life—anybody's life but their own, of course; who have no peace in themselves, no habit of sweet thought; whose lives are one long agony of excitement, objection, envy, hate, and unrest; the decently clad devils of society who may be known by their eternal carping, and who are already in torment, and doing their utmost to drag others after them. Putting them aside, as any one may who has the courage to face them—for they are terrible cowards—and taking the best of us, and the best intentioned among us, we find that all are apt to make some one trait in the characters, some one trick in the manners, some one incident in the lives of people we meet the text of an objection to the whole person. And a state of objection is a miserable state, and a dangerous one, because it stops our growth by robbing us of half our power to love, in which lies all our strength, and which, with the delight of being loved, is the one thing worth living for. When we know in ourselves that love is heaven, and hate is hell, and all the intervals of like and dislike are antechambers to either, we possess the key to joy and sorrow, by which alone we can attain to the mystery that may not be mentioned here, but beyond which ecstasy awaits us.

This is why such details are necessary.

Doctors-spiritual must face the horrors of the dissecting-room, and learn before they can cure or teach; and even we, poor feeble creatures, who have no strength, however great our desire, to do either, can help at least a little by not hindering, if we attend to our own mental health, which we shall do all the better for knowing something of our moral anatomy, and the diseases to which it is liable. We hate and despise in our ignorance, and grow weak; but love and pity thrive on knowledge, and to love and pity we owe all the beauty of life, and all our highest power.

---

[1] Tennyson, "Merlin and Vivien," *Idylls of the King*, lines 829-832.

IDEALA.

A STUDY FROM LIFE.

CHAPTER I.

SHE came among us without flourish of trumpets. She just slipped into her place, almost unnoticed, but once she was settled there it seemed as if we had got something we had wanted all our lives, and we should have missed her as you would miss the thrushes in the spring, or any other sweet familiar thing. But what the secret of her charm was I cannot say. She was full of inconsistencies. She disliked ostentation, and never wore those ornamental fidgets[1] ladies delight in, but she would take a piece of priceless lace to cover her head when she went to water her flowers. And she said rings were a mistake; if your hands were ugly they drew attention to them, if pretty they hid their beauty; yet she wore half-a-dozen worthless ones habitually for the love of those who gave them to her.

It was said that she was striking in appearance, but cold and indifferent in manner. Some, on whom she had never turned her eyes, called her repellent. But it was noticed that men who took her down to dinner, or had any other opportunity of talking to her, were never very positive in what they said of her afterwards. She made every one, men and women alike, feel, and she did it unconsciously. Without effort, without eccentricity, without anything you could name or define, she impressed you, and she held you—or at least she held *me*, always—expectant. Nothing about her ever seemed to be of the present. When she talked she made you wonder what her past had been, and when she was silent you began to speculate about her future. But she did not talk much as a rule, and when she did speak it was always some subject of interest, some fact that she wanted to ascertain accurately, or some beautiful idea, that occupied her; she

---

[1] A dress item that has some moveable part on it, so one can "fidget" with it; a "fidget ring," for example.

had absolutely no small talk for any but her most intimate friends, whom she was wont at times to amuse with an endless stock of anecdotes and quaint observations; and this made people of limited capacity hard on her. Some of these called her a cold, ambitious, unsympathetic woman; and perhaps, from their point of view, she was so. She certainly aspired to something far above them, and had nothing but scorn for the dead level of dull mediocrity from which they would not try to rise.

"To be distinguished among these people," she once said, "it is only necessary to have one's heart

> Dower'd with the hate of hate, the scorn of scorn,
> The love of love.[1]

There is no need to *do* anything; if you have the right *feeling* you may be as passive as a cow, and still excel them all, for they never thrill to a noble thought."

"Then, pity them," I said.

"No, despise them," she answered. "Pity is for affliction, for such shortcomings as are hereditary and can hardly be remedied—for the taint in nature which is all but hopeless. But these people are not afflicted. They could do better if they would. They know the higher walk, and deliberately pursue the lower. Their whole feeling is for themselves, and such things as have power to move them through the flesh only. I would almost rather sin on the impulse of a generous but misguided nature, and have the power to appreciate and the will to be better, than live a perfect, loveless woman, caring only for myself, like these. I should do more good."

They called Ideala unsympathetic, yet I have known her silent from excess of sympathy. She could walk with you, reading your heart and soul, sorrowing and rejoicing with you, and make you feel without a word that she did so. It was this power to sympathize, and the longing she had to find good in everything, that made her forgive the faults that were patent in a nature with which she was finally brought into contact, for the sake of the virtues which she discovered hidden away deep down under a slowly hardening crust of that kind of self-indulgence which mars a man.

---

[1] Tennyson, "The Poet," lines 3-4.

But her own life was set to a tune that admitted of endless variations. Sometimes it was difficult even for those who knew her best to
detect the original melody among the clashing chords that concealed
it; but, let it be hidden as it might, one felt that it would resolve
itself eventually, through many a jarring modulation and startling
cadence, perhaps, back to the perfect key.

I saw her first at a garden party. She scarcely noticed me when
we were introduced. There were great masses of white cloud drift-
ing up over the blue above the garden, and she was wholly occupied
with them when she could watch them without rudeness to those
about her; and even when she was obliged to look away, I could see
that she was still thinking of the sky.

"Do you live much in cloudland?" I asked, and felt for a moment I
had said a silly thing; but she turned to me quickly, and looked at me
for the first time as if she saw me—and when I say she looked at me,
I mean something more than an ordinary look, for Ideala's eyes were
a wonder, affecting you as a poem does which has power to exalt.

"Ah, you feel it too," she said. "Are they not beautiful? Will you sit
beside me here? You can see the river as well—down there, beneath
the trees."

I thought she would have talked after that, but she did not. When
I spoke to her once or twice she answered absently; and presently
she forgot me altogether, and began to sing to herself softly:

> Flow down, cold rivulet, to the sea,
>   Thy tribute wave deliver;
> No more by thee my steps shall be,
>   Forever and forever.[1]

Then suddenly recollecting herself, she stopped, and exclaimed,
in much confusion, "O please forgive me! That stupid thing has been
running in my head all day—and it is a way I have. I always forget
people and begin to sing."

She did not see in the least that her apology might have been
considered an adding of insult to injury, and, of course, I was careful
not to let her know that I thought it so, although I must confess that
for a moment I felt just a trifle aggrieved. I thought my presence had

---

[1] Tennyson, "A Farewell," lines 1-4.

bored her, and was surprised to see, when I got up to go, that she would rather have had me stay.

She cared little for people in general, and had few likings. It was love with her if anything; but those whom she loved once she loved always, never changing in her affection for them, however badly they might treat her. And she had the power of liking people for themselves, regardless of their feeling for her; indeed, her indifference on this score was curious. I once heard a lady say to her: "You are one of the few young married ladies whom I dare chaperon in these degenerate days. No degree of admiration or worship ever seems to touch you. Is it real or pretended, your unconsciousness?"

"Unconsciousness of what?"

"Of the feeling you excite."

"The feeling *I* excite?" Ideala seemed to think a moment; then she answered gravely: "I do not think I am conscious of anything that relates to myself, personally, in my intercourse with people. They are ideas to me for the most part—men especially so."

That way she had of forgetting people's presence was one of her peculiarities. If she liked you she was content just to have you there, but she never showed it except by a regretful glance when you went away. She was very absent, too. One day I found her with a big, awkward volume on her knee, heated, excited, and evidently put out.

"Is anything the matter?" I wanted to know.

"O yes," she answered desperately; "I've lost my pen, and I'm writing for the mail."

"Why, where are you looking for it?" I asked.

She glanced at me, and then at the book.

"I—I believe," she faltered, "I was looking for it among the p's in the French dictionary."

On another occasion I watched her revising a manuscript. As she wrote her emendations she gummed them on over the old copy, and she was so absorbed that at last she put the gum-brush into the ink-bottle. Discovering her mistake, she gave a little disconcerted sort of laugh, and took the brush away to wash it. She returned presently, examining it critically to see if it were perfectly cleansed, and having satisfied herself, she carefully put it back in the inkbottle.

But perhaps the funniest instance of this peculiarity of hers was one that happened in the Grosvenor Gallery on a certain occasion.[1] She had been busy with her catalogue, doing the pictures conscientiously, and not talking at all, when suddenly she burst out laughing.

"Do you know what I have been doing?" she said. "I wanted to know who that man is"—indicating a gentleman of peculiar appearance in the crowd—"and I have been looking all over him for his number, that I might hunt up his name in the catalogue!"

Her way of seeing analogies as plausible as the obvious relation of p to pen, and of acting on wholly wrong conclusions deduced from most unexceptionable premises, was another characteristic. She always blamed her early education, or rather want of education, for it. "If I had been taught to think," she said, "when my memory was being burdened with historical anecdotes torn from the text, and other useless scraps of knowledge, I should be able to see both sides of a subject, and judge rationally, now.[2] As it is, I never see more than one side at a time, and when I have mastered that, I feel like the old judge in some Greek play, who, when he had heard one party to a suit, begged that the other would not speak, as it would only poggle what was then clear to him."

But in this Ideala was not quite fair to herself.

It was not always—although, unfortunately, it was oftenest at critical moments—that she was beset with this inability to see more than one side of a subject at a time. The odd thing about it was that one never knew which side, the pathetic or the humorous, would strike her. Generally, however, it was the one that related least to herself personally. This self-forgetfulness, with a keen sense of the ludicrous, led her sometimes, when she had anything amusing to relate, to overlook considerations which would have kept other people silent.

"I saw a pair of horses running away with a heavy wagon the other day," she told us once. "It was in Cross Street, and there was a child in the way—there always is a child in the way!—and, as there

---

[1] Founded in London in 1877 by Sir Coutts Lindsay and his wife Lady Lindsay to exhibit the works of both traditional and more progressive artists.

[2] Ideala's comments here raise the issue of women's lack of education, and miseducation, in the nineteenth century. Women were not admitted to universities until 1869, when Girton College was founded, at Cambridge University. Even after the opening of Girton and other women's colleges, women were not permitted to receive degrees from either Cambridge or Oxford until well into the twentieth century.

was no one else to do it, I ran into the road to remove that child. I had to pull it aside quickly, and there was no time to say 'Allow me'—in fact, there was no time for anything—and in my hurry I lost my balance and fell in the mud, and the wagon came tearing over me. It was an unpleasant sensation, but I wasn't hurt, you know; neither the wheels nor the horses touched me. I got very dirty, though, and I have no doubt I looked as ridiculous as I felt, and for that I expected to be tenderly dealt with; but when I went to ask after the child, a few days later, a neighbour told me that its mother was out, and it was a good thing too, as she had been heard to declare she would 'go for that lady the next time she saw her, for flingin' of her bairn[1] about!'"

When she had told the story, Ideala was horrified to find that the fact, which she had overlooked, of her having risked her life to save the child struck us all much more forcibly than the ingratitude that amused her.

Although her sense of humour was keen, it was not always, as I said before, the humorous side of a subject that struck her. I found her one day looking utterly miserable.

"What has happened?" I asked. "You look sad."

"And I feel sad," she answered. "I was just thinking what a pity it is those gay, pleasure-loving, flower-clad people of Hawaii are dying out!"

She was quite in earnest, and could not be made to see that there was anything droll in her mourning poignantly for a people so remote.

Another instance of her absent-mindedness recurs to me. The incident was related at our house one evening, in Ideala's presence, by Mr. Lloyd, a mutual friend. A clever drawing by another friend, of Ideala trying to force a cabman to take ten shillings for a half-crown[2] fare—one of the great fears of her life being the chance of not giving people of that kind as much as they expected—had caused Ideala to protest that she *did* understand money matters.[3]

---

[1] Scottish word for child.

[2] A half-crown is only two shillings, sixpence.

[3] The point here seems to be that most men think women do not understand money, a common perception in the nineteenth century. For example, in Elizabeth Gaskell's *Cranford* (1853), the women in the novel start a tea business but they ask a man to figure out the financial aspects of the business.

"O yes, we all know that your capacity for business is quite extraordinary," Mr. Lloyd said, with a smile that meant something. And then, addressing us all, he asked: "Did I ever tell you about her coming to borrow five shillings from me one day? Shall I tell, Ideala?"

"You may, if you like," Ideala answered, getting very red. "But the story is not interesting."

We all began to be anxious to hear it.

"Judge for yourselves," Mr. Lloyd said. "One day the head clerk came into my private room at the Bank, looking perplexed and discomfited. 'Please, sir' he said, 'a lady wishes to see you.' 'A lady,' I answered. 'Ladies have no business here. What does she want?' 'She would not say, sir, and she would not send in her name. She said it did not matter.' I began to wonder what I had been doing. 'What is she like?' I asked. He looked all round as if in search of a simile, and then he answered: 'Well, sir, she's more like a picture than anything.' 'Show her in,' I said."

Here the story was interrupted by a shout of laughter. He laughed a little himself.

"I should have been polite in any case," he declared, apologetically. "The clerk ushered in a lady whose extreme embarrassment made me sorry for her. She changed colour half-a-dozen times in as many seconds, and then she hurled her errand at my head in these words, without any previous preparation to break the blow: 'Mr. Lloyd, can you lend me five shillings?' and before I had recovered she continued—'I came in by train this morning, and I've lost my purse, and can't get back if you won't help me—at least I think I've lost my purse. I took it out to give sixpence to a beggar—and—and—here is the sixpence!' and she held it out to me. She had given her purse to the beggar and carried the sixpence off in triumph. You may well say 'Oh, Ideala!'"

"And Mr. Lloyd was so very good as to take me to the station, and see me into the train," Ideala murmured; "and he gave me his bankbook to amuse me on the journey, and carried Huxley's *Elementary Physiology*,[1] which I had come in to buy, off in triumph!"

But with all her self-forgetfulness there were moments in which

---

[1] *Lessons in Elementary Physiology* (1866), by Thomas Huxley (1825-1895). Huxley was nicknamed "Darwin's bulldog" for his defense of Darwin's ideas.

she showed that she must have thought deeply about herself, weighing her own individuality against others, to see what place she occupied in her own age, and how she stood with regard to the ages that had gone before; yet even this she seemed to have done in a selfless way, having apparently examined herself coolly, critically, fairly, as she might have examined any other specimen of humanity in which she felt an interest, unbiased by any special regard.

"People always want to know if I write, or paint, or play, or what I do," she once said to me. "They all expect me to do something. My function is not to do, but to be. I make no poetry. I am a poem—if you read me aright."

And again, in a moment of despondency, she said, "I am one of the weary women of the nineteenth century. No other age could have produced me."

When she said she did nothing she must have meant she was not great in anything, for her time was all occupied, and those things in which she was interested were never so well done without her help. If any crying abuse were brought to light in the old Cathedral city; if any large measure of reform were set on foot; if the local papers suddenly became eloquent in favour of some good movement, and adroit in their powers of persuasion; if burdens had to be lifted from the oppressed, and the weak defended against great odds, you might be sure that Ideala was busy, and her work could be detected in it all. And she was especially active when efforts were being made to find amusement for the people. "That is what they want, poor things," she would say. "Their lives are such a dreary round of dull monotonous toil, and they have so little sun to cheer them. They ought to be taught to laugh, and have the brightness put into themselves, and then it would seem as if they had been relieved of half the atmospheric pressure beneath which they groan. Think what your own life would be if day after day brought you nothing but toil; if you had nothing to look back upon, nothing to look forward to, but the labour that makes a machine of you, deadening the power to care, and holding mind and body in the galling bondage and weariness of everlasting routine."

She thought laughter an unfailing specific for most of the ills of life. "We can none of us be thankful enough for the sensation," she said. "Nothing relieves the mental oppression, which does such moral and physical harm, like mirth; of course, I mean legitimate laughter, not levity, nor the ill-natured rejoicing of small minds in such subjects for sorrow as their neighbours' faults, follies, and mistakes. What I am thinking of is the pleasure without excitement which there is in sympathetic intercourse with those large, loving natures that elevate, and the laughter without bitterness which is always a part of it."

Like most people whose goodness is neither affected nor acquired, but natural to them, Ideala saw no merit in her own works, and would not take the credit she deserved for them; nor would she have had her good deeds known at all if she could have helped it. But knowledge of these things leaks out somehow, although probably not a third of what she did will ever be even suspected.

CHAPTER II.

SPEAKING to me of women one day, she said: "Certainly they are *vainqueurs des vainqueurs de la terre*[1] in any sense they choose; but the pity of it is that they do not choose to exercise their power for good to any great extent. I agree with Madame Bernier—if it were Madame Bernier—who said: '*L'ignorance où les femmes sont de leurs devoirs, l'abus qu'elles font de leur puissance, leur font perdre le plus beau et le plus précieux de leurs avantages, celui d'être utiles.*'[2] But hundreds of other quotations will occur to you, written by thoughtful men and women in all ages, and all to the same effect; it is impossible to over-estimate their restraining and refining influence as the companions and mothers of men—and almost equally impossible to make them realize their responsibility or care to use their strength. I would have every woman feel herself a power for good in the land—and if only half of them did, what a world of difference it would make to everybody's health and happiness![3] But women should, as a rule, be silent pow-

---

[1] Conquerors of the conquerors of the earth.

[2] According to Sarah Lewis's *Woman's Mission* (1839), it is Madame Bernier who said, "The state of ignorance women are in about their proper work, the misuse that they make of their ability, makes them lose the best and most precious of their advantages, those of being useful."

[3] Ideala's comments highlight "thought-influence," the nineteenth-century

ers. There are, of course, occasions when they *must* speak—and all honour to those who do so when the need arises—but our influence is most felt when it is quietly persistent and unobtrusive. There is no social reform that we might not accomplish if we agreed among ourselves to do it, and then worked, each of us using her influence to that end in her own family, and among her own friends, only. I once induced some ladies to try a little experiment to prove this. At that time the gentlemen of our respective families were all wearing a certain kind of necktie. We agreed to banish the necktie, and in a month it had disappeared, and not one of those gentlemen was ever able to tell us why he had given it up. We don't deserve much credit for our ingenuity, though," she added, lightly. "Men are so easily managed. All you have to do is to feed them and flatter them."

"I think that hardly fair," I commented.

"What? The feeding and flattering?"

"No, the conspiracy."

"Well, that occurred to me too—afterwards, when it was too late to do anything but repent. At the time, I own, I thought of nothing but the success of the experiment as an example and proof of our will-power."

"You considered one side of the subject only, as per usual, when you are eager and interested," I softly insinuated.

She frowned at me thoughtfully; then, after a pause, she resumed: "Ah, yes! You may be sure there is a great deal of good motive power in women, but most of it is lost for want of knowledge and means to apply it. It works like the sails of a windmill not attached to the machinery, which whirl round and round with incredible velocity and every evidence of strength, but serve no better purpose than to show which way the wind blows."

This question of the position of women in our own day occupied her a good deal.

"The women of my time," she said to me once, "are in an unsettled state, it may be a state of transition. Much that made life worth having has lost its charm for them. The old interests pall upon them. Occupations that used to be the great business of their lives are now thought trivial, and are left to children and to servants. Principles

---

idea that you could change the world by thinking good thoughts. For more on this, see Introduction.

accepted since the beginning of time have been called in question. Weariness and distrust have taken the place of peace and content, and doubt and dissatisfaction are the order of the day. Women want something; they are determined to have it, too; and doubtless they would get it if only they knew what it is that they want. They are struggling to arrive at something, but opinions differ widely as to what that something ought to be; and the result is that they have divided themselves into three classes, not exactly distinct: they dovetail into each other so nicely that it is hard to say where the influence of the one set ends and the other begins. There are, first of all, the women who in their struggles for political power have done so much to unsex us. They have tried to force themselves into unnatural positions, and the consequence has been about as pleasing and edifying as an attempt to make a goose sing. They clamour for change, mistaking change for progress. But don't let the puzzling dovetail confuse you. The people I speak of are not those who have so nobly devoted themselves to the removal of the wrongs of women, though they work together. But the object of all this class is good. They wish to raise us, and what they want, for the most part, is a little more common sense—as is shown in their system of education, for instance, which cultivates the intellectual at the expense of the physical powers, girls being crammed as boys (to their great let and hindrance also) are crammed, just when nature wants all their strength to assist their growth; the result of which becomes periodically apparent when a number of amiable young ladies are let loose on society without hair or teeth. But the thing they clamour for most is equality. There is a great deal to be said in favour of placing the sexes on an equal footing, and if social conventions are stronger and more admirable than natural instincts—and doubtless they are—the thing should be done; but the innate perversity of women will make it difficult—for, I know this, that, whatever the position of a true woman, and however much she may clamour for equality with men in general, the man she herself loves in particular will always be her master.

"But such ridicule as this party has brought upon itself would not have mattered so much had nothing worse come of it. Unfortunately, there seems to be no neutral ground for us women: we either do good or harm; and I hold that first class responsible for the existence of those people who clamour for change of any kind, regardless of the consequences. Their ideas, shorn of all good intention, have resulted in the production of a new creature; and have made it possible for women who have the faults of both sexes and the virtues of neither to mix in society. The bad work done by the influence of this second class is only too apparent. It is to them we owe the fact that there is less refinement, less courtesy, less of the really good breeding which shows itself in kindness and consideration for others, and, heaven help us! even less modesty among us now than there was some years ago.

"These are the women, too, who spend their time and talents on the production of cleverly-written books of the most corrupt tendency. Their works are a special feature of the age, and are doubly dangerous because they have the art of making the worst ideas attractive, by presenting them in forms too refined and beautiful to shock even the most delicate.

"Besides these two classes there is the third, which is more difficult to define. It is the one on which our hope rests. The women who belong to it are dissatisfied like the others, but they are less decided, and therefore their dissatisfaction takes no positive shape. They also want something, and go this way and that as if in search of it, but they are not really trying for anything in particular. They do good and evil indiscriminately, and for the same motive: they find distraction in doing something—anything. But the desire to do good is latent in all of them; show them the way, and it will make itself apparent."

"But what is the reason of all this dissatisfaction?" I asked. "Why don't you go to your husbands and brothers to be set right, as of old?"

"Ah! when you ask me that, you get to the first cause of the trouble," she answered. "The truth is that we have lost faith in our men. They claim some superiority for themselves, but we find none. The age requires people to practice what they preach, and yet expects us to be guided by the counsels of those whose own lives, we know, have rendered them contemptible. They are not fit to guide us, and we are not fit to go alone. I suppose we shall come to an understanding eventually—either they must be raised or we must be lowered. It is for the death of manliness we women mourn. We marry, and find we have taken upon ourselves misery, and lifelong widowhood of the mind and moral nature. Do you wonder that some of us ask: Why should we keep ourselves pure if impurity is to be our bedfellow? You make us breathe corruption, and wonder that we lose our health."

"But why do you talk of the death of manliness? Men have as much courage now as they ever had."

"Oh, of course—mere animal courage; there is plenty of that, but that is nothing. A cat will fight for her kittens. It is moral courage that makes a man, and where do you find it now? Are men self-denying? Are they scrupulous to a shadow of the truth? Are they disinterested? How many *gentlemen* have you met in the course of your life? I know about half-a-dozen."

"What do you call a gentleman, then?" I asked in surprise. "What makes a man one?"

"Why, truth and affection, of course," she answered; "the one is the most ennobling, and the other the most refining quality. As a child I used to think ladies and gentlemen never told stories; it was only the common people who were dishonourable, and that was what made them common. *Hélas*! one lives and learns!"

"I don't think the world is worse than it ever was," I said, drily.

"Not worse, when we know so much better!" she answered with scorn. "Not worse when we have learnt to see so clearly, and most of us acknowledge that

It is our will
Which thus enchains us to permitted ill![1]

It is nearly two thousand years since Christianity began its work, and it is still unaccomplished. Do you know, I sometimes think that all this talk of virtue, and teaching of religion, is a kind of practical joke, gravely kept up to find a church parade of respectability for states, a profession for hundreds, and a means of influencing men by making a tender point in their nervous system to be touched, as with a rod, when necessary—a rod that is held over them always *in terrorem*! We all talk about morality; but try some measure of reform, and you will find that every man sees the necessity of it for his neighbour only. Goodness is happiness, and sin is disease. The truism is as old

---

[1] Percy Bysshe Shelley, *Julian and Maddalo* (1824), lines 170-171.

as the hills, and as evident; but if men were in earnest, do you suppose they would go on for ever choosing sin and its ghastly companion as they do? Do you know, there are moments when I think that even their reverence for the purity of women is a sham. For why do they keep us pure? Is it not to make each morsel more delicious for themselves, that sense and sentiment may be satisfied together, and their own pleasure made more complete? Individuals may be in earnest, but the great bulk of mankind is a hypocrite. When the history of this age is written, moral cowardice and self-indulgence will be found to have been the most striking characteristics of the people. There is no truth to be found in the inward parts."

But Ideala did not often adopt this tone, and she would herself check other people who were preparing to assume it. She had a favourite quotation, adroitly mangled, to suit such occasions. "When we begin to inculcate morality as a science, we must discard moralising as a method," she declared; and she would also beg us to stop the hysteria. "It is the mortal malady of all well-beloved measures," she said; "and it spreads to an epidemic if the infected ones are not suppressed at once to prevent contagion."[1]

But, although she spoke so positively when taken out of herself by the interest and importance of a subject, she had no very high opinion of her own judgment and power to decide. A little more self-esteem would have been good for her; she was too diffident, "I have not come across people on whose knowledge I could rely," she told me. "I have been obliged to study alone, and to form my opinions for myself out of such scraps of information as I have had the capacity to acquire from reading and observation. I am, therefore, always prepared to find myself mistaken, even when I am surest about a thing—for

> What am I?
> An infant crying in the night:
> An infant crying for the light:
> And with no language but a cry![2]

---

[1] Possibly an adaptation of ideas from J. S. Mill's *Utilitarianism*, since Mill takes issue with Bentham's belief that morality is a science in Chapter 1 of *Utilitarianism* and argues that it is an art instead.

[2] Tennyson, *In Memoriam A. H. H.*, section 54, lines 17-20.

In practice, too, she frequently, albeit unconsciously, diverged from her theories to some considerable extent; as on one occasion, when, after talking long and earnestly of the sin of selfishness, she absently picked up a paper I had just cut with intent to enjoy myself, took it away with her to the drawing-room, and sat on it for the rest of the morning—as I afterwards heard.

CHAPTER III.

IDEALA held that dignity and calm are essential in a woman, but, like the rest of the world, she found it hard to attain to her own standard of excellence. Her bursts of enthusiasm were followed by fits of depression, and these again by periods of indifference, when it was hard to rouse her to interest in anything. She always said, and was probably right, that want of proper discipline in childhood was the reason of this variableness, which she deplored, but could neither combat nor conceal. Temperament must also have had something to do with it. Her nervous system was too highly strung, she was too sensitive, too emotional, too intense. She reflected phases of feeling with which she was brought into contact as a lake reflects the sky above it, and the bird that skims across it, and the boats that rest upon its breast; yet, like the lake's, her own nature remained unchanged; it might be darkened by shadows, and lashed by tempests till it raged, but the pure element showed divinely even in its wrath, and the passion of it was expended always to some good end.

But even her love of the beautiful was carried to excess. It was a passion with her which would, in a sturdier age, have been considered a vice. She delighted in the scent of flowers, the song of the thrushes in the spring; colour, and beautiful forms. Doubtless the emotion they caused her was pure enough, and it was natural that, highly-bred, cultivated, and refined as she was, she should feel these delicate, sensuous pleasures in a greater degree than lower natures do. There was danger, however, in the overeducation of the senses, which made their ready response inevitable, but neither limited the subjects, nor regulated the degree, to which they should respond. But it would be hard in any case to say where cultivation of love for the beautiful should end, and to determine the exact point at which the result ceases to be intellectual and begins to be sensual.

I have sat and watched Ideala lolling at an open window in the summer. The house stood on a hill, a river wound through the valley below, and beyond the river the land sloped up again, green and dotted with trees, to a range of low hills, crested with a fringe of wood.

"Do you know what there is beyond those hills?" Ideala asked me once, abruptly. "*I* don't know; but I love to believe that the sea is there, and that the sun is sinking into it now. Sometimes I fancy I can hear it murmur."

And then followed a long silence. And the scent of mignonette[1] and roses blew in upon her, and the twilight deepened, and I saw her grow pale with pleasure when the nightingale began to sing—and then I stole away and never was missed.

She would lie in a long chair for hours like that, scarcely moving, and never speaking. At first I used to wonder what she thought about; but afterwards I knew that at such times she did not think, she only felt.

I have some pictures of her as she was then, dressed in a gown of some quaint blue and white Japanese material, with her white throat bare—I was just going to catalogue her charms, but it seems indelicate to describe a woman, point by point, like a horse that is for sale. I have some other pictures of her, too, as she appeared to me one hot summer when I was painting a picture by the river, and she used to come down the towing-path to watch me work, and sit beside me on the grass for hours together, talking, reading aloud, reciting, or silent, according to her mood, but always interesting. It was then I learnt to know her best. And I am always glad to think of her as I used to see her then, coming towards me in one particular grey frock she wore, tight-fitting and perfect, yet with no detail evident. It was like an expression of herself, that dress, so quiet to all seeming, and yet so rich in material, and so complex in design. The wonder and the beauty of it grew upon you, and never failed of its effect.

---

[1] Member of the Resedaceae family, herbs and shrubs inhabiting arid regions, especially the Mediterranean; is a source of perfume and also yellow dye.

CHAPTER IV.

WHEN I first knew Ideala her religious opinions were all unsettled. "I neither believe nor disbelieve," she told me; "I am in a state of don't know; or perhaps it would be more exact to say that I both doubt and believe at one and the same time. I go indifferently to either church, Protestant or Catholic, and am thankful when any note of music, or thrill of feeling in the voice, or noble sentiment, elevates me so that I can pray. But I am told that both Catholics and Protestants consider me a weak waverer, and call me incorrigible. Sometimes I cannot pray for months together, and when I do it is generally to ask for something I want, not to praise or give thanks. But what a blank it is when one cannot pray; when one has lost the power to conceive that there is a something greater than man, to whom man is nevertheless all in all, and to whom we may look for comfort in all times of our tribulation, and for sympathy in all times of our wealth! To be able to give thanks to God when one is happy is the most rapturous, and to be able to call upon Him in the day of trouble is the most blessed state of mind I know. Yet I believe we should only pray for the possible. The leafless tree may pray for the time of buds and blossoms; will the time come the sooner? Perhaps not, but it will come."

"I must confess," she said on another occasion, "that I do have moments of pure scepticism; but when I cannot believe in the existence of a God, and a Beyond, I feel as if the sky were nearer, and weighed upon me, so that I could not lift my head."

She thought religion consisted much more in doing right than in believing right, and set morality above faith; but I think she had a leaning towards the Roman Catholic religion nevertheless.

"It is a grand old faith," she said, "only it has certain ramifications with which I should always quarrel, notably that of the Sacred Heart[1] with which Catholics deface their lovely Lady in the churches. I always feel that such bad art cannot be good religion. When the

---

[1] Metaphor for Jesus in the Catholic Church. Here, Ideala objects to the Catholic tradition of painting on the Virgin Mary's breast a heart with a cross, as a way to express Mary's devotion to Jesus.

Roman Catholic religion commanded respect it expressed itself better—as in the days when it carved itself in harmonies of solid stone, and wrote itself in tint and tone on glowing canvases, and learnt to speak in thundering mass and mighty hymns of praise! There are people who think these new shoots good as a sign of life in the tree, and this consideration might perhaps make their appearance welcome; but a great deal of strength is expended on their production, and it would be just as well to lop them off again. The old tree wants pruning and cutting back occasionally, and it is a false sentiment that is letting it fall to decay for the sake of these struggling branches.

"There is another thing, too, for which we should all quarrel with the Catholic religion. I think the fact has already been noticed by some writer; at all events, it is evident enough to have occurred to any one. I mean the fact that the Church, by its narrow views about education, and its most unspiritual ambition for itself, has retarded the world's progress for centuries by interfering with the law of natural selection. As a matter of course for ages all the best men went into the Church; it was the only career open to them; and so they left no descendants."

At our house, on another occasion, when the Roman Catholic religion happened to be under discussion, she launched forth some observations in her usual emphatic way. There were only two strangers present, a lady and her husband. Ideala asked the lady, who was sitting next to her, if she were a Catholic, to which the lady answered "No;" and Ideala, satisfied, proceeded to remark: "It may be the true religion, but it certainly is not the religion of truth. The doctrine of expediency,[1] or the latitude they allow themselves on the score of expediency—I don't quite know how they put it—but it has much to answer for. I never find that my Roman Catholic friends are true, as my Protestant friends are. There is always a something kept back, a reservation; a want of straightforwardness, even when there is no positive deception—I can't describe the thing I mean, but it is

---

[1] Here, Ideala uses the phrase in a religious context, to mean someone who uses scripture to justify their own ideas rather than finding truth in scripture. But this phrase also is used in more secular contexts in the nineteenth century. For example, Herbert Spencer (1820-1903) uses the phrase to introduce his argument about natural rights at the beginning of *Social Statics; or, The Conditions Essential to Human Happiness Specified, and the First of Them Developed* (1850).

quite perceptible, and causes an uneasy feeling of distrust, which is all the more tormenting from its vagueness and want of definition. The low-class Roman Catholics, I find, never hesitate if a lie will serve their purpose; and Roman Catholic servants are notoriously untrustworthy. That, of course, proves nothing, for one knows that low-class people of any religion are not to be depended on—still, there is no doubt that one finds deception more rife among Catholics than among Protestants, and one wonders why, if the religion is not to blame."[1]

My sister, Claudia, had tried to catch Ideala's eye, and stop her, but in vain; and the lady next her broke out the moment she paused: "Indeed, you are quite wrong. You cannot have known many Catholics. They are not untrue."

"O yes, I have known numbers," Ideala answered; "I speak from experience. Yet it always seems to me that the Roman Catholic religion is good for individuals. There is pleasure in it, and help and comfort for them. But then it is death to the progress of nations, and the question is: Would an individual be justified in adding a unit more for his own benefit to a system which would ruin his country? I think not."

Here, however, she stopped, seeing at last that something was wrong.

"What dreadful mistake did I make this evening?" she asked me afterwards. "Mrs. Jervois declared she wasn't a Catholic."

"But her husband is," I answered; "and he heard every word."

Ideala groaned.

Not long afterwards Mrs. Jervois wrote and told us she had entered the Catholic Church. "I had, in fact, been received before I went to you," she confessed.

"There!" Ideala exclaimed. "It is just what I said. A want of common honesty is a part of the religion; and you see she had begun to practice it while she was here."

---

[1] Here, it is clear that Ideala exhibits the strong anti-Catholic present in England, but she also exhibits the anti-servant feeling that was widespread during the nineteenth century, since she argues that "low-class people of any religion are not to be depended on." This distrust of certain classes stems from the master/servant relationship that was a part of daily life in England in the nineteenth century.

"What an eternal lie it is they preach when they tell us life is not worth having," she said to me once, speaking of preachers generally. "I have heard an oleosaccharine[1] priest preach for an hour on this subject, detailing the worthlessness of all earthly pleasures, with which he seemed to be intimately acquainted—his appearance making one suspect that he had not even yet exhausted them all himself—and giving a florid account of the glories of the life to come, about which he appeared to know as much but to care less; just as if heaven might not begin on earth if only men would let it."

One day I had to warn her about acting so often on impulse. She heard what I had to say very good-naturedly, and, after thinking about it for a while, she said: "What a pity it is one never sees an impulse coming. It is impossible to know whether they arise from below, or descend from above. I always find if I act on one that it has arisen; and as surely if I leave it alone it proves to have been a good opportunity lost. And how curiously our thoughts go on, often so irrespective of ourselves. I was in a Roman Catholic church the other day, and the priest—a friend of mine, who looks like the last of the Mohicans minus the feathers in his hair; but a good man, with nice, soft, velvety brown eyes—preached most impressively. He told us that the Lord was there—there on that very altar, ready to answer our prayers; and, oh dear! when I came to think of it, there were so many of my prayers waiting to be answered! I 'felt like' presenting them all over again, it seemed such a good opportunity. And then they sang the *O salutaris Hostia*[2] divinely—so divinely that I thought if the Lord really had been there He would certainly have made them sing it again—and I could not pray any more after that. You call this rank irreverence, do you not? *I* do. And I wish I had not thought it. Yet it was one of those involuntary tricks of the mind for which I cannot believe that we are to be held responsible. Theologians would say it was a temptation of the devil, but they are wrong. The first cause of these mental lapses is to be found in some habit of levity, acquired young, and not easily got rid of, but still not hopeless. But prevention is better than cure, and children should be taught right-mindedness

---

[1] From oleosaccharum, a mixture of oil and sugar to dilute the bad taste of medicine.

[2] Hymn to the Host, one of two hymns sung at the Benediction of the Blessed Sacrament in the Catholic Church.

early. I wish I had been. Happy is the child who is started in life with a set of fixed principles, and the power to respect."

I used to wish that there might be a universal religion, but Ideala did not share my feeling on this subject. "I suppose it is a fine idea," she said; "but while minds run in so many different grooves, it seems to me far finer for one system of morality to have found expressions enough to satisfy nearly everybody."

She had very decided views about what heaven ought to be.

"The mere material notion of abundance of gold and precious stones, which appealed to the early churchmen, has no charm for us," she declared. "We must have new powers of perception, and new pleasures provided for us, such, for instance, as Mr. Andrew Lang[1] suggests in an exquisite little poem about the Homeric Phæacia—the land whose inhabitants were friends of the gods, a sort of heaven upon earth." And then she quoted:—

> The languid sunset, mother of roses,
>   Lingers, a light on the magic seas;
> The wide fire flames as a flower uncloses;
>   Heavy with odour and loose to the breeze.

* * * * *

> The strange flowers' perfume turns to singing,
>   Heard afar over moonlit seas;
> The siren's song, grown faint with winging,
>   Falls in scent on the cedar trees.[2]

"Those lines were the first to make me grasp the possibility of having new faculties added to our old ones in another state of existence," she said, "faculties which should give us a deeper insight into the nature of things, and enable us to discover new pleasures in the unity which may be expected to underlie beauty and excellence in all their manifestations, as Mr. Norman Pearson puts it. Did you ever read that paper of his, 'After Death,' in the *Nineteenth Century*?[3] It

---

[1] Andrew Lang (1844-1912), poet, novelist, folklorist, and literary critic. His work on Homer (editions of the *Odyssey* and the *Iliad*, as well as critical books arguing for the unity of Homer) is particularly well known.

[2] Lang, "A Song of Phæacia," *Grass of Parnassus* (1888), lines 1-4, 9-12.

[3] John Norman Pearson (1787-1865), Church of England clergyman, chaplain to

embodies what I had long felt, but could never grasp before I found his admirable expression of it. 'I can see no reason,' he says, in one passage in particular which I remember word for word, I think, it gives me such pleasure to recall it—'I can see no reason for supposing that *some such* insight would be impossible to the quickened faculties of a higher development. With a nature material so far as the existence of those faculties might require, but spiritual to the highest degree in their exercise and enjoyment: under physical conditions which might render us *practically* independent of space, and *actually* free from the host of physical evils to which we are now exposed, we might well attain a consummation of happiness, *generally* akin to that for which we now strive, but idealized into something like perfection. The faculties which would enable us to obtain a deeper and truer view of all the manifestations of cosmic energy would at the same time reveal to us new forms of beauty, new possibilities of pleasure on every side: and—to take a single instance—the emotions to which the sight of Niagara now appeals might then be gratified by a contemplation of the fierce grandeur of some sun's chromosphere or the calmer glories of its corona.'[1] That satisfies, does it not?" she added, with a sigh. "It suggests such infinite possibilities."

★ ★ ★ ★ ★

One day, when she was making herself miserable for want of a religion, I tried to comfort her by talking of the different people whose lives had been good and pure and noble, although they had had no faith.

"I suppose my principles are right," she said; "but if they are, they have come right by accident. The children of the people are sent to

---

Marquess Wellesley, first principal of Islington College of the Church Missionary Society, and vicar of Holy Trinity Church, Tunbridge Wells. "After Death," which appeared in the August 1883 issue of the *Nineteenth Century*, examines indifference toward the afterlife and suggests that it should receive more attention than it has. Further, Pearson argues that the afterlife can be a joyous existence; however, he does not accept the conventional joyful heaven/tortuous hell dichotomy. In addition, he rejects the ideas held by non-materialist philosophers that heaven is a place of intellectual bliss only and argues that both intellect and emotions have a place in the afterlife.

[1] Here, Ideala quotes Pearson accurately. For more on Pearson's views about the afterlife, see "After Death," *Nineteenth Century* 14 (Aug. 1883): 262-284.

Sunday schools, and taught the difference between right and wrong; *we* seem to be expected to know it instinctively. I think if I had learnt I might have profited, because I cling so fondly to the one principle I ever heard clearly enunciated. It was on the sin of shooting foxes; and I cannot tell you the horror I have of the crime, even down to the present day. But, now I think of it, I did receive two other scraps of religious training. My governess taught me the ten commandments by making me say them after her when I was eating bread and sugar for breakfast before going to church on Sunday. The thought of them always brings back the flavour of bread and sugar. And the other scrap I got from a clergyman to whom I was sent on a single occasion when I was thought old enough to be confirmed. He asked me which was the commandment with promise,[1] and I didn't know, so he told me; and then I made him laugh about a horse of mine that used to have great fun trying to break my neck, and after that he said I should do. I did not agree with him, however, and I positively refused to be confirmed until I knew more about it. My mother said I was the most disagreeable child she had ever known, which was probably true, but as an argument it failed to convince. It was her last remark on the subject, happily, and after that the thing was allowed to drop."

Ideala was fourteen when she refused to be confirmed for conscientious scruples, and although she made light of it in this way, she had suffered a good deal and been severely punished at the time for her refusal, but vainly, for she never gave in.

In after life she held, of course, that Christianity was the highest moral revelation the world had ever known; but when she saw that legal right was not always moral right, I think she began to look for a higher.

By baptism she belonged to the Church of England, but she seems to have thought of the Sacrament always with the idea of transubstantiation in her mind.[2] She spoke of it reverently, but had never been able to take it, and for a curious reason: she said the idea of it nause-

---

[1] The Fifth Commandment, "Honor thy mother and father," called the commandment with promise because it promises "long life and prosperity" in return for keeping the commandment.

[2] She was baptized in the Anglican Church, which generally holds that the Sacrament of Communion is *symbolic* of the body and blood of Christ. Catholics believe that, through transubstantiation, the bread and wine actually *become* Christ's body and blood.

ated her. She felt that the elements were unnatural food, and therefore she could not touch them—and this feeling never left her but
once, when she was dangerously ill, and yearned, as she told me, for
the Sacrament more than for life and health. Day and night the longing never left her; but, not having been confirmed, she did not like to
ask for it, and as she recovered the old feeling gradually returned.

Religious difficulties always tormented her more or less. As she
grew older she felt with Shelley that belief is involuntary, and a man
is neither to be praised nor blamed for it;[1] and she was always ready
to acknowledge with Sir Philip Sidney that "Reason cannot show
itself more reasonable than to leave reasoning on things above reason,"[2] but nevertheless her mind did not rest.

I have also heard her quote, "Credulity is the man's weakness, but
the child's strength,"[3] and add that in matters of faith and religion
we are all children, and I have thought at times that she had been
able to leave it so; but something always fell from her sooner or later
which showed that the old trouble was rankling still—as when she
told me once: "I have never heard the Divine voice which has called
you and all my friends. I listen for it, but it does not speak. I call, but
there is no reply. I wait, but it does not come. The heaven of heavens
is dark to me, and the yearning of my soul meets no response. Will
it be so for ever?"

No, not for ever—but she was led by tortuous ways, and left to
work out her own salvation in very fear and trembling, till the dear
human love was given to her in pity to help her to know something
of that which is Divine. And then, I hope, above the trouble of her
senses, and the turmoil of the world, the Divine voice did call her,
and she was able at last to hear.

---

[1] A paraphrase of ideas about belief expressed by Percy Bysshe Shelley (1792-
1822) in *The Necessity of Atheism* (1811), the pamphlet which prompted Shelley's
expulsion from Oxford. A revised and expanded version of the pamphlet appeared as a note in *Queen Mab* (1813).

[2] Sidney (1554-1586), *New Arcadia* (1590), Book 3. Philanax inquires the oracle at
Delphi about whether Basilius should give his daughters up for marriage to Anax-
ius and his brothers. The oracle says no, since the women are reserved for someone else, and Philanax responds to the oracle's message with this quotation.

[3] Charles Lamb, "Witches and Other Night Fears," *Essays of Elia* (published in
book form in 1823). Lamb (1775-1834) was poet and an essayist and wrote, with
his sister Mary, the children's book *Tales from Shakespeare* (1807).

CHAPTER V.

IDEALA often recurred to the subject of work for women.

"There are so many thousands of us," she said, "who have no object in life, and nothing to make us take it seriously. My own is a case in point. I am not necessary, even to my husband. There is nothing I am bound to do for him, or that he requires of me, nothing but to be agreeable when he is with me, which would not interfere with a serious occupation if I had one, and is scarcely interest enough in life for an energetic woman. My household duties take, on an average, half an hour a day; and everything in our house is done regularly, and well done. My social duties may be got through at odd moments, and the more of a pastime I make them the better I fulfil them; and, with the exception of these, there is nothing in my life that I cannot have done for me by someone better able to do it than I am. And even if I had children I should not be much more occupied, for the things they ought to learn from their mothers are best taught by example. For all practical purposes, parents, as a rule, are bad masters for any but very young children. They err on the side of over-severity or the reverse. So you see I have no obligations of consequence, and there is, therefore, nothing in my life to inspire a sense of responsibility. And all this seems to me a grievous waste of Me. I remember Lord Liberal telling me, when we discussed this subject, that he was travelling once with a well-known editor, and, noticing the number of villas that had sprung up of late years along the whole line of rail they were on, he said: 'I wonder what the ladies in those villas do with their time? I suppose their social duties are limited, and they are too well off to be obliged to trouble themselves about anything.' 'It is the existence of those villas, my lord,' the editor answered, 'that makes the present profession of the novelist possible.' But I think," said Ideala, "that those women might find something better to do than to make a profession for novelists."

"But you do a good deal yourself, Ideala," I ventured.

"Yes, in a purposeless way. All my acts are isolated; it would make little difference if they had never been done."

"Then you are not content, after all, to be merely a poem?" I said, maliciously. "You would like to do as well as to be?"

She laughed. Then, after a little, she said earnestly: "Do you know, I always feel as if I *could* do something—teach something—or help others in a small way with some work of importance. I never believe I was born just to live and die. But I have a queer feeling about it. I am sure I shall be made to go down into some great depth of sin and misery myself, in order to learn what it is I have to teach."

She loved music, and painting, and poetry, and science, and none of her loves were barren. She embraced them each in turn with an ardour that resulted in the production of an offspring—a song, a picture, a poem, or book on some most serious subject, and all worthy of note. But she was inconstant, and these children of her thought or fancy were generally isolated efforts that marked the culminating point of her devotion, and lessened her interest if they did not exhaust her strength.

Perhaps, though, I wrong her when I call her inconstant. It seems to me now that each new interest was a step by which she mounted upwards, learning to sympathize practically and perfectly with all men in their work as she passed them on her way to find her own.

CHAPTER VI.

SHE knew the poor of the place well, and took a lively interest in all that concerned them; and occasionally she would confide some of her own odd observations and reflections to me.

"On Sunday morning all the women wash their doorsteps," she told me; "I think it is part of their religion."

And on another occasion she said: "They have such lovely children here, and such swarms of them. I am always hard on the women with lovely children. People say it is envy, hatred, malice, and all uncharitableness, that makes me so; but it really is because I think women who have nice children should be better than other women. It would be worse for one of them to do a wrong thing than for poor childless me."

This conclusion may be quarrelled with as illogical, but the feeling that led to it was beautiful beyond question; and, indeed, all her ideas on that subject were beautiful.

She went once, soon after she came among us, to comfort a lady in the neighbourhood who had lost a baby at its birth.

"It is sad that you should lose your child," Ideala said to her; "but you are better off than I am, for I never knew what it was to be a mother."

She would have thought it a privilege to have experienced even the sorrows of maternity.

Talking about the people, she told me: "They draw such nice distinctions. They speak of 'a lady' and 'a real lady.' A 'real lady' is a person who gives no trouble. If Mrs. Vanbrugh wants anything from the butcher, and he has already sent to her house once that day, she does not expect him to send again, she sends to him—and she is 'a real lady.' Mrs. Stanton is also thoughtful, but she is something more; she is sociable and kind, and talks to them all in a friendly way, just as if they were human beings; and she is something more than 'a real lady'—she's 'a real nice lady.'

"Do you know Mrs. Poulterer at the fish-shop? What a fine-looking woman she is! Middle-aged, intelligent, and a very good specimen of her class, I should think. She has eight children already, and would consider the ninth a further blessing. Her husband is a good looking man, too, and most devoted. In fact, they are quite an ideal pair with their eight children and their fish shop. He had to go to Yarmouth the other day to buy bloaters,[1] and while he was away she went by the five o'clock train every morning to choose the day's supply of fish for the shop, and he was quite unhappy about it. He was afraid she would 'overdo' herself, and rather than that should happen he desired her to let the business go to the — ahem! He made her write every day to say how she was, and was wretched till he returned to relieve her of her arduous duties. She made friends with me during the scarlet fever epidemic. Number eight was a baby then, and she was afraid he might catch the disease and be taken to the hospital and die for want of her; and I sympathized strongly with her denunciations of the cruelty of the act. Fancy taking little babies from their mothers! Barbarous, don't you think it? One day a lady came into the shop while I was there. She was dressed in a bright pink costume, with a

---

[1] Yarmouth, also known as Great Yarmouth, is in Norfolk, at the mouth of the Bure River on the North Sea. Yarmouth was known for its herring. Bloaters are cured herring or mackerel.

large hat all smothered in pink feathers. I thought of the Queen of Sheba,[1] and felt alarmed. Mrs. Poulterer told me afterwards she was 'just a lady,' rolling in recently-acquired wealth, and 'as hard to please as if she had never washed her own doorstep.' It was then I learnt the difference between 'a lady' and 'a real lady.'"

One of Ideala's exploits got into the paper somehow, and she was annoyed about it, and anxious to make us believe the account of the risk she ran had been greatly exaggerated. I was present when she gave her own version of the story, which was characteristic in every way.

"I heard frantic cries from the river," she said. "Someone was shrieking, 'The child will be drowned!' and I ran to see what was the matter. A man was tearing up and down on the bank, a child was struggling in the water, and as there was nobody else to be seen he looked to *me* for assistance! I advised him to go in and bring the child out, but the idea did not appear to commend itself to him, so he took to running up and down again, bawling, 'The child will be drowned!' And indeed it seemed very likely; so I was obliged to go in and bring it out myself. The man was overjoyed when I restored it to him. He clasped it in his arms with every demonstration of affection; and then he looked at me and became embarrassed. He evidently felt that he ought to say something, but the difficulty was what to say. At last a bright idea seemed to strike him. His countenance cleared, and he spoke with much feeling. 'I am afraid you are rather wet,' he observed; and then he left me, and a sympathetic landlady, who keeps a little public-house by the river, and had witnessed the occurrence, took me in and dried me. She gave me whisky and hot water, and entertained me for the rest of the afternoon. She is a remarkable woman, and I should visit her often were it not for her love of, and faith in, whisky and hot water. I tell her there are five things which make the nose red—viz., cold, tight-lacing, disease of the right side of the heart, dyspepsia,[2] and alcohol, and the greatest of these is alcohol; but she says a little colour anywhere would be an improvement to me, and I feel that I can have nothing in common with a woman who has such bad taste in the distribution of colour."

---

[1] Queen of an ancient country in southern Arabia, probably in the area that is now Yemen. She was known for her beauty and her visit to King Solomon.

[2] Disease of the right side of the heart is cor pulmonale, or cordia pulmonalia, which is caused by inability of the right ventricle to control the increased blood pressure produced on the left side of the body. Dyspepsia is indigestion.

CHAPTER VII.

IDEALA's notions of propriety were altogether unconventional. She never could be made to understand that it was not the proper thing to talk familiarly to any one she met, and discuss any subject they were equal to with them.

"It is good for people to talk, and natural, and therefore proper," she said. "If I can give pleasure to a stranger by doing so, or he can give pleasure to me, it would not be right to keep silent."

She carried this idea of her duty to her neighbour rather far sometimes.

I remember her telling me once about two old gentlemen she had travelled with the day before.

"The sun came in and bothered me, and one of them offered to draw the blind," she said, "and he remarked it was rather a treat to see the sun, we have so little of it now; and I said that was true, and told him how I pitied the farmers. I had to stay in my room the other day with a bad cold, and I amused myself watching one of them at work in some fields opposite. The state of his mind was expressed by his boots. On Monday the sun was shining, the air was mild, and it seemed as if we were going to have a continuance of fine weather, and the farmer appeared of a cheerful countenance, and his boots were polished and laced. On Tuesday there was an east wind, veering south, with showers, and his boots were laced, but not polished. On Wednesday there was frost, fog, and gloom, and they were neither laced nor polished. On Thursday there was a snowstorm, and he had no boots at all on; and after that I did not see him, and I wondered if he had committed suicide—in which case I thought the jury might almost have brought in a verdict of 'justifiable *felo-de-se*.'[1] And when

[1] Suicide. Until 1823, with the passage of 4 George IV. c 52, suicide was seen as unjustifiable and grounds for burial at a cross-roads rather than in a church cemetery. But several cases in the early 1820s, including the suicide of Lord Londonderry, a central political figure in the House of Commons, led the English to begin distinguishing between justifiable suicide on the basis of insanity and unjustifiable suicide, committed with a sound mind. For more on nineteenth-century suicide, see Barbara Gates, *Victorian Suicide: Mad Crimes and Sad Histories* (Princeton: Princeton University Press, 1988).

I told that story the other old gentleman shut his book, and began to
talk too. And I said I thought the weather was much colder than it
used to be, for I could remember wearing muslin dresses in May, and
I could not wear them at all now; but I did not know if the change
were in the climate or in myself—perhaps a little of both—though,
indeed, I knew that, to a certain extent, it was in the climate, which
had been very much altered in different districts by drainage, and cutting, or planting—altered for the better, however, as a rule. And one
old gentleman had heard that before, but did not understand it exactly,
so I explained it to him; and then I talked about changes of climate
in general, and the formation of beds of coal, and the ice period, and
sun spots, and the theory of comets, and about my husband getting
up to see the last one, and going out in a felt hat and dressing-gown
with a bed-candle to look for it—and about that dream of mine, did
I tell you? I dreamt the comet came into our drawing-room, and the
leg of a Chinese table turned into a snake and snorted at it, and the
comet looked so taken aback that I woke myself with a shout of
laughter. And then we talked of popular superstitions about comets,
and dreams, and ghosts—particularly ghosts, and I told a number of
creepy stories, and one old gentleman pretended he didn't believe
in them, but he did, and so did the other without any pretence; and
we talked about Darwinism, and the nature of the soul, and Nihilism, and the state of society—and—and a few other things.[1] And they
were such dear delightful old gentlemen, and they knew such a lot,
and were so clever; and one of them was a Railway Director, and the
other couldn't let his farms, and was bothered about his pheasants,
and wanted to have the trains altered to suit him. I should so like to
meet them both again."

"And how long did all this take, Ideala?"

---

[1] Darwinism is Charles Darwin's theory of evolution, explicated in *The Origin
of Species* (1859), where Darwin (1809-1882) argues for a natural and gradual
origin of species rather than an immediate and divine creation. Also in this
work, Darwin claims that new species arise and are perpetuated by natural
selection. Nihilism is a philosophy, originally Russian, that rejects social institutions such as marriage and parental authority. It became a more widespread
political and cultural movement in the mid-nineteenth century, when propo-
nents denounced traditional values, argued that human existence is useless,
and advocated destruction of the social system and its institutions.

"Oh, some hours. I fancy their dreams would be rather confused last night," she added, naïvely.

"Poor old gentlemen!" said I.

This sociability and inclination to talk the matter out, and, I may say, a certain amount of innocence and lack of worldly wisdom into the bargain, betrayed her occasionally into small improprieties of conduct that were not to be excused, and would possibly not have been forgiven in anyone but Ideala. But such things were allowed in her as certain things are allowed in certain people—not because the things are right in themselves, but because the people who do them see no harm in them. There are people, too, who seem to enjoy the privilege of making wrong right by doing it. Society, however, only accords this privilege to a limited and distinguished few.

When Ideala saw for herself that she had done an unjustifiable thing she was very ready to confess it. I always fancied she had some latent idea of making atonement in that way. It never mattered how much a story told against herself, nor how much malicious people might make of it to her discredit; she told all, inimitably, and with scrupulous fidelity to fact.

One day she was standing waiting for a train at the station at York, and in her absent way she fixed her eyes on a gentleman who was walking about the platform.

Presently he went up to her, and, without any apology or show of respect, remarked: "I am sure I have seen you before."

"Probably," Ideala rejoined, as if the occurrence were the most natural thing in the world, "but I do not remember you. Perhaps if I heard your name——?"

"Oh, I don't suppose you ever heard my name," he said.

"In that case I can never have known you," she answered, calmly. "I never know any one except by name. I suppose you are an Englishman?"

"Yes," he said, eagerly; "I am in the 5th——"

"Ah, I thought so," she interrupted, placidly. "Englishmen in the 5th, and some other regiments, are apt to have but the one idea——"

"And that is?"

"And that is a bad one."

He looked at her for a moment, and then, hat in hand, he made her a low bow, and left her without another word.

"I think he felt ill, and went to have some refreshment," she added, when she told me.

From what happened afterwards I am sure that at the time she had no idea of the real significance of the position in which she found herself placed on this occasion. But, as a rule, if she did or said the wrong thing, she became painfully conscious of the fact immediately afterwards—indeed, it was generally *afterwards* that she grasped the full meaning of most things. She was ready with repartee without being in the least quick of understanding; she had to think things over, and even then she was not sure to do the right thing next time.

"Mr. Graves is ten years younger than his wife," she told me once, "and only fancy what I said one day. It was in his studio, and she was there. I declared a woman could have no sense of propriety at all who married a man younger than herself—that no good could possibly come of such marriages—and a lot more. Then I suddenly remembered, and you can imagine my feelings! But what do you think I did? I went there the next year, and said the same thing again exactly!"

CHAPTER VIII.

WHEN we were a small party of intimate friends, and Ideala was quite at her ease with us, it was pleasant to see her lolling, a little languidly as was her wont (for physically her energy was fitful), in the corner of a couch, looking happy and interested, her face, which was sad in repose, lit up for the time with amusement, as she quietly listened to our talk, and observed all that was going on around her. Even when she did not speak a word she somehow managed to make her presence felt, and, as a rule, she spoke little on these occasions. But sometimes we managed to draw her out, and sometimes she would burst forth suddenly of her own accord, with a torrent of eloquence that silenced us all; and even when she was utterly wrong she charmed us. Her chance observations were generally noteworthy either for their sense or their humour. It was only her sense of humour, I think, that saved her from being sentimental; but she gave expression to it in season and out of season, and would let it carry her too far sometimes, for she made enemies for herself more than once by the way she exposed the absurdity of certain things to the very people who believed in them. Every lapse of this kind caused her infinite regret, but the fault seemed incurable: she was always either repenting of it or committing it, although, having so many quirks of her own, she felt that she, of all people in the world, should have dealt most tenderly with the weaknesses of others.

She knew how narrowly she escaped being sentimental, and would often joke about her danger in that respect. "This lovely summer weather makes me *sickly* sentimental," she told me once. "I feel like the heroine of a three-volume novel written by a young lady of eighteen, and I think continually of *him*. I don't know in the least who *he* is, but that makes no difference. The thought of him delights me, and I want to write long letters to him, and make verses about him the whole day long. And he wants me to be good."

She had two or three pet abominations of her own, any allusion to which was sure to make her outrageous—false sentiment, and affectation of any kind were amongst them. She had little habits, too, that we were all pleased to fall in with. Sitting in the corner of a couch, and of one couch in particular in every house, was one of these; and people got into the way of giving up that seat to her whenever she appeared. I think it would have puzzled us all to say why or wherefore, for she never said or looked anything that could make us think she wished to appropriate it; she simply took it as a matter of course when it was offered to her, and probably did not know that she invariably sat there.

Ideala was a splendid horsewoman, and swam like a fish; but she was not good at tennis or games of any kind, and she did not dance, for a curious reason: she objected to be touched by people for whom she had no special affection. She even disliked to shake hands, and often wished someone would put the custom out of fashion. With regard to dancing I have heard her say, too, that she sympathized entirely with the Oriental feeling on the subject. She thought it delightful to be danced to, to lie still with a pleasant companion near her who would not talk too much, and listen to the music, and enjoy the poetry of motion coolly and at ease. "I love to see the 'dancers dancing in tune,'"[1] she said; "but to have to dance myself would be

---

[1] Tennyson, "Maud: A Monodrama," (1855), Part I, line 867.

as great a bother as to have to cook my dinner as well as eat it. I suppose it is a healthy amusement—indeed, I know it is when you take it as I do; for when all you people come down the morning after a dance with haggard eyes and no power to do anything, I am as fresh as a lark, and have decidedly the best of it."

She was not good at games because she was not ambitious. She did not care to have her skill commended, and was content to lose or win with equal indifference—so long as only the honour of the thing was involved; but when the stakes were more material she showed a vice of which she was quite conscious.

"I daren't play for money," she said to me. "I never have, and I have always said that I never will. All the women of my family are born gamblers. My mother has often told me that regularly, when she was a girl, the day after she received her allowance she had either doubled it or lost it all; and before she was twenty she hadn't a jewel worth anything in her possession—and my aunts were as bad. One of them staked herself one night to a gentleman she was playing with, and he won, and married her. Gambling was more the custom then than it is now, but for me it is as much in the air as if it were still the fashion. When there is any talk of play I feel fascinated, and when I see a pack of cards the temptation is so irresistible that I have often to go away to save my resolution."

Which made me think of a favourite quotation of Lessing's from Minna:—"*Tous les gens d'esprit aiment le jeu à la folie.*"[1]

CHAPTER IX.

IDEALA's low esteem for "mere animal courage" was probably due to the fact that she possessed it herself in a high degree. Yet soon after I met her I began to suspect, and was afterwards convinced, that something in her manner which had puzzled me at first arose from fear. There was that in her life which made her afraid of the world, which would, had it guessed the truth, have pried with curious eyes into her sorrow, and found an interest in seeing her suffer. The trouble was her husband. She rarely spoke of him herself, and I think I ought to

---

[1] "All wits love silly games"; Gotthold Ephraim Lessing (1729-1781), German dramatist, whose *Minna von Barnhelm* (1767) was a comedy about marriage.

follow her example, and say as little about him as possible. He was jealous of her, jealous of her popularity, and jealous of every one who approached her. He carried it so far that she scarcely dared to show a preference, and was even obliged to be cold and reserved with some of her best friends. I was a privileged person, allowed to be intimate with her from the first, partly because I insisted on it when I saw how matters stood, and partly because my position and reputation gave me a right to insist. I never had occasion to brave insults for her sake, but, like many others, I would have done so had it been necessary. Her friends were constantly being driven from her on one pretext or another. People would have taken her part readily enough had she complained, but complaint was contrary to her nature and her principles. Some, who suspected the truth, blamed her reticence; but I always thought it right, and on one occasion when we approached the subject indirectly I told her "Silence is best." I ought to have qualified the advice, for she carried it too far, and was silent afterwards when she should have spoken—that is to say, when it had become evident that endurance was useless and degrading.

She fought hard to preserve her dignity, and was determined that "as the husband is, the wife is,"[1] should not be true in her case. But he did lower her insensibly, nevertheless. As her life became more and more unendurable she became a little reckless in speech; it was a sort of safety-valve by means of which she regained her composure, and I soon began to recognize the sign, and to judge of the amount she had suffered by the length to which she afterwards went in search of relief, and the extent to which suffering made her untrue to herself.

As a rule, when with him, she was yielding, but she had fits of determination, too, when she knew she was right. One night, as they were driving home from a ball together, her husband suddenly declared that he would not allow her to be one of the patronesses of a fancy fair which was to be held for a charitable purpose, although she had already consented and he had made no objection at the time.

"But why may I not?" Ideala asked.

---

[1] Tennyson, "Locksley Hall" (1842), line 47. The complete line reads: "As the husband is, the wife is: thou art mated with a clown," and is followed by the line: "And the grossness of his nature will have weight to drag thee down."

"Because I object. Do you hear? I will not have it, and you must withdraw."

"I must decline to obey any such arbitrary injunction," she answered, quietly.

He detained her on the doorstep until the carriage had driven round to the stables.

"Now, are you going to obey me?" he asked.

"Yes, if you give me a reason for what you require," she answered, wearily.

"Oh, you are obstinate, are you?" he rejoined, in a jeering tone. "Well, stay in the garden and think it over. Perhaps reflection will make you more dutiful. I shall tell your maid you will not want her to-night. When you have made up your mind you can ring." And so saying he walked into the house and shut the door upon her.

It was a summer night, but Ideala felt chilly with only a thin shawl over her ball dress. She walked about as long as she could, but fatigue overcame her at last, and she was obliged to lie down on one of the garden seats. She wrapped the train of her dress round her shoulders, and lay looking up at the stars. The air was heavy with the scent of flowers. The night was very still. Once or twice the rush of a passing train in the distance became audible; and the ceaseless, solemn, inarticulate murmur of the night was broken by a nightingale that sang out at intervals, divinely.

Ideala never thought of submitting; she simply lay there, waiting without expecting. The night air overcame her more and more with a sense of fatigue, but she could not sleep. She saw the darkness fade and the dawn appear, and when at last the servants began to move in the house she watched her opportunity and slipped in unobserved. She went to one of the spare rooms, undressed, rang, and got into bed. When the bell was answered she ordered a hot bath and hot coffee immediately. The maid supposed she had slept there, and seemed surprised; but as her mistress offered no explanation she could make no remark; and so the matter ended.

But I do not think Ideala suffered much on that occasion. Her strong young womanhood saved her somewhat—and there was a charm for her in the beauty of the night and the novelty of her position, which a less healthy organism would not have appreciated, had it been able to discover it—at such a time.

CHAPTER X.

IDEALA had been married eight years, and two months after that night the long delayed hope of her life, which she had begun to believe was beyond hope, was at last realized. Her child was a boy, and her joy in him is something that one is glad to have seen. But it was short-lived. I do not know if her husband were jealous of her happiness, or if he thought the child was more to her than he was, or if he were merely making a proposition, by way of experiment, which he never meant to carry into effect—probably the latter. At all events, he went to her one day when the child was about six weeks old, and told her he thought she must give up nursing him.

The mother's nature was up in arms in a moment. I suppose she had not quite regained her strength, for she had been very ill, and, being weak, she was excitable.

"I will not give my baby up! How can you think it?" she exclaimed.

"Oh, well," he answered, coolly, "just as you like, you know. But I should think you'd better—for the child's sake, at least."

"It isn't true. I don't believe it," she said, piteously.

"Ask the Doctor, then;" and he sauntered out, smiling, and perhaps not dreaming that she would.

But "for the child's sake" had alarmed Ideala, and she sent for the Doctor. It was hours before he could come to her, and, in the meantime, not knowing that her state of mind would affect the child, she had fidgeted and fretted herself into a fever, and when the Doctor saw her, he could only confirm her husband's verdict.

"I am afraid you must give up nursing," he said. "You are in such a nervous state it will do the child harm. But he's such a fine fellow! He'll thrive all right—you needn't be frightened."

Ideala said nothing, but she sat in her own room night after night for a week, and heard the child crying for her, and could not go to him—and even when he did not cry she fancied she heard him still. I think as the milk slowly and painfully left her, her last spark of affection for her husband dried up too.

The child died of diphtheria some time afterwards, and in a little while, Ideala, who was then in her 26th year, returned to her old pursuits, and no one ever knew what she felt about it:

> For, it is with feelings as with waters—
> The shallow murmur, but the deep are dumb![1]

CHAPTER XI.

My widowed sister, Claudia, was one of Ideala's most intimate friends. She was a good deal older than Ideala, whom she loved as a mother loves a naughty child, for ever finding fault with her, but ready to be up in arms in a moment if any one else ventured to do likewise. She was inclined to quarrel with me because, although I never doubted Ideala's truth and earnestness (no one could), knowing her weak point, I feared for her. I thought if all the passion in her were ever focused on one object she would do something extravagant—a prediction which Claudia, with good intent, rashly repeated to her once.

Claudia was mistress of my house, and she and I had agreed from the first that, whatever happened, we would watch over Ideala and befriend her.

My sister was one of the people who thought it would have been better for Ideala to have talked of her troubles. When I praised Ideala's loyalty, and her uncomplaining devotion to an uncongenial duty, Claudia said: "Loyalty is all very well; but I don't see much merit in a life-long devotion to a bad cause. If there were any good to be done by it, it would be different, of course; but, as it is, Ideala is simply sacrificing herself for nothing—and worse, she is setting a bad example by showing men they need not mend their manners since wives will endure anything. It is immoral for a woman to live with such a husband. I don't understand Ideala's meekness; it amounts to weakness sometimes, I think. I believe if he struck her she would say, 'Thank you,' and fetch him his slippers. I feel sure she thinks some unknown defect in herself is at the bottom of all his misdeeds."

"I don't think she knows half as much about his misdeeds as we do," I observed.

---

[1] Misquotation of Sir Walter Ralegh (also Raleigh) (1552-1618), "The Silent Lover," lines 1-2. The correct quotation is "Passions are liken'd best to floods and streams: / The shallow murmur, but the deep are dumb."

"Then I think it would be a charity to enlighten her," Claudia answered, decidedly. "One can't touch pitch without being defiled,[1] and when it is too late we shall find she has suffered 'some taint in nature,' in spite of herself. Will you kindly take us to the Palace this evening? The Bishop wants us to go in after dinner, and Ideala has promised to come too."

Ideala was fastidious about her dress, and being in one of her moods that evening she teased Claudia unmercifully, on the way to the Palace, about a blue woollen shawl she was wearing. "A delicate and refined nature expresses itself by nothing more certainly than elegant wraps," she said, parodying another famous dictum; "and I should not like to be able to understand the state of mind a lady was in when she bought herself a blue woollen shawl; but I could believe she was suffering at the time from a temporary aberration of intellect—only, if she wore it afterwards the thing would be quite inexplicable."

Claudia drew the wrap round her with dignity, and made no reply: then Ideala laughed and turned to me. "Certainly your friend," she said, alluding to a young sculptor who was staying with me, "can 'invest his portraits with artistic merit.' Claudia's likeness in the Exhibition is capital, and the fame of it is being noised abroad with a vengeance. But I think something should be done to stop the little newspaper-boy nuisance: the reports they spread are quite alarming."

"Ideala, what nonsense are you talking about sculptors and newspaper boys?" Claudia exclaimed.

"I'll tell you," said Ideala. "There was a small boy with a big voice standing at the corner of the market-place this afternoon. He had a sheaf of evening papers under his arm, and was yelling with much enthusiasm to an edified crowd:—'Noose of the War! Hawful mutilation of the dead! Fearful collision in the Channel! Eighty-eight lives lost! Narrative of survivors! Thrilling details! Shindy in Parl'ment! Hirish members to the front again! 'Orrible haccident in our own town! The Lady Claudia's bust!'"[2]

---

[1] Pitch is the dark resin produced by trees, so one cannot touch it without getting dirty. The proverb appears in Ecclesiasticus 8:1 in the Apocrypha.
[2] The newspaper boy is speaking in a typical working-class British accent, by pronouncing an "h" at the beginning of words starting with a vowel. "Shindy in Parl'ment" is slang for "uproar in Parliament."

"Ideala, how *dare* you?"—but just then the carriage stopped, and we had to get out.

The good Bishop met us in the hall, and the laugh was presently against Ideala for positively declining to go upstairs when he asked her.

"It is too much trouble," she said, not seeing in her absence what was meant. "I would rather leave my things here."

"But I am afraid I *must* trouble you," the Bishop answered, in despair. "The fact is, my wife is not so well this evening, and she was afraid of the cold, and is staying in her own sitting-room."

The "sitting-room" was a snug apartment, warm, cosy, luxurious, and we found a genial little party of intimate acquaintances there when we arrived. Ideala's husband was not one of them. He did not take her out much at that time. Probably he was engaged in some private pursuit of his own, and insisted on her going everywhere alone to keep her out of the way. A little while before he would scarcely allow her to pay a call without him. But, as a rule, whatever his mood was, she did as he wished—and provoked him sometimes, I think, by her patient compliance; a little resistance would have made the exercise of his authority more exciting.

When we entered the sitting-room "an ominous silence fell on the group," which was broken at last by one of the ladies remarking that a kind heart was an admirable thing. Another agreed, and made some observations on the merits of self-sacrifice generally.

"But some people are not satisfied with merely *doing* a good deed," a gentleman declared, with profound gravity. "They think there is no merit in it if they do not suffer for it in some way themselves."

There was a good deal more of this kind of thing, and we were beginning to feel rather out of it, when presently the preternatural gravity of the party was broken by a laugh, and then it was explained.

Ideala had gone to a neighbouring town one day by train, and before she started a poor woman got into the carriage. The woman had a third class ticket, but she was evidently ill, and when the guard came and wanted to turn her out, Ideala took pity on her, insisted on changing tickets, and travelled third class herself. The woman had been to the Palace, and described the incident to the Bishop's wife that morning, and she had just told her guests, wondering who the lady could have been, and they in turn had put their heads together and decided that there was no one in the community but Ideala who would have done the thing in that way.

"But what else could I have done?" she asked, when she saw we were laughing at her.

"Well, my dear," said the Bishop, who always treated her with the kind indulgence that is accorded to a favourite child, "you might have paid the difference for the woman, and travelled comfortably yourself, don't you know?"

Ideala never thought of that!

Presently the dear old Bishop nestled back in his chair, and with a benign glance round, which, his scapegrace[1] son said, meant: "Bless you, my children! Be happy and good in your own way, but don't make a noise!" he sank into a gentle doze, and the rest of the party relapsed into trivial gossip, some of which I give for what it is worth by way of illustration. It shows Ideala at about her worst, but marks a period in her career, a turning-point for the better. She was seldom bitter, and still more rarely frivolous, after that night.

"Clare Turner will take none of the blame of that affair on his own shoulders," someone remarked.

"Mr. Clare Turner is the little boy who always said 'It wasn't me!' grown up," Ideala decided, from the corner of her couch. "He is a sort of two-reason man."

"How do you mean 'a two-reason man,' Ideala?"

"Well, he has only two reasons for everything; one is his reason for doing anything he likes himself, which is always a good one; and the other is his reason why the rest of the world should not do likewise, which is equally clear—to himself. He thinks there should be one law for him and another for everybody else. I don't believe in him."

"Nor I," said one of the gentlemen. "Underhand bowling was all he was celebrated for at school; he bowled most frightful sneaks all the time he was there."

"Talking about Clare Turner," Charlie Lloyd put in, "I've brought a new book of poems—author unknown. I picked it up at the station to-day. There's one thing in it, called 'The Passion of Delysle,' that seems to be intense; but I've only just glanced at it, and don't really know what it's like. Shall I read it?"

"Oh, do!" was the general exclamation, and we all settled ourselves to enjoy the following treat.

Charlie began softly:—

---

[1] Rascal.

O day and night! O day and night! and is this madness?
O day and night! O day and night! and is this joy?
Whence comes this bursting sense of life, and love, and gladness,
This pain of pleasure, perfected, without alloy?
Lo, flowing past me are the restless rivers,
Or swelling round me is the boundless sea;
Or else the widening waste of sand that quivers
In shining stretches, shuts the world from me—
Or seems to shut it, while I would that what it seems might be.

O day and night! O day and night! this mountain island,
This saintly shrine, this fort—I scarce know what 'tis yet—
This sand, or sea-girt,[1] rocky, town-clad, church-crown'd highland,
This dull and rugged gem in golden deserts set,
Has some delicious, unknown charm to hold me,
To draw me to itself and keep me here;
The old grey walls, it seems, with joy enfold me—
Or is it I that make the dead stones dear,
And send the throbbing summer in my blood thro' all things near?

O day and night! O day and night! where else do flowers
Open their velvet lids like these to greet the light?
Or raise such sun-kissed lips aglow to meet cool showers?
Or cast more subtle scents abroad upon the night?
These trees and trailing weeds that climb the cliff-side steep,
The dusky pine trees, draped with wreaths of vine,
Make bowers where love might lie and list the sea-voice deep,
And drink the perfumed air, the light, like wine
Which threads intoxication through these hot, glad veins of mine.

* * * * *

O day and night! O day and night! I sought this haven,
From place and power, and wealth I flew in search of rest;
They forced and bound me to a hard, detested craven,
Who mocked my loathing with his head upon my breast.
With deathless love I moaned for my young lover;
To make me great they drove him from my side,
And foully wrought with shame his name to cover—
My boy, my lord, my prince! In vain they lied!
But should I always suffer for their false, inhuman pride?

---

[1] A piece of land nearly surrounded by the sea, such as a peninsula.

O day and night! O day and night! I left them flying,
I fled by day and night as flies the nomad breeze,
Across the silent land when light to dark was dying,
And onward like a spirit lost across the seas;
And on from sea and shore thro' apple-orchards blooming,
Till all things melted in a moving haze;
And on with rush and ring by tower and townlet glooming,
By wood, and field, and hill, by verdant ways,
While dawn to mid-day drew, and noon was lost in sunset blaze.

O day and night! O day and night! light once more waxing,
Still on with courage high, tho' strength was well-nigh spent;
Grim spectres of pursuit the wearied brain perplexing,
Fear-fraught, but ever met with spirit dedolent.
The landscape reeled, there came a sense of slumber,
And myriad shadows rose and wanned and waned,
And flitting figures, visions without number,
Took shape above the land till sight was pained,
And floated round me till at last the longed-for goal I gained.

O day and night! O day and night! with rest abounding,
The soothing sinking down on hard-earned holy rest,
With grateful ease that grew from all the calm surrounding,
A languid, dreamful ease, my soul became possessed.
The hoarse sea-wind comes soughing, sighing, singing,
Its constant message from the patient waves,
While high above cathedral bells were ringing,
Or falling voices chanted hymns of praise,
And all the land seemed filled with peace and promised length of days.

* * * * *

O day and night! O day and night! once, all unheeding,
By sun and summer wind with tender touch caressed,
I wandered where the strains, the sacred strains, were pleading,
And, kneeling in the fane,[1] my thoughts to prayer addressed.
And softly rose the murmur'd organ mystery,
And swell'd around the colonnaded aisle,
Where smiled the pictured saints of holy history
On prostrate penitents who prayed the while:
I could not pray there, but I felt that God Himself might smile.

---

[1] Temple or church.

O day and night! O day and night! while I was kneeling
There came the strangest sense of some loved presence near;
A re-awakening rush of well-remembered feeling
Thrill'd thro' me, held me still, with vague expectant fear.
Half turn'd from me, there stood beside the altar,
Where incense-clouds nigh veiled him from my sight,
A fair-haired priest—my quicken'd heart-beats falter!
Or is he priest, or is he acolyte,
Or layman devotee who prays in novice robes bedight?

O day and night! O day and night! whence comes this feeling?
For all unreal seem day and night and life and death,
And all unreal the hope that sets my senses reeling,
And stills my pulse an instant, checks my lab'ring breath.
Yet louder rolls the mighty organ thund'ring.
And downward slopes a beam of light divine,
The perfumed clouds are cleft: he looks up wond'ring—
Looks up—what does he there before the shrine?
He could not give himself to God, for he is mine, is mine!

O day and night! O day and night! I go forth trembling,
He did not meet my eyes, he never saw my face.
My bosom swells with joy and jealousy resembling
A war of good and evil waged in a holy place.
No longer soft the day, the sun in splendour
Pours all his might upon this green incline;
I lie and watch the cirrus clouds surrender,
Their glowing forms to one hot kiss resign—
How could he give himself to God when he is mine, is mine?

O day and night! O day and night! beneath your glory
The crimson flood of life itself has turned to fire!
The rugged brows of those old rocks, storm-rent and hoary,
Are quivering in their grim surprise at my desire.
The mother earth, throbbing with pain and pleasure,
Would sink her voices for the languid noon,
But light airs wake a reckless madd'ning measure,
And wavelets dance and sparkle to the tune,
And mock the mocking malice of yon day-dimm'd gibbous moon.

★ ★ ★ ★ ★

O day and night! O day and night! a fisher maiden
Is wand'ring up the path to where unseen I lie;
She comes with some light spoil from off the shore beladen,
And softly singing of the sea goes slowly by.
And slowly rise great sun-tipped white cloud masses,
Sublimely still their shadows flit and flee:
How silently the work of nature passes—
The roll of worlds, the growth of flower and tree!
Angels of God in heaven! Give him to me! give him to me!

O day and night! O day and night! the hours rolling
Bring ev'ry one its change, its song, or chant, or chime:
Now solemnly their sounds a distant death-knell tolling,
And now the bells above beat forth the flight of time.
I lie, unconsciously each trifle noting,
The far-off sailors toiling on the quay,
Or o'er the sand a broad-wing'd sea-bird floating,
Or passing hum of honey-laden'd bee—
Angels of God in heaven! Give him to me! give him to me!

O day and night! O day and night! the scene surrounding
Grows dim and all unreal beneath the sunset glow;
And all the heat and rage pass into peace abounding,
I moan, I fear no more, but wait, while still tears flow.
The warm sweet airs scarce move the flowerets slender,
A pause and hush have settled on the sea,
A bird trills forth its love-song low and tender:
O bird rejoice! thy love and thou art free—
Angels of God in heaven! Give him to me! give him to me!

★ ★ ★ ★ ★

O day and night! O day and night! ye knew it ever!
Ye saw it written in the world's first golden prime!
And smiled your giant smile at all my rash endeavour
To snatch the cup unfill'd from out the hand of Time.
He comes, O day and night! Spirits attending,
Swift formless messengers my ev'ry sense apprise!
He comes! the bright fair head o'er some old book low bending:
Dear Lord, at last! his eyes have met my eyes—
Gleam of light goes quivering across the happy skies!

* * * * *

O day and night! O day and night! Love sits between us.
Far out the rising tide comes sweeping o'er the sand.
The murmurous pine trees lend their purple shade to screen us,
And breathe their fragrant sighs above the quiet land.
And, like a sigh, the sunset blaze is over,
The folding grey has veiled its colours bright;
While swift from view fade out the gulls that hover,
As round us sinks at last, on pinions light,
The dark and radiant clarity of the beautiful still night.

O day and night! O day and night! no words are spoken,
Such pleasant joy profound no words could well express:
His wand'ring fingers smooth my hair in silent token,
And all my being answers to the tender mute caress.
My head is resting on his breast for pillow,
And as by music moved my soul is thrill'd;
Flow on and clasp the land, O bursting billow!
O breezes, tell the mountains many-rill'd!
Our hearts now know each other, and our hope is all-fulfill'd.

O day and night! O day and night! no shadow crosses
This long'd-for solemn hour of all-forgetful bliss;
No chilling thought, or stalking dread arising, tosses
A poison'd drop of bitterness to spoil the ling'ring kiss:
No mem'ries past or future fears assailing—
As soon might doubt bedim the stars that shine!
Or souls released reach Paradise bewailing
The end of pain, and clemency divine:
The glorious present holds us: I am his and he is mine!

* * * * *

O day and night! O day and night! and was it madness?
Lo! all is changing, even sky, and sea, and shore
The heaving water ebbs itself away in sadness,
The waves receding sigh, 'Delight returns no more!'
Far down the East the dawn is dimly burning,
Its first chill breath has shivered thro' my frame,
And with the light comes cruel Thought returning,
The air seems full of voices speaking blame;
Another day commences, but the world is not the same!

O day and night! O day and night! its rushes pass'd us,
We stand upon the brink and watch the strong deep tide,
And shrink already from the howls that soon must blast us,
The world that sins unchidden, and the laws that would divide.
"O Love, they rest in peace whom ocean covers!"
One plunge, one clasp supernal, one long kiss!
Then downward, like those old Italian lovers,
Descend for ever through the long abyss,
And float together, happy, all eternity like this!

The charm of the reader's voice had held us spellbound, and the poem was well received; but after the usual compliments there was a pause, and then Ideala burst out impetuously: "I am sick of those old Italian lovers," she said; "they float into everything. Their story is the essence with which two-thirds of our love literature is flavoured. We should never have received them in society; why do we tolerate them in books? I like my company to be respectable even there; and when an author asks me to admire and sympathize with such people he insults me."

"They must be brought in, though, for the sake of contrast," somebody observed.

"They should be kept in their proper place, then," she answered. "You may choose what you please to point a moral, but for pity's sake be careful about what you use to adorn a tale."

"Moral or no moral," said the young sculptor, "I think a new poem of any kind a thing to be thankful for."

"And do you call that kind of thing new?" said Ideala. "I should say it was a fine compound of all the poems of the kind, and several other kinds, that have ever been written, with a dash of the peculiarly refined immorality of our own times, from which nothing is sacred, thrown in to make weight. Such writing,

> Like a new disease, unknown to men,
> Creeps, no precaution used, among the crowd,
> . . . . and saps
> The fealty of our friends, and stirs the pulse
> With devil's leaps, and poisons half the young.[1]

---

[1] Tennyson, "Guinevere," *Idylls of the King*, lines 515-519.

It is the feeling of the day accurately defined. Nobody sighs for love and peace now. The cry is for the indulgence of some fiery passion for an hour, and then, perdition!—if you like—since that is the recognized price of it."

"Our loves are more intense than they used to be," said the sculptor, sighing.

"Love!" Ideala answered. "Oh, do not desecrate 'the eternal God-word, love!' There is little enough of that in the business that goes by its name now-a-days. I am a lady—I cannot use the right word. But it is none the less the thing I mean because it calls blasphemously on God Almighty to help it to fulfil itself."

"Well," said Charlie Lloyd, deprecatingly, "I didn't offer this, you know, as an admirable specimen of what our day can produce. I told you I hadn't read it, and now that I have I don't suppose anyone has offered it to the public as a serious expression of sentiment."

"You do not think people write books about what they really feel?" said Ideala. "I believe they do when the feeling is shameful. If you want to keep a secret, publish the exact truth in a book, and nobody will believe a word of it. I think people who publish such productions should be burned on a pile of their own works."

"The writer is young, doubtless," I said, apologetically. It gives one a shock to hear a woman say harsh things.

"He was evidently not too young to have bad thoughts," said Claudia, supporting her friend; "and he was certainly old enough to know better."

"He!" ejaculated Ideala. "It is far more likely to be *she*. Do you read the reviews? You will find that all the most objectionable books are written by women—and condemned by men who lift up their voices now, as they have done from time immemorial, and insist that we should do as they say and not as they do."

"I am afraid you are right," said Charlie Lloyd. "So many of our best women—I mean the women who are likely to make most impression on the age—are going that way now."

"But what horrid things you say, Ideala," one of the ladies chimed in, "and you make everybody else say horrid things. That 'Passion of Delysle' is not a bit worse than Tennyson's 'Fatima'—and there's a lot more in it—that part about 'the roll of worlds,' you know, is quite grand."

"I always liked that idea," Ideala observed.

"And—and—" the lady continued, "where she looks at every-thing, you know. She was very properly seeking distraction, and found it for a moment in the contemplation of nature, and that softened her mood, so that when the inevitable rush of recollec-tion comes and forces the thought of him back upon her, her feeling finds expression in a prayer—instead of—instead of——"

"A blasphemous remonstrance," Ideala put in. "Oh, I don't deny that there is just enough to be said in favour of all these things to make them sell—and this one has two unusual points of interest. It opens with a riddle, and the lady's lover is a priest, which gives an additional zest to the charm of wrong-doing, a *sauce piquante* for jaded appetites."

"Why do you call the opening verses a riddle?" said Charlie Lloyd.

"Because I fancy no one will ever guess what kind of a place it was—

> This mountain island,
> This saintly shrine, this fort—

I forget how it goes on."

"Oh, the description of the place is not bad," Charlie answered, after reading it over again to himself. "It would do for the Mont St. Michael in Normandy."[1]

"Well, let that pass, then," said Ideala; "also the dear familiar 'subtle scents abroad upon the night.' But what does she mean by 'On with rush and ring'?"

"She means the train, obviously."

"What an outlandish periphrasis![2] And how about

> The rugged brows of those old rocks, storm-rent and hoary,
> Are quivering in their grim surprise?"

---

[1] Also called Mont-Saint-Michel, a Benedictine abbey located on the French coast of the English Channel, along the border of Brittany and Normandy. Known for its fantastic location, the abbey is located on a small island, which is separated from the mainland by only a kilometer of water.

[2] Use of longer and more abstract phrasing, in place of a shorter, more direct form of expression. Can be an effective rhetorical device or produce a comical effect, as in the speech of Polonius in Shakespeare's *Hamlet*.

"That is a 'pathetic fallacy.'[1] She is not speaking of the things as they were, but as they appeared to her excited fancy. She chronicles her own death, though——"

"So did Moses," said Ideala. "If you really want to justify 'The Passion of Delysle' I can help you. You see she was dreadfully badly treated by her friends, poor thing! and her marriage after all was no marriage, because she loved another man all the time; and your husband isn't properly your husband if you don't love him, love being the only possible sanctification—in fact, the only true marriage. And then her lover, thinking he had lost her, became a priest, and vows made under a misapprehension like that cannot be binding—it would be too much to expect us to suffer always for such mistakes. And then the world—but we all know how cruel the world is! And appearances were sadly against them, poor things! No one would ever have believed that they had stayed out all night to discuss their religious experiences. Suicide is shocking, of course; but still, when people are driven to it like that, we can only be sorry for them, and hope they will never do it again!" She nestled back more comfortably on her couch, and then continued in an altered tone: "But it is appalling to think of the quantity of machine-made verses like those that are imposed on the public year by year, verses the mere result of much reading and writing, without a scrap of inspiration in them, and as far removed from even schoolboy efforts of genius as an oleograph[2] is from an oil painting. Poets are as rare now as prophets, and inspiration has left us for our sins. I think any fairly educated one of us, with a tolerable memory and the habit of composition, could write that 'Passion of Delysle' again in half-an-hour."

"Oh, could they, though!" said Ralph, the son of the house. "I dare bet anything you couldn't do it yourself in twice the time."

"Dare you?" she answered, with a little smile. "Well, to adopt your elegant phraseology, Master Ralph, I bet I will produce the same story, with the same conclusion, but a different moral, in an

---

[1] Tendency to ascribe human emotions to nature; used extensively in the late-eighteenth and nineteenth centuries and discussed by John Ruskin in *Modern Painters*, vol. 3 (1856). To describe rocks as "quivering in their grim surprise," as the author of "The Passion of Delysle" does, is a pathetic fallacy.

2 A lithograph printed on cloth to imitate an oil painting.

hour—since you allow me twice the time I named—if I may be permitted to write it in blank verse, that is, and, of course, with the
understanding that what I write is not intended to be anything but
mere versified prose."

"Done with you!" cried Ralph.

"Hush—h—h!" his mother exclaimed, deprecatingly. "Betting,
and before the Bishop, too!"

"What the Bishop don't know will do him no harm, Ma," said
the youth in a stage whisper. "Sit down, Ideala, and begin. It's ten
minutes to ten now."

The Bishop slept serenely; conversation flagged; and Ideala wrote
steadily for about three-quarters of an hour—then she gathered up
the manuscript, rose from the table, and returned to her old seat.

"'The Passion of Delysle' has become 'The Choice,'" she said.
"Will you read it for me, Mr. Lloyd? I think it should have that advantage, at least."

Charlie took the manuscript, and read:—

> Once on a time, not very long gone by,
> A noble lady had a noble choice.
> The daughter of an ancient house was she,
> Beauty, and wealth, and highest rank were hers,
> But love was not, for of a proud, cold race
> Her people were, caring for nought but lands,
> Riches, and power; holding all tender thoughts
> As weakly folly, only fit for babes.
> The lady learnt their creed; her heart seem'd hard—
> She thought it so; and when the moment came
> To choose 'twixt love, young love, and pride of place,
> She still'd an unwonted feeling that would rise,
> And saying calmly: "I have got no heart,
> And love is vain!" she chose to be the wife
> Of sinful age, corruption, and untruth,
> Scorning the steadfast love of one who yearn'd
> To win her from the crooked paths she trod,
> And break the sordid chains that bound her soul,
> And sweep the defiling dust of common thoughts
> From out her mind, until it shone at last
> With large imaginings of God and good.

She chose: no more they met: her life was pass'd
In constant round of pomp and proud display.
But when he went, and never more there came
The love-sad eyes to question and entreat,
The voice of music praising noble deeds,
The graceful presence and the golden hair,
She miss'd the boy; but scoff'd at first and said:
"One misses all things, common pets one spurn'd,
Good slaves and bad alike when both are gone,—
A small thing makes the habit of a life!"
But days wore on, and adulation palled.
She knew not what she lack'd, nor that she loath'd
The hollow semblance, the dull mockery,
Which she had gain'd for joy by choosing rank,
And money's worth, instead of peace and love.

Yet ever as the long days grew to months
More heavy hung the time, moved slower by,
And all things troubled her and gave her pain,
And morning, noon, and night the thought would rise,
And grew insistent when she would not hear:
"One loved me! out of all this crowd but one!
And he is gone, and I have driven him forth!"

Then in the silent solitude of night
An old weird story that she once had heard
Tormented her; a story speaking much
Of a rock-island on the Norman coast,
A mountain peak rising from barren sand,
Or standing sea-girt when the tide returns,
And beaten by the winds on ev'ry side,
With wall'd-in town, and castle on the height,
And high above the castle, strangely placed,
A grey cathedral with its summit tipp'd
By a gold figure of St. Michael[1] crown'd,
With burnished wings and flashing sword that shone
A beacon in the sunset, seen for miles,
As tho' the Archangel floated in the air.

---

[1] Generally, one of the principal angels who fought against Satan; his name was used in the battle cry of the good angels. More specifically, in Normandy, Michael is considered the patron of mariners.

The castle and the church a sanctuary
And refuge were, to which men often fled
For rest or safety, finding what they sought.
And as the lady thought about the place,
A notion came that she would like to kneel
And pray for peace at that far lonely shrine.
The longing grew: she rested not nor slept.
And should she fly and leave her wretched wealth?
And if she fled she never could return;
Yet if she stay'd she felt that she should die.
So go or stay meant misery for her—
But misery is lessened when we move.
Yes, she would go! and then she laugh'd to think
Of the wild fury of her harsh old Lord
When he should wake one day and find her gone—
Laugh'd! the first time for long and weary months.

By Mont St. Michael, on the Norman coast,
A restless river, changing oft its course,
Flows sullenly; and racehorse-like the tide,
Which, going, leaves a wilderness of sand,
Comes rushing back, a foam-topp'd, wat'ry wall;
And those who, wand'ring, 'scape the quicksand's grip,
Are often caught and drown'd ere help can come.
But fair the prospect from the Mount when bright
The sunshine falls on Avranches[1] far away,
A white town straggling o'er a verdant hill;
And on the tree-clad country toward the west,
On apple orchards, and the fairy bloom
Of feath'ry tam'risk bushes on the shore;
Whilst high above in silent majesty
Of hue and form the floating clouds support
The far-extending vault of azure sky.

Such was the shrine the lady sought, and there
In mute appeal for what she lack'd she knelt,
Not knowing what she lack'd; but finding peace
Steal o'er her soul there as she faintly heard
The slow and solemn chanting of the priests,
The mild monotony of murmured prayers,

---

[1] Town of Avranches, located relatively close to Mont-Saint-Michel, despite the lines in Ideala's poem suggesting otherwise.

And hush of pauses when she seemed to feel
The heart she deem'd so hard was melting fast,
And listen'd to a voice within her say—
"Love is not vain! Love all things and rejoice!"
And found warm tears were stealing down her cheeks.

The mystery of love, of love, of love,
Of hope, of joy, of life itself, she felt;
The crown of life, which she had sacrificed
In scornful pride for lust of power and place.

The lady bow'd her head, and o'er her swept
A wave of anguish, and she knew despair.
"Could I but see him once again!" she moan'd,
"See him, and beg forgiveness, and then die!"
Did the Archangel Michael, standing there
Upon her left in shining silver hear?
Who knows? Her prayer was answer'd like a flash;
For at that moment, clear and sweet o'er all
The mingled music of the chanting choir,
There rose a voice that thrill'd her inmost soul:
It breathed a blessing; utter'd soft a prayer.
No need to look: and yet she look'd, and saw
A hooded monk before the altar kneel,
A graceful presence, tho' in sordid dress.
And as she gazed the cowl slipp'd back and show'd
(But dimly thro' the incense-perfumed cloud)
A pure pale face, a golden tonsured head,
And blue eyes raised to heaven. Then the truth
Was there reveal'd to her that he had left
The world to watch and pray for such as she.

Out of the castled-gate she hurried forth:
What matter'd where she went, to east or west!
What matter'd peasant's warning that the sand
Was shifting ever, and the rushing tide
Gave them no quarter whom it overtook?
'Twas death she courted, and with heedless step
Onward to meet it swift the lady fled.
Death is too beautiful at such a time!
When all the land in summer sunshine lies,
And lapse of distant waves breaks pleasantly

The silence with a soothing dreamy sound,
And danger seems no nearer than the sky,
He tempts us from afar with hope of rest.
She hurried on in search of death, nor heard
That eager footsteps followed where she went.
The voice that call'd her was not real, she thought,
But a sweet portion of a strange sweet dream—
For now the terrible anguish quickly pass'd,
And sense of peace at hand was all she felt.

"O stop!"
        Ah! that was real. She turn'd and saw,
Nor saw a moment till she felt his grasp
Strong and determined on her rounded arm.
"Thou shalt not die!" he cried. "What madness this?"
"Madness!" she echoed: "nay, my love, 'tis bliss—
The first my life has known—to stand here still
With thee beside me, and to wait for death.
I know my heart at last, but all too late!
I may not love thee, I, another's wife;
Thou mayst not love me, thou hast wedded heaven.
We cannot be together in this world;
I cannot live alone and know thee here.
And thou art troubled! I for beneath that garb
Thy heart beats ever hot with love for me;
For love will not be quell'd by monkish vows.
But all things change in death! so let us die
Thus, hand in hand, and so together pass,
And be together thro' eternity!"

There was a struggle in the young monk's breast;
He would not meet her pleading eyes and yield,
But gazing up to heaven prayed for strength,
Strength to resist, and guidance how to act,
For death like that with her was luring—sweet—
A strong temptation, but he must resist,
And strive to save and show her how to live.
"We cannot make hereafter for ourselves,"
He answered softly; "all that we can do
Is so to live that we shall win reward
Of praise, and peace, and happy life to come.
Thy duty lies before thee; so does mine.

Let each return, and toil and watch and pray,
Knowing each other's heart is fix'd on heaven,
And do the good we can; not seeking death
Nor shunning it, but living pure and true,
With conscience clear to meet our God at last,
And win each other for our great reward."

The moving music of his words sank deep:
Her alter'd heart thrill'd high to holy thoughts.
"Be thou my guide," she said. "My duty now
Shall bring me peace; so shall I toil like thee
To win the love I yearn for in the end."

It might not be. The treach'rous, working sand
Already clutched their feet, and check'd their speed;
And dancing, sparkling, like a joyful thing,
A glitt'ring, glassy wall of foam-fleck'd wave
Towards them glided with that fatal speed
You cannot mark because it is so swift.
No use to struggle now: no time to fly!
He clasp'd her to him: "God hath will'd it thus.
Courage, my sister!" "Is this death?" she cried.
"Yes, this is death." "It is not death, but joy!"
And as she spoke the spot where they were seen
Became a wat'ry waste of battling waves:
While high above the summer sun shone on—
A passing seabird hoarsely shriek'd along!
All things were changed, with that vast change which makes
It seem as tho' nought else had ever been.

"Well done, Ideala!" said Ralph, patronisingly; "you certainly have a memory, and are quite as good at patchwork as the author of 'Delysle.' I could criticize on another count, but taking into consideration time, place, circumstances, and the female intellect, I refrain. That is the generous sort of creature I am. So, without expressing my own opinion further—except to remark that, though I don't think much of either of them, personally I prefer 'Delysle.' The other is wholesomer, doubtless, for those who like a mild diet. Milk and water doesn't agree with me. But I put it to the vote. Ladies and gentlemen, do you or do you not consider that this lady has won her bet?"

"Oh, won it, most decidedly!" we all agreed.

"By-the-by, what was the bet?" I asked.

"My Pa's gaiters against Ideala's blue stockings.[1] I regret to say that circumstances over which I have no control"—and he glanced at the unconscious Bishop—"prevent the immediate payment of my debt—unless, indeed, he has a second pair;" and he left the room hurriedly as if to see.

He did not come back to us that evening, but I believe he was to be heard of later at the sign of the "Billiard and Cue."

"Well," said the young sculptor, returning to the old point of departure, "for my own part, I find much that is elevating in modern works."

"So do I," said Ideala; "I find much that raises me on stilts."

"But even that eminence would enable you to look over other people's heads and beyond."

"It would," she answered, "if human nature didn't desire a sense of security; but, as it is, when I am artificially set up, I find that all I can do is to look at my own feet, and tremble lest I fall. Modern literature stimulates; it doesn't nourish. It makes you feel like a giant for a moment, but leaves you crushed like a worm, and without faith, without love, without hope. It excites you pleasurably, and when you see life through its medium you never suspect that the vision is distorted. It makes you think the Iconoclast the greatest hero, and causes you to feel that you share his glory when you help him with your approval to overthrow all the images you ever cherished; but when the work of destruction is over, and you look about you once more with sober eyes, you find you have sacrificed your all for nothing. Your false guide fails you when you want him most. He robs you, and leaves you hungry, thirsty, and alone in the wilderness to which he has beguiled you. There is no need for new theories of Life and Religion; all we require is strength and courage to perfect the old ones.[2] What the mind wants is food it can grow upon, not stimulants which inflate it for a time with a fancied sense of power

---

[1] This phrase identifies Ideala with the eighteenth-century intellectual circle of women referred to as "blue stockings," which included Elizabeth Vesey, Hannah More, Elizabeth Montagu, Elizabeth Carter, and others.

[2] She quite changed her mind upon this subject eventually, and held that there was not only need of new theories, but good hope that we should have them. [Grand's note.]

that has no real existence. But I have small hope for our nation when I think of the sparkling trash that the mind of the multitude daily imbibes and craves for. I mean our novels. What a fine affectation of goodness there is in most of them! And what a perfect moral is tacked on to them!—like the *balayeuse*[1] at the bottom of a lady's dress; but, like the *balayeuse*, it is only meant to be a protection and a finish, and, however precious it may be, it suffers from contact with the dirt, and sooner or later has to be cut out and cast aside, soiled and useless. Some doggerel a friend of mine scribbled on one book in particular describes dozens of popular novels exactly:—

> O what a beautiful history!
> Think what temptations they passed!
> Each one more cruelly trying,
> More tempting, indeed, than the last.
> And what a lesson it teaches;
> No passion from evil's exempted—
> Whilst admiring the moral it preaches,
> It makes you quite long to be tempted.

I agree with those who tell us that society is breaking up, or will break up unless something is done at once to stop the dissolution. We have no high ideals of anything. Marriage itself is a mere commercial treaty, and only professional preachers speak of it in other terms—and those young people, with a passion for each other, who are about to be united—a passion that dies the death inevitably for want of knowledge, and wholesome principle, and self-control to support it. Some of us like our bargains better than others, but you can judge of the estimation in which marriage is held when you see how much happiness people generally find in it. If men and women were kept apart, and made to live purely from their cradles, they would still scarcely be fit for marriage; yet any man thinks he may marry, and never cares to be the nobler or the better for it. And when you see that this, the only perfect state, the most sacred bond of union between man and woman, is everywhere lightly considered, don't you think there is reason in the fear that we are falling on bad times? Oh, don't quote the Romans to me, and the Inevitable. We

---

[1] A ruffle of silk or lace, sewed inside the lower edge of a skirt, to keep the train of the skirt from getting dirty.

know better than the Romans, and could do better if we chose. But we have to mourn for the death of our manhood! Where is our manhood? Where are our men? Is there any wonder that we are losing what is best in life when only women are left to defend it? Believe me, the degradation of marriage is the tune to which the whole fabric of society is going to pieces——"

"Eh, what!" exclaimed the Bishop, waking up with a start—"whole fabric of society going to pieces? Nonsense! When so many people come to church. And then look at all the societies at work for the—for the—ah—prevention of everything. Why, I belong to a dozen at least myself; the Prevention of Cruelty to Animals, and the Rational Dress Reform,[1] for doing away with petticoats—no, by-the-by, it is my wife who belongs to that. But, at any rate, everything is being done that should be done, and you talk nonsense, my dear"—looking at Ideala severely—"because you don't know anything about it."

"The faults we are hardest on in others are those we are most conscious of in ourselves—perhaps because we know how easy it would be to conquer them," Ideala observed vaguely.

"Oh, come, now, my dear," said the Bishop, beaming round on all of us, "you must not believe what you hear about society being in such a bad state. I know idle people say so, and it is very wrong of them. Why, I never see anything wrong."

"Of course not," said Ideala. "We are all on our best behaviour before you."

The Bishop patted his apron good-humouredly. "Well, now, take yourself for example," he said. "I am sure *you* never do wrong—tell stories, you know, and that kind of thing."

---

[1] The Society for the Prevention of Cruelty to Animals was founded in 1824 by Richard Martin, M.P., also known as "Humanity Dick." In the 1840s, Queen Victoria was sufficiently impressed with the work of the society to approve the alteration of its name to the *Royal* Society for the Prevention of Cruelty to Animals. The Rational Dress Reform was a movement to change women's fashion, so women would be more comfortable in their own clothes. Led by members of the Rational Dress Society, founded by Lady Harberton and Emily King in 1881, this movement focused especially on restrictive corsets and the health risks for women who wore them. The cause of rational dress was taken up by a number of women's magazines of the period, including the Society's own paper, *The Rational Dress Society's Gazette*.

"Haven't I, though!" she answered, mischievously. "Not that it was much use, for I always repented and confessed; and now I have abandoned the practice to the best of my ability. It is horrid to feel you don't deserve the confidence that is placed in you, Bishop, isn't it?"

"Ideala!" Claudia protested.

The Bishop looked puzzled.

"I can assure you I have suffered agonies of remorse because, in an idle moment, I deceived my cat—a big, comfortable creature, who used to come to me every day to be fed, and preferred to eat out of my hand. He was greedy, though, and snapped, and one day I offered him a piece of preserved ginger, and he dashed at it as usual, and swallowed it before he knew what it was. Then he just looked at me and walked away. He trusted me, and I had deceived him. It was an unpardonable breach of confidence, and I have always felt that I never could look that cat in the face again."

The Bishop smiled and sighed at the little reminiscence. "I think you are right, though, in one way, Ideala," he presently observed. "The powers of Light and Darkness are certainly having a hard fight for it in our day; but we have every reason to hope.

> Oh, yet we trust that somehow good
> Will be the final goal of ill."[1]

"And, granted that the popular literature of the day is corrupt," the young sculptor put in, "and that the standard of society is being yearly lowered by it, still there is Art——"

"But there is so little of it," said Ideala; "I mean so little that elevates. Most of the subjects chosen are not worth painting; and what profit is there in contemplating a thing that is neither grand nor beautiful in itself, nor suggestive, by association, of anything that is grand or beautiful? The pictures one generally sees are not calculated to suggest anything to the minds that need suggestion most. The technical part may be good and gratifying to those who understand it, but that is the mere trade of the thing. We prefer to

---

[1] Tennyson, *In Memoriam A.H.H.*, section 54, lines 1-2. This section of *In Memoriam*, in which the death of Tennyson's friend Arthur Hallam serves as the impetus for exploration of issues of faith and doubt, is one in which trust is mixed with doubt. The bishop interprets this line of Tennyson as more hopeful than doubtful.

see it well done, of course, but if the canvas has nothing but the paint to recommend it, the artist might have saved himself the trouble of putting it on, for all the good it does or the pleasure it gives."

"Oh, Ideala, do you know nothing of the charm of colour?" asked a lady who painted.

"I do," said Ideala, "but I may be supposed to have enjoyed exceptional advantages. And it is hardly charm we want to elevate us. There will always be enough in all conscience to appeal to the senses. But there is an absence even of charm."

"Many a noble thought has been expressed in a coat of colour," said the lady.

"I know it has," Ideala answered; "and all best thoughts give pleasure. I have been so thrilled by a noble idea, well expressed, that I could do nothing but sit with closed eyes and revel in the joy of it. But if such an idea were placed before you, and you did not know the language in which it was written, what good would it do you? An uneducated person seeing a picture of a donkey in a field sees only a donkey in a field, however well it may be painted; and I fancy very exceptional ability would be required to make any of us think a grey donkey sublime, or believe an ordinary green field to be one of the Elysian."[1]

"Talking about charm," the sculptor broke in, enthusiastically, "I suppose you haven't seen the new picture, 'Venus getting into the Bath?' That is a feast of colour, and realism, if you like! She is standing beside the bath with a dreamy look on her face. Her lovely eyes are fixed on the water. One arched and blue-veined foot is slightly raised as if the touch of the marble chilled her. Her limbs are in an easy attitude, and beautifully modelled. She is represented as a slight young girl, and the figure stands out in exquisite nudity from a background of Pompeian red,[2] and the dark green of myrtles. With one hand she is holding aloft the masses of her rich brown hair—the attitude suggests the stretching of the muscles after repose; with the other"—but here his memory failed him. "What *is* she doing with her other hand?"

"Scratching herself!" slipped from Ideala, involuntarily, to her

---

[1] Place where the blessed dwell after life; paradise.

[2] Brownish or greyish red; called such because it is the same color as the walls of houses in Pompeii in its last days.

own horror and the delight of some. But she recovered herself quickly, and turning to the good Bishop, who was looking mildly astonished and much amused, she said: "There, my Lord, is an instance of the corrupt state of society in our own day. You see, even your restraining presence doesn't always keep us in order. I hope," she whispered to me, "I'm not going to be made the horrid example to prove the truth of all my theories."

Soon after this the party broke up. Claudia returned in her wraps to say good-night to the Bishop's wife.

"Claudia!" Ideala exclaimed, "you have forgotten that detestable old blue shawl."

Claudia tried to stop her with a significant gesture, but in vain. Ideala was obtuse.

"Claudia came out this evening in the most extraordinary covering I ever saw a lady wear," she said to the Bishop's wife. "I really think she must have borrowed it from one of the maids."

"I am afraid you must mean the blue shawl I lent to Lady Claudia the other evening," the Bishop's wife replied, with a hurt smile.

"Oh!" said Ideala, disconcerted for a moment. "But, really, Bishopess, you deserve to be upbraided. You should set a better example, and not provoke us to scorn on the subject of your shawls."

Later, when I was alone with my sister, I said: "Ideala did nothing but put her foot in it this evening. What was the matter with her? I never heard her speak so strongly before, except when she was alone with us. And I don't think she ought to discuss such subjects with such people; it is hardly delicate."

Claudia sighed wearily. "Who knows what pain is at the bottom of it all?" she said. "But one thing always puzzles me. Ideala rails at evils that never hurt her, and yet she speaks of marriage, which has been her bane, as if it were a holy and perfect state, upon which it is a privilege to enter."

"Plenty of people have condemned marriage simply because their own experience of it has been unfortunate," I answered; "but Ideala is above that. She will let no petty personal mishap prejudice her judgment on the subject. She sees and feels the possibility of infinite happiness in marriage when there is such love and such devotion on both sides as she herself could have brought to it; and she understands that her own unhappy experience need only be exceptional."

"I wish it were!" sighed Claudia.

Some years later, Ideala confessed to me that she had written "The Passion of Delysle" herself, but had had no idea of its significance until she heard it read aloud that night, and then, as she elegantly expressed it, she could have cut her throat with shame and mortification, which I consider a warning to young ladies not to trust to their poetical inspirations, for—if the shade of Shelley will pardon the conclusion—alas! *apparently*, they know not what they do when they write verses!

"I can't think how you could have criticized it like that, Ideala," I said, "now that I know you wrote it."

"Neither can I," she answered.

"You ought to have confessed you had written it, or have said nothing about it," I told her, frankly.

"Yes," she assented. "Not doing so was a kind of falsehood. But neither course occurred to me." And then she explained: "I never see the meaning of what I write till the light of public opinion is turned upon it, or some cold critic comes and damps my enthusiasm. When a subject possesses me, and shapes itself into verse, it boils in my brain, and my pen is the only way of escape for it, the one safety-valve I have to ease the pressure. And I can't judge of its merits myself for long enough after it *is* written, because the boiling begins again, you see, whenever I read it, and then there is such a steam of feeling I cannot see to think. For the verses, however poor they appear to you, contain for me the whole poem as I have it in my inner consciousness. It is beautiful as it exists there, but the power of expression is lacking. If only I could make you feel it as I do, I should be the greatest poet alive."

It was Ideala's trick of missing the true import of a thing—often an act of her own—until the occasion had passed, or of seeing it strangely distorted, as she frequently did at this time—though that gradually ceased altogether as she grew older; but it was this peculiarity, so strongly marked in her, which first helped me to comprehend a curious trait there is in the moral nature of men and women while it is still in process of development. Many men, Frenchmen especially, have thought the trait peculiar to women. La Bruyère declares that "Women have no principles as men understand the word. They are guided by their feelings, and have full faith in their guide. Their notions of propriety and impropriety, right and wrong, they get from the little world embraced by their affections."[1] And Alphonse Karr says: "Never attempt to prove anything to a woman: she believes only according to her feelings. Endeavour to please and persuade: she may yield to the person who reasons with her, not to his arguments"[2]—opinions, however, which apply to men as often as not, and only to the young, impressible, passionate, and imperfectly educated of either sex. But there is scarcely a generalisation for one sex which does not apply equally to the other, so perfectly alike in nature are men and women. The difference is only in circumstance. Reverse the position of the sexes, require men to be modest and obedient, and they will develop every woman's weakness in a generation. If a man would comprehend a woman, let him consider himself; the woman has the same joys, sorrows, hopes, fears, pleasures, and passions—expressed in another way, that is all. But, certainly, for a long time Ideala's guide was her feeling about a thing. I have often said to her, when at last she decided to take some step which had obviously been the only course open to her from the first: "But, Ideala, *why* have you hesitated so long? You knew it was right to begin with."

"Yes," she would answer, "I *knew* it was right; but I have only just now *felt* that it was."

She had never thought of acting on the mere cold knowledge. For feeling to knowledge, in young minds, is like the match to a fire laid in a grate; knowledge without feeling being as cheerless and impotent as the fire unlit.

---

[1] Jean de La Bruyère (1645-1696), French writer best known for *Les Caractères de Théophraste, traduits du grec; avec Les Caractères ou les mœurs de ce siècle* (1688). The first part is a translation of Theophrastus, and the rest is made up of character sketches, maxims, and literary discussions. La Bruyère had strong opinions about various aspects of society including the economy and the nobility, but he was not necessarily a reformer. Here, Ideala is rephrasing aphorism 54 in "Of Women," Chapter 3 in *Les Caractères*: "Most women hardly have principles; they are led by their passions, and form their morals and manners after those whom they love."

[2] Alphonse Karr (1808-1890), French novelist and journalist, who edited *Le Figaro* and founded *Les Guêpes* beginning in 1839 and founded *Le Journal* in 1848. The quotation here is from Chapter 3 in *Les Femmes*.

CHAPTER XII.

A LITTLE while after that evening at the Palace we learnt to our dismay that Ideala's husband had taken a house in one of the rough manufacturing districts, to which he meant to remove immediately. Business was the pretext, as he had money in some great ironworks there; but I think the nearness of a large city, where a man of his stamp would be able to indulge all his tastes without let or hindrance, had something to do with the change.

Ideala had kept up very well while she was among us, but soon after she went away we gathered from the tone of her letters that there was a change in her which alarmed us. Her health, which had hitherto been splendid, seemed to be giving way, and it was evident that her new position did not please her, and that, even after she had been there for months, she continued to feel herself "a stranger in a strange land." The people were uncongenial, and I think it likely they regarded Ideala's oddities with some suspicion, and did not take to her as we had done. She had not that extreme youth which had been her excuse when she came to us, and which, somehow, we had not missed when she lost it; and her habitual reserve on all matters that immediately concerned herself must also have tended to make her unpopular with people whose predominant quality was "an eminent curiosity."

"They are far above books," Ideala wrote to Claudia; "what they study is each other, and in the pursuit of this branch of knowledge they are indefatigable. When they can get nothing out of me about myself, they question me about my husband and friends, and it is in vain that I answer them with those words of wisdom (I feel sure I misquote them)—'All that is mine own is yours till the end of my life; but the secret of my friend is not mine own'—they persevere.

"Our house is near the town. Eighteen big chimneys darken our daylight and deluge us with smuts[1] when the wind brings the smoke our way; and besides the smoke we are subject to unsavoury vapours from chemical works in the other direction, so that when the wind shifts we only exchange evils. They say these chemical fumes are

---

[1] Soot, from a chimney

not unwholesome, and quote the death-rate, which is lower than any other place of the size in England. In fact, scarcely anybody dies here. They go away as soon as they begin to feel ill—perhaps that accounts for it. But those horrid chemical fumes have a great deal to answer for. They have killed the trees for miles around. It is the oaks that suffer principally. The tops are nipped first, and then they gradually die downwards till the whole tree is decayed all through. The absence of trees makes the country bleak and desolate, and I cannot help thinking the unlovely surroundings affect us all. The people themselves are unlovely in thought, and word, and deed; but I have found a good deal of rough kindliness amongst them nevertheless. They did mob me on one occasion, and made most unkind remarks about my nether garments, when I was obliged to walk through the town in my riding habit;[1] but, as a rule, the mill girls merely observe 'That's a lady,' and let me go by unmolested—unless I happen to be carrying flowers. They do so love flowers, poor things! and I cannot resist their pathetic entreaties when they beg for 'One, missus, on'y one!' Some of my lady friends are not let off so easily as I am. The girls chaff them unmercifully about their dress and personal peculiarities, and if they show signs of annoyance they call them names that are not to be repeated. The mill girls wear bright-coloured gowns, white aprons, and nothing on their heads. If a policeman catches them at any mischief they either clatter off in their clogs with shrieks of laughter, or knock him down and kick him most unmercifully. They are as strong as men, and as beautiful, some of them, as saints; but they are very unsaintlike creatures really—irresponsible, and with little or no idea of right and wrong. One scarcely believes that they have souls—and I am always surprised to find that anything not cruel and coarse can survive in the hearts of people begrimed, body and mind, like these, by their hard surroundings; but it is there, nevertheless—the human nature, and the poetry, and the something ready to thrill to better things. A gentleman has a lovely place, not far from us, where the trees have been spared by a miracle. Nightingales seldom wander so far north, but a few years ago a stray one was heard there, and the wonder and the beauty of

---

[1] Nether garments are under garments, and, in the nineteenth century, a lady's riding habit consisted of a masculine, tailored jacket and often a very long skirt, since women rode side saddle.

its voice brought hundreds from the mills and crowded streets to hear it sing. Special trains were run from the neighbouring city to accommodate the crowds that came nightly to wait in the moonlight and listen; and an enterprising trader set up a stall, and sold gingerbeer. The story ends there, but I like it, don't you? especially the gingerbeer part of it. It was told me by one who remembers the circumstance.

"My greatest pleasure in life is in my flowers, they are dearer to me than any I ever had before, because they are all so delicate, and require such infinite care and tenderness to keep them alive in this uncongenial climate. I have my thrushes also—two, which I stole from a nest in a wood one moonlight night, and brought up by hand on bread and milk and scraped beef. I had to get up at daylight, and feed them every hour until dark; but the clergy will not allow that this obligation was a proper excuse for staying away from church, and just now I am unhappy in the feeling that their religion must be inhuman. But my thrushes have well repaid the trouble. They call me when I go into the room, and come to me when I open the door of their cage, and perch on my shoulder. One of them, Israfil,[1] sings divinely. People who come to hear him see only a little brown bird with speckled breast, and call him a thrush; but *I* know he is Israfil, 'the angel of song, and most melodious of God's creatures;' and *he* thinks that I have wings. He told me so!

"I wish you would send me a basket of snails packed up in lettuce leaves. I don't know why, but I can find none here, and I cannot hear of one ever having been seen in the county. But please do not send them unless you are quite sure you can spare them."

"Ideala is trying to hide herself behind these pretty trivialities," Claudia said. "I always suspect that there is something more wrong than usual when she adopts this playful tone and childlike simplicity of taste."

"It must be trying to have a friend who believes so little in one as you do in Ideala," I answered.

"Oh, how exasperating you are!" Claudia exclaimed. "You know what I mean quite well enough."

---

[1] In the Koran, one of four important angels; Gabriel, Michael, and Azrael are the others. Israfil is the angel of song, who will blow the trumpet on Judgment Day. Israfil, Gabriel, and Michael warned Abraham of Sodom's destruction.

Later, Ideala wrote:—"You are anxious about my health. The fact is, I have developed a most extraordinary talent for taking cold. I went by train to see the museum in the city the other day. I took off my cloak while I was there, and stayed an hour, and when I came away, the antiquary, who knew I was a precious specimen, wrapped me up carefully himself. Nevertheless I caught cold. Then I went to stay with some people near here who clamoured much for the pleasure of my company. They live in a palace and are entertaining. The lady's papa took me in to dinner the first evening. He asked me about Major Gorst, and wanted to know, in an impressive tone of voice, if I had heard that he was the next heir but one to the Hearldom of Cathcourt.[1] He also told me that he had sent twenty-seven baskets of grapes to his son-in-law at York since Christmas; and I sympathized with him, and wanted to know why his vines had failed this year, and said it was a pity. I wonder why he wouldn't talk to me any more after that![2]

"The next day my hostess said to her husband: 'Dearest, do let me ride Oscar,' and he replied: 'No, my darling, I can't till I know he's safe. I must get some one to try him first'—and he looked at me—'Perhaps you wouldn't mind?'

"They had never seen me on horseback, and I was longing to distinguish myself. I did distinguish myself. Oscar was a merry horse, but one never knew how he would take things. The first bridge we came to—I was 'sitting easy to a canter' with my foot out of the stirrup and my leg *over* the third crutch—a bad habit I learnt from a foreign friend—and an express train rushed by. Oscar went on abruptly, but I remained. The next difficulty was at a brook. We ought to have crossed it together; but Oscar changed his mind at the last moment, so he remained and I went on. And after that we came to crossroads, and had a difference of opinion about which was the right one. That ended in our coming over together, which made me feel solemn—disheartened, in fact—and then I thought we should never understand each other and be friends, so I gave him up. I did not talk much about riding to those people after that.

---

[1] Here begins a section that was deleted from the Donohue, Henneberry and Co. edition.

[2] This is the end of a section deleted from the Donohue, Henneberry and Co. edition.

"But I wore my summer habit that day, and of course I caught cold. And when that was nearly well I went downstairs to be civil to some people who had driven a long way to see me. The drawing-room was damp from disuse, and the fire had only just been lighted—and of course I caught cold. When that was better I went for a drive. The wind was East, and the carriage was open—and of course I caught cold. I don't know how it may strike you, but argument seems to me useless when a person has such a constitution."

"Can you read between the lines of that letter?" Claudia asked me.

"She seems to be dreadfully *don't care*," I said.

"Exactly. She is more reckless, and therefore more miserable, than she used to be. I wouldn't live with him."

"Ideala won't shirk her duty because it is hard and unpalatable," I answered.

"I believe she likes it!" Claudia exclaimed; and then, smiling at her own inconsistency, she explained, "I mean if she really is miserable she ought to speak and let us do something."

"It is contrary to her principles. She would think it wrong to disturb *your* mind for a moment because her own life is a burden to her. That is why she always tries to seem happy, and is cheerful on the surface. If she made lament, we should suffer in sympathy, and all the more because there is so very little we could do to help her. Silence is best. If she ever gives way, she will not be able to bear it again."

"But why *should* she bear it?" Claudia demanded.

"It is her duty."

"I know she thinks so, and is sacrificing her life to that principle. But will you kindly tell me where a woman's duty to her husband ends and her duty to herself begins? I suppose you will allow that she has a duty to herself? And the line should be drawn somewhere."

Claudia's mind was a sort of boomerang just then, returning inevitably to this point of departure; but I could make no suggestion that satisfied her. And I was uneasy myself. Ideala refused to come to us, and had made some excuse to prevent it when Claudia offered to go to her. This puzzled me; but we induced her at last to promise to meet us in London in May. It was April then, and we thought if she could be persuaded to stay two months of the season in town with us, and go with us afterwards to a place of mine in the North which she loved, she would probably recover her health and spirits.

CHAPTER XIII.

IN the meantime, however, something decisive happened, as we afterwards learnt.

It seems that after they left our neighbourhood Ideala had, by accident, made a number of small discoveries about her husband which had the effect of destroying any remnant of respect she may still have felt for him. She found that he was in the habit of examining her private papers in her absence, and that he had opened her letters and resealed them. His manner to her was unctuous as a rule; but she knew he lied to her without hesitation if it suited his purpose—and that alone would have been enough to destroy her liking for him, for it is not in the nature of such a woman to love a man who has looked her in the face and lied to her.

These things, and the loneliness he brought upon her by driving from her the few people with whom she had any intellectual fellowship, she would have borne in the old uncomplaining way, but he did not stop there.

One day she drove into town with a friend who got out to do some shopping. Ideala waited in the carriage, which had stopped opposite a public-house, and from where she sat she could see the little sitting-room behind the bar, and its occupants. They were her husband and the barmaid, who was sitting on his knee.

Ideala arranged her parasol so that they might not see her if they chanced to look that way, and calmly resumed the conversation when her friend returned.

She dined alone with her husband that evening, and talked as usual, telling him all she had done and what news there was in the paper, as she always did to save him the trouble of reading it. In return he told her he had been at the ironworks all day, only leaving them in time to dress for dinner, a piece of news she received with a still countenance, and her soft eyes fixed on the fire.

She was standing on the hearth at the time, and as he spoke he laid his hand upon her shoulder caressingly, but she could not bear it. Her powers of endurance were at an end, and for the first time she shrank from him openly.

"How you do loathe me, Ideala," he exclaimed.

"Yes, I loathe you," she answered.

And then, in a sudden burst of rage, he raised his hand and struck her.

Ideala's determination to be faithful to what she conceived to be her duty had kept her quiet hitherto, but now a sense of personal degradation made her desperate, and she forgot all that. Her first impulse was to consult somebody, to speak and find means to put an end to her misery; but I was not there, and to whom should she go for advice? Her impatience brooked no delay. She must see some one instantly. She thought of the Rector of the parish, but felt he would not do. He was a fine-looking, well-mannered old gentleman, much engaged in scientific pursuits, who always spoke of the Deity as if he were on intimate terms with Him, and had probably never been asked to administer any but the most formal kind of spiritual consolation in his life.

The training and experience of a Roman Catholic priest, accustoming them as it does to deal with every phase of human suffering and passion, would have been more useful to her in such an emergency, but she knew none of the priests in that district, and did not think of going to them. But while she was considering the matter, as if by inspiration, she remembered something an acquaintance had lately written to her. This lady was a person for whom she felt much respect, and that doubtless influenced her decision considerably. The lady wrote:—"It must be convenient to be only twenty minutes by train from such a big place. I suppose you go over for shopping, &c.? When you are there again I wish you would go and see my cousin Lorrimer. He is Adviser in General at the Great Hospital[1]—a responsible position; and I am sure, if you go, he will be glad to do the honours of the place, which is most interesting."

---

[1] Most likely modeled after the Great Hospital in Norwich, Norfolk, which was founded as St. Giles's Hospital in 1249 and later became the Great Hospital. In a letter to Walter Powell, dated 7 Dec. 1923, Grand states that Norwich had been the setting for all three novels in the Morningquest trilogy, of which *Ideala* was the first. See Teresa Mangum, *Married, Middlebrow, and Militant: Sarah Grand and the New Woman Novel* (Ann Arbor: University of Michigan Press, 1998), 60.

Ideala had felt from the first that she would rather consult a stranger who would be disinterested and unprejudiced. This gentleman's name promised well for him, for he belonged to people whose integrity was well known; and his position vouched for his ability—and also for his age to Ideala, whose imagination had pictured a learned old gentleman, bald, spectacled, benevolent, full of knowledge of the world, "wise saws and modern instances."[1] No one, she thought, could be better suited for her purpose; and accordingly, next day, after attending to her household duties, she went by an early train to consult him.

CHAPTER XIV.

THE Great Hospital had been founded by an eccentric old gentleman of enormous wealth for an entirely original purpose. He observed that great buildings were erected everywhere to receive patients suffering from all imaginable bodily ills, chronic mania, of course, when the brain was diseased, being one of them; but no one had thought of making provision for such troubles, mental, moral, and religious, as affect the mind; and he held that such suffering was as real, and, without proper treatment, as incurable and disastrous, as any form of physical ailment. He therefore determined to found a hospital for these unhappy ones, which should contain every requisite that Divine Revelation had suggested, or human ingenuity could devise, for the promotion of peace of mind. The idea had grown out of some great mental trouble with which he himself had been afflicted in early life, and for which the world, as it was, could offer him no relief.

The first thing he did towards the carrying out of his plan was to buy a site for his hospital near a growing town on the banks of a big river. The building was to be surrounded by green fields, for the colour is refreshing; and within sight of a great volume of calmly flowing water, the silent power of which is solemn and tranquil-

---

[1] Shakespeare, *As You Like It*, 2.7.156. Part of Jaques's well known speech that begins "All the world's a stage / And all the men and women merely players" and describes the seven stages of a man's life. Stage five, Justice, has man understanding the laws of the world and making judgments about it.

lizing to the spirit; and human society was to be within easy reach, for many people find it beneficial. As soon as he had found the site, which was entirely satisfactory, he set about maturing his plan for the building. Such a scheme could not be carried out in a moment, and he spent thirty years in travelling to study human nature, and architecture, and all else that should help to bring his work to perfection. At the end of thirty years he had finished a plan for the building to his own entire satisfaction; but Mr. Ruskin[1] had been growing up in the meantime, and had begun to write, and the founder, happening to come across his works by accident one day, discovered his own ideas to be wrong from beginning to end. However, as it was the Truth he was aiming at, and not a justification of himself, he calmly burnt his plans, put his fingers in his ears (figuratively speaking) that he might not hear the rest of the world bray, and for ten years more devoted himself to the study of Mr. Ruskin. At the end of that time he knew something about proportion, about masses and intervals of light and shade; about the grandeur and sublimity of size, and the grace and beauty of ornament; about depth and harmony of colour, and all the other wonders that make one sick with longing to behold them; and when he had mastered all this he determined to begin at the very beginning, that is to say, with the walls that were to enclose his vast experiment. Everything was to be real, everything was to be solid, everything had to be endowed with a power of expression that could not fail of its effect. And as soon as he felt he might safely begin, he hastened away to inspect the long neglected site for his wonderful building. But here an unexpected check awaited him. While he himself had been so hard at work, his future neighbours had not been idle. The town had grown to a city; the river's banks were crowded with wharves and human habitations; the river itself cradled a fleet on its bosom, its waters, once so sublimely clear and still, were turbid and yellow, befouled by the city sewers, and useful only; and all that remained to remind him of what had once been were a few acres of weeds enclosed by an iron railing—an eyesore to the inhabitants of that region, as the Corporation told him, with a polite hope that he would either build on it

---

[1] Ruskin, in *The Stones of Venice* (1851-53), argued for a return to Gothic architecture, since it more fully embraced the unique craftsmanship of the worker instead of the cookie-cutter look of manufactured designs.

soon or leave it alone, which was their diplomatic way of request-
ing him to hand the lot over to themselves. And this he might have
done had they said "Please;" but when he found the young city so
ignorant, he thought it his duty to teach it manners, so he took a
year or two more to consider the matter. Then he perceived that if
he built his house on the site as it was now, he should do even more
good than he had intended, for the constant contemplation of such
a stately pile would help to elevate the citizens outside the building, while those within might find comfort in seeing themselves surrounded by even greater misery than their own.

And so the building rose and grew to perfection, and they found
after all that no better site could have been chosen for it; for from
every side as you approached it it was seen to advantage, and the majesty and power of it were made manifest. Outside the design was so
evident in its grandeur that the mind was not wearied and perplexed
by an effort to understand; it was simply elevated to a state of enjoyment bordering on exaltation—exaltation without excitement, and
near akin to peace. And the interior of the building as you entered it
maintained this first impression. Such ornament as there was touched
you, as the clouds do, with a sense of suitability that left nothing to be
desired. Art was so perfectly hidden that there seemed to have been
no striving for effect in decoration or construction, it looked like a
work of Nature, accomplished without effort, and beautiful without
design; and the mind brought under its influence, and left free of conjecture, was gently compelled to revel in the peace which harmoni-
ous surroundings insensibly produce. Disturbing thoughts vanished
as being too common and mean, too human, for such a place, and the
spirit was soothed with a sense of repose—of sensuous restfulness,
really, for the pleasure, as intended, affected the senses more than the
intellect, which could here make holiday. Work-wearied brains were
thus eased from pressure, and minds a prey to doubts and other disturbing thoughts which impaired their strength, if they did not render
them useless, were at once relieved. And this was the beginning of
the treatment which was afterwards continued in other parts of the
building, and by other means, until the cure was complete—arrangements being made for the removal of cases that proved to be hopeless
to those older establishments which have long existed at the expense
of the country, or as the outcomes of private enterprise.

Of course the staff of such a place had to be formed of men of a high order. Some of these had been patients themselves, and had been chosen on that account, it being thought that those who had suffered from certain ills would be apt to detect the symptoms in others, and able to devise remedies for them, which proved to be the case. The establishment was munificently endowed and liberally supported, and the Master, as he was reverently called, lived just long enough to see that it was a success.

He had not thought of extending the charity to women, being under the impression that no such provision was necessary for them. He acknowledged that they had a large share of physical suffering to endure, but asserted that Nature, to preserve her balance, must have arranged their minds so as to render them incapable of suffering in any other way. Sentimentality, hysteria, and silliness, he said, were at the bottom of all their mental troubles, which did not, therefore, merit serious attention.

CHAPTER XV.

BUT of all this Ideala knew little or nothing when she went there, except that the Great Hospital existed for some learned purpose. She felt the power of the place, however, preoccupied as she was, and stopped involuntarily when she saw the building, ceasing for a moment to be conscious of anything but the awe and admiration it inspired. Then she passed up the broad steps, beneath the massive pillars of the portico, and entered the hall. A man-servant took her card to Mr. Lorrimer, and, returning presently, requested her to follow him. They left the great hall by a flight of low steps at the end of it, and, turning to the right, passed through glass doors into quite another part of the building. A long, dimly-lighted gallery led away into the distance. A few doors opened on to it, and at one of these the servant stopped and knocked. A tall gentleman opened the door himself, and, begging Ideala to enter, bade her be seated at a writing-table which stood in the middle of the room, and himself took the chair in front of it, and looked at Ideala's card which lay before him. Another gentleman, whom Lorrimer introduced as "My brother Julian," lounged on a high-backed chair at the other side of the table. The room was a good size, but so crowded with things that there was scarcely space to turn round. The light fell full upon Lorrimer as he sat facing the window, and Ideala saw a fair man of about thirty, not at all the sort of man she had imagined, and quite impossible for her purpose.

An awkward pause followed her entrance. She was unable to tell him the real reason of her visit, and at a loss to invent a fictitious one.

"I don't suppose you know in the least who I am," she said, seeing that he glanced at her card again, and then she explained, telling him what his cousin had written to her.

"And you would like to see the Hospital?" he asked.

"Please."

He rose, took down a bunch of keys, and requested her to follow him. She felt no interest in the place, and knew it was a bore to him to show it to her; but the thing had to be done. He led her through halls and lecture rooms, places of recreation and places for work; he showed her picture galleries, statuary, the library, and a museum, and told her the plan of it all clearly, like one reciting a lesson, and indifferently, like one performing a task that must be got through somehow, but making it all most interesting, nevertheless.

Ideala began to be taken out of herself.

"What a delightful place!" she said, when they came to the library. "And there is a whole row of books I want to consult. How I should like to come and read them."

"Oh, pray do," he answered, "whenever you like. Ladies frequently do so. You have only to write and tell me when you wish to come, and I will see that you are properly attended to."

"Thank you," Ideala rejoined. "It is just the very thing for me, for I am writing a little book, and cannot get on till I have consulted some authorities on the subject."

In the museum they stopped to look at a mummy.

"Oh, happy mummy!" burst from Ideala, involuntarily.

"Why?" asked Lorrimer, aroused from his apathy.

"It has done with it all, you know," she answered.

Then he turned and looked at her, and she saw that he was something more than cold, pale-faced, and indifferent, which had been her first idea of him. His eyes were large, dark grey, and penetrating. She would have called his face fine, rather than handsome; but the upper part was certainly beautiful, in spite of some hard lines on it. There was something in the expression, more than in the formation, of the mouth and chin, however, that did not satisfy. His head and throat were splendid; the former narrowed a little at the back, but the forehead made up for the defect, which was not striking. He made Ideala think of Tito Melema and of Bayard.[1]

That remark of hers having broken the ice, they began to talk like human beings with something in common. But Ideala's mood was not calculated to produce a good impression. The failure of her enterprise brought on a fit of recklessness such as we understood, and she said some things which must have made a stranger think her peculiar. Lorrimer had begun to be amused before they returned to the great entrance hall. Once or twice he looked at her curiously. "What sort of a person are you, I wonder?" he was thinking,

"I was dying of dulness," she said, telling him about the place she came from, "and so I came to see you."

He left her for a moment, but presently returned with his brother.

"You had better come and have some luncheon before you go back," he said.

And she went.

As they left the building, Lorrimer asked her: "Where on earth did my cousin meet *you*?"—with the slightest possible emphasis. Ideala understood him, and laughed. "Upon my word I don't know who introduced her," she answered, standing on her dignity nevertheless. "I can't remember."

They went to the refreshment-room at the station. It was crowded, but they managed to get a table to themselves. There was a vacant seat at it, and an old gentleman begged to be allowed to occupy it as there was no other in the room. The three chatted while they waited, each hiding him, or her, self beneath the light froth of easy conversation; and people, not accustomed to look on the surface for signs of what is working beneath, would have thought them merry enough. As she began to know her companions better, Ideala

---

[1] Tito Melema is a character in George Eliot's *Romola* (1862-63) who is handsome but unscrupulous, and Bayard may be Pierre Terrail, seigneur de Bayard (1476-1524), a French soldier known for his chivalry, or Hippolyte Bayard (1801-1887), one of the earliest photographers.

was more and more drawn to Lorrimer. His brother, who was a dark man, and very different in character, did not attract her.

The old gentleman, meanwhile, was absorbed in his newspaper, and he marked his enjoyment of it by inhaling his breath and exhaling it again in that particular way which is called "blowing like a porpoise."

Lorrimer, by an intelligent glance, expressed what he thought of the peculiarity to Ideala, who remarked:—"It is the next gale developing dangerous energy on its way to the North British and Norwegian coasts."

The laugh that followed caused the old gentleman to fold up his paper, and look benignly at the young people over his pince-nez.

It was early in the season, and peas were a rare and forced vegetable. A small dish of them was brought, and handed to the dangerous gale, who absently took them all.

"You have taken all the peas, sir; allow me to give you all the pepper," said Lorrimer, dexterously suiting the action to the word.

The dangerous gale, though disconcerted at first, was finally moved to mirth.

"Ah, young people! young people!" he said, and sighed—and being a merry and wise old gentleman, he found pleasure in their pleasure, and entered into their mood, little suspecting that Black Care[1] was one of the party, or that a black bruise which would have aroused all the pity and indignation of his honest old heart, had he seen it, was almost under his eyes.

And they all loved him.

Presently he rose to go; but before he departed, he observed, looking kindly at Ideala and Lorrimer:—"You're a handsome pair, my dears! Let me congratulate you; and may your children have the mother's sweetness and the father's strength, and may the love you have for each other last for ever—there's nothing like it. Thank God for it, and remember Him always—and keep yourselves unspotted from the world." And so saying, he went his way in peace.

---

[1] A dark presence that cannot be outrun; depression. The phrase comes from Horace, who writes, in *Odes* 3.1, "But Fear and Threats climb up with the master, and black Care doesn't withdraw from the bronze ship and sits behind the calvaryman" (sed Timor et Minae / scandunt eodem quo dominus, neque / decedit aerata triremi et post equitem sedet atra Cura).

"Dear embarrassing old man!" said Lorrimer, regretfully. "I wish I hadn't spilt the pepper on his plate."

"Is there a chance for Lorrimer?" his brother asked.

But Ideala only stared at him. There was something in his tone that made her feel ill at ease, and brought back the recollection of her misery in a moment. Then all at once she became depressed, and both the young men noticed it.

"I'm afraid you're rather down about something," Julian said. "You'd better tell us what it is. Perhaps we could cheer you up. And I'm a lawyer, you know. I might be able to help you."

Lorrimer was looking at her, and seemed to wait for her to speak; but she only showed by a change of expression that the fact of his brother being a lawyer possessed a special interest for her.

"If you will trust us," he said at last, "perhaps we *can* help you."

"I wish I could," she answered, wistfully; "I came to tell you."

"This sounds serious," Julian said, lightly. "You will have to begin at the beginning, you know. Come, Lorrimer, we'll go down the river. And," to Ideala, "you might tell us all about it on the way, you know."

"Yes, come," said Lorrimer.

Ideala rose to accompany them without a thought. It all came about so easily that no question of propriety suggested itself—and if any had occurred to her she would probably have considered it an insult to these gentlemen to suppose they would allow her to put herself in a questionable position; and when Julian lit a cigarette without asking her permission, she was surprised.

On the way to the river Ideala's spirits rose again, and they all talked lightly, making a jest of everything; but while they were waiting for a boat, Julian took up a bunch of charms that were attached to Ideala's watch chain and began to examine them coolly, and the unwonted familiarity startled her. With a sudden revulsion of feeling she turned to Lorrimer. She was annoyed by the slight indignity, and also a little frightened. Whatever Lorrimer may have thought of her before, he understood her look now, and his whole manner changed.

Julian left them for a moment.

"I *am* so ashamed of myself," Ideala said. "I have made some dreadful mistake. I have done something wrong."

"I am very sorry for you," he answered, gravely—and then, to his brother, who had returned—"You can go on if you like. I am going back."

"Oh, we can't go on without you," Ideala interposed; "and I would rather go back too."

They began to retrace their steps, and Lorrimer, as they walked, managed, with a few adroit questions, to learn from Ideala that the trouble had something to do with her husband.

"Regy Beaumont is coming to me this afternoon," he said to his brother. "Would you mind being there to receive him?"

They exchanged glances, and Julian took his leave.

"Now, tell me," Lorrimer said to Ideala.

But an unconquerable fit of shyness came over her the moment they were left alone together. "I cannot tell you," she answered. "It is too dreadful to speak of."

"Your husband has done you some great wrong?" he said.

"Yes."

"Something for which you can get legal redress?"

"Yes."

"And that made you desperate?"

"Yes."

"And what did you do?" He put the question abruptly, startling Ideala, as he had intended.

"I? Oh, I—did nothing," she stammered.

There was a pause.

"My ideal of marriage is a high one," he said at last, "and I should be very hard on any shortcomings of that kind."

Ideala longed to confide in him, but her shyness continued, and she walked by his side like one in a dream.

He took her to the station, and when they parted he said "You will write and tell me?"

Ideala looked up. There were no hard lines in his face now; he was slightly flushed.

"Yes, I will write," she answered, almost in a whisper.

And then the train, "with rush and ring," bore her away through the spring-country; but she neither saw the young green of the hedgerows, nor "the young lambs bleating in the meadows,"[1] nor

---

[1] Likely a reference to Elizabeth Barrett Browning's poem "The Cry of the Children" (1843), which contrasts the images of lambs bleating in a meadow to the grinding of mechanical wheels in order to show the plight of children working in England's factories.

the broad river as she passed it, nor the fleecy clouds that flecked the blue. She was not really conscious of anything for the moment, but that sudden great unspeakable uplifting of the spirit, which is joy.

CHAPTER XVI.

THE following week Ideala came to London, but not to us—she had promised to stay with some other people first. She wrote three times to Lorrimer while she was with them—first to thank him for his kindness, to which he replied briefly, begging her to confide in him, and let him help her.

In her second letter Ideala told him what had occurred. His reply was business-like. He urged her to let him consult his legal friends about her case; pointed out that she could not be expected to remain with her husband now; and showed her that she would not have to suffer much from all the publicity which was necessary to free her from him.[1] She replied that her first impulse had been to obtain legal redress, but that now she could not make up her mind to face the publicity. She would see him, however, when she returned, and consult him about it; and she would also like to consult those books in the library. Her buoyant spirit was already recovering under the influence of a new interest in life.

Lorrimer's answer was formal, as his other notes had been. He begged her to make any use of the library she pleased, only to let him know when to expect her, that she might have no trouble with the officials; and offered her any other help in his power.

In the meantime my sister Claudia had seen Ideala, and had been pleased to find her, not looking well, certainly, but just as cheerful as usual. "It is evident the place does not agree with her," Claudia said; "but a few weeks with us will set her all right again."

They drove in the park together one afternoon, and talked, as

---

[1] Grand does not specify the exact year in which the novel takes place, but it seems to take place after 1857, when the Marriage and Divorce Bill made obtaining a divorce easier than it had been. Still, the grounds for men asking for a divorce were different from the grounds for women. Men had to prove only that their wives had been unfaithful; women had to prove that the adultery was especially unusual (i.e., bigamy or incest). For more about about legislation related to women's rights, see Introduction.

usual, of many things, the state of society being one of them. This was a subject upon which my sister descanted frequently, and it was from her that Ideala learnt all she knew of it.

"Can you wonder," Claudia said on this occasion, "that men are immoral when ladies in society rather pride themselves than otherwise on imitating the *demi-monde*?"[1]

"Have you ever noticed," Ideala answered, indirectly, "how frequently a word or phrase which you know quite well by sight, but have never thought of and do not understand, is suddenly brought home to you as it were? You come across it everywhere, and at last take the trouble to find out what it means in self-defence. That expression—*demi-monde*—has begun to haunt me since I came to town, and I feel I shall be obliged to look it up at once to stop the nuisance. We went to a theatre the other night, and when we were settled there I saw my husband in the stalls with a lady in flame-coloured robes. I didn't know he was in town. The rest of our party saw him, too, and the gentlemen had a mysterious little consultation at the back of the box. Then one of them left us, but returned almost immediately, and told us the carriage had not gone, and hadn't we better try some other theatre—the piece at that one was not so good as they had supposed. But I knew they had taken a lot of trouble, entirely on my account, to get a box there, as I had expressed a wish to see that particular piece, and I said I had come to enjoy it, and meant to. I did enjoy it, too. It was so absorbing that I forgot all about my husband, and don't know when he left the theatre. I only know that he disappeared without coming near us. When we got back, Lilian came to my room and told me they were all saying downstairs that I had behaved splendidly, and I said I was delighted to hear it, particularly as I did not know how, or when, or where I had come to deserve such praise. And then she asked me if I knew who it was my husband was with. I said, no; some alderman's wife, I supposed. 'Nothing half so good,' she answered. 'That woman is notorious: she is one of the *demi-monde*!' 'Well,' I said, 'I don't suppose she is in society.' And then Lilian said, 'Good gracious, Ideala! how can you be so tranquil? You *must* care. I think you are the most extraordinary person I ever met.' And I told her that the only extraordinary thing about me just then

---

[1] Women marginalized by society because of their questionable character and/or class status; often incorrectly applied to courtesans.

was a great 'exposition of sleep' that had come upon me.[1] And then she left me; but she told me afterwards that she thought I was acting, and came back later to see if I really could sleep."

"And you did sleep, Ideala?"

"Like a top—why not? But now you are following suit with your ill-conducted people, and your *demi-monde*. I want to know what you mean by that phrase?"

Then Claudia explained it to her.

"But I thought all that had ended with the Roman Empire," Ideala protested.

Claudia laughed, and then went on without pity, describing the class as they sink lower and lower, and cruelly omitting no detail that might complete the picture.

"But the men are as bad," said Ideala.

"Oh, as bad, yes!" was the answer.

Ideala was pale with disgust. "And we have to touch them!" she said.

Her ignorance of this phase of life had been so complete, and her faith in those about her so perfect, that the shock of this dreadful revelation was almost too much for her. At first, as the carriage drove on through the crowded streets, she saw in every woman's face a hopeless degradation, and in every man's eyes a loathsome sin; and she exclaimed, as another woman had exclaimed on a similar occasion: "Oh, Claudia! why did you tell me? It is too dreadful. I cannot bear to know it."

"How a woman can be at once so clever and such a fool as you are, Ideala, puzzles me," Claudia remonstrated, not unkindly.

She had warmed as she went on, and forgot in her indignation to take advantage of this long-looked-for opportunity to speak to Ideala about her own troubles; and afterwards, when she showed an inclination to open the subject, Ideala put her off with a jest.

"'*Le mariage est beau pour les amants et utile pour les saints*,'"[2] she

---

[1] Shakespeare, *A Midsummer Night's Dream*, 4.1.38-39: "But, I pray you, let none of your people stir me; I have an exposition of sleep come upon me."

[2] "Marriage is appealing to lovers and of service to saints." From George Sand's *Historie de ma vie* (1854-55). Sand was known for her legal separation from her husband Baron Dudevant, her relationships with the composers Franz Liszt and Frédéric Chopin, and her unconventional masculine dress.

quoted, lightly. "Class me with the saints, and talk of something interesting."

A few days later Claudia came to me in dismay.

"What do you think?" she said. "Ideala is not coming to us at all! She says she must go back at once."

"Go back!" I exclaimed, "and why?"

"She is going to write something, for which she requires to read a great deal, and she says she must go back to work."

"But that is nonsense," I protested. "She can work as much as she likes here—I can even help her."

"I know that," Claudia answered; "but she spoke so positively I could not insist. I suppose the truth is her husband has ordered her back, and she is going to be a good, obedient child, as usual."

"Does she seem at all unhappy?"

"No, and that is the strange part of it. She has coolly broken I don't know how many other engagements to return at once, and instead of seeming disappointed, she simply 'glows and is glad.'[1] She says nothing, but I can see it. I don't know what on earth she is up to now." And Claudia left the room, frowning and perplexed.

When I heard she was not unhappy, this sudden whim of Ideala's did not disturb me much; indeed, I was rather glad to think she had found something to be enthusiastic about. Her fits of enthusiasm were rarer now, and I thought this symptom of one a good sign. It was odd, though, that I had not seen her while she was in town. I was half inclined to believe she had avoided me.

CHAPTER XVII.

To give the story continuity it will be necessary to piece the events together as they followed. Many of them only came to my knowledge some time after they occurred, and even then I was left to surmise a good deal; but I am able now, with the help of papers that have lately come into my possession, to verify most of my conjectures and arrange the details.

---

[1] This phrase appears in Algernon Swinburne's "By the North Sea" (1880), lines 33-34, but with the genders reversed: "In the pride of his power she rejoices, / In her glory he glows and is glad."

The summer weather had begun now. Laburnums and lilacs were in full flower, the air was sweet with scent and song, and to one who had borne the heavy winter with a heavy heart, but was able at last to lay down a load of care, the transition must have been like a sudden change from painful sickness to perfect health. Ideala went to the Great Hospital at once. She had written to fix a day, and Lorrimer was waiting for her. She was not taken to his room, however, as on the previous occasion, but to another part of the building, a long gallery hung with pictures, where she found him superintending the arrangement of some precious things in cabinets. Ideala looked better and younger that day in her summer dress than she had done in her heavy winter wraps on the occasion of their first meeting; but when she found herself face to face with Lorrimer she began to tremble, and was overcome with nervousness in a way that was new to her. He saw the change in her appearance and manner at a glance, and, smiling slightly, begged her to follow him, and led the way through long passages and many doors, passing numbers of people, to his own room. He spoke to her once or twice on the way, but she was only able to answer confusedly, in a voice that was rendered strident by the great effort she had to make to control it. He busied himself with some papers for a few minutes when they reached his room to give her time to recover herself, and then he said, standing with his back to the fireplace, looking down at her, and speaking in a tone that was even more musical and caressing than she remembered it—"Well, and how are you? And how has it been with you since your return?"

"I am utterly shaken and unnerved, as you see," she answered— then added passionately—"I cannot bear my life; it is too hateful."

"There is no need to bear it," he said. "Nothing is easier than to get a separation after what has occurred. Was there any witness?"

"No; and I don't think any one in the house suspects that there is anything wrong. And none of my friends know. I have never told them. I wonder why I told you?"

"You wanted me to help you," he suggested.

"I don't think I did," she said. "How could I want you to help me when I don't mean to do anything? I fancy I told you because I was afraid you would think me a little mad that day, and I would rather you knew the truth than think me mad. I don't mean to try for a separation. I can't leave him entirely to his own devices. If I did, he would certainly go from bad to worse."

"And if you don't what will become of you? I think much more of such a life would make you reckless."

She was silent for a little, then she exclaimed, "Help me not to grow reckless. I am so alone."

He took her hands and looked down into her eyes. A sudden deep flush spread over his face, smoothing out all the lines, as she had seen it do once before, and transforming him.

"It is like walking on the edge of a precipice in the dark," he said in a low voice, and his grasp tightened as he spoke.

There was something mesmeric in his touch that overpowered Ideala. She felt a change in herself at the moment, and she was never the same woman again.

"I will help you, if I can," he said, after another pause, and then he let her go.

After that they talked for some time. He tried to persuade her to reconsider her decision and leave her husband. He honestly believed it was the best thing she could do, and told her why he thought so. She acknowledged the wisdom of his advice, but declined to follow it, and he was somewhat puzzled, for the reasons she gave were hardly enough to account for her determination. They wandered away from that subject at last, however, and talked of many other things. He told Ideala of his first coming to the Great Hospital as a patient, and gave her some of the details of his own case, and told her enough of his private history to arouse her sympathy and interest; but of the nature of these confidences I know nothing. Ideala felt in honour bound not to repeat them, as they were made to her in the course of a private conversation, and she was always scrupulously faithful to all such trusts. I know, however, that he was a man who had suffered acutely, both from unhappy circumstances and from those troubles of the mind which beset clever men at the outset of their career, and sometimes never leave them entirely at peace. But this man was something more than a clever man; he was a man in a thousand. He had in a strong degree all that is worst and best in a man. The highest and most spiritual aspirations warred in him with the most carnal impulses, and he spent his days in fighting to attain to the one and subdue the other.

Ideala had never known a man like this man. His talents, his rapid changes of mood, as sense or conscience got the upper hand, and his versatility charmed her imagination and excited her interest; and he had, besides, that magnetic power over her by which it is given to some men to compel people of certain temperaments to their will. While she was with him he could have made her believe that black was white, and not only believe it, but be glad to think that it was so; and he always compelled her to say exactly what she had in her mind at the moment, even when it was something that she would very much rather not have said.

"But I am forgetting my other object in coming," Ideala broke off at last. "May I look at the books?"

Lorrimer took out his watch. "You ought to have some lunch first," he said. "If you will come now and have some, we can return and look at the books afterwards."

Ideala acquiesced, fearing it was his own lunch time, and knowing it would detain him if she did not accompany him.

They went as before to the station close by, and sat down side by side, perfectly happy together, chatting, laughing, talking about their childhood, and making those trifling confidences which go so far to promote intimacy, and are often the first evidence of affection.[1] Now and then they touched on graver matters. He upheld all that was old, and believed we can have no better institutions in the future than those which have already existed in the past. Ideala had begun to think differently.

"I am sure it is a mistake to be for ever looking back to the past for precedents," she said. "The past has its charm, of course, but it is the charm of the charnel house—it is the dead past, and what was good for one age is bad for another."

"As one man's meat is another man's poison?" he said.

"Proverbs prove nothing," she answered lightly. "Have you noticed that they go in pairs? There is always one for each side of an argument. 'One man's meat is another man's poison' is met by 'What is sauce for the goose is sauce for the gander'—and so on. But don't you think it absurd to cling to old customs that are dying a

---

[1] The Donohue, Henneberry & Co. edition includes an additional phrase at the beginning of this sentence. "Ladies not being allowed to lunch at the Great Hospital, they . . ."

natural death? Learn of the past, if you like, but live in the present, and make your laws to meet its needs. It is this eternal waiting on the past to copy it rather than to be warned by its failures, to do as it did, under the impression, apparently, that we must succeed better than it did, following in its footsteps though we know they led to ruin once, and, because the way was pleasant, being surprised to find that it must end again in disaster—it is this abandonment of all hope of finding new and efficacious remedies for the old diseases of society that has checked our progress for hundreds of years, and will keep the world in some respects just as it was at the time of the crucifixion. For my own part, I cannot see that history does repeat itself, except in trifling details, and in the lives of unimportant individuals.

"I think," he rejoined, "if you have studied the decline of the Roman Empire, you must have seen a striking analogy between that and our own history at the present time. With the exception of changes of manners, which only affect the surface of society, we are in much the same state now as the Romans were then."

"I know many people say so, and believe it," Ideala answered; "and there is evidence enough to prove it to people who are trying to arrive at a foregone conclusion; but it is not the resemblances we should look to, but the differences. It is in them that our hope lies, and they seem to me to be essential. Take the one grand difference that has been made by the teaching for hundreds of years of the perfect morality of the Christian religion! Do you think it possible for men, while they cling to it, to 'reel back into the beast and be no more'?"[1]

"But are men clinging to it?"

"Yes, in a way, for it has insensibly become a part of all of us, and has made it possible for us to show whole communities of moral philosophers now in a generation; the ancients had only an occasional one in a century."

"But such a one!"

"The old moral philosophers were grand, certainly, but not grander than our own men are, of whom we only hear less because there are so many more of them."

"But do you mean to say society is less sinful than it was?"

---

[1] Tennyson, "The Last Tournament," *Idylls of the King*, line 125.

"There is one section of society at the present day, they tell me, which is most desperately wicked. It is worse than any class was when the world was young, because it knows so much better. But I believe the bulk of the people like right so well that they only want a strong impulse to make them follow it. I feel sure sometimes that we are all living on the brink of a great change for the better, and that there is only one thing wanting now—a great calamity, or a great teacher—to startle us out of our apathy and set us to work. We are not bold enough. We should try more experiments; they can but fail, and if they do, we should still have learnt something from them. But I do not think we shall fail for ever. What we want is somewhere, and must be found eventually."

"They tried some experiments with the marriage laws in France once," Lorrimer observed, tentatively.

"Yes, and failed contemptibly because their motive was contemptible.[1] They did not want to improve society, but to make self-indulgence possible without shame. I think our own marriage laws might be improved."

"People are trying to improve them," he said, with a slight laugh. "A friend of mine has just married a girl who objected to take the oath of obedience. How absurd it is for a girl of nineteen to imagine she knows better than all the ages."

"I think," said Ideala, "that it is more absurd for 'all the ages' to subscribe to an oath which something stronger than themselves makes it impossible for half of them to keep. Strength of character must decide the question of place in a household as it does elsewhere; and it is surely folly to require, and useless to insist on, the submission of the strong to the weak. The marriage oath is farcical. A woman is made to swear to love a man who will probably prove unlovable, to honour a man who is as likely as not to be undeserving of honour, and to obey a man who may be incapable of judging what is best either for himself or her. I have no respect for the ages that uphold such nonsense. There was never any need to bind us

---

[1] France adopted more progressive policies regarding civil marriage and divorce after the Revolution in 1789, with new legislation on both matters passing in 1792. Ideala's response, in which she questions the motives of the French reformers, possibly reflects Grand's purity feminism. See Introduction for more on this topic.

with an oath. If men were all they ought to be, wouldn't we obey them gladly? To be able to do so is all we ask."

"Well, it is a difficult question," he answered, "and I don't think we need trouble ourselves about it any way. Do you like flowers?"

"Yes," she burst out in another tone; "and easy chairs, and pictures, and china, and everything that is beautiful, and all sensual pleasures."

She said it, but she knew in a moment that she had used the wrong word, and was covered with confusion.

Lorrimer looked at her and laughed.

"And so do I," he said.

"Oh! if only I could unsay that!" thought Ideala; but the word had gone forth, and was already garnered against her.

Then came an awful moment for her—the moment of going and paying. It was hateful to let him pay for her lunch, but she could not help it. She was seized with one of those fits of shyness which made it just a degree less painful to allow it than to make the effort to prevent it.

They returned to Lorrimer's room and pored together over a catalogue, looking up the books she wanted. When they had found their names and numbers Lorrimer sent for them from the library, but it was too late to do anything that day, and so she rose to go.

Lorrimer walked with her to the station, and saw her into the train. On the way they talked of little children. He loved them as she did.

"A friend of mine," he said, "has the most beautiful child I ever saw. Just to look at it makes me feel a better man."

CHAPTER XVIII.

IN the days that followed a singular change came over Ideala. No external circumstance affected her. She moved like one in a dream; thought had ceased for her; all life was one delicious sensation, and at times she could not bear the delight of it in silence. She would tell it in low songs in the twilight; she would make her piano speak it in a hundred chords: and it would burst from her in some sudden glow of enthusiasm that made people wonder—the apparent cause being too slight to account for it. While this lasted nothing hurt her. She saw the sufferings of others unmoved. She met her husband's brutalities with a smiling countenance, and bore the physical discomfort of a bad sprain without much consciousness of pain. And she knew nothing of time, and never asked herself to what she owed this joy.

The utter forgetfulness of everything that came upon her when she was alone was almost incredible. One evening she spent two hours in walking a distance she might easily have done in forty minutes. She had been to see a sick person, and when she found herself in the fresh air, after having spent some time in a small, close room, the dream-like feeling came over her, and her spirit was uplifted with inexpressible gladness. The summer air was sweet and warm, a light rain was falling, and she took off her hat and wandered on, looking up, but noting nothing, and singing Schubert's "Hark! hark! the lark,"[1] to herself softly as she came. A man standing at a cottage door begged her to go in and shelter. She looked at him, and her face was radiant—the rain drops sparkled on her hair. He was only a working man, "clay—and common clay," but the light in her eyes passed through him, and the memory of her stayed with him, a thing apart from his daily life, held sacred, and not to be described. A man might live a hundred years and never see a woman look like that.

"I did not know it was raining," she said. "It is only light rain, and the air is so sweet, and the glow down there in the west is like heaven. How beautiful life is!"

"Ay, lady!" he answered, and stood there spellbound, watching her as she passed on slowly, and listening to her singing as she went.

A few days later she saw Lorrimer again. She found him in his room this time. He knew she was coming, and flushed with pleasure when he met her at the door. Ideala was not nervous; it all seemed a matter of course to her now. The books he had got for her from the library were where she had left them. He placed a chair for her beside his writing-table, and then went on with his own work. She had understood that she was to read in the library, but she did not think of that now; she simply acquiesced in this arrangement as she would have done in any other he might have made for her. A secre-

---

[1] One of three Shakespearian songs composed by Franz Peter Schubert (1797-1828) in 1826.

tary was busy in another part of the room when she entered, but after awhile he left them. Then Lorrimer looked up and smiled.

"You are looking better to-day," he said. "Tell me what you have been doing since I saw you."

"Lotus-eating,"[1] she answered. "How lovely the summer is! Since I saw you I have wanted to do nothing but rest and dream."

"You have been happy, then?"

"Yes."

"Is he kind to you?"

"Oh—he! He is just the same. There is no change in my life. The change is in me."

"Then you mean to be happy in spite of him? I call that the beginning of wisdom. I know two other ladies who hate their husbands, and they manage to enjoy life pretty well. And I don't see why *you* should be miserable always because you happen to have married the wrong man. How was it you married him? Were you very much in love with him?"

"No, not in the least."

"Spooney,[2] then?"

"Not even 'spooney,' as you call it. I was very young at the time. Very young girls know nothing of love and marriage."

"Very young," he repeated thoughtfully. He was drawing figures with his pen on the blotting-paper before him. "But why did you marry him, then?"

"I can give you no reason—except that I was not happy at home."

"You all say that," slipped from him, with a gesture of impatience.

"I wish I had been more original," said Ideala.

She took up her book again, and he resumed his writing, and for some time there was silence. But Ideala's attention wandered. She began to examine the room, which was, as usual, in a state of disorder. One side of it was lined with cabinets of various sizes and periods. Labels indicated the contents of some of them. Only one picture hung on that side of the room—it was the portrait of a gentleman—

---

[1] Reference to Homer's *Odyssey*, in which Odysseus's soldiers eat the lotus flower, inducing a dreamy state.

[2] Silly or foolish, sentimentally in love.

but several others stood on the ground against the cabinets. The walls were painted some dark colour. A Japanese screen was drawn across the door, and beside it was a hard narrow settee covered with dark green velvet. Books were piled upon it, and heavily-embroidered foreign stuffs, and near it a number of Japanese drawings stood on a stand. The mantelpiece was crowded with an odd mixture of china and other curios, all looking as if they had just been unpacked. Above it another picture was hung, a steel engraving. The writing-table by which they sat was nearly in the middle of the room. In the window was another table, covered also with a miscellaneous collection of curios; and on every other available article of furniture books were piled. The high backs of the chairs were elaborately carved, the seats being of the same green velvet as the settee. A high wire guard surrounded the fire place, and this unusual precaution made one think, that the contents of the room must be precious. The occupant of this apartment might have been an artist, a man of letters, or a virtuoso—probably the latter; but whatever he was, it was evident that his study was a workshop, and not a showroom.

From the room Ideala looked to her companion. He was writing rapidly, and seemed absorbed in his subject. He was frowning slightly, his face was pale and set, and he looked older by ten years than when he had spoken last, and seemed cold and unimpassioned as a judge; but Ideala thought again that the face was a fine one.

Presently he became conscious of her earnest gaze. He did not look up, but every feature softened, and a warm glow spread from forehead to chin; it was as if a deep shadow had been lifted, and a younger, but less noble, man revealed.

"How you change!" Ideala exclaimed—"not from day to day, but from moment to moment. You are like two men. I wish I could get behind that horrid veil of flesh that hides you from me. I want to see your soul."

He smiled. "You are getting tired," he said. "Do let me persuade you to come and have some lunch. When you begin to speculate, I know you have done enough."

But Ideala could not go through the ordeal of who should pay for lunch again. She preferred to starve. The *camaraderie* between them was mental enough to be manlike already, but only as long as there was no question of material outlay.

"Mayn't I stay here and read?" she said. "I can have something by-and-by, when I want it. Do go and leave me."

And he was obliged to go at last, wondering somewhat at her want of appetite.

When he returned she was still working diligently, and they spent the rest of the afternoon together, reading, writing, and chatting, until it was time for Ideala to go. Lorrimer saw her into her train, and fixed another day for her to return and go on with her work.

And so the thing became a settled arrangement. Whenever she could spare the time she went and worked beside him, and he was always the same, kindly, considerate, helping her now and then, but not, as a rule, interfering with her. She just came and went as she pleased, and as she would have done had he been her brother. Sometimes they were alone together for hours, sometimes his secretary worked in the room with them, and always there were people coming and going. There was nothing to suggest a thought of impropriety, and they were soon on quarrelling terms, falling out about a great many things—which is always the sign of a good understanding; but after the first they touched on no dangerous subject for a long time. At last, however, there came a change. Ideala noticed one day that Lorrimer was restless and irritable.

"Am I interfering with your work to-day?" she said. "Do tell me. Any other day will suit me just as well."

"Oh, no," he answered. "I am lazy, that is all. How are you getting on? Let me see," and he took the paper she was engaged upon, and looked at it.

She watched him, and saw that he was not reading, although he held it before his eyes for some time. He was paler than usual, and there was a look of indecision in his face, very unlike its habitual expression, which was serene and self-contained.

Looking up all at once, he met her eyes fixed on him frankly and affectionately, but he did not respond to her smile.

"How do you suppose all this is going to end?" he said, abruptly.

"Won't it do?" she answered, thinking of her paper. "Had I better give it up, or re-write it?"

He threw the paper down with a gesture of impatience, and got up; and then, as if ashamed of his irritability, he took it again, and gave it back to her. In doing so his hand accidentally touched hers.

"How cold you are," he said. "Let me warm your hands for you."

"They *are* benumbed," she answered, letting him take them and rub them.

After a moment he said, without looking at her, "Do you know, it is very good of you to come here like this."

"Why?" she asked. "It suits my own convenience."

"I know. But it is refreshing to find some one who will suit their own convenience so."

"That sounds as if it were not the right thing to do!" she exclaimed.

"Nonsense!" he answered. "You misunderstand me."

Ideala withdrew her hands hastily, and half rose.

"What is the matter?" he said. "Come, don't be idle! You should have mastered that book by this time."

But Ideala was disturbed. "I can't read," she said. "Tell me what you thought of me when I came to you that first day? I fancied you were old. And I have been afraid since, in spite of your cousin's suggestion, that you may have considered it odd of me to introduce myself like that."

"Oh, it is quite customary here," he answered. "But even if it had not been, we can't all be bound by the same common laws. The ordinary stars and planets have an ordinary course mapped out for them, and they daren't diverge an inch. But every now and then a comet comes and goes its own eccentric way, and all the lesser lights wonder and admire and let it go."

"That would be very fine for us if only we were comets among the stars," she said.

"Oh, you might condescend to claim a kindred with them," he answered lightly.

"The only heavenly body I ever feel akin to is one of those meteors that flash and fall," she said. "They go their own way, too, do they not, and are lost?"

"There is no question of being lost here," he interposed. "The most scrupulous have made an exception in favour of one person, and the world has not blamed them. After having endured so much you are entitled to some relaxation. I should do as I liked now, if I were you."

She looked at him inquiringly. It seemed as if he were not expressing himself, but trying the effect of what he said upon her.

He was sitting in his usual place now, drawing figures on the blot-
ting pad.

"You have read, I suppose?" he added, after a pause, and without
looking up.

"I wish I had never read anything," she exclaimed passionately. "I
wish I could neither read, write, nor think."

But the trouble now was, if only she could have recognised it,
that she did not think; she only felt.

She got up and went to the mantelpiece; he remained where
he was, sitting with his back to her. Presently she began to look at
the china, absently at first, but afterwards with interest. There were
some new specimens, just unpacked, and all crowded together.

"What a lovely lotus-leaf," she said at last. "Satsuma, I suppose—
no, Kioto;[1] but what a good specimen. And it is broken, too. What a
pity! I should so like to mend it."

"Would you?" he said, rousing himself. "Then you shall."

He went to one of the cabinets and got out the materials, and in
a few minutes they were bending busily over the broken plaque, as
interested and eager about it as if no subject of more vital importance had ever distracted them. They were like two children together,
often as quarrelsome, always as inconsequent; happy hard at work,
and equally happy idling; apt to torment each other at times about
trifles, but always ready to forget and forgive; and with that habit in
common of forgetting everything utterly but the occupation of the
moment.

They talked on now for a little longer, but not brilliantly. They
were both considered brilliant in conversation, but somehow on
these occasions neither of them shone. I suppose when two such
bright and shining lights come together they put each other out.

Then it was time for Ideala to go. A bitter wind met them in the
face on their way to the station, and before they had gone far Ideala
noticed that Lorrimer's mood had changed again. His face grew

---

[1] Different types of porcelain produced in Japan. Traditionally, Satsuma was
produced in southwest Kyushu, and Kioto (Kyoto) in Kyoto. Now, Satsuma also
is produced in Kyoto, though it looks somewhat different from that produced
in Kyushu.

pale, his step less elastic, his manner cold and formal. All the brightness, all the sympathy, which made their intimacy seem the most natural, because it was the pleasantest thing in the world to Ideala, had gone; he was like a man seized with a sudden fit of remorse, disgusted with himself, and moved to repent.

"I should bear with your husband, if I were you," he said at last, breaking the silence. "He behaves like a brute, but I dare say he can't help it. A man can't help his temperament, and probably you provoke him more than you think."

Ideala was surprised, it was so long since they had mentioned her husband.

"I fear I am provoking," she answered, humbly. "But how am I to help it? I have tried so hard, and for so long, to be patient. And I only want to do right."

They were parting then, and he looked down at her in silence for some seconds, and when Ideala saw the expression of his face her heart sank. In that one moment she realised all that his friendship had been to her, and foresaw the terrible blank there would be for her if it should ever end. That there was any danger, that there could be anything but friendship between men and women who must not marry, had not even yet occurred to her. Her intimacy with myself had prepared the way for Lorrimer, and made this new intimacy seem also perfectly right.

"What is the matter with you to-day?" she said. "What spirit of dissatisfaction has got hold of you?"

"I *am* dissatisfied," he said, raising his hat, and brushing his hand back over his hair. Then he looked at her. "Why don't you help me?" he asked.

"How can I help you?" she answered. "I don't understand you."

"You ought to. I wish to goodness you did"—and then his face cleared. "But you will come again," he added, in the old way. "I shall expect you soon."

And so he let her go; and Ideala was glad, because an unpleasant jar was over. She did not trouble herself about his private worries; if he wished her to know he would tell her. Lorrimer had a temper—but then she had known that all along; and Lorrimer was Lorrimer—that was all about it.

CHAPTER XIX.

HE let her go, somewhat bewildered, and not understanding herself or him, nor caring to understand, only happy, dangerously happy. The train bore her through an enchanted region of brightness and summer, and, although the power of thought was for the moment suspended, she was conscious of this, and her own delight was like the unreasoning pleasure of earth when the sun is upon it.

There was no carriage to meet her at the station, and she set off to walk home. It was the first time she had been alone on foot in the squalid disorderly streets of that dingy place, and her way, which she was not quite sure of, took her through some of the worst of them. They were filled with loud-laughing uncleanly women, and skulking hang-dog looking men, and the grime-clogged atmosphere was heavy with foul odours, but she noticed nothing of this. The golden glow the sun made in his efforts to shine through the clouds of smoke might have been a visible expression of her own ecstatic feeling, and she would have thought so at any other time, but now she never saw it.

In a somewhat open and more lonely part of the road she met a tramp, a great rude, hulking, common fellow, with fine blue eyes. He stopped in the middle of the road and stared at Ideala as she came up to him, walking, as usual, with a slight undulating movement that made you think of a yacht in a breeze, her face up-raised and her lips parted. He took off his cap as she approached. The gesture attracted her attention, and, thinking he wanted to beg or ask some question, she stopped, and looked at him inquiringly.

"Well, you *are* a nice lady!" he exclaimed.

He hadn't the gift of language, but she saw the soul of a man in his eyes, and she understood him.

"Thank you," she answered, and passed on, unsurprised.

In the next street a breathless creature came running after her, a tawdry, painted, dishevelled girl. She stopped Ideala and stood panting, with hot dry lips, and eyes full of animal suffering. Her clothes exhaled the smell of some vile scent that was overpowering. Involuntarily Ideala shrank from her, and all the joy left her face.

"I've run"—the girl gasped—"such a way—they said you'd gone this road. I've waited about all day to catch you. Come, for God's sake!"

"But where?"

"There's a girl dying"—and she clutched Ideala's arm, trying to drag her along with her—"or she would die and have done with it, but she can't till she's seen you. She've something on her mind—something to tell you. Come, my lady, come, for the love of the Lord and the Blessed Virgin. No harm'll happen to you."

Ideala made a gesture. "Show me the way," she said. "But you don't seem able to walk. There's an empty cab coming. Get in and tell the man where to drive to."

They stopped at a row of many-storied houses in a low by-street. A stout elderly woman with an evil countenance met them at the door. She began some speech in a cringing tone to Ideala, but the tawdry girl pushed her aside rudely.

"Hold your jaw, and get out of the way," she said. "I'll show the lady up."

The woman muttered something which Ideala fortunately did not hear, and let them pass. They went upstairs to the very top of the house, and entered a low room, furnished with a broken chair and a small bed only. On the bed lay a girl, who, in spite of disease and approaching death, looked not more than twenty, and was probably two years younger. She turned her haggard face to the door as it opened, and a gleam of satisfaction caused her eyes to dilate when she saw Ideala. They were large dark eyes, but her face was so distorted with suffering and discoloured by disease, it was impossible to imagine what it once had been.

"Here she is, Polly," said the Tawdry One, triumphantly. "I said I'd bring her, now didn't I?"

Ideala knelt down by the bed.

"My! but you're a game un!" said the Tawdry One, admiringly. "You ain't afraid of catching nothing! Now, I'd have asked what was up before I'd have done that; and I wouldn't touch her with the tongs, nor stay in the room with her was it ever so. You just holler when you want me and I'll come back." And so saying she left them.

"You are not afraid to touch me—you don't mind?" said the

dying girl when Ideala had taken off her gloves, and knelt, holding her hands.

"Afraid? Mind?" Ideala whispered, her eyes full of pity. "I only wish you would let me do something for you."

At that moment they were startled by an uproar downstairs. A man and woman were quarrelling at the top of their voices. At first only their tones were audible, but these grew more distinct, and in a few seconds Ideala could hear what was said, and it was evident that the combatants were approaching.

"I tell you the lady's all right," the woman Ideala had seen downstairs was heard to shriek, with sundry vile epithets. "Polly's dying, and she've come to visit her."

"Seein' 's believin'," the man rejoined, doggedly. "Just show me the lady and shut up, you foul-mouthed devil you."

The door was flung open, and there stood the fat harridan, and towering over her was a great red-haired policeman, who seemed both relieved and abashed when he saw Ideala.

"What is the meaning of this?" she said, rising, and drawing herself up indignantly. "Don't you see how ill this girl is? Such an uproar at such a time is indecent."

The woman shrank from her gaze and slunk away. The policeman wiped his hot face with a red handkerchief.

"I saw the girl fetch you here, ma'am," he said, apologetically, "and I thought it was a trap. It ain't safe for a woman, let alone a lady, to come to no such a place. I'll just wait and see you safe out of it."

He shut the door, and Ideala heard him walking up and down on the landing outside.

The dying girl seemed scarcely conscious of what was passing. Ideala looked round for something to revive her. There was not even a cup of water in the room. She knelt once more beside the bed, and raised her in her arms, and let her head rest on her shoulder. All the mother in her was throbbing with tenderness for this poor outcast. The girl drew a long deep sigh.

"Could you take anything?" Ideala asked.

"No, lady, not now. The thirst was awful awhile ago, and I cried and cried, though I knew no one would listen to me, or come if they heard. They'd rather we'd die when we get ill. It's a bad thing for the house." She could only speak in gasps.

"And what have you had?" Ideala asked.

"The scarlet fever, ma'am. There's an awful bad kind about, and I caught it. They all die that gets it."

Ideala drew her closer, and laid her own cool cheek on her damp forehead.

"Tell me why you wished to see me," she said.

"You are so good," the girl answered—"I thought you'd better know—and get—away from—that low brute."

Ideala understood, and would fain have stopped the story, but it seemed a relief to the girl to speak, and so she listened. It was the old story, the old story aggravated by every incident that could make it more repulsive—and her husband was the hero of it.

"Shall I go to hell?" the girl asked, shrinking closer.

"For these Christ died," Ideala murmured. The words flashed through her mind, and the meaning of them was new to her. Her heart was wrung for the desolate girl, dying alone in sin and sorrow without a creature to care for her—dying alone in the arms of a strange woman, with a policeman outside guarding her. Ideala cried in her heart with an exceeding bitter cry: "God do so to him, and more also."

"Pray for me, lady."

But Ideala could not pray with a curse on her lips—and, besides, the power to pray had been taken from her for many a weary day before that. She thought of the policeman, and called him in.

"See, she is dying," she said, looking up at him helplessly; "and she has asked me to pray, and I can't. Will you?"

And, quite simply and reverently, as if it had been part of his ordinary duty, he took off his helmet and knelt down, a great rough-looking man in a hideous dress, and prayed: "Dear Lord, forgive her!"

They were the last words she heard.

CHAPTER XX.

THE people seemed to have deserted the house. Even the Tawdry One had disappeared, and Ideala was obliged to lay out the poor dear girl herself, and make her ready for decent burial. As soon as she could leave the place she went, escorted by the policeman, to the fever hospital[1] to have her things fumigated. The risk of infection had not troubled her till she remembered the likelihood of taking it to others, but as soon as she thought of that she took the necessary precautions to prevent it. She sent a message from the hospital to her maid, telling her to pack up some things and meet her at the station in time for the mail at eleven o'clock that night. She had thought of some friends who lived a nine hours' journey from her home, and had determined to go to them for a time.

She wrote to her husband also from the hospital. "The girl, Mary Morris, died of scarlet fever this afternoon in the house to which you sent her when you were tired of her," she said. "I was with her when she died. I am going to the Trelawneys to-night; but at present I have formed no plans for the future."

During the first few days of her stay with the Trelawneys she just lived from hour to hour, not thinking of anything, past, present, or to come; but out of this apathy a desire grew by degrees. She wanted to see Lorrimer. She could speak to him, and she was sure he would help and advise her. She wrote to him, telling him she particularly wished to see him on a certain day, and asking him to meet her at the station, adding by way of postscript: "I do not think I quite know what you meant when you advised me to go my own way; but if any wrong doing were part of the programme I should not be able to carry it out. However, I feel sure that you would be the last person in the world to let me do wrong, even if I were inclined to."

She knew that her husband was away from home, and her intention had been to sleep there that night, and go on to Lorrimer the next morning; but she had been misinformed about the trains, and after many changes and tedious waits, she found herself alone in the middle of the night at a little railway junction, with no chance of a train to take her on for several hours; and what was worse, without money enough in her purse to pay her bill if she went to an hotel. The waiting-rooms were all closed for the night, and there seemed

---

[1] A temporary hospital set up during epidemics. "Fever" covered a number of different diseases, including scarlet fever but also cholera, influenza, and typhus. All of these fevers were particularly active in the late-1830s and 1840s, in part because of the development of the railroad, which caused disease to spread more easily.

nothing for it but to wander about the station till the train came and released her. She told her dilemma to an old Scotch guard who was waiting to see what she meant to do. He gave the matter his best consideration, but it evidently perplexed him.

"If you was a box," he said, rubbing his chin thoughtfully, "we could put you in the left-luggage office."

"But I am not a box," Ideala answered, as if only the most positive denial would prevent mistake on the subject.

It was raining hard, and bitterly cold. Only part of the platform was roofed in, and every now and then a gust of wind splashed the raindrops into their faces as they stood beside Ideala's luggage in a circle of yellow light cast upwards by a lantern which the guard had put on the ground at their feet.

"There's me and Tom, the porter," he said at last; "we've got to wait for the two o'clock down and the four o'clock up. Tom, he'll come 'ome and sit over the kitchen fire with me. I suppose, now, you wouldn't like to do that?"

"Indeed I should be very glad to," Ideala answered; "that is," she added quickly, "if it would not inconvenience you."

He made an inexplicable gesture, and seemed to consider the matter settled.

"I'll just put this here luggage in the office," he said, shouldering a box and taking up a portmanteau; but he muttered as he went: "It's a pity, now, you wasn't luggage."

Ideala followed him meekly from the luggage office out into the lane, and down a country path to a little cottage. The door opened into the kitchen, and a young man in a porter's uniform was sitting over a cheery fire reading a newspaper by the light of a tallow candle. The kitchen was large for the size of the house. Besides the door they had entered by there were two others, both closed. The walls were panelled from floor to ceiling with wood darkened by age. Several of the panels were doors of cupboards that projected slightly from the wall, and shelves had been sunk in flush with it, and placed angle-wise in the corners. The shelves were covered with old china. There was a row of brass candlesticks of good design on the high mantelpiece, and more china stood behind them. On a panel above the mantelpiece a curious design of dogs and horses in a wood had been carved with much patience and some skill. The furniture of the place was an old oak table standing in the window—the window itself had a deep sill, on which was arranged a row of flowerpots, from which a faint perfume came at intervals—a long narrow oak chest, carved and polished, with the date, 1700, on the side of it, a settle, and a dresser covered with the ordinary crockery used by poor people. The brick floor was *rudded*[1] and sanded, the hearth-stone was yellow, and the part under the grate was white. One high-backed old-fashioned chair stood on each side of the hearth. Tom the Porter was sitting in one of them, and at his elbow was a small round table with a pipe, tobacco jar, and two or three books upon it. A square table in the middle of the room was laid out for supper with a dish, two plates, a beer mug, and half a loaf of bread. Some potatoes were roasting on the hob.[2]

"The old woman's asleep, I expects. You'll mind and not make a noise," the guard said to Ideala, as if he were warning a child to be good.

Tom the Porter rose, and gazed at the lady with his mouth open in a state of astonishment that was justified by the time and place of her advent; but he offered her his chair with the courtesy of a gentleman, and the old guard bade her make herself at home, which she did by removing her hat and wraps and taking off her gloves. In a higher sphere of life those two men would have stared her out of countenance, but Tom the Porter and the old guard, not from want of appreciation, but from the refinement that seems natural to people who come of an old stock, whatever their station, and have had china and carved oak in their possession from one generation to another—forebore even to look at her lest she should be embarrassed by their curiosity. They did the honours of the house with dignity, and without vulgar apology for a state of things that was natural to them, and Ideala at once adapted herself to the circumstances, and burnt her fingers while attending to the baked potatoes, which Tom had somewhat neglected.

She always declared afterwards that there was nothing so good in the world as baked potatoes and salt, provided the company was agreeable; and now and then she would thrill us with reminiscences of that evening's entertainment—with wonderful accounts of rail-

---

[1] Typically means "to make red" but can also mean "to rub or polish."
[2] Projection on a fireplace where cooked items can be kept warm.

way accidents—and of one in particular that happened on a pitch-
dark night when fires had to be made to light the workers as they
toiled fearfully amongst the wreck of the trains, searching for the
mangled and mutilated, the dying and the dead, while the air was
filled with horrid shrieks and groans.

For it seems these three, when they had finished the baked potatoes, drew their chairs to the fire and talked. And one can well imagine what Ideala's stories were—her tales of the Japanese with whom
she had lived; of Chinese prisons into which she had peeped; of
earthquakes, tornadoes and shipwrecks, and other perils by land and
sea, all told in a voice that thrilled you, whatever it said. Tom the Porter and the old Scotch guard were in luck that night, and they knew
it. When at last it was time for Ideala to go, and in return for her
thanks for his kind hospitality, and the contents of her purse, which
had rather more in it than she had fancied, the guard expressed his
appreciation with an earnest smack.

"Well," he said, "you're rare good company. I shan't mind when
you come along this way again."

The train was late in arriving, and she had only time to rush up
to the house, change her dress, and return to the station to catch
the one by which she had asked Lorrimer to meet her. Perhaps it
was the thought of what she had come to tell him that made her
heart beat nervously as the train drew up at her destination, and
she leant forward to look for him among the people on the platform. She looked in vain—he was not there. Something, of course,
had happened to detain him; doubtless he had sent a message to
explain. She waited a little, but nobody appeared to be looking for
her. Then she left the station and walked in the direction of the
Hospital, thinking he had missed the train, and she should probably
meet him on the way. Her nervousness increased as she went. She
was not used to be alone in crowded streets, and she began to feel
faint and bewildered. Her heart seemed to stop whenever she saw
a fair-headed man, but she reached the Hospital at last, and no Lorrimer had met her.

Then a new fear disturbed her. Perhaps he was ill. She went up to
the door, and there, just coming out, Lorrimer's secretary met her.

"I was just coming to meet you, madam," he said; "I am sorry I
am too late. Mr. Lorrimer has been detained by visitors, and sent me

to apologise for his absence. If you will be so good as to come to the library, he will join you there as soon as he is disengaged."

When she was settled in the library a servant brought her books to her. She had not come to read, but work was the daily habit of her life, and she went on now, mechanically, but carefully as usual, though with a curious sinking of the heart and benumbing sense of loss and pain. As she came along in the train she had been thinking how it would amuse Lorrimer to hear of her night's adventure, and of the relief it would be to tell him of all the other things she had come to tell; but now she felt like one bidden to a bridal and brought to a burial. People were going and coming continually in the library. A gentleman sat at a table near her, busily writing. Servants went backwards and forwards with books. Another gentleman came in and looked at her curiously, and then went away. She began to feel uncomfortable, and wondered what was keeping Lorrimer so long. She thought, too, of leaving the place at once and going back by an earlier train than she had intended, but it would hardly have been polite. A servant came and told her the library was closed to visitors at two.

"I am waiting for Mr. Lorrimer," she said.

"Oh, in that case——" and the man withdrew. The name was an open sesame to all parts of the building.

At last he came. She rose with a great sense of relief.

"Let me take your books," he said.

"I have done with them," she answered.

And without another word he led the way to his own room.

They took their accustomed seats.

"I am sorry I could not meet you," he said. "I hope you do not think me rude. Some wretched people turned up at the last moment, and wanted to see everything. Just look at the room!"

Every cabinet seemed to have been ransacked, and treasures of all kinds were lying about in most admired disorder. Lorrimer looked round him desperately, and pushed his hat back from his forehead. Ideala smiled. It was so like him to forget he had it on.

Outside a heavy thundercloud gathered and darkened the room. Presently big drops of rain splashed against the window, and it began to lighten. Long claps of thunder rolled and muttered incessantly away in the distance, and every now and then one would burst directly above them, as it seemed, with splendid effect.

Lorrimer looked up at the window straight before him, and played with a pen; and Ideala, half turning her back to him, sat silent also, watching the storm.

There were some high houses opposite of which only the upper storeys were visible. Two children were playing in a dangerous position at an open window in one of them. Above the houses a strip of sky, heavy and dark and changeful, was all that showed.

Ideala felt cold and faint. The long fast and fatigue were beginning to tell upon her. She was nervous, too; the silence was oppressive, but she could not break it. She felt some inexplicable change in her relations with Lorrimer which made it impossible to speak. Furtively she watched him, trying to discover if he felt it too. The look of age was on his face, and it was clouded with discontent. Anxiously she sought some sign of sickness to account for it. But, no. There was no trace of physical suffering; the trouble was mental.

"You are not looking well," Lorrimer said at last. "I suppose you have been starving yourself since I saw you. You have had no lunch to-day again. You will kill yourself if you go on like that. I was speaking about you to a doctor the other day. He said you could not fast as you do without taking *something*—stimulants or sedatives."

Ideala winced. "What an insulting thing to say," she exclaimed, indignantly. "I will not allow you to adopt that tone with me. You have no right to scold me."

"I have, and shall," he retorted. "I suppose you want to kill yourself. Perhaps it is the best thing people can do who hate their lives."

"I don't hate my life; I don't want to die," she rejoined.

"The other day you said you loathed your life."

"You are accusing me of inconsistency," she said. "You! who are in two states of mind every time I see you!" She got up. "And I *do* mean what I say," she resumed. "I loathed the old life, but that is done with. I am living a new life now——"

He turned to look at her, red chasing white from his face at every breath; then, yielding to an irresistible impulse, he went to her, grasped her folded hands in both of his, and looked into her eyes for one burning moment. The hot blood flamed to her face. She was startled.

"Don't let us quarrel," he said, hoarsely.

"Why do you try to?" she retorted. "It is always you who begin."

"I think you want pluck," he said.

"Oh, no; not that," she answered.

"Just now you do."

"Then I think you want discernment," she retorted with spirit.

And so they went on, as if neither of them had ever heard of such a thing as conventional propriety.

Lorrimer did not answer that last remark. He was standing at a little distance from her, watching her. Ideala was looking grave.

"What is your conscience troubling you about now?" he asked. "I never listen to my conscience."

"I don't believe you," she answered, promptly.

"That is polite," he observed.

Then there was another pause.

"It must be time for me to go," she said, at last.

The rain was still falling in torrents.

"Oh, no!" he exclaimed. "You mustn't go yet. Your train does not leave for another hour. Why do you want to go?"

She was struggling with the button of a glove, and he went to help her, but she repulsed him, half unconsciously, as she would have brushed off a troublesome fly.

The gesture irritated him.

"I cannot believe you are not conscientious," she said, with a frown of intentness. "When a man of talent ceases to be true, he loses half his power."

He turned from her coldly, sat down at the writing table, and began to write.

Ideala was still putting on her gloves.

Outside, the rain fell lightly now, and the clouds were clearing. The children were still playing at the open window of the house opposite. Lorrimer had often been obliged to answer notes when she was there; she thought nothing of that; but he was a long time, and at last she interrupted him. "Forgive me if I disturb you," she said, "but I am afraid I shall miss my train."

"Oh, pardon me," he answered, jumping up, and looking at his watch. "But it is not nearly time yet. I cannot understand why you are in such a hurry to-day."

"Yet you know that I always go when I have done my work," she said.

"You have done unusually early then," he replied; "and I wish to goodness I had." He looked round the room pettishly, like a school-boy out of temper. "I shall have to put all these things away when you're gone—a task I hate, but nobody can do it but myself."

"Why wait till I've gone? Let me help you," said Ideala.

His countenance cleared, and they set to work merrily, he explaining the curious histories of coins and cameos, of ancient gems, ornaments of gold and silver, and valuable intaglios,[1] as they returned them to their places, and both forgetting everything in the interest of the collection; so that, when the last tray was completed, they were surprised to find that two trains had gone while they were busy, and another had become due, and there was only time to jump into a hansom to catch it.

Lorrimer was still irritable.

"Why on earth does a lady always carry her purse in her hand?" he said, as they drove along.

Ideala laughed, and put hers in her pocket.

"When are you coming to go on with your work?" he asked.

"I will write and fix a day," she said.

"I shall be away a good deal for the next three weeks," he contin-ued. "The twenty-third or twenty-sixth would be the most conven-ient days for me, if they would suit you."

"Thank you," she answered, and hurried down the platform, without having said a word or given a thought to what she had come to say.

And then at last the twenty-four hours' fasting, fatigue, and men-tal suffering overcame her. A little later she was lying insensible on the floor of her room, and she was alone. The servants had not seen her enter, and there was not a creature near her to help her.

---

[1] Type of design in gem cutting, in which the design is carved below the sur-face. Intaglio is the opposite of cameo: in a cameo gem, the design is engraved on the top layer and the remainder is carved away leaving the design in relief.

CHAPTER XXI.

IDEALA was unable to exert herself for many days after this. At last, however, she began to think of work again, and of Lorrimer. She was uneasy about him. He had not been himself on that last occasion. Something was wrong, she could not think what, but she felt anxious; and out of her anxiety arose an intense longing to see him again. So she wrote, first of all fixing the twenty-third for her visit; but when the day came she found herself unequal to the exertion, and wrote again, begging him to expect her on the twenty-sixth instead.

He did not reply. He was generally overwhelmed with correspondence, and she had therefore begged him not to do so if the days she named suited him.

Up to this time she had never heard Lorrimer mentioned by any one; but now, suddenly, his name seemed to be in everybody's mouth. She thought of him incessantly herself, and it was as if the strength of her own mind compelled all other minds to think of him while she was present, and to yield to her will and tell her all they knew. For, curiously enough, she had begun to want to know about him. I call it curious because she was so confiding, so unsuspicious, and also so penetrating, she never seemed to care to know more of people than she learnt from intercourse with them. But with regard to Lorrimer, she had evidently begun to distrust her own judgment, which is significant.

One night, at a dinner-party, she was thinking of a gratuitous piece of information an old woman, who brought her some milk on one occasion at the Great Hospital, had given her. Ideala had noticed that the old woman had a bad cough, and had asked her, in her usual kindly way, if she were subject to it, and what she did for it, remarking that the north country air was trying to people with delicate chests, and warmer clothing and greater care were more necessary there than in the south; and thereupon the old woman had launched forth, as such people will upon the slightest provocation, with minute details of her own sufferings, and the sufferings of all the people she ever knew, from "the bronchitis" during the winter and spring, Mr. Lorrimer being included among the number.

"Does Mr. Lorrimer suffer in that way?" Ideala had asked with interest.

"Indeed, yes," was the answer, given with many shakings of the head and that air of importance and pleasure which vulgar bearers of bad news assume. "He was very bad in the spring. He coughed so as never was, and had to give in at last and keep his room, which he should have done at first; but it takes a deal to make him give in, for he takes no care of hisself though not strong, and we *were* in a way! Eh! but it would be a bad thing for this place if anything happened to Mr. Lorrimer!"

Ideala gave the woman half-a-crown.

"People may have bronchitis without being delicate," she asserted. "Mr. Lorrimer is very kind to all of you, I suppose?"

"If I was to tell you all his good deeds, Ma'am," the woman said, impressively, "I'd not have done before to-morrow morning. But as to his not being delicate," she continued—in the hope, perhaps, of scoring another on that point—"why, it just depends on what you call delicate."

Ideala absently gave her another half-crown, and another after that, but she could not get her to say that Mr. Lorrimer's chest was strong. Later, when Lorrimer returned, and they were both at work, he was interrupted in the middle of some cynical remarks on over-population, and the good it would do to check it by allowing the spread of epidemics and encouraging men to kill each other, by the arrival of another old woman in great distress.

His manner changed in a moment. "I am afraid he is worse," he said to her most kindly.

She could only shake her head.

"There is the order," he went on, giving her a paper—"get him these things at once, and tell him I will come as soon as I am disengaged."

When they were alone again, Ideala looked at Lorrimer and laughed. "Another instance, I shrewdly suspect, of the difference between theory and practice," she observed.

He brushed his hand back over his forehead and hair, a trifle disconcerted. "He was the only son of his mother, and she was a widow," he said.

"And one can approve of capital punishment without having the

nerve to see it inflicted, I suppose," Ideala commented, "and be convinced that it would be good for the human race to have a certain
number of their children drowned, like kittens, every year, and yet
not be able to see a single one disposed of in that way without risk-
ing one's own life to save it. Verily, I have heard this often, and yet
I think I am more surprised to find it true than if I had never been
warned! But that is always the way. Things surprise us just as much
as we expect them to. When we went up the river to Canton and
saw the Pagoda, we all exclaimed, 'Why, it is just like the pictures—
river, and junks, and all!'[1] If we had not seen the pictures I believe
we should scarcely have noticed it, and certainly we should not have
been surprised at all."

"Haven't you done being surprised yet?" Lorrimer asked.

"No. Have you?"

"Quite. Nothing ever surprises me."

"I have read somewhere," she said, trying hard to recall the passage, "that fast men, stupid men (*I think*), and rascals, profess to feel
no surprise at anything."

The colour flew over his face, he seemed about to speak, but
took up his pen again as if the thing were not worth the trouble of
a word, and went on with his work. The habit of treating men as
ideas is not to be got rid of in a moment, and it was only when she
thought it over at dinner this evening that she saw anything to hurt
him in what she had said. Now that she did think of it, however, it
certainly seemed natural that he should object to being classed in
any category which included fast men, stupid men, or rascals; but
even while she blamed herself, and credited him with much forbear-
ance in that he had allowed her rudeness to pass unpunished, she
was conscious of the existence, in that substratum of thought which
goes on continually irrespective of our will, of a doubt as to whether
he might not after all be one of these—say, a fast man. For what
did she know about him? Nothing, except that his manners were

---

[1] Also called Guangzhou, Canton is the capital of Kwangtung province in
southeastern China. It has two famous pagodas, or Asian temples: the five-
story red pagoda, built in 1380, and the seventeen-story Flower Pagoda, built in
537 A.D., as part of the Six Banyan Temple. Junks are Chinese ships, which have
bluff lines, a high poop deck, little or no keel, high pole masts, and a deep rud-
der. Grand herself traveled extensively in Asia while her husband was active in
the military and likely saw many of the places she describes in this novel.

agreeable. True, she had heard of his good deeds, and there is never smoke without fire; but a man may balance his accounts, and many men do, in that way, topping up the scale of good deeds pretty high when the bad ones on the other side threaten to turn it; and, seeing that she knew nothing definitely about his private character, suppose she had been deceived in him? But, no! The thing was impossible. And just as she thought it, a gentleman, sitting opposite, one whom she had not met before, looked across the table and asked her if she knew Mr. Lorrimer.

"I have seen him," she answered, with a burning blush, being taken unawares.

"He's a charming fellow—don't you think so?"

"Yes, I think so," she agreed, with an indescribable sense of relief.

And the next day a young clergyman whom she stopped to speak to in the street began at once about Lorrimer.

"I met him at dinner the other night," he said. "I suppose you know him? There is much truth in 'birds of a feather.' He fascinated us all with his talk of art and literature. He gave us such new ideas—described such varied experiences, and all with such grace and power."

"Yes," she answered, thoughtfully. "I believe he is brilliant."

"Many people are that," was the reply, given with hearty enthusiasm; "but Lorrimer is something more. He is good. He makes you feel it, and know it, and believe in him, without ever saying a word about himself."

"Ah!" she sighed, "there is power in that. What lovely summer weather! It makes me dream. Don't you love the time of nasturtiums? Their pungent scent, and their colours? They seem to penetrate and glow through everything, and make the time their own."

And so she left him.

But that same day, an old gentleman, who came from another county, and looked as if he had come from another century—an old gentleman with curious wavy hair, parted in the middle, who worshipped the Idol of Days—the past and all that belonged to it—and, for evening dress, wore knee-breeches, frilled shirt, black silk stockings, and diamond buckles in his shoes; and had a bijou house,[1] filled with a thousand relics of his Idol of Days, where

---

[1] A small but elegant house.

noble ladies were wont to loll and listen to him, and drink tea out of his wonderful cups, and love him—so it was said—this gentleman called on Ideala. He came to charm and to be charmed; and he, of all people in the world the one from whom she would least have expected it, although she knew they had met, began to sing Lorrimer's praises.

"He raises the tone of everything he is engaged upon," this gentleman said. "He has not quite kept faith with me about a matter he promised to look into for me a year ago, but doubtless he is busy. I suppose you know him?"

"Yes, I know him. He seems to be very much above the average."

"Oh, very much above the average," was the warm response. "He's a charming fellow, and a thoroughly good fellow, too."

This was the chorus to everything, and there was only one dissentient voice—that of a man who admired Ideala, and was a good soul himself, having gone out of his way to pay her trifling attentions, and even found occasion to do her some small acts of kindness. He began with the rest to praise Lorrimer, but when he saw he was doing so at his own expense, by diverting her attention from himself to his subject, he somewhat lowered his tone.

"Every one seems to like Mr. Lorrimer," Ideala said.

"O yes, he's certainly a nice fellow; but he puts a lot of side on."

"And well he may, being so very good and well-beloved," she answered, smiling.

"So spoilt and conceited, you might say," was the rejoinder; but she felt that there was jealousy in the tone, and only laughed.

"What an interesting face he has," a lady remarked, who was having tea with Ideala, *tête-à-tête*, one afternoon, and had brought the conversation round to Lorrimer, as seemed inevitable in those days. "He must make a charming portrait."

"Yes, it is a fine face," Ideala answered, dreamily—"a face for a bust in white marble; a face from out of the long ago, not Greek, but Roman, of the time when men were passing from a strong, simple, manly, into a luxuriously effeminate, self-indulgent stage; the face of a man who is midway between the two extremes, and a prey to the desires of both. I wish I had been his mother."

"His mother was a noble woman."

"I know; but she was not omniscient, and she never could have understood the boy. I daresay he was not enough of an ugly duckling to attract special attention, and with many other chicks in the brood he could not have more than the rest, and yet he required it. He ought to have been an only child. If he had been mine, I should have known what his dreaminess meant, why he loved to wander away and be alone; what was the conflict that began in his cradle—or earlier. Surely a mother must remember what there was in her mind to influence her child; she must have the key to all that is wrong in him; she must know if his soul is likely to be at war with his senses"—and then Ideala forgot her listener, and burst out with one of those curious flashes of insight, irrespective of all knowledge, to which she was subject: "If I were only a soul to be saved, he would save me; but I am also a body to be loved, and whether he loves me or not, he suffers. It is the eternal conflict of mind and matter, spirit and flesh, two prisoners chained together—the one despising the other, yet ruled by him, and subservient to the needs of his lower nature."

The lady stared at her.

"You know Mr. Lorrimer very well, then, I suppose?" she remarked.

"Let me see," said Ideala, awaking from her trance, "that is a question I often ask myself. And sometimes I say I *do* know him very well, and sometimes I say I don't. I go to the Great Hospital frequently to read, and to look up information, and he helps me. He is a man who makes an instant impression, but he is many-sided, and, now you ask me, I think on the whole that I do not know him well. I should not be surprised to hear any number of the most contradictory things about him."

"It is not a nice character to have," the lady said.

"No," Ideala answered, "not at all nice, but very interesting."

When at last the day arrived she felt an unusual impatience to see him. And she was in a strange flutter of nervous excitement. Should she tell him of those things which she had not been able to confide to him on the last occasion of their meeting? Could she? No; impossible! But she must see him, nevertheless. The desire was imperative.

The servant she had been accustomed to see met her at the door of the Great Hospital. She fancied he looked at her peculiarly. He said he had heard something about Mr. Lorrimer being absent that day, but he would enquire. He left her, and, returning in a few minutes, told her Mr. Lorrimer was not there.

"Did he leave no note, no message for me?" Ideala asked, faintly.

"No, madam, nothing," was the reply.

CHAPTER XXII.

For quite three months we heard nothing of Ideala, but we were not alarmed, as she often neglected us in this way when she was busy. At last, however, Claudia received a note from her, written in pencil, and in her usual style.

"It has been dull down here to a degree," she said. "I am beginning to think we are all too respectable. Are respectability and imbecility nearly allied, I wonder? But don't tell me; I don't want to know. All the trouble in the world comes from knowing too much. And then, I'm so dreadfully clever! If people take the trouble to explain things to me, I am sure to acquire some of the information they try to impart. I heard of the block system[1] the other day. It sounded mysterious. I like mystery, and I went about in daily dread of having it all made plain to me by some officious person. One day I was sitting on a rail above the line watching the trains. A workman came and sat down near me. It is very hard to have a workman sit down near you and not to talk to him, so we talked. And before I knew what was coming, he had explained the whole of that block system to me. Only fancy! and I may never forget it! It is quite disheartening.

"He said he was a pointsman, and I asked him if he would send a train down a wrong line for fifty pounds. He said fifty pounds was a large sum, and he had a mother depending on him! The people here are delicious. I think I shall write a book about them some day.

"Have you felt the fascination of the trains? My favourite seat here is a lovely spot just above where they pass. I can look down on them, and into them. The line winds, rather, through meadows and between banks, where wild flowers grow; and under an ivied bridge

---

[1] System of running railroad trains that uses danger signals to create safe spacing of trains. The signals appear at the beginning of specified lengths, or blocks, of track, and are kept at "Danger" when a train is on the block.

or two, and by some woods. And the trains rush past—some slow, some fast; and now and then comes one that is just a flash and roar, and I cling to the railing for a moment till it passes, and quiver with excitement, feeling as if I must be swept away. I look at the carriage windows, too, trying to catch a glimpse of the people, and I always hope to see a face I know. In that lies all the charm.

"I seem to be expected in town, and some Scotch friends have asked me to pay them a visit *en route*. I should like to go that way above everything; one would see so much more of the country! But I daren't go to London while the Bishop is there. He is making a dead set at me again (confirmation this time), and I am afraid if he heard of my arrival he would do something rash—dance down the Row in his gaiters,[1] perhaps—which might excite comment even if people knew what he was after."

And then she went on to say she had been a little out of sorts, and very lazy, and she thought the north country air would brace her nerves, and, if we would have her, she would like to go to us at once.

She arrived late one afternoon, and I did not see her until she came down to the drawing-room dressed for dinner.

I had not thought anything of her illness, she made so light of it, and I was therefore startled beyond measure when she appeared.

"Why, my dear!" I exclaimed, involuntarily, "what have they done to you? You're a perfect wreck!"

"Well, so *I* thought," she answered; "but I did not like to tell you. I was afraid you might think I was trying to make much of myself—wrecks are so interesting."

There was a large party staying in the house, and I had no opportunity of speaking to her that evening; but the next morning she came into my studio with a brave assumption of her old manner. I cannot tell how it was that I knew in a moment she had broken down, but I did know it, and I could only look at her. Perhaps something in my look showed her she had betrayed herself, for all at once her false composure forsook her, and she stretched out her hands to me with a piteous little gesture:

"What am I to do?" she said. "Will it always be like this?"

But I could not help her. I turned to the picture I was working

---

[1] Dance down in the street in nothing but stockings.

at, and went on painting without a word. By-and-by she recovered herself, and began to talk of other things.

I blamed myself afterwards. I ought to have let her tell me then; but I had no notion of the truth. I only thought of her husband, and I selfishly shrank from encouraging her to speak. Complaint seemed to be beneath her. But I know now that she never wanted to make any complaint of him to me. It was of her new acquaintance that she longed to tell me. She had settled the difficulty with her husband without consulting any one. She had returned to his house, and remained there as his wife nominally, and because he particularly wished that the world should know nothing of the rupture. I believe that she had done it sorely against the grain, and only because he represented that by so doing she would save his reputation. But from that time forward she would accept nothing from him but house-room, for she held that no high-minded woman could take anything from a man to whom she was bound by no tie more sacred than that of a mere legal contract.

She was very quiet when she first came to us, but beyond that I noticed nothing unusual in her manner, and after the first I was inclined to think that being out of health accounted for everything. My sister Claudia, however, was not so easily deceived. She declared that Ideala was suffering from some serious trouble, either mental or bodily; and as the days wore on and there was no change for the better in her, but rather the contrary, I began to share Claudia's anxiety.

Ideala grew paler and thinner, and more nervous. She was oftenest depressed, but occasionally had unnatural bursts of hilarity that would end suddenly in long fits of brooding.

It seems she had at first believed that Lorrimer's absence was an intentional slight, and the humiliation, coming as it did upon the long train of troubles which had weakened her already both in body and mind, nearly killed her. She had been lying for weeks between life and death, and we had known nothing of it. But as her strength returned she began to think she had been unjust to Lorrimer. She could account for his absence in many ways. He had been called out suddenly, and had left no message because he expected to be back before she arrived, but had been detained; or perhaps he had left a message with one of the servants whom she had not seen—there were so many about the place; or it was just possible that he had never received her letter at all—a certain number are lost in the post every day; and altogether it was more difficult to think badly of him than to believe that there had been some mistake. But still there was a doubt in her mind, and she bore the torment of it rather than ask for an explanation which might only confirm her worst fears.

CHAPTER XXIII.

About a month after she came to us, Ideala caught a bad cold. The doctor said her chest was very delicate. There was no disease, but she required great care, and must not go out of doors. Soon afterwards he ordered her to remain in two rooms, and my sister had a favourite sitting-room turned into a bedroom for her. It opened into the blue drawing-room, and we took to sitting there in the evening, so that Ideala might join us without change of temperature. Ideala had always been careless about her health, and we expected some trouble with her now, but she acquiesced in all our arrangements without a word. It was easy to see, however, that her docility arose from indifference. The one idea possessed her, and she cared for nothing else. Did he, or did he not, mean it? was the question she asked herself, morning, noon, and night, till at last she could bear it no longer. Anything was better than suspense. She must write to him, she must know the truth one way or the other.

I had stayed up in the blue drawing-room to read one night after the rest of the party had gone to their rooms, but my mind wandered from the book. Ideala had been very still that evening, and I could not help thinking about her. Once or twice I had caught her looking at me intently. It seemed as if she had something to say, but when I went to speak to her she answered quite at random. I was much troubled about her, and something happened presently which did not tend to set my mind at rest. The room was large, and the fire, though bright, and one shaded lamp standing on a low table, left the greater part of it in shadow. When I gave up the attempt to read, I had gone to the farther end of it to lie on a sofa which was quite in the shade. About midnight the door into Ideala's room opened and she stood on the threshold with a loose white wrapper round her. She could not see me, and I ought to have spoken and let her know I was there, but I was startled at first by her sudden appearance, and afterwards I was afraid of startling her. She was so nervous and fragile then that a very little might have led to serious consequences. I did not like to play the spy, but it was a choice of two evils, and I thought she had come for a book or something, and would go directly, and if she did discover me she would suppose me to be asleep. She walked about the room, however, for a little in an objectless way; then she sank down on the floor with a low moan beside a chair, and hid her face on her arm. Presently she looked up, and I saw she held something in her hand. It was a gold crucifix, and she fixed her eyes on it. The lamplight fell on her face, and I could see that it was drawn and haggard. Claudia had maintained latterly that her illness arose more from mental than from physical trouble; did this explain it? And was it a religious difficulty?

A weary while she remained in the same attitude, gazing at the crucifix; but evidently there was no pity for her pain, and no relief. She neither prayed nor wept, and scarcely moved; and I dared not. At last, however, a great drowsiness came over me; and when I awoke I almost thought I had dreamt it all, for the daylight was streaming in, and I was alone.

Later in the day when I saw Ideala she had just finished writing a letter.

"Shall I take it down for you?" I asked. "The man will come for the others presently."

She handed it to me without a word. On the way downstairs I saw that it was addressed to Lorrimer, of whom I had not then heard, but somehow I could not help thinking that this letter had something to do with what I had seen the night before.

For a day or two after that Ideala seemed better. Then she grew restless, which was a new phase of her malady; she had been so still before; and soon it was evident that she was devoured by anxiety which she could not conceal. I felt sure she was expecting someone, or something, that never came. For days she wandered up and down, up and down, and she neither ate nor slept.

One afternoon I went to ask if she had any letters for the post. At first she said she had not, then she wanted to know how soon the post was going. In a few minutes, I told her. She sat down on the impulse of the moment, and hurriedly wrote a note, which she handed to me. It was addressed to Lorrimer; but I asked no questions.

Two days afterwards a single letter came by the post for Ideala. I took it to her myself, and saw in a moment that it was what she had waited for so anxiously: the cruel suspense was over at last.

That evening she was radiant; but she told us she must go home next day, and we were thunderstruck. It was the depth of winter; the weather was bitterly cold, and she had not been out of the house for months, and under the circumstances to take such a journey was utter madness. But we remonstrated in vain. She was determined to go, and she went.

CHAPTER XXIV.

IN a few days she returned to us, and we were amazed at the change in her. Her voice was clear again, her step elastic, her complexion had recovered some of its brilliancy; there was a light in her eyes that I had never seen there before, and about her lips a perpetual smile hovered. She was tranquil again, and self-possessed; but she was more than that—she was happy. One could see it in the very poise of her figure when she crossed the room.

"This is delightful, is it not?" Claudia whispered to me in the drawing-room on the evening of her return.

"Delightful," I answered, but I was puzzled. Ideala's variableness was all on the surface, and I felt sure that this sudden change, which looked like ease after agony, meant something serious.

She did not keep me long in suspense. The next morning she came to my studio door and looked in shyly.

"Come in," I said. "I have been expecting you," and then I went on with my painting. I saw she had something to tell me, and thought, as she was evidently embarrassed, it would be easier for her to speak if I did not look at her. "I hope you are going to stay with us some time now, Ideala," I added, glancing up at her as she came and looked over my shoulder at the picture.

Her face clouded. "I—I am afraid not," she answered, hesitating, and nervously fidgeting with some paint brushes that lay on a table beside her. "I am afraid you will not want me when you know what I am going to do. I only came back to tell you."

My heart stood still. "To tell me! Why, what are you going to do?"

"It is very hard to tell you," she faltered. "You and Claudia are my dearest friends, and I cannot bear to give you pain. But I must tell you at once. It is only right that you should know—especially as you will disapprove."

I turned to look at her, but she could not meet my eyes.

"Give us pain! Disapprove!" I exclaimed. "What on earth do you mean, Ideala? What are you going to do?"

"An immoral thing," she answered.

"Good heavens!" I exclaimed, throwing down my palette, and rising to confront her. "I don't believe it."

"I mean," she stammered—the blood rushing into her face and then leaving her white as she spoke—"something which you will consider so."

"I cannot believe it," I reiterated.

"But it is true. He says so."

"*He*—who, in God's name?"

"Lorrimer."

"And who on earth is Lorrimer?"

"That is what I came to tell you," she answered, faintly.

I gathered up my palette and brushes, and sat down to my easel again.

"Tell me, then," I said, as calmly as I could.

I pretended to paint, and after a little while, still standing behind me so that I could not see her face, she began in a low voice, and told me, with her habitual accuracy, all that had passed between them.

"And what did you think when you found he was not there?" I asked, for at that point she had stopped.

"At first I thought he did not want to see me, and had gone away on purpose," she answered; "then I was ill; but after that, when I began to get better, I was afraid I had been unjust to him. There might have been some mistake, and I was half inclined to go and see, but I was frightened. And every day the longing grew, and I used to sit and look at my watch, and think—'I could be there in an hour;' or, 'I might be with him in forty minutes.' But I never went. And after a while I could not bear it any longer, and so I came to you. But the thought of him came with me, and the desire to know the truth grew and grew, until at last I could bear that no longer either, and then I wrote; and day after day I waited, and no answer came; and then I was sure he had done it on purpose, but yet I could not bear to think it of him. And I began not to know what people said when they spoke to me, and I think I should have killed myself; but I come of an old race, you know, and none of us ever did a cowardly thing, and I would rather suffer for ever than be the first—*noblesse oblige.*[1] I don't deserve much credit for that, though, for I knew I should die if I did not see him again—die of grief, and shame, and humiliation because of what I had written, for as the days passed, and no answer came, I was afraid I had said too much, and he had misunderstood me, and would despise me. If I had only been sure that he did not want to see me again, of course I should never have written; but so many people have lost their only chance of happiness because they had not the courage to find out the truth in some such doubtful matter; and I *did* believe in him so—I could not think he would do a *low* thing. I was in a difficult position, and I did what I thought was right; but when no answer came to my letter I began to doubt, and then in a moment of rage, feeling myself insulted, I wrote again. Yet I don't know what made me write. It was an impulse—the sort of thing that makes one scream when one is hurt. It does no good, but the cry is out before you can think of that. All I said was: 'I understand your silence. You are cruel and unjust. But I can keep my word, and if I live for nothing else, I promise that I will make you respect me yet.' I never expected him to answer that second note, but he did, at once. And he offered to come here and explain—he was dreadfully distressed. But I preferred to go to him."

"And you went?"

"Yes. And I was frightened, and he was very kind."

By degrees she told me much of what had passed at that interview. She seemed to have had no thought of anything but her desire to see him, and have her mind set at rest, until she found herself face to face with him, and then she was assailed by all kinds of doubts and fears; but he had put her at her ease in five minutes—and in five minutes more she had forgotten everything in the rapid change of ideas, the delightful intellectual contest and communion, which had made his companionship everything to her. She did just remember to ask him why he had not answered her first letter.

He searched about amongst a pile of newly-arrived documents on his writing table. "There it is," he said, showing her the letter cov-

---

[1] Concept that aristocratic heritage requires virtuous actions.

ered with stamps and postmarks. "It only arrived this morning—just in time, though, to speak for itself. I was abroad when you wrote, and it was sent after me, and has followed me from place to place as you see, so that I got your second letter first. You might have known there was some mistake."

"Pardon me," Ideala answered. "I ought to have known."

And then she had looked up at him and smiled, and never another doubt had occurred to her.

"But, Ideala," I said to her, "you used the word 'immoral' just now. You were talking at random, surely? You are nervous. For heaven's sake collect yourself, and tell me what all this means."

"No, I am not nervous," she answered. "See! my hand is quite steady. It is you who are trembling. I am calm now, and relieved, because I have told you. But, oh! I am so sorry to give you pain."

"I do not yet understand," I answered, hoarsely.

"He wants me to give up everything, and go to him," she said; "but he would not accept my consent until he had explained, and made me understand exactly what I was doing. 'The world will consider it an immoral thing,' he said, 'and so it would be if the arrangement were not to be permanent. But any contract which men and women hold to be binding on themselves should be sufficient now, and will be sufficient again, as it used to be in the old days, provided we can show good cause why any previous contract should be broken. You must believe that. You must be thoroughly satisfied now. For if your conscience were to trouble you afterwards—your troublesome conscience which keeps you busy regretting nearly everything you do, but never warns you in time to stop you—if you were to have any scruples, then there would be no peace for either of us, and you had better give me up at once.'"

"And what did you say, Ideala?"

"I said, perhaps I had. I was beginning to be frightened again."

"And how did it end?"

"He made me go home and consider."

"Yes. And what then?" I demanded impatiently.

"And next day he came to me—to know my decision—and—and—I was satisfied. I cannot live without him."

I groaned aloud. What was I to say? What could I do? An arrangement of this sort is carefully concealed, as a rule, by the people concerned, and denied if discovered; but here were a lady and gentleman prepared, not only to take the step, but to justify it—under somewhat peculiar circumstances, certainly—and carefully making their friends acquainted with their intention beforehand, as if it were an ordinary engagement. I knew Ideala, and could understand her being over-persuaded. Something of the kind was what I had always feared for her. But, Lorrimer—what sort of a man was he? I own that I was strongly prejudiced against him from the moment she pronounced his name,[1] and all she had told me of him subsequently only confirmed the prejudice.

"Why was he not there that day to receive you?" I asked at last.

"I don't know," she said. "I quite forgot about that. And I suppose he forgot too," she added, "since he never told me."

"Oh, Ideala!" I exclaimed, "how like you that is! It is most important that you should know whether he intended to slight you on that occasion or not. It is the key to his whole action in this matter."

"But supposing he did mean to be rude? I should have to forgive him, you know, because I have been rude to him—often. He does not approve of my conduct always, by any means," she placidly assured me.

"And does he, of all people in the world, presume to sit in judgment on you?" I answered, indignantly. "I always thought *you* the most extraordinary person in the world, Ideala, until I heard of this—*gentleman*."

"Hush!" she protested, as if I had blasphemed. "You must not speak of him like that. He *is* a gentleman—as true and loyal as you are yourself. And he is everything to me."

But these assurances were only what I had expected from Ideala, and in no way altered my opinion of Mr. Lorrimer. I knew Ideala's peculiar conscience well. She might do what all the world would consider wrong on occasion; but she would never do so until she had persuaded herself that wrong was right—for *her* at all events.

"He may be everything to you, but he has lowered you, Ideala," I resumed, thinking it best not to spare her.

"I was degraded when I met him."

---

[1] A lorimer is a maker of riding gear, such as bits and spurs. Dawne appears to object to Lorrimer because of the class implications in his name.

"Circumstances cannot degrade us until they make us act unworthily," I rejoined.

"Oh, no, he has not lowered me," she persisted; "quite the contrary. I have only begun to know the difference between right and wrong since I met him, and to understand how absolutely necessary for our happiness is right-doing, even in the veriest trifle. And there is one thing that I must always be grateful to him for—I can pray now. But I belied myself to him nevertheless. He asked me if I ever prayed, and I was shy; I could not tell him, because I only prayed for him. It was easier to say that sometimes I reviled. Ah! why can we not be true to ourselves?

"But I can't always pray," she went on sorrowfully; "only sometimes; generally when I am in church. The thought of him comes over me then, and a great longing to have him beside me, kneeling, with his heart made tender, and his soul purified and uplifted to God as mine is, possesses me—a longing so great that it fills my whole being, and finds a voice: 'My God! my God! give him to me!'"

"'Angels of God in heaven! give him to me! give him to me!'" I answered, bitterly.

"Yes, I remember," she rejoined, "I said it in my arrogant ignorance. I did not understand, and this is different."

"It is always *different* in our own case," I answered. "Do you remember that passage Ralph Waldo Emerson quotes from Lord Bacon: 'Moral qualities rule the world, but at short distances the senses are despotic'?[1] it seems to me that when you call upon God in that spirit you are worshipping Him with your senses only."

"Then I believe it is possible to make the senses the means of saving the soul at critical times," she answered; "and at all events I know this, that I more earnestly desire to be a good woman now than I ever did before."

"It would be a dangerous doctrine," I began.

"Only in cases where the previous moral development had not been of a high order," she interrupted.

I felt it was useless to pursue that part of the subject, so I waited a little, and then I said: "Am I to understand, then, that you are going to give up your position in society, and all your friends, for the sake of this one man, who probably does not care for you, who certainly

---

[1] Emerson, "Manners," *Essays*, 2nd series (1844).

does not respect you, and of whom you know nothing? Verily, he has gained an easy victory! But, of course, you know now what his object has been from the first."

"I know what you mean," she answered, indignantly; "but you are quite wrong; he does care for me. And if I give up my position in society for his sake, he is worth it, and I am content. And it is my own doing, too. I know that there cannot be one law for me and another for all the other women in the world, and if I break through a social convention I am prepared to abide by the consequences. Do you want to make me believe that his sympathy was pretended, that he deliberately planned—something I have no word to express—and would have carried out his plan absolutely in cold blood, without a spark of affection for me? It would be hard to believe it of any man; it is impossible to believe it of him. He is a man of strong passions, if you will, but of noble purpose; and if I make a sacrifice for him, he will be making one for me also. He may have been betrayed at times by grief, or other mental pain, which weakened his moral nature for the moment, and left him at the mercy of bad impulses; but I can believe such impulses were isolated, and any action they led him into was bitterly repented of; and no one will ever make me alter my conviction that I wronged him when I doubted him, even for a moment."

"This is all very well, Ideala," I said, trying not to irritate her by direct opposition, "if you appeared to him as you appear to me. Do you think you did? Was there anything in your conduct that might have given him a low estimate of your character to begin with? Anything that might have led him to doubt your honesty, and think, when you made your confession, that you were trying to get up a little play in which you intended him to take a leading part? That you merely wished to ease your mind from some inevitable sense of shame in wrong-doing by finding an excuse for yourself to begin with—an excuse by which you would excite his interest and sympathy, and save yourself from his contempt?"

"Oh!" she exclaimed, "could he—could anyone—think such a thing possible?"

"Such things are being done every day, Ideala, and a man of the world would naturally be on his guard against deception. If he thought he was being deceived, do you think it likely he would feel bound to be scrupulous?"

"But he *did* believe in me," she declared, passionately.

"He pretended to; it was part of the play. You see he only kept it up until he thoroughly understood you, and then his real feelings appeared, and he was rude to you. For I call his absence on that occasion distinctly rude, and intentionally so too, since he sent no apology."

"He was only rude to me to save me from myself, then, as Lancelot was rude to Elaine,"[1] she answered.

"Or is it not just possible that he was disappointed when he found you better than he had supposed? that he felt he had wasted his time for nothing, and was irritated——"

She interrupted me. "I forgive you," she said, "because you do not know him. But I shall never convince you. You are prejudiced. You do not think ill of me: why do you think ill of him?"

I made no answer, and she was silent for a little. Then she began again, recurring to the point at issue:

"If he did slight me on that occasion," she said—"and I maintain that he did not—but if he did, it was accidentally done."

"The evidence is against him," I answered, drily.

"Many innocent persons have suffered because it was," she said, with confidence.

"You are infatuated," I answered, roughly. And then my heart sent up an exceeding great and bitter cry: "Ideala! Ideala! how did it ever come to this?"

She was silent. But her eyes were bright once more, her figure was erect, there was new life in her—I could see that—and never a doubt. She was satisfied. She was happy.

"Must I give you up?" she said at last, tentatively.

"No, you must give him up," I answered.

"Ah, that is impossible!" she cried. "We were made for each other. We cannot live apart."

"Ideala," I exclaimed, exasperated, "he never believed in you. He thought you were as so many women of our set are, and he showed it, if only you could have understood, when you saw him at the Hospital on that last occasion. You felt that there was some change, as

---

[1] Reference to Tennyson, "Lancelot and Elaine," *Idylls of the King,* line 981. Elaine professes her love for Lancelot, and he responds by leaving without saying goodbye to her, the "one discourtesy that he used."

you say yourself, and that was it. You talked to him of truth then, and it irritated him as the devil quoting Scripture might be supposed to irritate; and when you went back again he showed what he thought of you by his unexplained absence. He thought you were not worth consideration, and he gave you none."

"It would have been paying himself a very poor compliment if he had thought that only a corrupt woman could care for him," she answered, confidently. "But, I tell you, I am sure there is some satisfactory explanation of that business. I only wish I had remembered to ask for it, that I might satisfy you now. And, at any rate," she added, "whatever he may have thought, he knows better by this time."

I could say no more. Baffled and sick at heart, I left her, wondering if some happy inspiration would come before it was too late, and help me to save her yet.

CHAPTER XXV.

I WENT to consult my sister Claudia. The blow was a heavy one for her also; but I was surprised to find that she did not share my contempt for the person whom I considered responsible for all this trouble.

"Ideala is no common character herself," Claudia argued; "and it isn't likely that a common character would fascinate her as this man has done."

"Will you speak to her, Claudia, and see what your influence will do?"

"It is no use my speaking to her," she answered, disconsolately. "Ideala is a much cleverer woman than I am. She would make me laugh at my own advice in five minutes. And, besides, if she be infatuated, as you say she is, she will be only too glad to be allowed to talk about him, and that will strengthen her feeling for him. No. She has chosen you for her confidant, and you had better talk to her yourself—and may you succeed!" she added, laying her head on the table beside which she was sitting, and giving way to a burst of grief.

I tried to comfort her, but I had little hope myself, and I could not speak at all confidently.

"I believe," Claudia said, before we parted, "that there is nothing for her now but a choice of two evils. If she gives him up she will never care for anything again, and if she does not, she will have done an unjustifiable thing; and life after that for such a woman as Ideala would be like one of those fairy gifts which were bestowed subject to some burdensome condition that made the good of them null and void."

I did not meet Ideala again until the evening, and then I was not sorry to see that her manner was less serene. It was just possible that she had been thinking over what I had said, and that some of the doubts I had suggested were beginning to disturb her perfect security.

After dinner she brought the conversation round to those social laws which govern our lives arbitrarily. I did not see what she was driving at, neither did the good old Bishop, who was one of the party, nor a lawyer who was also present.

"You want to know something," said the latter. "What is it? You must state your case clearly."

"I want to know if a thing can be legally right and morally wrong," Ideala answered.

"Of course not," the Bishop rashly asserted.

"That depends," the lawyer said, cautiously.

"If I signed a contract," Ideala explained, "and found out afterwards that those who induced me to become a party to it had kept me in ignorance of the most important clause in it, so that I really did not know to what I was committing myself, would you call that a moral contract?"

"I should say that people had not dealt uprightly with you," the Bishop answered; "but there might be nothing in the clause to which you could object."

"But suppose there *was* something in the clause to which I very strongly objected, something of which my conscience disapproved, something that was repugnant to my whole moral nature; and suppose I was forced by the law to fulfil it nevertheless, should you say that was a moral contract? Should you not say that in acting against my conscience I acted immorally?"

We all fell into the trap, and looked an encouraging assent.

"And in that case," she continued, "I suppose my duty would be to evade the law, and act on my conscience?"

The Bishop looked puzzled.

"I should only be doing what the early martyrs had to do," she added.

"That is true," he rejoined, with evident relief.

"But I don't see what particular contract you are thinking of," said the lawyer.

"The marriage contract," Ideala answered, calmly.

This announcement created a sensation.

The lawyer laughed: the Bishop looked grave.

"Oh, but you cannot describe marriage in that way," he declared, with emphasis.

"Humph!" the lawyer observed, meditatively. "I am afraid I must beg to differ from your Lordship. Many women might describe their marriages in that way with perfect accuracy."

"Marriages are made in heaven!" the Bishop ejaculated, feebly.

"Let us hope that some are, dear Bishop." Claudia sweetly observed, and all the married people in the room looked "Amen" at her.

"I think an ideal of marriage should be fixed by law, and lectures given in all the colleges to teach it," Ideala went on; "and a standard of excellence ought to be set up for people to attain to before they could be allowed to marry. They should be obliged to pass examinations on the subject, and fit themselves for the perfect state by a perfect life. It should be made a reward for merit, and a goal towards which goodness only could carry us. Then marriages might seem to have been made in heaven, and the blessing of God would sanctify a happy union, instead of being impiously pronounced in order to ratify a business transaction, or sanction the indulgence of a passing fancy. But only the love that lasts can sanctify marriage, and a marriage without such love is an immoral contract."

"Marriage an immoral contract!" the Bishop exclaimed. "O dear! O dear! This is not right, you know; this is not at all right. I must make a note of this—I really must. You are in the habit of saying things of this sort, my dear. I remember you said something like it once before; and really it is not a subject to joke about. Such an idea is quite pernicious; it must not be allowed to spread—even as a joke. I wish, my dear, you had not promulgated it, even in that spirit. You have—ah—a knack of making things seem plausible, and of giving weight to opinions by the way you express them, although the opinions themselves are quite erroneous, as on the present occasion. Some of your ideas are so very mistaken, you know; and you really ought to leave these matters to those who understand them, and can judge. It is very dangerous to discuss such subjects, especially—ah—when you know nothing about them, and—ah—cannot judge. I really must preach a sermon on the subject. Let me see. Next Sunday—ah, yes; next Sunday, if you will kindly come and hear me."

We all thanked him as enthusiastically as we could.

Later, I found Ideala alone in one of the conservatories. She took my arm affectionately, and we walked up and down for a time in silence. She was smiling and happy; so happy, indeed, that I found it hard to say anything to disturb her. For a moment I felt almost as she did about the step she proposed to take. There had been little joy in her life, and she had borne her cross long and bravely; what wonder that she should rebel at last, and claim her reward?

"Do you remember how you used to talk about the women of the nineteenth century, Ideala," I said at last, "and describe the power for good which they never use, and rail at them as artificial, milliner-made, man-hunting, self-indulgent *animals*?"[1]

"I know," she answered; "and now you would say I am worse than any of them? I used to have big ideas about woman and her mission; but I always looked at the question broadly, as it affects the whole world; now my vision is narrowed, and I see it only with regard to one individual. But I am sure that is the right way to look at it. I think every woman will have to answer for one man's soul, and it seems to me that the noblest thing a woman can do is to devote her life to that soul first of all—to raise it if it be low, to help it to peace if peace be lacking, and to gather all the sunshine there is in the world for it; and, after that, if her opportunities and powers allow her to help others also, she should do what she can for them.

---

[1] This notion of the nineteenth-century woman as "artificial, milliner-made, man-hunting, self-indulgent *animals*" is seen in Grand's nonfiction, in articles such as "The New Woman and the Old," in which she compares the woman of previous generations to the woman of the late-Victorian period. This essay, which first appeared in *Lady's Realm* in 1898, is reprinted in Ann Heilmann and Stephanie Forward, *Sex, Social Purity and Sarah Grand: Volume 1: Journalistic Writings and Contemporary Reception* (London: Routledge, 2001), 69-76.

I do not know all the places which it is legitimate for women to fill in the world, but it seems to me that they are many and various, and that the great object in life for a woman is to help. To be a Pericles I see that a man must have an Aspasia.[1] Was Aspasia vile? some said so—yet she did a nobler work, and was finer in her fall, if she fell, than many good women in all the glory of uprightness are. And was she impure? then it is strange that her mind was not corrupting in its influence. And was she low? then whence came her power to raise others? It seems to me that it only rests with ourselves to make any position in life, which circumstances render it expedient for us to occupy, desirable."

"And you propose to be an Aspasia to this modern Pericles?"

"If you like to put it so. The cases are not dissimilar, as there was an obstacle in the way of their marriage also."

"The law was the obstacle."

"Yes; another of those laws which are more honoured in the breach than in the observance. They might not marry because she came from Militus![2] and Lorrimer may not marry me because I came out of the house of bondage. Unwise laws make immoral nations."

"But you have gone about this business in such an extraordinary way, Ideala," I said. "You seem to have tried to make it appear as bad for yourself as you can. Why did you not leave your husband when Lorrimer advised you to?"

"If I had gone then I should have been obliged to live somewhere else—a long way from Lorrimer; and I might never have seen him again."

"And do you mean to say you decided to endure a life that had become hateful to you in every way, simply for the sake of seeing this gentleman occasionally?"

---

[1] Pericles was an Athenian statesman who lived from c.495–429 B.C. and created a number of democractic reforms in Athens during his tenure, including salaries for all Athenians and encouraging all citizens to run for office. He also supported the arts and architecture, including the building of the Parthenon, and he fought in the Peloponnesian War. Aspasia was Pericles's mistress and is thought to have advised him. She appears in ancient texts by Aeschines the Socratic, Plato, and Xenophon, as well as the writings of the nineteenth-century poet Walter Savage Landor, who wrote "Pericles and Aspasia" (1836).

[2] Also spelled Miletus; an Ionian Greek city on the western coast of Anatolia (now Turkey).

"Yes. Ah! you do not know how good he is, nor how he raises me! I never knew the sort of creature I was until he told me. He said once, when we quarrelled, that I was fanciful, sentimental, lackadaisical, hysterical, and in an unhealthy state of mind, and yet——"

I made a gesture of impatience, and she stopped.

"But, Ideala," I asked her, after a little pause, "have you never felt that what you are doing is wrong?"

"I cannot say that exactly," she answered. "I knew that certain social conventions forbade the thing—at least I began to acknowledge this to myself after a time. At first, you know, I thought of nothing. I was wholly absorbed in my desire to see him; that excluded every other consideration. Do you know what it is to be sure that a thing is wrong, and yet not to be able to feel it so—to have your reason acknowledge what your conscience does not confirm?"

I made no answer, and we were silent for a little; then she spoke again:

"One day when I was in Japan," she said, "I was living up in the hills at Hakone,[1] a village on a lake three thousand feet above the level of the sea. The Mayor of the village was entertaining me, and whenever I went out he sent his son and several of his retainers, as an escort, that I might not be subject to annoyance or insult from strangers. One day I was crossing the hills by a mountain path there is between Hakone and Mianoshita, and after I passed Ashynoyou,[2] where the sulphur springs are, I found myself in a dense fog. I could not see anything distinctly three yards in front of me. Kashywaya and the other men never walked with me; they used to hover about me, leaving me to all intents and purposes alone if I preferred it. The Japanese are very delicate in some things; it was weeks before I knew that I had a guard of honour at all. On that particular day I lost sight of them altogether, but I could hear them calling to each other through the fog; and I sat down feeling very wretched and lonely. I thought how all the beauty of life had been spoiled for me; how,

---

[1] A region in central Japan, Hakone is known for its mountains, especially Mt. Fuji. Also, there are many religious shrines, including The Hakone Shrine (built in 757), and hot springs in the area.

[2] Mianoshita, also spelled Miyanoshita, is a spa town in the Hakone region, and Ashynoyou, also spelled Ashinoyu, is one of seven hot springs in the same region.

past, present, and to come, it was all a blank; and I wished in my heart that I might die, and know no more. And, do you know, just at that moment the fog beneath me parted, and I saw the sea, sapphire blue and dotted with boats, and the sand a streak of silver, and the green earth, and a low horizon of shining clouds, and over all the sun! Dear Lord in heaven! how glad a sight it was!" She pressed her handkerchief to her eyes. "And I was wandering," she continued, "in some such mental mist, lost and despairing, when Lorrimer came into my life, and changed everything for me in a moment, like the sun. Would you have me believe that he was sent to me then only for an evil purpose? That the good God, in whom I scarcely believed until in His mercy He allowed me to feel love for one of His creatures, and to realise through it the Divine love of which it is surely the foreshadowing—would you have me believe myself degraded by love so sent? Would you have me turn from it and call it sin, when I feel that God Himself is the giver?"

I was silent, not knowing how to answer her.

Presently I asked: "But why not have a legal separation, a divorce, from your husband now?"

"I cannot," she answered, sadly. "At one time I had written proof of his turpitude, but I could not make up my mind to use it then, and I destroyed it eventually; so that now my word would be the only evidence against him, and that would not do, I suppose, although you all know, better than I do, I fancy, what his life has been."

Other people had by this time come into the conservatory, and we were therefore obliged to change the subject.

In the days that followed every one seemed to become conscious of some impending trouble. We were all depressed, and one by one our party left us, until at last only Ideala remained, for we had not the heart to ask other guests, even if it had been expedient, and, under the circumstances, Claudia did not consider it so.

Ideala spent much of her time in writing to Lorrimer. Some of these letters were never sent. I fancy she wrote exactly as she felt, and often feared when she had done so that she had been too frank. How these two ever came to such an understanding I am at a loss to imagine, and I have searched in vain for any clue to the mystery. Only one thing is plain to me, that when at last Ideala understood her feeling for Lorrimer, she cherished it. After she found that her husband had broken every tie, disregarded every obligation, legal and moral, that bound her to him, she seems to have considered herself free. But I feel quite sure she had not acknowledged this, even to herself, when she returned to Lorrimer, and that simply because she had not contemplated the possibility of being asked to take any decided step. When the time came, however, she apparently never questioned her right to act on this fancied freedom. The circumstances under which they had met were probably responsible for a great deal. The whole of their acquaintance had had something unusual about it which would naturally predispose their minds to further unaccustomed issues when any question of right or expediency arose. The restrictions which men and women have seen fit to place upon their intercourse with each other are the outcome of ages of experience, and they who disregard them bring upon themselves the troubles against which those same restrictions, irksome at times as they must be, are the only adequate defence.

One letter I have here shows something of the strength and tenderness of Ideala's devotion; and I venture to think that, even under the circumstances, it must be good for a man to have been loved once in his life like that. The letter begins abruptly—"Oh, the delight of being able to write to you," she says, "without fear and without constraint. If it were possible to step from the dreary oppression of the northern midnight into the full blaze of the southern noon, the transition would not be greater than is the sense of rest and relief that has come to me after the weary days which are over. Do you know, I never believed that any one person could be so much to another as you are to me; that any one could be so happy as I am! I think I am *too* happy. But, dear, I want you! I want you always; but most of all when anything good or beautiful moves me; I feel nearer to you then, and I know you would understand. Every good thought, every worthy aspiration, everything that is best in me, and every possibility of better things, seems due to your influence, and makes me crave for your presence. You have been the one thing wanting to me my whole life long. I believe that no soul is perfect alone, and that each of us must have a partner-soul *somewhere*, kept apart from us—by false marriages, perhaps, or distance, or death, but still to be ours, if not in this state, then in some other, when both are perfect enough to make the union possible. We are not all fit for that love which is the beginning of heaven, and can have no end.[1] Does this seem fanciful to you? It would comfort me if we were ever separated. If—I cannot tell you how it makes my heart sink just to look at that word, although I know it does not suggest anything that is possible in our case. What power would take you from me now, when there is no one else in the whole wide world for me *but* you? and always you! and only you! You, with your ready sympathy and perfect refinement; your wit, your rapid changes, your ideality, your kindness, your cruelty, and the terrible discontent which makes you untrue to yourself. You are my world. But unless I can be to you what you are to me, you will always be one of the lonely ones. Tell me, again, that my absence makes a blank in your life. You did not write the word, you only left a space, and do you know how I filled it at first? 'It was such a *relief* when you left off coming,' I read, and I raged at you.

"I have heard it said lately that you are fickle, but these people do

---

[1] While *Ideala* was in the press, the author read *Lord Brackenbury*, by Miss Amelia B. Edwards, and found the same idea at the beginning of Chapter XL., expressed in almost identical language. The inborn passionate longing of the human soul for perfect companionship doubtless accounts for the coincidence, which also shows how deeprooted and widely spread the hope of eventually obtaining the desired companionship is. Some will maintain that the desire for such a possibility has created the belief in it, but others claim to have met their partner-souls, and to have become united by a bond so perfect that even distance cannot sever it, there being some inexplicable means of communication between the two, which enables each to know what befalls the other wherever they may be. The idea might probably be traced back to that account of Adam which describes him as androgynous, or a higher union of man and woman—a union of all the attributes of either, which, to punish Adam for a grievous fault, was subsequently sundered into the contrast between man and woman, leaving each lonely, imperfect, and vainly longing for the other. [Grand's note.] What Ideala says is very close to a conversation in Chapter XL of Edwards's novel. In this conversation a young man who identifies himself as Romeo tries to convince a young woman named Giulietta that they are soulmates. In addition to drawing on Edwards's novel, Grand may also have been drawing on Socrates's account of the teaching of Diotima in the *Symposium* and Aristophanes's speech about "circle" beings, who possessed two sets of body parts, though Aristophanes does not apply the concept of an androgynous ideal to Adam directly. In the Donohue, Henneberry & Co. edition, the beginning of the note is slightly different. The first sentence is replaced with the following: "This passage might have been taken from Plato verbatim, but Ideala had not read Plato at the time it was written."

not understand you. You are true to your ideal, but the women you have hitherto known were only so many imperfect realizations of it, and so you went from one to the other, always searching, but never satisfied. And you have it in you to be so much happier or so much more miserable than other men—I should have trembled for you if your hopes had never been realized.

"But what *would* satisfy you? I often long to be that mummy you have in the Great Hospital, the one with the short nose and thick lips. When you looked at me spirit and flesh would grow one with delight, and I should come to life, and grow round and soft and warm again, and talk to you of Thebes,[1] and you would be enchanted with me—you could not help it then. I should be so old, so very old, and genuine!

"Dear, how I laugh at my fears now, or rather, how I bless them. If I had never known the horror of doubt, how could I have known what certainty is? And I did doubt you; I dare acknowledge it now. I wonder if you can understand what the shame of that doubt was? When I thought your absence and your silence were intentional slights, I knew how they felt when 'they called on the rocks to cover them,' and I wished—oh, *how* I wished!—that a thousand years had passed, and my spirit could be at the place where we met, and see the pillars broken, and the ivy climbing over the ruins, and the lizards at home amongst them, and the shameless sunlight making bare the spot where we stood.[2]

"It was as if I had been punished for some awful unknown sin, and when I seemed to be dying, and I dared not write to you, and all hope of ever knowing the truth had departed, I used to exclaim in my misery: 'Verily, Lord, if Thy servant sinned she hath suffered! for the anguish of death has been doubled, and the punishment of the lost has begun while yet the tortured mind can make its lament and moan with the tortured body!'[3]

---

[1] Ancient Greek city, northwest of Athens.

[2] Rephrasing of Revelation 6:15-17, "Then the kings of the earth and the great men and the generals and the rich and the strong, and every one, slave and free, hid in the caves and among the rocks of the mountains, calling to the mountains and rocks, 'Fall on us and hide us from the face of him who is seated on the throne, and from the wrath of the Lamb; for the great day of their wrath has come, and who can stand before it?'"

[3] While this particular quote does not appear in the Bible, the idea of double

"But all that bitter past only enhances the present.

"I wonder where you will be to-day. I believe you are always in that room of yours. You only leave it to walk to the station with me, after which you go back to it, and work there till it is dark; and then you rest, waiting for the daylight, and when it comes you go to work again. I cannot fancy you anywhere else. I should not like to realize that you have an existence of which I can know nothing, a life through which I cannot follow you, even in imagination.

"But sometimes you come to me, and then how glad I am! You come to me and kiss me, and it is night and I am dreaming, and not ashamed.

"Yes, the days do drag on slowly, for after all I am never quite happy, never at peace even, never for a moment, except when I am with you. I am sorry I feel so, for it seems ungrateful in the face of all the kindness and care that is being lavished on me by my friends. One lady here has seven children—another instance of the unequal distribution of the good things of this world. She has lent me one of them to comfort me because I am jealous. He sleeps in my room, and is a fair-haired boy, with eyes that remind me of you. Will he also, when he grows up, have 'the conscience of a saint among his warring senses'?[1] I hope not, I should think when sense and conscience are equally delicate, and apt to thrill simultaneously, life must be a burden. Would such a state of things account for moods that vary perpetually, I wonder?"

Here she breaks off, and I think these last reflections account for the fact that the letter was never sent.

CHAPTER XXVI.

IDEALA lingered unwillingly, but the reason of her reluctance to go was not far to seek. Now that Lorrimer knew she loved him she was ashamed to go back. It would have been bad enough had he been

---

punishment can be found in two biblical passages. In Jeremiah 16:16-18, God says through the prophet Jeremiah that his people will not be able to hide from him, "and I will doubly repay their iniquity." In Isaiah 40:2, Isaiah says that the people of Israel can find comfort because they have paid double for their sins and will soon return to their homeland from exile.

[1] Tennyson, "Guinevere," *Idylls of the King*, lines 634-635.

able to come to her; but going to him was like reversing the natural order of things and unsexing herself. I suppose, however, that she forgot her shyness in her desire to be with him as the time went on, and the effort it cost her to conquer her fear and go to him was not so dreadful as the blank she would have been obliged to face had she stayed away. At all events, she fixed a day at last, and one morning she announced to us, sadly enough, that on the morrow she must say farewell. She made the announcement just after breakfast, and Claudia rose and left the room without a word. My sister had never been able to speak to Ideala on the subject, but she did not cease to urge me to expostulate, and she had suggested many arguments which had affected Ideala, and made her unhappy, but without altering her determination.

I could not find a word to say to her that morning, and during the slow hours of the long day that dragged itself on so wearily for all of us, nothing new occurred to me.

"It will be a relief when it is over," I said to my sister.

"Yes," she answered; "it is worse than death."

In the evening she came to my study and said: "Ideala is alone in the south drawing-room. I wish you would go to her, and make a last effort to dissuade her."

I consented, hopelessly, and went.

Ideala was standing in a window, looking out listlessly. She was very pale, and I could see that she had been weeping. I sat down near the fire; and presently she came and sat on the floor beside me, and laid her head against my knee. In all the years of my love for her she had never been so close to me before, and I was glad to let her rest a long, long time like that.

"Were you happy while you were with Lorrimer, Ideala?" I asked at last.

She did not answer at once, and when she did, it was almost in a whisper.

"No, never quite happy till this last time," she said; "never entirely at ease, even. It was when I left him, when I was alone and could think of him, that the joy came."

"There was nothing real in your pleasure, then," I went on; "it was purely imaginary—due to your trick of idealizing everything and everybody, you care for?"

"I do not know," she said.

"Do you think it was the same with him?" I asked again—"I mean all along. Did it always make him happy to have you there?"

"I cannot tell," she said. "Yes, I think at times he was glad. But a word would alter his mood, and then he would grow sad and silent."

"Even on the last occasion?"

"No, not on the last occasion. He was happy then"—and she smiled at the recollection—"ah, so happy! It was like new life to him, he was so young, so fresh, so glad—like a boy."

"But before, when his moods varied so often, did it ever seem to you that he was troubled and dissatisfied with himself? that the intimacy had begun on his part under a misapprehension, and that when he began to know you better, he had tried to end it, and save you, by not seeing you on that occasion?"

"Ah, *that occasion* again!" she ejaculated. "I forgot to tell you, but I asked for an explanation just to satisfy you. Here it is!" And she took a note from her pocket-book and handed it to me. It was one which she had written to him.

"I do not understand," I said.

"Read it," she answered, "and you will find I asked him to expect me on *Monday*, the 26th. It was a clerical error. Tuesday was the 26th, and I went on Tuesday. He waited for me the whole long Monday, and that night he had to set off suddenly for the Continent on business connected with the Great Hospital. He went, wondering what had detained me, and expecting an explanation. When he returned he inquired, but nobody could tell him whether I had been or not. So he waited, and waited, as I did, expecting to hear, and as much perplexed and distressed as I was, and as proud, for he never thought of writing to me—nor did he think of looking at my note again until I wrote the other day, and then he discovered the mistake. Now, are you satisfied?"

"About that—yes," I answered, reluctantly. It was no relief to find him blameless.

"But what did he mean when he talked of conscience and scruples?"

"He used to laugh at my 'troublesome conscience,' as he called it," she answered, evasively.

"Would he have known you had a conscience, do you think, if he had had none himself?" I asked her. "Did he ever say anything that showed he was yielding to a strong inclination which he could not justify and would not conquer?"

"Oh, no!" she said; then added, undecidedly: "at least—he did say once: 'Of course, in the opinion of the world the thing cannot be justified,' but then he went on as if it had slipped from him involuntarily: 'Bah! I am only doing as other men do.'"

"Which shows he was not exactly satisfied to be only as other men are."

"That is what I have often told you," she said; "his ideal of life, both for himself and others, is the highest possible, and he suffers when he falls below it, or even belies himself with a word."

"Passion never lasts, and love does not lead to evil," I continued, meditatively; "if you love him, Ideala, how will you bear to feel that he has degraded himself by degrading you?"

"Oh! do not speak like that!" she exclaimed. "There is no degradation in love. It is sin that degrades, and sin is something that corrupts our minds, is it not? and makes us unfit for any good work, and unwilling to undertake any. This is very different."

"Ideala, do you remember telling me once that you had a strange feeling about yourself? that you thought you would be made to go down into some great depth of sin and suffering, in order to learn what it is you have to teach?"

"Ah, yes!" she answered, "but I have not gone down. I must obey my own conscience, not yours; and my conscience tells me the thing is right which you hold to be wrong. I am quite willing to believe it would be wrong for you, but for me it is clearly right. You said the other day he had lowered me. What a fiction that is! In what have I changed for the worse? Do I fail in any duty of life since I knew him in which I previously succeeded? Oh, no! he has not lowered me! Love like this rounds a life and brings it to perfection; it could not wreck it."

"But, Ideala, you are going to fail in a duty; you are going to fail in the most important duty of your life—your duty to society."

"I owe nothing to society," she answered, obstinately.

"I have always admired you," I pursued, "for not letting your own experience warp your judgment. Oh, what a falling off is here!

I have heard you wish to be something more than an independent unit of which no account need be taken. How can we, any of us, say we owe nothing to society, when we owe every pleasure in life to it? Do we owe nothing to those who have gone before, and whom we have to thank for the music, the painting, the poetry, and all the arts which would leave a big blank in *your* life, Ideala, if they ceased to exist? You would have been a mere savage now, without refinement enough to appreciate that rose at your waistbelt, but for the labour and self-denial which the hundreds and thousands who lived, and loved, and suffered in order to make you what you are have bestowed on you, and on all of us. You would not say, if you thought a moment, that society had done nothing for you; and no one can honestly think that they owe it nothing in return. It seems to me that a rigid observance of the laws which hold society together, and make life possible for all of us, and pleasant for some, is the least we can do; and do you know, Ideala, when a woman ever thinks of doing what you propose to do, she has already gone down to a low depth—of ingratitude, if of nothing else."

"I do not propose to do anything that will injure any one," she answered, coldly. "I am free, am I not, to dispose of myself as I like— to give myself to whomsoever I please?"

"We are none of us free in that sense of the word," I replied.

> "All are but parts of one stupendous whole
> Whose body Nature is, and God the soul.[1]

You are, as I know you have desired to be, part of a system, and an important part. All the toil and trouble of the world, and all the work which began with the life of man, is directed towards one great end—the doing away with sin and suffering, and the establishment of purity and peace. And this work seems almost hopeless, not because the multitude do not approve of it, but because individuals are cowardly, and will not do their share of it. Every act of yours has a meaning; it either helps or hinders, what is being done to further this, the object of life. Lately, Ideala, you have been talking wildly, without for a moment considering the harm you may be doing. You have expressed opinions which are calculated to make people

---

[1] Alexander Pope, *An Essay on Man* (1733-34), epistle 1, line 267.

discontented with things as they are. You rob them of the content which has made them comfortable heretofore, and yet you offer them nothing better in return for it. You would have society turned topsy-turvy, and all for what? Why, simply to make a wrong thing right for yourself! If your example were followed by all the unhappy people in the world, how would it end, do you think? There must be moral laws, and it is inevitable that they should press hardly on individuals occasionally; but it is clearly the duty of individuals to sacrifice themselves for the good of the community at large."

"I do not understand your morality," she said. "Do you think that, although I love another man, it would be right for me to go back and live with my husband?"

"Right, but, under the circumstances, not advisable. And, at any rate, nothing would make it moral for you to go to that other man."

"Oh! do not fill my mind with doubt," she pleaded, piteously. "I love him. Let me go."

I did not answer her, and after a while she began again, passionately—"We *are* free agents in these things. Individuals *must* know what is best for themselves. If I devote my life to him, as I propose, who would be hurt by it? Should I be less pure-minded, and would he be less upright in all his dealings? When things can be legally right though morally wrong, can they not also be morally right though legally wrong?"

"I have already tried to show you, Ideala," I answered, preparing to go over the old ground again, patiently, "that we none of us stand alone, that we are all part of this great system, and that, in cases like yours, individuals must suffer, must even be sacrificed, for the good of the rest. When the sacrifice is voluntary, we call it noble."

"If I go to him I shall have sacrificed a good deal."

"You will have sacrificed others, not yourself. He is all the world to you, Ideala; the loss would be nothing to the gain"—she hid her face in her hands—"and what is required of you is self-sacrifice. And surely it would be happier in the end for you to give him up now, than to live to feel yourself a millstone round his neck."

"I do not understand you," she said, looking up quickly.

"The world, you see, will know nothing of the fine sentiments which made you determine to take this step," I said. "You will be spoken of contemptuously, and he will be 'the fellow who is living with another man's wife, don't you know,' and that will injure him in many ways."

"Do you think so?" she asked, anxiously.

"I know it," I replied. "And look at it from that or any other point of view you like, and you must see you are making a mistake. A woman in your position sets an example whether she will or not, and even if all your best reasons for this step were made public, you would do harm by it, for there are only too many people apt enough as it is at finding specious excuses for their own shortcomings, who would be glad, if they dared, to do likewise. And you would not gain your object after all. You would neither be happy yourself, nor make Lorrimer happy. People like you are sensitive about their honour—it is the sign of their superiority; and the indulgence of love, even at the moment, and under the most favourable circumstances of youth, beauty, and intellectual equality, does not satisfy such natures, if the indulgence be not regulated and sanctified by all that men and women have devised to make their relations moral."

This was my last argument, and when I had done she sat there for a long time silent, resting her head against my knee, and scarcely breathing. She was fighting it out with herself, and I thought it best to leave her alone—besides, I had already said all there was to say; repetition would only have irritated her, and there was nothing now for it but to wait.

Outside, I could hear the dreary drip of raindrops; somewhere in the room a clock ticked obtrusively; but it was long past midnight, and the house was still. I thought that only the night and silence watched with me, and waited upon the suffering of this one poor soul.

At last she moved, uttering a low moan, like one in pain.

"I do see it," she said, almost in a whisper; "and I am willing to give him up."

"God in His mercy help you!" I prayed.

"And forgive me," she answered, humbly.

She was quite exhausted, and passively submitted when I led her to her room. I closed the shutters to keep out the cheerless dawn, and made the fire burn up, and lit the lamps. She sat silently watching me, and did not seem to think it odd that I should do this for her. She clung to me then as a little child clings to its father, and, like a father, I ministered to her, reverently, then left her, as I hoped, to sleep.

My sister opened her door as I passed. She was dressed, and had been watching, too, the whole night long.

"Well?" she asked.

I kissed her. "It is well," I answered; and she burst into tears.

"Can I go to her now?" she said.

"Yes, go." I went to Claudia's room, and waited. After a long time she returned.

"She is quiet at last," she told me, sorrowfully.

And so the long night ended.

CHAPTER XXVII.

IDEALA had returned to us quite under the impression that if she took the step she proposed we should think it right to cast her off; and that little tentative: "Must I give you up?" was the only protest she had offered. But such was not our intention. Far from it! We do not forsake our friends in their bodily ailments, and we are poor, pitiful, egotistical creatures indeed when we desert them for their mental and moral maladies, leaving them to struggle against them and fight them out or succumb to them alone, according to their strength and circumstances. The world will forsake them fast enough, and that is sufficient punishment—if they deserve punishment. Of course, Ideala could never have come back to us as an honoured guest again, after taking such a step, but she would have continued to fill the same place in our affections, if not in our esteem.

"And you will drive everybody else away, and keep the house empty all the year round, in order to be able to receive her—*and* Mr. Lorrimer—whenever they choose to visit us," Claudia had declared when we discussed the subject.

That was not quite what I intended; but I had made Ideala understand that nothing she could do would affect her intercourse with us. I told her so at once, because I would not have her alter her determination for any consideration but the highest. She might at the last have hesitated to separate herself from us for ever; but I felt sure if that were the case, and it was not a better motive entirely which deterred her, she would not be satisfied eventually; and I know now that I was right.

Ideala wrote to Lorrimer, and when she had finished her letter I found that she intended to impose a terrible task upon me.

"Until you know him yourself you will always misjudge him," she said. "I want you to take him my letter, and make his acquaintance."

I hesitated.

"It is the least you can do," she pleaded. "I shall be easier in my mind if you will. It will be better for him to see you, and hear all the things I cannot tell him in my letter; and—and—if I must not see him myself it will be a comfort to see somebody who has. Do go. I shall be pained if you refuse."

This decided me, and I went at once.

It was a long journey, the same that Ideala herself had taken under such very different circumstances so short a time before. I thought of her going in doubt and uncertainty, her own feelings col-ouring the aspect of all she saw on the way; and returning in the first warm glow of her great and unexpected joy—her new-found happiness which was destined, alas! to be so short-lived. Miserable fate which robbed her of all that would have made her life worth having—a husband on whom she could rely; her child; and now the man upon whom she had been prepared to lavish the long pent-up passion, the concentrated devotion of her great and noble nature! Poor starved heart, crushed back upon itself, suffering silently, suf-fering always, but never hardening—on the contrary, growing ten-derer for others the more it had to endure itself! Would it always be so? Was there no peace on earth for Ideala? No one who could be all her own? I felt responsible for this last hard blow; had I done well? The rush and rattle of the train shaped itself into a sort of sub-chorus to my thoughts as we sped through the pleasant fields: *Was it right? Was it right? Was it right?* And I saw Ideala, with soft, sad eyes, pleading—mutely pleading—pleading always for some pleasure in life, some natural, womanly joy, while youth and the power to love lasted. By an effort of will I banished the question. I told myself that my action in the matter had been expedient from every point of view; but presently:

> The rush of the grinding steel!
> The thundering crank, and the mighty wheel!

took me to task again, and the chorus now became: *Expediency right!*
Expediency right! Expediency right! which, when I banished it, resolved
itself into: *Cold, proud Puritan! Cold, proud Puritan!* for the rest of the
way.

But the journey ended at last—though that was little relief with
the task I had before me still unaccomplished.

A bulbous functionary took my card to Lorrimer when I pre-
sented myself at the Great Hospital next day, and returning presently
informed me that Mr. Lorrimer was disengaged, and would see me
at once, if I would be so good as to come this way. How familiar
the whole proceeding seemed! And how well I knew the place! the
soothing silence, the massive grandeur, the long, dimly lighted gallery to the right, the door at which the servant stopped and knocked,
the man who opened it, and met my eyes fearlessly, bowing with
natural grace, and bidding me enter—a tall, fair man; self-contained
and dignified; cold, pale, and unimpassioned—so I thought—but my
equal in every way: the man who was "all the world" to Ideala.

When I saw him I understood.

* * * * *

Lorrimer, after dismissing his secretary, was the first to speak.

"You come to me from Ideala?" he said. "Is there anything wrong?
Is she ill?"

And I fancied he turned a trifle paler as the fear flashed through
his mind.

I reassured him. "Physically she is better," I said.

"But mentally?" he interposed. "You give her no peace."

I was silent.

"I know you are no friend of mine," he added.

"On the contrary," I answered. "I hope I am the best friend you
have just now."

"I know what that means," he said. "You have tried to dissuade
Ideala, and having failed, you have come here to use your influence
with me."

"No," I answered. "I have not come to discuss the subject. I have brought you a letter from Ideala at her special request, and I am ready to take her any reply which you may think fit to send."

I gave him the letter, and rose to go, but he detained me.

"Stay till I have read it, if you can spare me the time," he said. "It is just possible that there is something in it which we *ought* to discuss."

I turned to the mantelpiece, and tried to interest myself in the lovely things with which it was crowded; but never in my life did my heart sink so for another; never have I endured such moments of pained suspense.

I heard him open the envelope; I heard the paper rustle as he turned the page; and then there was silence—

> Full of the city's stilly sound—

a moment only, but filled with

> Something which possess'd
> The darkness of the world, delight,
> Life, anguish, death, immortal love.
> Ceasing not, mingled, unrepress'd,
> Apart from space, withholding time—[1]

a moment's silence, and then a heavy fall. Lorrimer had fainted.

* * * * *

I stayed three days at the Great Hospital, three days of the most delightful converse. At first, Lorrimer had rebelled, not realizing that Ideala's last decision was irrevocable.

"You have over persuaded her," he said.

"No," I answered; "I have convinced her. And I shall convince you, too."

He pleaded for her pathetically, not for himself at all. "She has had so little joy!" he said; using the very words that had occurred to me. "And I wanted to silence her. I wanted to save her from her fate. For she is *une des cinq ou six créatures humaines qui naissent, dans tout*

---

[1] Tennyson, "Recollections of Arabian Nights" (1830), lines 103 and 71-75. The last line is a misquotation; the line should read: "Apart from place, withholding time—"

un siècle, pour aimer la vérité, et pour mourir sans avoir pu la faire aimer des autres.[1] She must suffer terribly if she goes on."

This was a point upon which we differed. He would have given her the natural joys of a woman—husband, home, children, friends, and only such intellectual pursuits which are pleasant. *I* had always hoped to see her at work in a wider field. But she was one of those rare women who are born to fulfil both destinies at once, and worthily, if only circumstances had made it possible for her to combine the two.

Before I had been with him many hours, I began to be sensible of that difference of feeling on certain subjects which would have made their union a veritable linking of the past to the future—his belief that nothing can be better than what has been, and that the old institutions revised are all that the world wants; and her faith in future developments of all good ideas, and further discoveries never yet imagined. For one thing, Lorrimer considered famine and war inevitable scourges of the human race, necessary for the removal of the surplus population, and useless to contend against, because destined to recur, so long as there is a human race; but he would have limited intellectual pursuits for women, because culture is held to prevent the trouble for which the elder expedients only provided a cure—a point upon which Ideala did not agree with him at all. "Nothing is more disastrous to social prosperity," she held, "or more likely to add to the criminal classes, than families which are too large for their parents to bring up, and educate comfortably, in their own station. If the higher education of women is a natural check on over production of that kind, then encourage it thankfully as a merciful dispensation of providence for the prevention of much misery. I can see no reason in nature or ethics for a teeming population only brought into existence to be removed by famine and war. Why, this old green ball of an earth would roll on just as merrily without any of us."

* * * * *

Lorrimer wrote to her at last. He had been obliged to acquiesce; and I took Ideala his letter; but she, womanlike, though nothing would have altered her decision, was not at first satisfied with his

---

[1] George Sand, *Jacques* (1834), "one of five or six human beings in any century born to love truth, and die having made others love it."

compliance. It seemed to her too ready; and that made her doubt if she might not have been to blame after all. They wrote to each other once again, and when she received his last letter, she spoke to me about it.

"He must have seen it as you do from the first, for he has said no word to alter my determination—rather the contrary," she told me. "We are not to meet again, nor to correspond; and doubtless it is a relief to him to have the matter settled in this way; but one thing puzzles me. In my last letter I bade him good-bye, adding 'since that is what you wish,' and he has replied: 'I never said I wished it; will you remember that?' I do remember it, and it comforts me; but why?"

I knew that Lorrimer had said little in order to make her sacrifice as easy for her as possible; and I was silent, too, for the same reason. I thought if she felt herself to blame, her pride would come to the rescue and make her loss appear rather inevitable than voluntary. For, say what we will, we reconcile ourselves to the inevitable sooner than to those sorrows which we might have saved ourselves had we deemed it right.

"You insinuated once that it was all *my* fault," she said. "Perhaps it was—if fault there be. But if I tempted him, it must have been generosity that made him yield to the temptation. He pitied me, and was ready to make me happy by devoting himself to me, since that was what I seemed to require. And I agree with you now. I don't think we should either of us have found any real happiness in that way. But, oh, how I long for him! for his friendship! for his companionship! for his love! It is hard, hard, hard if he does not miss me as I do him."

Then I told her: "But he does. And he did not yield to your decision until I had convinced him that he could never make you happy in such a position."

A great sigh of relief escaped her. And then I saw that I ought to have been frank with her from the first. It strengthened her to know that they still had something left to them in common, though that something was only their grief.

I tried to comfort her by speaking of the many ways in which she might still find happiness. She listened patiently until I was obliged to stop for want of words, then she said:

"This is all very well, but you know you are talking nonsense.

What is the use of offering people everything but the one thing needful? What I say to myself is:

> Well, I have had my turn, have been
>   Raised from the darkness of the clod,
> And for a glorious moment seen
>   The brightness of the skirts of God.[1]

And I try to think I have no right to complain, but still I am not better satisfied than the child that has eaten its cake and wants to have it too. And I suppose there are many who would call me wretched, and say that my life, with my sorrowful marriage—which was no marriage, but a desecration of that holy state, and a sin—and my hopeless love, is a broken life. Certainly *I* feel it so. And yet I don't know. With his nature it seems to me that some wrongdoing was inevitable. Do you think my suffering might be taken as expiation for his sins? Do you think we are allowed the happiness of bearing each other's burdens in that way if we will? If I were sure of that I should not fancy, as I used to, that I had a work to do in the world; I should know that my work is done, and that now I may rest. Ah, the blessing of rest!"

Not long after this a cruel rumour reached us, on good authority, that Lorrimer was engaged to be married. I confess that my feeling about it was one of unmitigated contempt for the man, and I trembled for the effect of the news upon Ideala. She made no sign, however, when first she heard it. I was surprised, and fear I showed that I was, in spite of myself, for she spoke about it.

"You do not understand," she said. "One event in his career is not of more consequence to me than another, because all are of the greatest consequence. But I have none of the dog-in-the-manger spirit. I think there must be something almost maternal in my feeling for him, which is why it does not change. Were I less constant it would prove that my affection is of a lower kind, less enduring because less pure. I do not care to talk about him, but I think of him always. I think of him as I saw him last with the sun on him. Do you know his hair is like light gold with the sun on it. Sometimes the memory of him fades a little, and I cannot recall his features, and

---

[1] William Cullen Bryant, "Life" (1864), lines 33-36.

then I am tormented; but of course he comes back to me—so vividly that I have started often when I looked up and found myself alone. The desire to be with him never lessens; it burns in me always, and is both a pain and a pleasure. But my love is too great to be selfish. His wishes for himself are my wishes, and what is best for him is happiest for me. Am I never jealous? Jealous! No! Do you not know that he is mine, mine through every change? Neither time nor distance separates us really. No common tie can keep him from me. Let him be bound as, and to whomsoever he pleases, his soul is mine, and must return to me sooner or later. I like him to be happy in any way that is right, for I know that what he gives to others is not himself. I was not fit for the dear earthly love, but perhaps, if I keep myself pure, body and soul, for him, I shall be made worthy at last, and of something better. And my love is so great it would draw him in spite of himself; but it will not be in spite of himself, for he will find by-and-by that he cannot live with a smaller soul, and then he will come to me. Do you not understand what I want? His soul—purified, strengthened, ennobled—nothing less will satisfy me; and his mother might ask as much. If I might be made the means of saving it——" Then after a little pause, she added: "Ah, how beautiful death is! He will be glad, as I should be now, to meet it—and yet more glad! for then the end will have come for him, but I should have still to wait."

The rumour of Lorrimer's engagement, however, proved to be false. It was another Lorrimer, a cousin of his.

"Lorrimer is restored to your good graces now, I suppose," Claudia said, in her half sarcastic way, when the mistake was explained. I had not told her what was in my mind; she had read my thoughts. "You think that a man whom Ideala has loved should consider himself sacred," she added.

I did not answer. But I hold that all men who have felt or inspired great love will be sanctified by it if there be any true nobility in their nature; and I knew that one man, whom Ideala did not love, had been so sanctified by love for her, and held himself sacred always.

But it was a relief to my mind to know that Lorrimer was not unworthy. He was a distinguished man then, and I felt sure that he would become still more distinguished eventually. He was not one of the many who come and go, and are forgotten; but one of those destined to live for ever

In minds made better by their presence.[1]

The good in his nature was certainly as far above the average as were his splendid abilities, and Ideala was right when she declared that she could answer for his principles. It is impulse that is beyond calculation, and for his own or another's impulses no wise man will answer.

Ideala continued to droop.

"She will never get over it;" I said to Claudia one day, when we were alone together.

"Indeed she will," Claudia answered, confidently. "Out of the depth of your profound ignorance of natural history do you speak, my brother. I dread the reaction, though. When it comes she will be overwhelmed with shame; but it will come. All this is only a phase. She is in a state of transition now. It is her pride that makes her nurse her grief, and will not let her give him up. She cannot bear to think that she, of all women in the world, should have been the victim of anything so trivial as a passing fancy. Not that it would have been a passing fancy if they had not been separated; but as it is—why, no fire can burn without fuel."

Claudia had evidently changed her mind, and she might be right; but my own fear was that her first impression would be justified, and that Ideala would never be able to take a healthy interest in anything again.

"I cannot care," was her constant complaint. "Nothing ever touches me either painfully or pleasurably. Nothing will ever make me glad again."

She said this one evening when she was sitting alone with Claudia and myself, and there was a long silence after she had finished speaking, during which she sat in a dejected attitude, her face buried in her hands.

All at once she looked up.

"It is very strange," she said, "but half that feeling seems to have gone with the expression of it."

"I think," Claudia decided, in her common-sense tone, "that you are nursing this unholy passion, Ideala. You are afraid to give

---

[1] George Eliot, "O May I Join the Choir Invisible" (1867), line 3.

it up lest there should be nothing left to you. Can you not free your mind from the trammels of it, and grasp something higher, better, and nobler? Can you not become mistress of yourself again, and enter on a larger life which shall be full of love—not the narrow, selfish passion you are cherishing for one, but that pure and holy love which only the best—and such women as you may always be of the best—can feel for all? If you could but get the fumes of this evil feeling out of yourself, you would see, as we see, what a common thing it is, and you would recognize, as we recognize, that your very expression of it is just such as is given to it by every hysterical man or woman that has ever experienced it. It is a physical condition caused by contact, and kept up by your own perverse pleasure in it—nothing more. Everyone grows out of it in time, and anyone with proper self-control could conquer it. You are wavering yourself. You see, now that you have crystallised the feeling into words, that it is a pitiful thing after all, that the object is not worth such an expenditure of strength—certainly not worth the sacrifice of your power to enjoy anything else. Such devotion to the memory of a dead husband has been thought grand by some, although for my part I can see nothing grand in any form of self-indulgence, whether it be the indulgence of sorrow or joy, which narrows our sphere of usefulness, and causes us to neglect the claims of those who love us upon our affection, and the claims of our fellow creatures generally upon our consideration; but in your case it is simply——" Claudia paused for want of a word.

"You would say it is simply degrading," Ideala interposed. "I do not feel it so. I glory in it."

"I know," said Claudia, pitilessly. "You all do." And then she got up, and laid her hand on Ideala's shoulder. "It is time," she said, earnestly,

> "It is time, O passionate heart and morbid eye,
> That old hysterical mock-disease should die."[1]

---

[1] Tennyson, "Maud," Part 3, lines 32-33.

CHAPTER XXVIII.

I HOPED Claudia's plain speaking had made an impression, but for a long time after that it seemed as if Ideala's interest in life had really ended, that her sphere of usefulness had contracted, and that she herself would become like the rest—a doer of unconnected trifles that have meaning only as the straws have meaning which show which way the current sets. One cannot help thinking how many of these significant straws must go down to the ocean and be lost, their little use unrecognized, their little labour unavailing: because it does so little good merely to know which way the stream is setting, or what ocean will receive it at last, if we have no power to profit by the knowledge. At this time Ideala's own life was not unlike one of these hapless straws, and it seemed a wretched failure of its early promise, that ending as a straw on the common stream, when so little might have made her influence in her own sphere like the river itself, strong and beautiful. Those who loved her watched her in her trouble with eager hope that some good might yet come of it; but the hope diminished always as the days wore on. At first her mind had raged and stormed; one could see it, though she said so little. Her renunciation was perfect, but nevertheless she could not reconcile herself to it. She would not go back, but she could not go on, and so she remained midway between the past, which was hateful to her, and the future, which was a blank, raging at both. But gradually the storm subsided; and then came a period of calm, but whether it was the calm of apathy or the calm of resignation it was hard to say—and meantime she lost her health again, and became so fragile that my sister only expressed what I felt when she was speaking of her one day, and said, sadly:

> "Her cheek is so waxenly thin
> As if deathward 'twere whitening in,
> And the cloud of her flesh, still more white,
> Were clearing till soul is in sight.

* * * * *

Her large eyes too liquidly glister!
Her mouth is too red.
                    Have they kissed her—
The angels that bend down to pull
Our buds of the Beautiful,
And whispered their own little Sister?"[1]

We were anxious to take her abroad, but she would not accompany us. She talked of going alone, but she did not go, and after a time we gave up thinking about it. Then one day, quite suddenly, she said: "It *is* time this old hysterical mock-disease should die," and she told us that she had at last decided to travel—somewhere; nothing more definite than that, for she said she had no fixed plans. We concluded, however, that she meant to be away some time, for she said something about perils of the deep, and the uncertainty of life generally, and she confided her private papers to my care, telling me to look at them if they would interest me, and make what use of them I pleased; and that was how those from which I have gathered much of her story came into my possession. And then she left us, and for a whole year we heard nothing of her, not one word. Claudia chafed a little, and complained, as women will when things do not arrange themselves exactly as they would have ordered them; but I was content to wait, and, because I expected nothing, the time did not seem so long as perhaps it might have done. We lived our usual life—part of the year in one of the Eastern counties, and part in London, and then we came North again. It was winter weather, frosty and clear and bright, and I was tempted out a great deal, taking long rides, begun before sunset and ending by moonlight, and generally alone. And always when the world seemed most beautiful I thought of Ideala, and how she had loved its beauty—mountain and plain, flood and field, forest and flower, the snow and the sunshine, and all the alternations of light and shade; the wonders of form, and the depth and harmony of colour; the blue sky by day, with its glories of sunrise and sunset; the dark sky by night, with its moonlight and starlight—the sky always! that cloudland to which, when we are

---

[1] Gerald Massey, "The White Child," lines 22-25 and 34-39. Massey (1828-1907) is best known as an Egyptologist, but he published a number of poetry collections. "The White Child" appeared in *A Tale of Eternity and Other Poems* (1869).

wearied by the more monotonous earth, we had only to lift our eyes
and there the scene is changing for ever—the sky—and the sea:

> In all its vague immensity![1]

Would she ever see it again in the old way? When she left us one
might have said of her mental state—

> O dark, dark, dark, amid the blaze of noon—
> Irrecoverably dark, total eclipse
> Without all hope of day![2]

And where was she now? and was she learning to see again? I own
I sometimes had the presumption to think that if she had stayed
with us I might have helped her. It seemed hardly credible that she
should be able to stand alone at such a time, not to speak of the
strength required to take her out of herself. And was not the loneliness itself an added misery? She never could bear to be alone, and
I always thought the worst trial of her married life was the mental
solitude to which it had reduced her by making her feel the necessity for reserve, even with her best friends. Of course she had chosen to go alone; it was quite her own doing; but I could not help
thinking, uneasily at times, that she would not have gone at all if
she had not noticed how anxious we were about her, and fancied
she could relieve us of our trouble by relieving us of her presence.
That would have been so like Ideala! And then my thoughts would
wander off, recalling her numberless little deeds of love, her perfect
selflessness, and all the depth and beauty of her great and tender
nature, as we do recall such things of one who has gone and will
nevermore return, as in the old days, to make us glad. There was
the day I had seen her from the club window stoop to pick up a little ragged barefooted child that was crying in the street, and wrap
her furs about it and carry it off, smiling and happy, in her arms,
with no more thought of the attention such an action would attract
than if she had been alone with her waif in the desert. But many
and many a time, and in many a way, she had made glad hearts by

---

[1] Henry Wadsworth Longfellow, Part 5, "The Inn at Genoa," *Christus—The Golden Legend* (1872-73), line 2.
[2] John Milton, *Samson Agonistes* (1671), lines 80-82.

deeds like that, and now where was she? And was there never a one in the whole wide world to help her to bear her own sorrow and ease her pain?

One evening in particular I had been more than usually tormented by such thoughts. I had been blaming myself bitterly for having allowed her to go away alone, and when I rode up to my own door I was conscious of a half-formed resolution to follow her without delay and bring her back.

Claudia was standing on the steps in the crisp, fresh evening air, apparently watching for me. She put her arms round my neck when I alighted, and kissed me.

"Has she written?" I exclaimed, for Claudia was not demonstrative, and this meant something.

"She is here," was the answer.

My heart gave a great leap, but I could not ask if it were well with her. I could only look at Claudia, and wonder if it were the moonlight that made the expression of her face so singularly content and sweet.

I went into the lighted house, and being somewhat dazed and altogether too eager to see her at once, I dressed for the evening, leisurely, and then I went to find her. There was a change in the house already. It was lighted from top to bottom as befits a time of rejoicing, and our other guests, whom I passed in my search, seemed gayer—or I fancied so. She was not among them, but I took the liberty of going to her rooms and knocked at the sitting-room door, and entered. She rose to receive me, stretching out her hands, and my first impression was that she had grown! afterwards I understood that it was a change in the fashion of her dress that made it appear so. She wore a long robe, exquisitely draped, which was loose, but yet clung to her, and fell in rich folds about her with a grace that satisfied. I cannot describe the fashion of this robe, or the form, but I have seen one like it somewhere—it must have been in a picture, or on a statue of a grand heroic woman or a saint; and it suggested something womanly and strong, but not to be defined.

It was Ideala, herself—not as she had been, but as I always hoped she would be, and felt she might. She showed the change in every gesture, but most of all in her clear and steady eyes, which made you feel she had a purpose now, and a future yet before her. She looked as women look when they know themselves entrusted with a work, and have the courage and resolution to be true and worthy of their trust. She was very gracious, but somehow in the first moment of our meeting I felt abashed—abashed before this woman who had gone down to the verge of dishonour, but whose goodness, with the vitality of all goodness, had raised her again above the best; whose trouble had been to her, because of this goodness, as is a painful operation which must be gone through if the patient would ever be strong.

I fancy she thought me cold because my great respect made me shy, and I hesitated to show her all the joy I felt.

"Won't you kiss me once after my long, long voyage?" she said, holding up her face like a child to be kissed. And it made me inexpressibly glad, to perceive that, while gaining in dignity and purpose, her character had lost none of the childlike faith and affection which had been one of the greatest charms of the old Ideala. I could not help examining her curiously, looking for traces of a conflict, for those lines of suffering which are generally left by fierce mental troubles like scars after a battle, showing that the fight has been no child's play, but a struggle for life or death. Such a conflict there must have been, but all trace of it was swept away by the wonderful peace that had succeeded it. Ideala looked younger, certainly, but the change showed itself most in her perfect serenity, and in the steadfast earnestness of her wonderful eyes.

But I had no time to talk to her, for Claudia, in diamonds and velvet and lace—her donning of which is her one way of expressing a satisfaction too deep for words—blazed in upon us. If it had occurred so her, she would certainly have had the bells of the parish rung—provided my authority as lay Rector could have accomplished such an extravagance. She took us away with her now to join our other guests, and when dinner was announced I offered Ideala my arm. She was silent as we went, but looked about her with a grave little smile on her lips, renewing her acquaintance with familiar objects, and noting every change. And so busy was she with her own reflections, so thoroughly absorbed, that, when we were seated at table, she put her serviette beside her plate and her bread on her lap mechanically, and took up her knife and fork to eat her soup. She seemed puzzled for a moment when she found that the implements did not answer, and then she laughed! Such a fresh, girlish laugh! It did one's heart good to hear her! Yes, verily! Ideala was herself again, absent-mindedness and all.

And before dinner was over a wonderful thing had happened. For whereas we had hitherto been the most commonplace and prosaic party imaginable, getting along smoothly, taking no particular interest in each other, or in anything else, and only remarkable for a degree of dulness which would have astonished us by its bulk could it have been weighed and measured—to-night, for no apparent reason, we suddenly woke up and astounded ourselves by more originality than we had been accustomed to believe was left in the world altogether—while something put into our conversation just the right amount of polite friction to act as a counter-irritant, so that, when we left the table, each felt that he had been at his best—had been brilliant, in fact, and shone with lustre enough to make any man happy.

Once in a London theatre I saw an actress walk across the stage. She did not utter a word, she never looked at the audience, she was apparently unconscious of everything but what she had in her own mind; yet before she was half across the stage the people rose to their feet with a roar. Ideala's coming amongst us had produced some such startling effect; but *her* power was altogether occult. The audience knew what the actress meant, but we did not understand Ideala, and yet we applauded by laying our best before her, and acknowledged the charm of her presence in every word. She spoke very little, however. Indeed, I remember nothing she said until we went to the drawing-room. On the way thither Claudia had picked up a crumpled paper, and, glancing at it, had exclaimed—"Why, Ideala, here are some of your verses! Do you still write verses?"

It was curious that we all spoke as if she had been away for years.

"Yes," she answered, tranquilly; and Claudia coolly proceeded to read the verses aloud, a difficult task, as they were scribbled in pencil on half a sheet of note paper, and were scarcely decipherable. Ideala, meanwhile, listened, with calm eyes fixed on vacancy, like one trying to be polite, but finding it hard for lack of interest.

"By Arno, when the tale was o'er,
At sunset, as in days of yore,
  I wandered forth and dreamed.
The sky above, the town below,
The solemn river's silent flow,
The ancient story-haunts I know,
  In varied colours gleamed.

By Arno calm my steps I stayed,
Just where the river's bank displayed
  A tangled growth of weeds;
Tall houses near, and on the right
An arched bridge upreared its height,
And boats drew near, and passed from sight—
  I heard the tramp of steeds.

I heard, and saw, but heeded not;
My feet were rooted to the spot,
  A fancy checked my breath.
'Twas here that Tito lay, I knew,
His fair face upward to the blue,
His velvet tunic soaking through,
  Most beautiful in death.

But Baldassarre was not there.
'Twas I that stooped to kiss the hair,
  Besprent with ooze and dew.
Ah, God! light gold the locks caressed—
I saw no Greek in velvet dressed—
But wildly to my bosom pressed—
  Not Tito, love, but you!

The massive, godlike head and throat
Belonged not to those days remote,
  The fine grey eye—the limb;
It was the soul I know so well,
So full of earth, and heaven, and hell,
That came from out that time to dwell
  In you and make you him.

And I, the victim of your smiles,
And I, the victim of your wiles,
  My vengeance shall prevail.
The river Time shall float you nigh,
And earth and hell your soul shall fly,
And only heaven remain when I
  The deed triumphant hail!"

It surprised me to find that Claudia could read those verses to the end, their import—to me, at least—was so obvious. But Ideala continued unmoved; and when the little buzz of friendly criticism had subsided, she remarked, with unimpassioned directness:

"I am quite sure that all my verses are rubbish; but nevertheless they delight me. I should feel dumb without the power to make verses; it is a means of expression that satisfies when nothing else will. I always carry my last about in my pocket. I know them by heart, of course, but still it is a pleasure to read them; and so it continues until I write some more; and then I immediately perceive that the old ones are bad, and I destroy them—when I remember. Those were condemned ages ago, so please oblige me, Claudia, by putting them into the fire."

Claudia was about to obey, but I interposed. I had a fancy for keeping those verses. They are rubbishy if you will; but the sentiment which struggles to find expression in them is far from despicable.

No one smoked that evening; no one played billiards; no one cared for music; we just sat round the fire in a circle, and talked.

"And where have you come from, Ideala?" was the first question.

"From China," she answered.

There was a general exclamation.

"I have been with the missionaries in China," she added.

"Oh, isn't it very strange, the life in China?" someone asked.

"It looks different," she said, "but it feels like our own. To begin with, one is struck by the strange appearance of the people, and the quaint humour of their art; but when the first effect wears off, and you learn to know them, you find after all that theirs is the same human nature, only in another garb; the familiar old tune, as it were, with a new set of variations. The like in unlikeness is common enough, but still the finding of a remarkable similarity in things apparently unlike continues to surprise us."

"But, Ideala, you cannot compare the Chinese to ourselves! Think of the state of degradation the people are in! Every crime is rife among them—infanticide is quite common!"

"Yes," said Ideala, as if it were the most natural thing in the world.[1] "I learnt something about that from a missionary lady in Central Chekiang.[2] Of course, as I do not speak the language I had to get all my information second-hand, from the missionaries."

"Don't you speak the language, Ideala?" Claudia asked.

Ideala laughed. "No," she said. "And I don't think such a collection of unintelligible sounds should be dignified with the name of language.[3] I only learnt two words while I was there, and I'm not sure that I know them properly. They sounded like 'nin sek,' and I believe they meant second course, for the butler always bawled them out at the cook when he took out the soup, and that was how I learnt them. One gentleman, who speaks three European languages perfectly, told me that after living two years among the people at Canton, hearing nothing but Chinese spoken, and working hard at the language the whole time, he was only just able to make himself understand a little, and could scarcely make out anything that was said to him. Yet some of the audacious missionary ladies actually blame themselves severely for still finding it difficult to preach to the people in Chinese, after a lengthy residence of fifteen months in the country!"

"But don't they find it very hard to get amongst the people?"

"Yes, at first. In new districts women fly from them terrified."

"How absurd!"

"It seems so; but I fancy if all our nearest and dearest friends, those whom we have most confidence in, assured us with one accord that a stranger's only object in coming amongst us was to make medicine of us, we should not meet them ourselves with all the cordiality they

---

[1] This is the beginning of a section that was deleted from the Donohue, Henneberry & Co. edition.

[2] Also called Zhejiang, Chekiang is a small province along the East China Sea.

[3] Imperialist biases of the Victorian period are evident in some of Ideala's comments about the Chinese. For more on Grand's investment in the British Empire, see Iveta Jusová, The New Woman and the Empire (Columbus: Ohio State University Press, 2005).

might expect at our hands. The Chinese women are very affectionate and kind when once you know them—just like ourselves. In fact,
a Chinese lady is the same idea translated into a foreign language;
she loses something, but she also gains by the translation. She has
the advantage of possessing a bigger brain. After the great typhoon
in Hong Kong a few years ago—you remember my telling you about
it, Claudia? twenty thousand people were killed, according to the
official report.[1] I was there at the time. Afterwards, they weighed the
brains of some of the women of the coolie class—the lowest grade
of Chinese society, you know—who had perished, and they found
that the average weight was 45 1/2 ounces, which is one ounce and
a half above the European, and half an ounce above the average
Scotchman![2] One of the first missionary ladies who went to Peking
told some curious stories about the northern women. She said that,
possibly owing to the introduction of the Manchu element, they differed slightly from the southerns; but I didn't find, myself, that there
was as much difference as there is between an English woman and
a Scotch one. They are excessively timid. At first she could scarcely
get a glimpse of her neighbours. When she surprised one of them
standing at her gate, and, anxious to ingratiate herself, inquired
effusively, with a benign smile: 'Have you eaten your rice?' the lady
invariably turned and fled, and if she had a child in her arms she
would hide its face on her bosom to keep it from the missionary's
'evil eye.' But when at last they came to understand that the foreign
lady had really kind intentions and she began to know them, she
found them shrewd and clever regarding anything that had fallen

---

[1] Grand writes about this typhoon, which took place on September 22, 1874, in
"The Great Typhoon," which appeared in *Aunt Judy's Magazine for Young People*,
1 April 1881, 358-370. This article is reprinted in Ann Heilmann and Stephanie
Forward, *Sex, Social Purity and Sarah Grand: Volume 4: Selected Shorter Writings (2)*
(London: Routledge, 2001), 33-46.

[2] This comment points to the nineteenth-century belief that the weight of a
person's brain determined his or her intelligence: supposedly, the heavier the
brain, the smarter the person was. Also, the English often assumed European
brains to be heavier than those of non-Europeans, so Ideala is poking fun at
this assumption by pointing out that a Chinese woman of the lower class had
a heavier brain than a European. In 1895, *The Woman's Signal*, a feminist newspaper that admired Grand's work, questioned this assumption too, in an article
titled "Weight in Sex," 29 August 1895, 131.

within their range, very quick to learn; and they have much tact and delicacy of feeling. In fact, all classes have that. Once, in the Tung-chow district, at one of the An-hing villages two foreign ladies were sitting on a "kong,"[1] eating their breakfast. Thirty people crowded into the room to see them; four boys stood on the table to have a better view, and some enterprising youths outside tore holes in the paper window to have a glimpse at the Foreign children."

"I thought they called strangers 'Foreign Devils,'"[2] I interrupted.

"Yes, generally, but you see they were disposed to be friendly that day, and the term referred to their estimate of the intellectual capacity of their guests. The room was suffocating, and the glare of so many eyes not so pleasant.

"'Do you know,' one of the Foreigners asked an old lady, 'what I have been doing? I have been counting the number of persons in this room.' For a moment the old lady looked disconcerted, then she said apologetically: 'We have never seen any heavenly people before,' which, you must acknowledge," Ideala added, "was a magnificent compliment.

"But the ladies are really well-bred, and many of them well-educated, accomplished, and thoroughly good housekeepers, not at all 'suppressed,' I am told, after all these centuries of degradation and ill-usage. The elasticity of their nature is wonderful, and so is their desire to learn and improve themselves, and their unconquerable perseverance. Strength of character in its women is an element of greatness and a source of longevity in a nation, and I believe China owes the fact that she has continued to flourish, while so many other nations have decayed and crumbled away, entirely to the pluck and constancy of her women."

"But I always thought," Claudia objected, "that Chinese women

---

[1] A kong is a bed, with space under it to place coals to keep the sleepers warm in the winter. It also is used as a sitting bench, where people eat meals. The location, in the Tung-chow district, likely is near Peking, since there is a Tung-chow pagoda near the city.

[2] This term also appears in Grand's "Ah, Man: A Study from Life," a story about the relationship between Chinese servants and their European masters, which appeared in *Woman at Home*, vol. 1, no. 1, 1893, 24-30. This article is reprinted in Ann Heilmann and Stephanie Forward, *Sex, Social Purity and Sarah Grand: Volume 4: Selected Shorter Writings (2)* (London: Routledge, 2001), 48-54.

were mere slaves, and had no voice whatever either in the affairs of the nation or of the household."

"Ah, then you have never heard of the Queens Regent of China!" Ideala replied. "I went out with much the same idea, and was not surprised to find that we were constantly asked: 'In your country, do the women rule?' But when our position was explained to them, I *was* surprised to hear that they answered: 'Ah! the right of final decision lies with the men, does it? That is just as it is here; we consult together, and the man decides.' The Chinese will not allow that they ill-use their women. There was a meeting at Swatow[1] in 1879 to discuss this question, and the native speakers argued so strongly in proof of the ill-usage that they made the men feel uncomfortable, it seems—which, in China, is tantamount to producing a strong impression here. But they got out of the difficulty by asserting that the women did not always treat *them* well! And, really, if you were a Chinaman, with your mother at the head of your house, ruling you, and your wife, and your children, with a word that is not to be gainsaid, you might think so too."

"But are the missionaries successful? Do they make many converts?"

"Yes, considering the tenacity with which the people cling to their convictions, and the strength of their prejudices, a great many; and that reminds me of the missionary lady's story, which I was going to tell you when you spoke of infanticide. A certain Mrs. Chang, described as a bright young woman, the wife of a native preacher, said to this lady once: 'We have often spoken to my mother about the doctrine of salvation, in which we ourselves find so much peace and joy, but she laughs, and says she does not find so much difference between old Buddha and Jesus Christ. That many a time Buddha has answered her prayers. "And what if the priest *does* get a few cash out of me, do we not all 'k 'ao tien ch 'ih fan?'"[2] Sometimes she gets angry, and says she will give me a taste of a green bamboo for my impertinence. "You say your religion teaches you to respect your

---

[1] Also called Shantou, this city is a port on the South China Sea and was opened as a Treaty Port in 1861. The meeting referred to here was likely held by one of the mission groups that worked in the area to convert the Chinese to Christianity.

[2] We depend on Heaven for our food.

father and mother, and this is the way you do it, by telling mother she is going to hell." (Here follow sundry choice expressions.) 'What is the use of talking to her?' Mrs. Chang added, thoughtfully; and then after a pause she went on to say, 'I am the first of a family of eight. My mother tells me that, at my birth, she was angry because I was a girl, but, thinking I should be useful in cooking the rice, and washing the clothes, she did her best for me.' The missionary congratulated Mrs. Chang upon her immunity from those strange sicknesses and accidents which so frequently befall girls of a few days old. Then she said, 'Two brothers were born, who are still alive—afterwards three girls in succession, none of whom lived beyond a few hours. The fact is my mother drowned them all.'[1] Yes, doubtless, the lower classes in China kill their children; here, in certain districts, they insure them," Ideala concluded gravely.

"But then," said Claudia—"Oh! Ideala, I don't think you can establish your parallel. We all know the sort of a life a Chinese lady leads."

"When the lady is not at the head of her house it is certainly vacuous," Ideala agreed, "like the lives of our own ladies when they are not forced to do anything. Why, at Scarborough this year they had to take to changing their dresses four times a day; so you can imagine how they languish for want of occupation."

"Well, at all events, English girls are not sold into a hateful form of slavery," someone observed contentedly.

"Are they not?" Ideala rejoined with a flash. "I can assure you that both women and men, fathers, husbands, and brothers, of the same class in England, do sell their young girls—and I can prove it."

"We have the pull over them in the matter of marriage, then. We don't give our daughters away against their will as they do."

"That is not a fair way of putting it. A Chinese girl expects to be so disposed of, and accepts the arrangement as a matter of course. And the system has its advantages. The girl has no illusions to be shattered, she expects no new happiness in her married life, so that any that comes to her is clear gain. As to our daughters' inclinations not being forced, I suppose they are not, exactly. But have you never been conscious of the tender pressure that is brought to bear when a

---

[1] This is the end of a section deleted from the Donohue, Henneberry & Co. edition.

desirable suitor offers? Have you never seen a girl who won't marry when she is wanted to, wincing from covert stabs, mourning over cold looks, and made to feel outside everything—suffering a small martyrdom under the general displeasure of all for whom she cares, her world, without whose love life is a burden to her; whom she believes to know best about everything? As Mrs. Bread said about Madame de Cintré: 'She is a delicate creature, and they make her feel wicked,'[1]—and she ends by thinking any sacrifice light at the moment, if only it wins her back the affection and esteem of her friends."

"You are hard on us, Ideala," said Claudia, laughing. "At all events, we don't bind our feet."[2]

Ideala looked dangerous. "No," she said; "we only change the shape of them every time it pleases the shoemaker to alter the fashion of our shoes; and we raise ourselves on heels which alter the proper equilibrium of the body, and cause the displacement of vital organs; and we make ourselves V-shaped with stays, enduring the pressure downwards with a fortitude worthy of a better cause, and with the help of stimulants; enduring the shortness of breath and low state of vitality which comes from defective circulation when the diaphragm is paralysed by the pressure and will not act——"

Ideala was interrupted by an indignant exclamation: "Everyone doesn't tight-lace who wears stays!"

"Everybody says so," she answered imperturbably; "and everyone who has worn them also complains that she cannot sit up without them. Now, why cannot she sit up? Because, the circulation having been stopped by pressure, the muscles that should support the body have become attenuated for want of nourishment, and the artificial support of steel, and bones, and buckram has been made a necessity. Girls have the strength to withstand the effects of injurious dress; it is not as a rule till thirty that the evil is positively permanent. At thirty

---

[1] Henry James, *The American* (1877), Chapter 22.

[2] This is the beginning of a section deleted from the Donohue, Henneberry & Co. edition. Ideala's argument about the parallel between Chinese foot-binding and the fashions worn by English women can be found in the discourse of the Dress Reform Movement. For example, it appears in the writings of Mary Eliza Haweis, who in *The Art of Beauty* (1878) and *The Art of Dress* (1879) argued that the use of corsets and tight-lacing done by Englishwomen was the equivalent, if not worse than, Chinese foot-binding, since vital organs were affected.

a woman's strength naturally begins to decline; but it should decline
imperceptibly, and leave her many years of young womanhood and
uninterrupted enjoyment of life. This, however, is not the case with
Englishwomen who have worn stays. At thirty they are faded, generally; but even when their appearance has suffered a little, their nerves
are not to be depended on; they are often in the doctor's hands, often
on the sofa. Their pleasures end in exhaustion, and their pursuits
have to be given up one after the other. The ball at night means hours
in bed next day. The ride ends in a backache. The walk is done gently
and gingerly in the tight, high-heeled boots, and the consequence
has to be met by the mild stimulation of tea, or something stronger.
Sal volatile[1] becomes part of the preparation for everything, and not
unfrequently the day's work begins with a stimulant and ends with
a backache as inevitably as the rising and setting of the sun. That
'backache,' which means a crowd of small ailments, is the origin of
bad temper, and the bane of everybody's life; but still it is endured
with the stays, and groaned under patiently, although it was not one
of the evils which our hapless flesh was originally made heir to. The
so-called limp, æsthetic ladies are laughed at now, but the woman
who has the strength of mind to give up stays and assume a graceful,
dignified dress, will have the laugh on her own side eventually, for,
verily, her children will rise up and call her blessed!"[2]

Ideala had been carried away by her earnestness, and now she
stopped abruptly, somewhat disconcerted to find everyone listening
to her. The ladies—milliner-made all of them—sat with their eyes
on the floor, the gentlemen exchanged glances, but no one spoke for
some time.[3]

At last my sister made a move, and the spell was broken. We
separated for the night, and many were the ladylike whispers that
reached my ears, all ending in: "So like Ideala!"

But, as Ideala herself remarked on another occasion, "You can't
sweep a room that requires it without raising a dust; the thing is to
let the dust settle again, and then remove it."

---

[1] Use of smelling salts to keep from fainting.
[2] This is the end of a section deleted from the Donohue, Henneberry & Co.
edition.
[3] The phrase "milliner-made all of them" is missing from the Donohue, Henneberry & Co. edition.

CHAPTER XXIX.

CLAUDIA did not see the change in Ideala all at once. She said: "She is looking her best, and is our own Ideala again—faults and all! How she talked last night!"

"Just in the old way," I agreed, "but with a difference; for in the old days she talked at random, but now I feel sure she has a plan and a purpose, and all that she says is part of it."

This suggested new possibilities to Claudia, and when Ideala joined us presently, she asked, abruptly: "Are you going back to China?"

Ideala answered deliberately: "I did think of becoming a missionary—that was why I went out there. But I know all radical reforms take time, and when I saw what the Chinese women were doing for themselves, and compared their state with our own, it seemed to me that there was work in plenty to be done at home, and so I returned. Someone was triumphant on the subject of foot-binding last night.[1] Certainly, the Chinese women of the day bind their feet. When a girl is seven or eight years old, her mother binds them for her, and everybody approves. If the mother did otherwise, the girl herself would be the first to reproach her when she grew up. It is wonderful how they endure the torture; but public opinion has sanctioned the custom for centuries, and made it as much a duty for a Chinese woman to have small feet as it is for us to wear clothes! And yet they do a wonderful thing. When they are taught how wrong the practice is, how it cripples them, and weakens them, and renders them unfit for their work in the world, they take off their bandages! Think of that! and remember that they are timid and sensitive in a womanly way to a degree that is painful. When I learnt that, and when I remembered that my countrywomen bind every organ in their bodies, though they know the harm of it, and public opinion is against it, I did not feel that I had time to stay and teach the heathen. It seemed to me that there was work enough left yet to do at home."

"But, Ideala," Claudia protested, "what is the use of drawing

---

[1] This sentence was deleted from the Donohue, Henneberry & Co. edition.

degrading comparisons between ourselves and other nations? You
gave great offence last night."

"I said more than I intended," she answered; "I always do. It was
Tourgenieff,[1] was it not, who said that the age of talkers must precede
the age of practical reformers? I seem to have been born in the age
of talkers. But I shall not say much more. Last night I did not really
intend to say anything. You led me on. But I *do* want to make their
hearts burn within them, and if I succeed, then I shall not care about
the offence. An Englishwoman is nothing if she is not patriotic. She
will not bear the humiliation, if she is made to see that she is really
no better, with all her opportunities, than a much-despised Chinese.
She would not like the contempt the women of that nation feel for
her if she were made to acknowledge the truth—that she deserved
it. And so much depends on our women now.[2] There are plenty of
people, you know, who believe that no nation can get beyond a certain point of prosperity, and that when it reaches that point it cannot
stay there, but must begin to go down again; and they say that the
English nation has now reached its extreme point. They compare it
with Rome in the days which immediately preceded her decline and
fall—when men ceased to be brave and self-denying, and became
idle, luxurious, and effeminate; and women traded on their weakness, and made light of their evil deeds. It is a question of the sanctity of marriage now, as it was in the days of the decline of Rome. De
Quincey traces her fall to the loosening of the marriage tie. He says

---

[1] The Russian short story writer and novelist Ivan Turgenev (1818-1883). It is not
clear where Turgenev said this, but William Hazlitt, in *The Spirit of the Age* (1825),
wrote: "the present is an age of talkers, not of doers, and the reason is that the
world is growing old." The idea that talking happens before action is explored by
Grand in her essay, "The New Aspect of the Woman Question" (1894), where she
argues that women have been talking about their social status for some time but
only started to do something about it more recently. This essay is reprinted in Ann
Heilmann and Stephanie Forward, *Sex, Social Purity and Sarah Grand: Volume 1:
Journalistic Writings and Contemporary Reception* (London: Routledge, 2001), 29-35.
[2] The idea that England's future depended on the work of its women is evident in
several of Grand's essays, particularly "The Case of the Modern Spinster" (1913),
which first appeared in the *Pall Mall Gazette* and highlights how "noble" single
women focus on the betterment of the nation by channeling their motherly instincts into helping less fortunate English citizens. This essay is reprinted in Ann
Heilmann and Stephanie Forward, *Sex, Social Purity and Sarah Grand: Volume 1: Journalistic Writings and Contemporary Reception* (London: Routledge, 2001), 138-145.

that few indeed, if any, were the obligations in a proper sense *moral* which pressed upon the Roman. The main fountains of moral obligation had in Rome, by law or custom, been thoroughly poisoned. Marriage had corrupted itself through the facility of divorce, and through the consequences of that facility (viz., levity in choosing, and fickleness in adhering to the choice), into so exquisite a traffic of selfishness, that it could not yield so much as a phantom model of sanctity. The relation of husband and wife had, for all moral impressions, perished amongst the Romans.[1] And, although it is not quite so bad with ourselves at present, that is what it is coming to.

"But there are two sides to every question, and the one which we must by no means lose sight of just now is not that which shows the respects in which we resemble the Romans, so much as the one which shows the respects in which we differ from them. It is therein that our hope lies. And we differ from them in two important respects. We differ from them in the matter of experience, and in the use we are disposed to make of our experiences. We are beginning to know the rocks upon which they split, and we shall soon be making use of our knowledge to steer clear of them. But there is another respect in which we differ from all the older nations, not even excepting the Jewish. I mean morality. We have the grandest and purest ideal of morality that was ever preached upon earth, and, if we do but practice it, there is no doubt that the promise will be fulfilled, and our days as a nation will be prolonged with rejoicing.

"The future of the race has come to be a question of morality and a question of health. Perhaps I should reverse it, and say a question of health and morality, since the latter is so dependent on the former. We want grander minds, and we must have grander bodies to contain them. And it all rests with us women. To us is confided the care of the little ones—of the young bodies and the young minds yet unformed. Ours will be the joy of success or the shame of failure, and we should fit ourselves for the task both morally and physically by the practice of every virtue and by every art known to the science and skill of man."[2]

---

[1] Beginning with the phrase "were the obligations...", a direct quote from Thomas De Quincey's *Confessions of an English Opium Eater* (revised edition, 1856).

[2] Here, Ideala articulates a social purity perspective, but her view also anticipates eugenics, which advocated not restraint from reproduction (as social pu-

"But how would you begin," asked the practical Claudia.[1]

"By dressing properly!" was the prompt response.

"Oh Ideala! you are not taking up the dress question? Why, it seems quite *infra dig.*[2] for you after such lofty aspirations."

"Well, perhaps it would be if that were all—if it were only the dress question, as you call it, that I am taking up," Ideala answered good-humouredly. "And yet even that alone is a question of vital importance to the race. There is not a household that would not be the happier for having a wholesome mistress. And that they never will have while women are weighed down with pounds of petticoats, and trussed up out of all natural shape in stays. And if you doubt it, ask their husbands about their tempers, or the chemists and quack doctors they employ about their bills for drugs, and then judge yourself how wholesome women living under such conditions generally are! Healthy and beautiful clothing for us is the Alpha of all changes for the better. It is the beginning of wisdom for women. It means freedom for them, room to stretch their pinioned limbs and breathe! And for men it means health, and strength, and glorious nerve power, such as comes to them from vigorous mothers only. Other nations see the truth of this, and have already begun to reform; but with us it is always

> 'Let that be done which Mat doth say'—
> 'Yea,' quoth the Earl, *'but not to-day!'*[3]

Oh, why are we so backward? Why do we only talk?"

"But it will not be so for ever," she burst out after a pause.[4] "Eng-

---

rity did) but participation in reproduction for the purpose of improving the population. For more on Grand and eugenics, see Angelique Richardson, *Love and Eugenics in the Late Nineteenth Century: Rational Reproduction and the New Woman* (Oxford: Oxford University Press, 2003) and the section on "Eugenics and Social Hygiene" in Ann Heilmann and Stephanie Forward, *Sex, Social Purity and Sarah Grand: Volume 4: Selected Shorter Writings* (2) (London: Routledge, 2001).

[1] This is the beginning of a section that was deleted from the Donohue, Henneberry & Co. edition.

[2] Below one's dignity.

[3] Sir Walter Scott, *Chronicles of the Canongate*, 1st series, (1827), Chapter 1.

[4] This is the end of a section that was deleted from the Donohue, Henneberry & Co. edition.

lishwomen could not sit still and know that their lovely homes will be wrecked eventually, and left desolate; that this country of theirs will become a wilderness of ruin, such as Egypt is, but rank and overgrown, its beauty of sweet grass and stately trees, and all its rich luxuriance of flowers and fruits and foliage plants, only accentuating the ruin—bearing witness to the neglect. No, our greatness shall not depart. The decay may have begun, but it shall be arrested. I am not afraid."

"But if it is the fate of nations, Ideala——"

"I propose to conquer fate," said Ideala. "Fate itself is no match for one woman with a will, let alone for thousands! When horrid war is threatened, men flock to fight for their country; and they volunteer for every other arduous duty to be done. Do you think women are less brave? No. When they realize the truth they will fight for it. They will fly to arms. They will use the weapons with which nature has provided them: love, constancy, self-sacrifice, their intellectual strength, and will. And so they will save the nation."

Claudia, the unimaginative, sat silent and perplexed.

"I would join," she said at last, "if I were quite sure—— Oh, Ideala! it is not a sort of Woman's Rights business, and all that, you are going in for, is it? A woman can do good in her own sphere only."[1]

Ideala laughed. "But 'her own sphere' is such a very indefinite phrase," she observed. "It is nonsense, really. A woman may do anything which she can do in a womanly way. And don't you think it is time we had done talking about the relative superiority of the sexes also?" she asked.[2] "It has been proved by statistics, I believe, that in that respect there is about six of one and half-a-dozen of the other. Some Chinese gentlemen told me they objected to the higher education of women, because if the women were better educated they would want to rule. That must be what Englishmen think, though they do not say it.[3] They say that our brains are lighter, and that

---

[1] Claudia's comment typifies the "separate-spheres" doctrine that predominated in mid-century England. Ruskin's "On Queen's Gardens," in *Sesames and Lilies* (1865), is the most famous articulation of this doctrine. J. S. Mill's *The Subjection of Women* (1869) is a well-known rebuttal of the separate-spheres doctrine.

[2] This is the beginning of a section that was deleted from the Donohue, Henneberry & Co. edition.

[3] This is the end of a section that was deleted from the Donohue, Henneberry & Co. edition.

therefore we must not be taught too much. But why not educate us to the limit of our capacity, and leave it there? Why, if we are inferior, should there be any fear of making us superior? We must stop when we cannot go any farther, and all this old-womanish cackle on the subject, the everlasting trying to prove what is already said to be proved—the looking for the square in space after laying it down as a law that only the circle exists—is a curious way of showing us how to control the 'exuberance of our own verbosity.'[1] They say we shall not be content when we get what we want, and there they are right, for as soon as our own 'higher education' is secure we shall begin to clamour for the higher education of men. For the prayer of every woman worth the name is not 'Make me superior to my husband,' but, 'Lord, make my husband superior to me!' Is there any more pitiful position in the world than that of a right-minded woman who is her husband's superior and knows it! There is in every educated and refined woman an inborn desire to submit, and she must do violence to what is best in herself when she cannot. You know what the history of such marriages is. The girl has been taught to expect to find a guide, philosopher, and friend in her husband. He is to be head of the house and lord of her life and liberty, sole arbiter on all occasions. It is right and convenient to have him so, the world requires him to fill that position, and the wife prefers that he should. But the probabilities are about equal that he, being morally her inferior, will not be fit for it, and that, therefore, she will find herself in a false position. There will then be an interval of intense misery for the wife. Her education and prejudices will make her try to submit at first to what her sense knows to be impossible; but eventually she is forced out of her unnatural position by circumstances. To save her house and family she must rebel, take the reins of government into her own hands, and face life, a disappointed and lonely woman."

"Heaven help her!" said Claudia. "One knows that the future of a

---

[1] Rephrasing of statement by Benjamin Disraeli, novelist and British Prime Minister, about his rival, Prime Minister William Gladstone: "A sophistical rhetorician, inebriated with the exuberance of his own verbosity, and gifted with an egotistical imagination that can at all times command an interminable and inconsistent series of arguments to malign an opponent and to glorify himself." From a speech given July 27, 1878, quoted in the *Times* on July 29, 1878.

woman in that state of mind is only a question of circumstance and temperament; she may rise, but——"

Ideala looked up quickly. "But she may fall, you were going to say—yes. But you know if she does it is her own fault. She *must* know better."

"She may not be quite mistress of herself at the time—she may be fascinated; she may be led on!" I interposed, quickly. Claudia seemed to have forgotten. "But one thing is certain, if she has any real good in her she will always stop before it is too late."

"I think," said Claudia, "it would be better, after all, if women were taught to expect to find themselves their husband's equals—the disappointment would not be so great if the husband proved inferior; but when a woman has been led to look for so much, her imagination is full of dreams in which he figures as an infallible being; she expects him to be her refuge, support, and comfort at all times; and when a man has such a height to fall from in any one's estimation, there can be but little of him left if he does fall."

Ideala sighed, and after a short pause she said: "I have been wondering what makes it possible for a woman to love a man? Not the flesh that she sees and can touch, though that may attract her as the colour of the flower attracts. It must be the mind that is in him—the scent of the flower, as it were. If she finds eventually that his mind is corrupt, she must shrink from it as from any other form of corruption, and finally abandon him on account of it, as she would abandon the flower if she found its odour fetid—indeed, she has already abandoned her husband when she acknowledges that he is not what she thought him." She paused a moment, and then went on passionately: "I cannot tell you what it was—the battling day by day with a power that was irresistible because it had to put forth no strength to accomplish its work; it simply was itself, and by being itself it lowered me. I cannot tell you what it was to feel myself going down, and not to be able to help it, try as I would; to feel the gradual change in my mind as it grew to harbour thoughts which were reflections of his thoughts, low thoughts; and to be filled with ideas, recollections of his conversations, which had caused me infinite disgust at the time, but remained with me like the taste of a nauseous drug, until I almost acquired a morbid liking for them. Oh, if I could save other women from that!"

Claudia hastily interposed to divert her. "That is a good idea, the higher education of men," she said. "I don't know whether they have abandoned hope, or whether they think themselves already perfect, certain it is the idea of improving themselves does not seem to occur to them often. And we want good men in society. If the clergy and priests are good, it is only what is required of them, what everybody expects, and, therefore, their goodness is accepted as a matter of course, and is viewed as indifferently as other matters of course. One good man in society has more effect as an example than ten priests."

"But you have not told us what you propose to do, Ideala?" I said.

"I hope it is nothing unwomanly," Claudia interposed, anxiously.

Ideala looked at her and laughed, and Claudia laughed too, the moment after she had spoken. The fear of Ideala doing anything unwomanly was absurd, even to herself.

"An unwomanly woman is such a dreadful creature," Claudia added, apologetically.

"Yes," said Ideala, "but you should pity her. In nine cases out of ten there is a great wrong or a great grief at the bottom of all her unwomanliness—perhaps both; and if she shrieks you may be sure that she is suffering; ease her pain, and she will be quiet enough. The average woman who is happy in her marriage does not care to know more of the world than she can learn in her own nursery, nor to see more of it, as a rule, than she can see from her own garden gate. She is a great power; but, unfortunately, there is so very little of her!

"What I want to do is to make women discontented—you have heard of a noble spirit of discontent? I thought for a long time that everything had been done that could be done to make the world better; but now I see that there is still one thing more to be tried. Women have never yet united to use their influence steadily and all together against that of which they disapprove. They work too much for themselves, each trying to make their own life happier. They have yet to learn to take a wider view of things, and to be shown that the only way to gain their end is by working for everybody else, with intent to make the whole world better, which means happier. And in order to accomplish this they must be taught that they have only to *will* it—each in her own family and amongst her own friends; that, after having agreed with the rest about what they mean to put down, they have only to go home and use their influence to that end, quietly, consistently, and without wavering, and the thing will be done. Our influence is like those strong currents which run beneath the surface of the ocean without disturbing it, and yet with irresistible force, and at a rate that may be calculated. It is to help in the direction of that force that I am going to devote my life.[1] Do not imagine," she went on hurriedly, "that I think myself fit for such a work. I have had conscientious scruples—been sorely troubled about my own unworthiness, which seemed to unfit me for any good work. But now I see things differently. One may be made an instrument for good without merit of one's own. So long as we do not deceive ourselves by thinking we are worthy, and so long as we are trying our best to become so, I think we may hope; I think we may even know that we shall eventually——" She stopped and looked at me.

"Be made worthy," said Claudia, kissing her; "and if it were not so, Ideala, if everybody had to begin by being as good themselves as they want others to be, there would be no good workers left in the world at all."

At this moment a noisy party burst in upon our grave debate and carried Ideala off for a ride. We saw them leave the house, and watched them ride away until the last glimpse of them was veiled by the misty brightness of the frosty air and the morning sunshine.

"How well she looks!" Claudia exclaimed, "better than any of them. She has quite recovered, and is none the worse."

"I do not know about recovery," I answered, dubiously. "She will never——"

But Claudia interrupted hotly: "I know what you are going to say, and I do wish you would leave off speaking of Ideala in that way. Anyone to hear you would suppose she had committed a sin, and you know quite well that that was not the case. If she acted without common prudence, and I will not deny that she did, it was entirely your own fault. She has never been intimate with any man but yourself, and you have made her believe that all men are like

---

[1] This section reflects the philosophy of thought-influence. For more on this philosophy, see the Introduction.

you. How could she harbour suspicion when she did not know what to suspect? Of course she saw everything wrongly and awry. The old life had become impossible to her, and she nearly made a mistake as to what the new one should be, that was all. I know she wavered for a moment, but the weakness was more physical than moral, I think. Her vision was clouded at the time, but as soon as she was restored to health she saw things clearly enough. She is a great and good woman, pure-hearted, and full of charity. God bless her for all her tenderness, and for her wonderful power to love. He alone can count the number who have reason to wish her well."

"That is true," I answered. "And I was merely going to remark, when you interrupted me, that she will never think herself 'none the worse'——"

"I don't see what difference that makes," Claudia again interposed. "She always did think herself least of the least when she thought of herself at all, and that was not often. You are dwelling too long on the past, really, and making too much of it. Men, when they are saints, are twice as bad as women."

I pointed out to my sister something confusing in her way of expressing the fact, but my kindness seemed to exasperate her.

"You know what I mean quite well," she said tartly.

"Yes, I know," I rejoined; "but I wanted to help you to make yourself intelligible to other people."

Claudia made a gesture of impatience, but laughed, and left me; and I remained for a long time thinking over all that Ideala had said, and also thinking of her as she looked at the time; and the subject was so inspiring that, although my strong point is landscape, in an ambitious mood I began to paint an allegorical picture of her as a mother nursing the Infant Goodness of the race. She saw it when it was nearly finished, but did not recognize herself, and exclaimed: "What a gaunt creature! and that baby weighs at least twelve stone!"[1]

The picture was never finished.

---

[1] One stone is equivalent to fourteen pounds, so a twelve-stone baby would weigh 168 pounds.

CHAPTER XXX.

WE soon found that Ideala, having at last put her hand to the plough, worked with a will, and although she was true to her principle that a woman's best work is done beneath the surface, I think her own labours will eventually make themselves felt with a good result in the world. But the life she has chosen for herself is martyrdom, and her womanly shrinking from the suffering she would alleviate is never lessened by use. Yet she does not waver. Other women admire her devotion, and follow in her footsteps; they do not doubt but that she has chosen the better part; but I fancy that most men who have seen her draw the little children about her and forget everything for a moment but her delight in them, have felt that there must be something wrong in the world when such a woman misses her vocation, and has to scatter her love to the four winds of heaven, for want of an object upon which to concentrate it in all its strength.

I do not know if her feeling for Lorrimer has changed. My sister declares in her positive way that of course it has, completely; but my sister is not always right. Ideala has never mentioned his name since she returned to us, nor given us any other clue by which we could judge. Only on one occasion, when some allusion was made to the course she had intended to pursue in the past, she exclaimed: "Oh, how could I!" and covered her face with her hands.

From where I sit just now I can see her walking up the avenue. She is as straight as an arrow, young-looking, and fresh. Her step is firm and light and elastic, and she moves with an easy grace only possible when every muscle is unconstrained. Her dress is a work of art, light in weight, but rich in colour and texture.

"What a beautiful woman!" I think involuntarily.

I see her daily, and pay her that tribute every time we meet, for—

> Age cannot wither her, nor custom stale
> Her infinite variety.[1]

Her intellect and selflessness preserve her youth. She is changed,

---

[1] Shakespeare (1564-1616), *Antony and Cleopatra*, 2.2.234-235.

certainly. She has arisen, and can return no more to the lower walks, to the old purposeless life, and desultory ways; but yet she is the same Ideala, and holds you always expectant—you, who see beneath the surface. The world will call her cold and self-contained till the end, and so she is and will be—a snow-crowned volcano, with wonderful force of fire working within. And she will not stop where she is; there is something yet to come—some further development—something more—something beyond! and she makes you feel that there is. What she says of other women is true of herself. "Do not stand in their way," she begs; "do not hinder them—above all, do not stop them. They are running water; if you check them they stagnate, and you must suffer yourself from their noisome exhalations. For the moral nature is like water; it must have movement and air and sunshine to stay corruption and keep it sweet and wholesome: and its movement is good works; its air, faith in their efficiency; its sunshine, the evidence of this and hope."

Comparative anatomists have proved that the human brain, from its first appearance as a semi-fluid and shapeless mass, passes in succession through the several structures that constitute the permanent and perfect brains of fishes, reptiles, birds, and mammalia; but ultimately it passes beyond them all, and acquires a marvellous development of its own. And so it is with the human soul. It must rise through analogous stages, and add to its own strength and beauty by daily bread of love and thought, growing to greatness by help of these aliments only, and reaching ultimately to such perfection as we cannot divine, for the end is not here. But we might reach it sooner than we do were it not for our own impatience. Growth is so exquisitely minute, it bursts upon us an accomplished fact. We know this, and yet we would see the process; and not seeing it we lose faith, waver, hesitate, stop, and recoil—a going back *pour mieux sauter*[1] it is with the choicer spirit; but we all are deficient in hope, all have our retrograde moments of despair. We do not look about us enough to see what is being done for others, how they are progressing, by what strange paths they are led. We keep our eyes on our own ground too much, and, because we will not compare cheerfully, we think our own way the roughest, our own journey the longest—if there be

---

[1] French phrase, meaning "to go back in order to move forward" or "to give a little in order to achieve a better position."

any end to it at all! Yet all the time we might see the end if only we would look up. And we need never despair and lag, need never be cold and comfortless, if we would but love and remember.

> For, while the tired waves, vainly breaking,
>   Seem here no painful inch to gain,
> Far out, through creeks and inlets making,
>   Comes silent, flooding in, the main![1]

Ideala raises her eyes to mine now, and smiles as she passes beneath my window.

Another woman—a woman whom Claudia had long refused to know—is leaning on her arm, talking to her earnestly. And that is Ideala's attitude always. She gathers the useless units of society about her, and makes them worthy women. There is no kind of sorrow for which she has not found comfort, no folly she has not been successful in checking, no vice she has not managed to cure, and no form of despair which she has not relieved with hope. Her own experiences have taught her to sympathize with every phase of feeling, and be lenient to every shortcoming and excess. Wherever she is you may be sure that another woman is there also—someone with a sorrowful history, probably; and you may be equally sure that she is leaning on Ideala. God bless her!

THE END.

---

[1] Arthur Hugh Clough, "Say Not the Struggle Naught Availeth" (1862), lines 9-12.

APPENDIX

I. Anonymous, "Ideala," *Saturday Review*, 1 Sept. 1888, 227.

The anonymous author of *Ideala* describes his or her work as a Study from Life. Without departing widely either from accuracy or from the character of the phrase selected by the author, we might describe it as a modest essay in Naturalism, using that word in the modern French sense. It is the story of a nasty-minded woman. It is, unhappily, the fact that there are some nasty-minded women about—not counting those who do not prate about their "purity." They are noisy out of all proportion to their numbers, and odious out of all proportion to their noise. Whether it is a good thing to have written a sentimental prose epic describing a specimen of the class with considerable spirit and accuracy is a question which different people will probably answer differently, according to whether they are "naturalists" or otherwise.

The story, of which there is not much, can be shortly indicated. It is narrated by an elderly person of aristocratic birth, considerable means, and, as we are expressly told, of the male sex. He once insinuates that he cherishes a senile and unrequited passion for his heroine, and it seems likely, upon the whole, that this was so. Ideala was a married lady ranging from about twenty-five to thirty in the course of the events narrated. She had a dissolute and probably vulgar husband, and took a great dislike to him, which increased after the death of her only child. At last he struck her, not without provocation, and she determined that she could live with him no longer. She wanted some one to consult with and remembered that a lady friend had referred to a cousin of hers, named Lorrimer, the head of a ridiculous hospital founded by a lunatic, as the proper person to be applied to by any one who wanted to visit the establishment. She thought the head of a hospital would be old, respectable, and a suitable person to confide her conjugal woes to, so she went to see Lorrimer. He turned out to be thirty, handsome, and not at all the sort of person to consult. Ideala, therefore, consulted him, but only by letter, and not until a day or two after her first visit. The natural result was a commonplace flirtation rapidly developing into an intrigue, which they presently arranged should be consummated by Ideala's running away from the wicked Idealus and becoming Lorrimer's mistress. But there is often more bark than bite about a nasty-minded woman, and Ideala was true to her character. When the time came for open sin her heart failed her, and she took her venerable biographer into her confidence. For a considerable time they went through the form of argument whether she should go to Lorrimer or not, and had long talks about "purity," and love, and the true union of marriage, and the like. At last, on the eve of the day fixed for Ideala's flight, her biographer pointed out to her that, among other consequences of her proposed action, "you will be spoken of contemptuously, and he will be 'the fellow who is living with another man's wife, don't you know,' and that will injure him in many ways." Ideala admitted the force of this remarkably profound and original argument with all the candour of a character in one of Mr. Gilbert's comedies, and announced in the course of the evening that she had changed her mind, and that the biographer must go and acquaint Lorrimer with the circumstances. He did so, and Lorrimer fainted. When he revived they talked the matter over for three days, at the end of which time Lorrimer agreed that Ideala was quite right, and that, all things considered, the eternal separation of two pining spirits was as romantic as adultery and less practically inconvenient. Ideala went to China for a year to extirpate the roots of her affection for Lorrimer, and to find a substitute for it in the employment of her mental energies. She decided to improve the lot of women, and incidentally that of men. This will be done by improving women's minds, the first step to which is to abolish their stays. "We want grander minds, and we must have grander bodies to contain them." But women's bodies will not be grander "while women are weighed down with pounds of petticoats and trussed up out of all natural shape in stays."

This rather slender thread, remarkable perhaps chiefly for the astonishing bathos at the end of it, suffices as best it may for the exhibition of the character of a nasty-minded woman as conceived by the author of *Ideala*. For we are given to understand that she was a person of such genius as to dominate entirely the society she happened to be in, and to convince her friends that when she undertook the regeneration of women women were as good as regenerated, even though the first step was nothing newer or more tremendous than the denunciation of tight-lacing. The main topics of Ideala's many discourses are two; her own overpowering love for any human beings (except her husband) whom she happens to come across, and for all and sundry whom she does not come across; and the wickedness, selfishness, and "impurity" of men. Her manners and language are alleged to have been fascinating in no ordinary degree, but this must be taken on trust, as what we read of her remarks indicates less of genius than of verbosity, dulness, and rudeness. One of her weaknesses was an affectation of absent-mindedness. She would suddenly begin to sing when a new acquaintance was talking to her, and then apologize for not listening to him. She would also—which was ingenious—tell exciting stories of how she rescued children from being drowned or run over, and affect, when complimented on her heroism, to have forgotten to consider the matter from that point of view. Once she stared at a stranger in a railway station until, under a natural mistake, he accosted her. She replied with an epigram, and said when innocently telling the story to her biographer, "I think he felt ill, and went to have some refreshment." But all her absent-mindedness disappeared when she was in Lorrimer's company. The first time she met this personage she had lunch with him—at his expense—in a restaurant. An old gentleman sat down at the same table, and, being short of breath, puffed audibly.

> Lorrimer, by an intelligent glance, expressed what he thought of the peculiarity to Ideala, who remarked:—"It is the next gale developing dangerous energy on its way to the North British and Norwegian coasts."

Then a small dish of peas was handed to the old gentleman. The portion was intended for the whole party, but the old gentleman thought it was only for him, and took it all. Lorrimer said, "you have taken all the peas, sir; allow me to give you all the pepper," and emptied the pepper-pot on the old gentleman's plate. Ideala was very much amused. The third time they met Lorrimer asked her how it was she married her husband. "Were you very much in love with him?" "No," said Ideala, "not in the least." "Spooney, then?" asked Lorrimer. She thought him the incarnation of nobility, and presently said to him, "I wish I could get behind that horrid veil of flesh that hides you from me. I want to see your soul."

Ideala deserves notice because it is a clever book, and illustrates the nasty-minded woman vividly and picturesquely. She is self-conscious, rather vulgar, and morbidly and intensely sorry for herself. In her talk she hovers sometimes on this and sometimes on that side of the verge of indecency. She commits adultery in her heart with the first cleverish man she comes across after the rupture with her husband, and fails to do so in fact only because she lacks the courage of her appetite. Hers is a depraved and despicable character, and the most satisfactory thing about it is that it is much less common than one might suppose from reading the newspapers.

II. Anonymous, "Ideala," *Spectator*, 12 Jan. 1889, 55-56.

How far the author of this remarkable book has drawn what he has called a "Study from Life" from an actual personality, living through actual or possible circumstances, and how far the character of his study is the result of the accumulated experience and impressions gathered from intercourse and contact with many phases of life and character which have found their expression in the portrayal of one leading character, we cannot, of course, tell. Ideala stands to us in the light of a real living character; and in so far as that result is attained, the writer has, so to speak, fulfilled the chief part of the unwritten contract which exists between a good author and his readers. Whether the heroine is a portrait, and how far she is a true or a natural one, is a matter for the author and his intimates alone, and beyond our concern. To concentrate the whole interest of a story upon the delineation of a single character, and this, so far as the reader is concerned, a fictitious one; to make this interest sufficient, even intense and absorbing, without the aid of any incident except that which is wholly subordinate, or of any other character, save one, which is intended to be of the slightest importance, argues a very uncommon power and capacity in the line which the author has taken up. There is something defective in the manner of narration, and there are certain inequalities of production which seem to us at times carelessly and aggressively bald and inartistic. These, and the impression left by what appears to us one or two slight inconsistencies of character and perhaps of jarring speech, are all of which we have to relieve ourselves in the spirit of fault-finding, before coming to dwell upon the main features of the book. And then we find ourselves left with little but that to which the expression of very high praise is due.

Far as we seem led into a knowledge of Ideala's nature, we feel in the end that there remain depths which we have not sounded, and much is still vague to us. All we learn of Ideala is either expressed in her own words or judged of from the impression which her character and conversation have made upon one, the truest of her friends, who tells the story of a certain period of her life, and who possesses much, if not all, of her confidence. The disadvantage, of course, of thus learning so much of a heroine, real or fictitious, from her own lips is that what one gains in actual knowledge is often at the expense of that respect for the reserve and want of self-consciousness in her character, which in the case before us at least, the author is evidently anxious we should retain. The extract we subjoin will show, we think, where he has gone a step too far in allowing Ideala to enlarge upon herself, and will give, too, a slight example of her absent-mindedness, of which the earlier chapters are so amusingly full:—

> "But, although she spoke so positively when taken out of herself by the interest and importance of a subject, she had no very high opinion of her own judgment and power to decide. A little more self-esteem would have been good for her; she was too diffident. 'I have not come across people on whose knowledge I could rely,' she told me. 'I have been obliged to study along, and to form my opinions for myself out of such scraps of information as I have had the capacity to acquire from reading and observation. I am, therefore, always prepared to find myself mistaken, even when I am surest about a thing—for
>
> > "What am I?
> > An infant crying in the night:
> > An infant crying for the light:
> > And with no language but a cry!'"

In practice, too, she frequently, albeit unconsciously, diverged from her theories to some considerable extent; as on one occa-

sion, when, after talking long and earnestly of the sin of selfishness, she absently picked up a paper I had just cut with intent to
enjoy myself, took it away with her to the drawing-room, and sat
on it for the rest of the morning—as I afterwards heard."

We have advanced some way in the story, and are familiar with
many of her opinions and many little traits of character peculiar to
her, before we know in the least who Ideala is. Gradually we rather
infer than are directly told, that her childhood has been an unusual and an unhappy one, that she has been early married to a man
uncongenial to her in every way. When the book opens, some years
of gradual recognition of the gulf which lies between them have
helped to make the spirit in which she meets her trial a hard and
somewhat reckless one, while preparing her for discoveries in regard
to him which render her position unnatural and degrading. That
this spirit is contrary to her nature, which is as loving and noble as it
is impulsive and unconventional, is shown partly by the intimate and
affectionate relation existing between her and her friends, and partly
by the peculiar fascination and charm which she seems to have exer-
cised over her inferiors in social position. Having learnt so much of
her nature and circumstances, it is not hard to guess what will prove
the temptation and the tragedy of her life. What we know of her
hitherto has been leading up to her appreciation of the kind of spirit
which she puts forth to meet it.

We cannot enter into the circumstances of Ideala's meeting with
Lorrimer, which, together with the intercourse which follows and
the mutual attraction of their natures, brings about the inevitable
result. Her subsequent suffering and temptation, the temporary
yielding of a mind which seems to have satisfied its higher prompt-
ings while yielding to its passionate impulses, the constantly recurring struggles which, without being directly told them, we infer
from the slightness of the guiding impetus which brings her right at
last,—all this can only be fully understood by one who will follow
out the working of the story for himself. It would be impossible
by any extract to give an example of the successive stages of the
growth of her feeling for Lorrimer; and we are half-afraid of detract-
ing from the completeness of the chapter which tells of the crisis of
her life by giving the closing page:—

"'This was my last argument, and when I had done she sat there for a long time silent, resting her head against my knee, and scarcely breathing. She was fighting it out with herself, and I thought it best to leave her alone—besides, I had already said all there was to say; repetition would have irritated her, and there was nothing now for it but to wait. Outside, I could hear the dreary drip of raindrops; somewhere in the room, a clock ticked obtrusively; but it was long past midnight, and the house was still. I thought that only the night and silence watched with me, and waited upon the suffering of this one poor soul. At last she moved, uttering a low moan, like one in pain.—'I do see it,' she said, almost in a whisper; 'and I am willing to give him up.'—'God in his mercy help you!' I prayed.—'And forgive me,' she answered, humbly.—She was quite exhausted, and passively submitted when I led her to her room. I closed the shutters to keep out the cheerless dawn, and made the fire burn up, and lit the lamps. She sat, silently watching me, and did not seem to think it odd that I should do this for her. She clung to me then as a little child clings to its father, and, like a father, I ministered to her, reverently, then left her, as I hoped, to sleep. My sister opened her door as I passed. She was dressed, and had been watching, too, the whole night long.—'Well?' she asked.—I kissed her. 'It is well,' I answered; and she burst into tears.—'Can I go to her now?' she said.—'Yes, go.'—I went to Claudia's room, and waited. After a long time she returned.—'She is sleeping at last,' she told me, sorrowfully. And so the long night ended.'"

To appreciate fully the nature of the struggle through which Ideala is passing, the reader must understand how far she has justified to herself—of course wrongly—the step which she has been about to take. This perhaps too easy justification, and her entire ignorance of ordinary conventionalities in one of her experiences of life, strike us as somewhat inconsistent. We share in the perplexity of one of her friends, who says somewhere in the course of the book,—"how a woman can be at once so clever and such a fool as you are, Ideala, puzzles me."

The hopeless apathy which succeeds Ideala's self-conquest is the beginning of what might have been a striking close; but we cannot help thinking that there is a bathos about the chapter which precedes the closing scene. The long harangue about Chinese women and tight-lacing is inappropriate, and Ideala's aspirations, though impressive, are very vague. We find the same kind of inappropriateness earlier, in the description of the Great Hospital, a marvellously impossible building, where the accumulated treasures of art and science minister to the needs of tired minds, but where the chief consulter, as we have it three times forced upon our attention, cannot even get his lunch without going to the refreshment-room of a neighbouring railway-station.

We have not space to dwell upon Lorrimer's chracter. In many respects, though incomplete, it is a very striking one. It is impossible to read a book of such undoubted power, and given to us in so agreeable a form, without some guesses about its author, whose name nowhere appears. That it is a woman's work, we have little doubt. The slight inconsistencies and want of artistic finish do not seem sufficient to mark it as the work of a young writer, a conjecture which the style and subject likewise forbid, though we should say that there is something of the fierceness of youth in the working of the attack upon the "decently clad devils of society" in the preface. We should rather say that the conception of the book had so strong a root in actual observation or experience, as to make a successor to it improbable, one of equal merit impossible.

III. From Margaret Oliphant, "The Old Saloon," *Blackwood's Edinburgh Magazine*, 146 (1889), 256-262.

A very different matter is the volume which stands by, in a modest costume and colour, which courts no notice, but with the sacred inscription of "fourth edition" on its title-page, to shame those who have not yet made acquaintance with the very charming woman of the period whose history, or at least a piece of her history, is herein given. 'Ideala' is one of the books which show the condition of the public mind, and what it is which secures the deepest attention at this particular moment among a large class at least of the more "thoughtful" readers. It is not like 'Robert Elsmere,' and does not take advantage of any religious question to secure attention. But it is equally the expression of a fashion of the varying public intelligence. It is not so forcible a study as to have demanded attention at a time when men's minds, or rather women's minds, were drawn in any other direction; but it is the expression of a great many thoughts of the moment, and of a desire which is stronger than it ever has been before, cultivated by many recent agitations and incidents, for a new development of feminine life, for an emancipation, which even those who wish for it most strongly could not define and scarcely understand. It is not to be supposed that we imply any contempt, or even a want of respect, in so characterising it. There is nothing worthy of slight or scorn in 'Ideala,' or in the feeling which is expressed and responded to in this book. Of all works of fiction women are the chief audience, and he who scorns such hearers had better hang his harp upon something quite apart from the book-shelves of Messrs Mudie, and betake himself to science or philosophy: though even there he may not escape. The "ladies who had intelligence in love" were the chosen audience to whom Dante and the medieval poets appealed: so that this regiment of women is at least nothing new.

But 'Ideala' has to do with women in something different from this broad and general way. The heroine of this book is an example of the new sentiment which has been developed by, or which has been the cause of—we do not know which to say—the singular and scarcely recognized revolution which has taken place in the positions and aspirations of women during the last generation. This has been very great, though there may be many people who are unconscious of it. In Parliament, indeed, and elsewhere, men still use the old phraseology, and talk as if there was no important difference in the life or sentiments of the women by whom they are surrounded; but if we look back, we will find that the difference is immense, almost incalculable. Exceptional women always have done whatever might happen to be necessary for those they loved, with a defiance of all restrictions; but they were exceptional, and did not alter the rule. It is now, however, the rule that is altered; and hosts of young and ardent minds, once kept fairly in discipline and order, have begun to think and to wish and to struggle for their own career and destiny in a manner inconceivable to their mothers—or at least to their grandmothers, let us say—for the mothers have veered round in sympathy with them to the new standing-point. A certain number of martyrs have made the way and bore the brunt; have been called many bad names, and sometimes have deserved them—for to be a pioneer even in a good way is not always a good, and very seldom is a pretty thing. There are some still, and those naturally the most prominent,

who justify all the old vulgar commonplaces about the interference
of women in matters which do not concern them; but the evil effect
of these undesirable leaders is dying away in the general change
which has come over the spirit of our dream. Our daughters are
becoming what our sons used alone to be—independent existences,
conscious of warm individual life and wants and ambitions, and no
longer hampered in the means of fulfilling these ambitions. It is only
those whose aspirations are political who come prominently before
the public; and these are the most easy to laugh at or to put down
with a jeer (though also the most difficult; for the political women
have come to be quite contemptuous of jeers which once would
have fired them to passion). The other revolutionaries are much less
easy to deal with, and they are everywhere. It is not a sect or a party,
but an atmosphere, and it breathes through almost every educated
household in the land.

A book like 'Ideala' is one of the most significant emanations
of this atmosphere. It is a section of the story of a woman who has
no story in the ordinary sense of the word, to whom nothing particular happens, yet who occupies from first to last the little stage,
attracting by her thoughts and variations of mind what is evidently
the absorbed attention of a very large audience. That her career is
crossed by an impassioned episode of love, as unlike the ordinary
and well-worn love-story as can be conceived, dangerous almost
fatal episode, yet done all in honour, and vanquished at the critical
moment by the higher sense of duty and moral obligation, is scarcely
a necessary point in the history when that which is most important
is herself, the new woman, the offspring of a changed world. Ideala
is actually, as we regret to say, something of a prig: but she is so
naturally placed before us, and is so entirely the new woman she is
professed to be, that we take no exception to that part of her character, but allow her to prelect from page to page without objection,
with a pleasure in her attitude of mind, in the wisdom and want of
wisdom, which runs through a great deal of talk, without resent-
ment or even weariness. We should probably have been very tired of
her twenty years ago, but we are not so now. Her absences of mind
are sometimes amusing, as when she comes into a lawyer's office
very much flustered and embarrassed, to ask him to lend her five
shillings, as she has lost her purse.

"'At least I think I have lost my purse. I took it out to give six-pence to a beggar—and—and here is the sixpence,' and she held it out to me. She had given the purse to the beggar, and carried the sixpence off in triumph. 'You may well say, O Ideala!'

"'And Mr. Lloyd was so very good as to take me to the station, and see me into the train,' Ideala murmured; 'and he gave me his bank-book to amuse me on the journey, and carried Hux-ley's 'Elementary Physiology,' which I had come in to buy, off in triumph!'"

There is a great deal of suppressed and quiet humour mingled with the lengthened utterances which one ought to be tired of, but is not. Ideala is not very sure about anything. She is very impartial, sometimes a little profane without meaning it, in her completely human way of treating everything, knowing no higher method: con-fused in life and many of its practical questions by the fact of being married to a brute, who is scarcely introduced into the book, but is indicated as a great deal too bad and brutal for anything, which is the general weakness of such representations. It is improbable, we think, that a man who betrayed his wife's confidence in the imme-morial way by coarse vice, would also have shut her out of the house and compelled her to spend a night in the garden, in order to subdue her to his will about a trifling matter which she had prom-ised but he in pure caprice forbade. The man who did the one thing probably would not do the other; but it is a very common error to paint an objectionable husband entirely in black. It is perfectly true, however, to the idea of the modern woman, that, having once been compelled to recognize what her husband is, she is not frantic by his offences, as the woman, for instance, of the late Mrs. Norton's time, would have been. She slips into the house as soon as it is opened in the morning, and goes on as if nothing had happened, putting aside the incident with pride which belonged to a much earlier age—the days when family feeling and a proud determination not to be talked about made women lock up such sorrows in their own bosoms. The fact of the brutal husband, however, as we have said, confuses many things to Ideala, and makes her rush upon what would have been her doom in the last generation. A friend recommends her, should she be in any trouble, to ask the advice of a certain Mr. Lorrimer, a functionary at a great hospital in a town near her, a man whom everybody consults, and in whose hands she would be safe. When things come to the point with Ideala that she can endure no longer—with the natural feeling that it would be easier to submit the difficult circumstances of her lot to a stranger than to the faithful advisers whom she has at hand, and in the belief that the person so recommended to her must be an old man—she betakes herself to the hospital, and asks for Mr. Lorrimer. He proves to be young and handsome, and so is she; and the inevitable result occurs. The two fall passionately in love with each other. There is a period during which this passion grows unconsciously in the woman's fine nature, and the desire to be with him, to tell him everything, to receive his sympathy and the record of his experience in return. At last she gets ill, distracted, miserable; and circumstances occur which make her believe that he is forsaking her, though all this while not a word has been said of love. She comes at last to the house of a friend who tells the story, with a look of recovered health and happiness, in which there is something, however, which holds him in anxiety.

"'I hope you are going to stay with us some time now, Ideala,' I added, glancing up at her as she came and looked over my shoulder at the picture.

"Her face clouded. 'I—I am afraid not,' she answered hesitating, and nervously fidgeting with some paint-brushes that lay on a table. 'I am afraid you will not want me when you know what I am going to do. I only came back to tell you.'

"My heart stood still. 'To tell me! Why, what are you going to do?'

"'It is very hard to tell,' she faltered. 'You and Claudia are my dearest friends, and I cannot bear to give you pain. But I must tell you at once. It is only right that you should know, especially as you will disapprove.'

"I turned to look at her, but she would not meet my eyes. 'Give us pain! disapprove!' I exclaimed. 'What on earth do you mean, Ideala? What are you going to do?'

"'An immoral thing,' she answered.

"'Good heavens!' I exclaimed, throwing down my palette, and rising to confront her. 'I don't believe it.'

"'I mean,' she stammered, the blood rushing into her face,

then leaving her white as she spoke, 'something which you will consider so.'

"'I cannot believe it,' I reiterated.

"'But it is true—he says so.'

"'He—who, in God's name?'

"'Lorrimer.'

"'And who on earth is Lorrimer?'

"'That is what I came to tell you,' she answered, faintly."

She then tells with much simplicity and straightforwardness the story of their intercourse, and of a misunderstanding between them which had brought matters to a crisis.

"'But, Ideala,' I said to her, 'you used the word "immoral" just now. You were talking at random, surely? You are nervous. For heaven's sake, collect yourself, and tell me what all this means.'

"'No, I am not nervous,' she answered. 'See! My hand is quite steady. It is you who are trembling. I am calm now and relieved, because I have told you. But oh, I am sorry to give you pain.'

"'I do not yet understand,' I answered hoarsely.

"'He wants me to give up everything and go to him,' she said; 'but he would not accept my consent until he had explained and made me understand exactly what I was doing. "The world will consider it an immoral thing," he said, "and so it would be if the arrangement were not to be permanent. But any contract which men and women hold to be binding on themselves should be sufficient now, and will be sufficient again, as it used to be in the old days, provided we can show good cause why any previous contract should be broken. You must believe that, you must be thoroughly satisfied now. For if your conscience were to trouble you afterwards—your troublesome conscience, which keeps you regretting nearly everything you do, but never warns you in time to stop you—if you were to have any scruples, then there would be no better peace for either of us, and you had better give me up at once."'

"'And what did you say, Ideala?'

"'I said, perhaps I had. I was beginning to be frightened again.'

"'And how did it end?'

"'He made me go home and consider.'

"'Yes; and what then?' I demanded impatiently.

"'And next day he came to me to know my decision—and—
and—I was satisfied. I cannot live without him.'

"I groaned aloud. What was I to say? What could I do? An
arrangement of this sort is carefully concealed, and denied, if
discovered; but here were a lady and gentleman prepared not
only to take the step, but to justify it—under somewhat peculiar circumstances certainly—and carefully making their friends
acquainted with their intention beforehand, as if it were an ordinary engagement."

Of course every inducement this kind friend can bring to bear
upon her is produced, for a long time with no effect. Ideala con-
founds the bishop, who is one of the figures in the background of
the picture, and a lawyer who is with him, by asking whether a contract could be valid, one of the parties to which had been kept in
ignorance of a most important clause in it? The bishop unsuspecting
falls into the trap; but is horrified when she informs him that it is the
marriage-contract she means, and can only get out of the dilemma
by promising to preach on the subject, a promise which does little
good to any one. The argument continually renewed is, however, at
length brought to a crisis as follows: the whole question has been
reasoned over again, and she ends by asserting that her life will be no
less pure if she devotes it to her lover, and that nobody but herself
can be hurt by the step she takes.

"'When things can be legally right though morally wrong,'
she says, 'can they not also be morally right though legally
wrong?'

"'I have clearly tried to show you, Ideala,' I answered, preparing to go over the old ground again patiently, 'that we none of us
stand alone; that we are all a part of this great system, and that in
cases like yours individuals must suffer—must even be sacrificed
for the good of the rest. When the sacrifice is voluntary we call it
noble.'

"'If I go to him I shall have sacrificed a good deal.'

"'You will have sacrificed others, not yourself. He is all the
world to you, Ideala; the loss would be nothing to the gain,'—she
hid her face in her hands,—'and what is required of you is self-
sacrifice. And surely in the end it would be happier for you to give

him up now, than to live to feel yourself a millstone round his neck.'

"'I do not understand you,' she said, looking up quickly.

"'The world, you see, will know nothing of the fine sentiments which made you determine to take this step,' I said. 'You will be spoken of contemptuously, and he will be "the fellow who is living with another man's wife, don't you know," and that will injure him in many ways.'

"'Do you think so?' she asked anxiously.

"'I know it,' I replied. 'A woman in your position sets an example whether she will or not; and even if all your best reasons for this step were made public, you would do harm by it, for there are only too many people apt enough as it is at finding spurious excuses for their own shortcomings, who would be glad if they dared to do likewise. And you would not gain your object after all. You would neither be happy yourself nor make Lorrimer happy. People like you are sensitive about their honour—it is the sign of their superiority: and the indulgence of love even at the moment, and under the most favourable circumstances of youth, beauty, and intellectual equality, does not satisfy such natures, if the indulgence be not regulated and sanctified by all that men and women have devised to make their relations moral.'

"This was my last argument, and when I had done she sat there for a long time silent and scarcely breathing. She was fighting it out with herself, and I thought it best to leave her alone— besides, I had already said all that there was to say; repetition would only have irritated her, and there was nothing now for it but to wait.

"Outside I could hear the dreary drip of the raindrop: somewhere in the room a clock ticked obtrusively: but it was long past midnight, and the house was still. I thought that only the night and silence watched with me and waited upon the suffering of this one poor soul. At last she moved, uttering a low moan like one in pain.

"'I do see it,' she said, almost in a whisper, 'and I am willing to give him up.'

"'God in his mercy help you,' I prayed.

"'And forgive me,' she answered humbly.

"My sister opened her door as I passed. She was dressed, and had been watching too all the night long. 'Well?' she asked.

"I kissed her. 'It is well,' I answered, and she burst into tears."

Thus the fatal step is stopped, and never takes place. The tragedy is forestalled. It is a tragedy still in many ways, and the different characterisation of the man, who is of much less importance in the piece, yet is well developed too, is very good in its way,—a man not carried away by the passion which forces Ideala; thinking, indeed, more of her than himself; grudging that she should not have a little happiness, a motive which would in itself have been death to her happiness. She triumphs over this strange catastrophe *manqué*, by which the power of her youth, high purpose, and modernism, perhaps the last most of all; and the book ends with a queer postscript of a chapter describing her return. She comes back as a reformer of women, in a beautiful and novel dress, and, as the first portion of her programme, determines to devote herself to the annihilation of *stays!* If this is intended as a final jeer at the whole system of feminine superiority, or if it is merely a specimen of the bathos into which a too highly strained endeavour is apt to fall, we are quite unable to say. It adds to the curious effect, so much a fashion of the time, of the episode which even the chief actors in it consider as nothing more than an episode bursting into the current of life without having any radical effect upon that persistent stream. Perhaps the conclusion means that among the victims of fate, the delicate women incapable of shame who are put wrong with life by a bad marriage, there is nothing to be done save by dignified endurance: and that really, on the whole, in their class there is so little hardship, that after the tragedy is over there is nothing worse to assail than the tyranny of clothes. Teufelsdrock had the same mission after that supreme moment when he saw his love pass him by in the joy of her honeymoon; but his was at once a larger and more deeply reaching trouble than the undue pressure of a woman's stays.

To turn from 'Ideala,' in which one of the chief charms is the revelation of a truth which is more or less fiction, and in which fact is proved to be the least important thing in the world—to the absolute truth of the Scotch village set before us by Mr Barrie, which is simple matter of fact, comprehended, perceived, and understood by genius, is the strangest step, greater perhaps than the step from one planet to another, if we had any knowledge on that point.

IV. Anonymous, "New Writers," *Bookman*, 4 (July 1893), 107-108.

The author of the 'Heavenly Twins' belongs on one side of her family to an old Quaker stock. Her grandfather was turned out of the community for hunting, and her mother, an enthusiastic woman, despised the peaceful Quakers, and kept her child aloof from their influences. In spite of this, it is not difficult to detect in Sarah Grand traces of Quaker ancestry. Strangers among the Friends have been known to recognize her by some mysterious sign as one of themselves. She began to write at a very early age, and it is a curious fact that she found the greatest difficulty in acquiring the art of penmanship. Her head was full of ideas long before her hand was able to inscribe them. As a child she used to pray fervently that she might be allowed to write well, meaning to write a good hand. Hearing a friend remark once that our prayers are never answered as we expect, she took this to mean that she would be made to write a very large hand, while her ambition yearned after a clear, delicate, small one. Her first long story, 'Singularly Deluded,' appeared in *Blackwood's Magazine*, and has been republished in volume form this year. Her second book 'Ideala,' which may be taken as a prelude to the 'Heavenly Twins,' is a work of remarkable genius, and with a better chance at starting, would have made her reputation. Both these novels were anonymous. The *nom de plume* "Sarah Grand" was suggested in a vivid dream. She awoke on a dark winter morning to find that the last proof-sheets of the 'Heavenly Twins' had arrived, and that the title-page was awaiting her name. Then and there she wrote upon it "Sarah Grand." By her express desire her real name remains a secret from the public. The reason for its concealment is no doubt a sorrowful one, and the persistent curiosity on the subject has caused her much annoyance.

Goethe once said to Eckermann that the name he would prefer to all others was "Befreier." It is possible that Sarah Grand may be known to the rising generation as "Die Befreierin." Ideas which have grown with higher education, and have floated more or less vaguely before the minds of cultured women, find in her sharp and startling expression. Her ideal women claim freedom for themselves, freedom to live the highest life, and secure the fullest development. Their lives are a contradiction of Lord Melbourne's remark to the Queen, that no woman, whatever her position, can afford to stand alone. Ideala and Evadne are ready to stand alone. They will face the social desert, but not disobey the heavenly vision. There is even a certain proud joy in their recognition of the fact that "Dieu n'a voulu pour elles que les grands et âpres sentiers." Yet with all their independence they are the most womanly of women. Sarah Grand has not the faintest sympathy with the bold and noisy female agitator. Her heroines have other things to do than to storm platforms. She is never happier than when describing a peaceful home-life, such as Gertrude's in 'Singularly Deluded,' or Angelica's at the close of the 'Heavenly Twins.'

There is a remark in the preface to 'Ideala' which may, without unfairness, be applied to its author. "It would be wrong to take any one of Ideala's opinions here given as final." There is much in the 'Heavenly Twins' which Sarah Grand's warmest admirers will accept as transitional. Her power is still half-developed, and her best work to come. She herself confesses that her knowledge of life has been confined to a somewhat narrow circle. She has no conception of the commonplace struggles which beset the lives of ordinary women. Her characters are the queens and princesses of the sex, and with all their charm, they do not tread the beaten highway. In the characters of Ideala and Evadne there is a certain superhuman element. The former, when she reappears in the 'Heavenly Twins,' moves with a shadowy splendour. Plain people refer to her in awestruck accents as "the other great lady." She looks on life as Juno might have done, if she had come as a curious visitor to some Greek peasant's home. One could not imagine Ideala making a small economy. Walter Besant's first care for a favourite hero is to fill his purse; Sarah Grand does not recognise the possibility of a purse being empty. Those who know her, however, are aware that the problem of the lives of poor women in London is at present engaging her deepest interest. And in their own sphere her strongest characters are the most helpful. The need of loving keeps their souls alive. "Love is one thing worth living for"—not a selfish independence. "Ideala gathers the useless units of society about her and makes them worthy women. Wherever she is, you may be sure that another woman is there also—someone with a sorrowful history, probably, and you may be equally sure that she is leaning on Ideala."

V. Anonymous, "Our Library Table: *Ideala: A Study from Life*," *The Woman's Herald*, 12 Oct. 1893, 537.

The tremendous success of "The Heavenly Twins" has created a demand for a new edition of the book to which it is a sequel. One naturally wishes to know something of the woman for whose sake Lord Dawne remained a bachelor. It must be confessed that at first Ideala is a little disappointing. She is strikingly original certainly, but in a way that must have made her friends anxious as to her sanity. It requires a lively imagination to conceive how an intelligent girl on losing her pen should expect to find it among the p's in the French dictionary. As the story advances, however, one forgets these peculiarities, and can find little but sympathy and admiration for the many noble qualities of a very complex character. The story of the wrongs which made shipwreck of Ideala's happiness, and nearly drove her into wild revolt against all established law, is the beginning of that fearless denunciation of social evils which later found such eloquent utterance in "The Heavenly Twins."

VI. From Anonymous, "Sarah Grand and Mr. Ruskin," *The Woman's Signal*, 25 Jan. 1894, 57.

RUSKIN AND "IDEALA"

"Ideala" was finished in 1883. It was sent the round of the publishers, by all of whom it was rejected. The tone of superiority affected by some of them, as I flip through those grim letters of refusal, read in the light of to-day like the lines of a farce. Sarah Grand finally sent it to Mr. George Allen, of Orpington, Mr. Ruskin's publisher, and asked him if he would kindly give her his opinion of the book and tell her if he thought it worth publishing at all. He replied that he not only thought it worth publishing, but was ready to publish it himself if Mr. Ruskin approved. He explained, however, that his agreement with Mr. Ruskin was such that he could bring out no book of which the latter disapproved. I remember Sarah Grand's delight on receipt of that appreciative letter, but it was not destined to live long. Ruskin did not approve, and shortly afterward the manuscript was returned, with expression of regret from Mr. Allen. Mr. Ruskin, it is to be presumed, in practising that chivalry towards women which he, together with the old school of believers in the subordination of women, held to be the proper practice of man to woman, used his giant strength after reading only a few pages of the manuscript which has since borne its writer to fame, and pettishly scribbling on it that he "didn't like the title" and "couldn't bear queer people, however nice," he returned it to the publisher. But Sarah Grand was unconvinced. She locked the book up for five years, however. But in the summer of 1888 she took it out again, read it carefully through, and, finding her confidence unshaken, she determined to publish it at her own risk. It appeared in a yellow paper back, was an instant success, was taken up by Bentley at his own request after it became famous—he having before refused it—and was published by him in a more ambitious form. The original yellow back is now sought after keenly by the collectors. A pretty strange and rare career for a first novel.

THE TRAGEDY OF WOMANHOOD

In "Ideala," as one of her critics has truly said, "Sarah Grand struck the keynote of her genius." It is the life story of a deeply sensitive, highly bred, delicately nurtured woman, married to a man of loose morals. Born with a light-hearted nature, she, a pure-souled woman, governed by a mistaken sense of duty, tries to live cheerfully beside the noisome being to whom she is tied, and from whom our revolting man-made social laws give her no means of escape except in disgrace. The anguish and degradation of the position are poignantly and powerfully suggested, yet suggested with a rare delicacy of touch. It requires a highly disciplined nature to live through such a partnership unsullied. "Ideala" is much more than a novel, it is the voice of a great-hearted woman speaking to her fellow women out of the innermost depths of her soul. The author herself calls it a study from life; it might well have been called "The Tragedy of Womanhood." Sarah Grand is ambitious for her sex. She cries to women to arise from the apathy which the slothful solitude of surrender has bred in them. But she is intensely feminine in her point of view and on the methods which she advocates. She wishes to see every woman making herself a power in the land; but always, when possible, a quiet power and never a blatant one.

VII. From Jane T. Stoddart, "Illustrated Interview: Sarah Grand,"
Woman at Home, 3 (1895), 247-252.

Immediately after the appearance of the 'Heavenly Twins,' I had
the pleasure of being Madame Sarah Grand's first interviewer. I met
her then at the Pioneer Club, before she had found a settled home in
London. She has now taken a flat in Kensington. It would be difficult
to imagine a more delightful home for a literary worker. A private
road divides the two blocks of buildings, and there I found Sarah
Grand enjoying the summer air on the afternoon of my visit. She
had been spending some weeks in the country, and was in London
for a few days on her way to the Continent. As we climbed the many
steps leading to her door, she told me that although she finds a top
flat an excellent workshop, she much prefers to write in the country
[. . . .] I could not help thinking as I sat with Sarah Grand what a
wholly false impression many people have of her opinions about
women.

"So many people suppose," she remarked, "that when an author
develops a character with great care and fulness, his own views may
be safely identified with those expressed by that character. I have
found this in the case of more than one personage in the 'Heavenly
Twins.' The views of Evadne or Angelica, for example, are not necessarily to be accepted as my views, in fact cannot be, for they are
even opposed to each other, yet people frequently write, wondering
how I can possibly defend such opinions."

"I have always understood," I suggested, "that your true view of
the position of women—your philosophy, if I may use the word—is
represented more fully in 'Ideala' than by any of the characters in
the 'Heavenly Twins.'"

"You are quite right," said Sarah Grand, "and I shall always be
glad that the success of the 'Twins' gave a fresh lease of life to 'Ideala,' for it is my own favourite among my books." Speaking of the
misrepresentations which have appeared in the press, she said, "Even
good critics, I think, are often unfair to authors by generalising upon
the slightest grounds. One very clever writer accused me of failing
to appreciate Fielding, simply because I had said I did not care for
Tom Jones—the person, not the book."

"Looking back on the last year or two, do you think there are any special reasons which account for the success of the 'Heavenly Twins'?"

"I think," said Sarah Grand slowly, "that the time was ripe for such a book. I had the strongest conviction that there was something very wrong in the present state of society, and in the 'Heavenly Twins' I did what I could to suggest a remedy. That the thought of cultured readers, both in England and America, had been running in the same direction, was shown by the welcome which my theories received. I have had the kindest letters from entire strangers, thanking me for speaking so fearlessly [. . . .]"

VIII. From Sarah A. Tooley, "The Woman's Question: An Interview with Madame Sarah Grand," *Humanitarian*, 8 (1896), 161-169.

When writing her first story, *Ideala*, Madame Grand found that social questions would get into it. The story was a study from life, and in drawing the characters she simply reproduced people with whose lives she was intimately acquainted. "I do not," she said, "like to see puppets in a book who are placed there for the purpose of saying certain things, and to give expression to a writer's theory. To be true to life should be the first aim of an author, and if one deals with social questions, one must study them in the people who hold them, not invent a puppet to give forth one's views. One thing has struck me as being very significant, and that is that literal facts are so often received by critics with incredulity. The story of Evangeline in *Our Manifold Nature*, is a case in point; it has been attacked as 'melodramatic' and 'impossible,' yet it is a true story from beginning to end, ungarnished by fictional embellishments."

After the publication of *Ideala*, a long interval elapsed before Madame Grand brought out the notable book which has done so much to rouse men and women to a thoughtful consideration of the evil it seeks to expose. The *Heavenly Twins* took two years to write and three years to find a publisher. One publisher to whom it was offered replied that it was a neurotic novel, and could not be expected to succeed, adding that "it was calculated to give great pain to the majority of novel readers, who were ladies." Another was known to have said that it was the book which no respectable house would publish, but, after it had achieved success, this same publisher was most anxious to publish her next book. "Success makes such a difference, don't you know?" said Madame Grand with a smile, as she referred to these little incidents. The criticism evoked by the *Heavenly Twins* was, as most people know, almost wholly adverse. Nearly all the reviews were against it, but from private correspondents the author received many sympathetic and encouraging communications, and even still the letters continue to come as the book penetrates into the remoter regions of civilization.